TREACHERY WITHIN

Wrapped in her thoughts, it was a moment before Rilsin realized there was something wrong. There was no guard outside her private quarters. She dropped Sola's hand.

"What is it? What's wrong?"

"Go get the guards." She was unarmed except for a slender knife she wore at her waist, a gift from the Iron Guild, more ornament than weapon. She drew this and opened the door to her quarters. She was peripherally aware that Sola was still beside her, that he had not gone to get the guards, and that he had drawn his sword.

The first thing Rilsin saw was Chilsa. The big cat was limp, half curled up on the floor right inside the door. He lay in a pool of blood, and his silver fur was matted.

Sola had moved ahead into the other rooms. She heard him say something, more a strangled noise than a word, and she ran forward. To her daughter's room . . .

Ace books by Noel-Anne Brennan

THE SWORD OF THE LAND
THE BLOOD OF THE LAND

THE
BLOOD
OF THE
LAND

NOEL-ANNE BRENNAN

ACE BOOKS, NEW YORK

THE BLOOD OF THE LAND

An Ace Book / published by arrangement with
the author

PRINTING HISTORY
Ace mass market edition / April 2004

ISBN: 0-441-01154-3

ACE®
Ace Books are published by The Berkley Publishing Group,
a division of Penguin Group (USA) Inc.,
375 Hudson Street, New York, New York 10014.
ACE and the "A" design
are trademarks belonging to Penguin Group (USA) Inc.

10 9 8 7 6 5 4 3 2 1

For L, Ph.D.

1

Rilsin ran a hand through her short brown hair in exasperation and glared at her councilors. They continued to argue.

"Quiet!" Her voice, pitched to carry, cut through the noise, and in the resulting silence Rilsin's ears rang. "When I invited you to speak your opinions, I did not mean all at once. I want open trade with Runchot; you know I have long advocated for that. The last thing I want is another war. But we cannot permit the Runchot to build up their forces to attack us under pretext of peaceful trade. Especially since circumstances here are not yet settled."

The circumstances she spoke of were known all too well to those present. It was not quite a year since Rilsin had won the SaeKet's chair back from her cousin Sithli in a civil war. Although the people had been behind her, not all of the nobles had.

"I think we must assume they want peace, SaeKet. If we have good relations with Runchot, they are more likely to turn over Sae Sithli. And Sae Kepit." Sola dira Mudrin was a member of the honored class, not an aristocrat. He was an inventor, a magician, many called him, who was responsible for the introduction of steam and of the fire-tube, the devastating new weapon that promised to give the land of Saeditin an advantage in war. He had no desire to be at this council meeting. He hated politics, but he was there because Rilsin had asked him to be there. He was lean and wiry, with long, braided dark hair, but without the gems or ornamentation many members of the upper classes seemed addicted to.

"They will not give us Sithli sae Melisin and Kepit sae Lisim. They will take everything they can from us and stall until it is too late. Sithli will have time to grow stronger, to build her army. I will not permit her to do that!" Rilsin slammed her hand down on the table.

The councilors avoided looking at one another. They remembered all too well the temper of the former SaeKet. Rilsin was not Sithli, but she was the SaeKet, and the memories were too raw. Rilsin saw the looks.

"My apologies. I will not permit her to do that," she repeated more quietly. "I know how strange it seems for me to appear to be against trade after advocating it with Sithli for so long, but I will give the Runchot nothing until Sithli sae Melisin and Kepit sae Lisim are turned over to me. That will be a sign of their good faith." She put no credence at all in the good faith of the Runchot.

"It may come to war, then, SaeKet." Essit sae Tillit was young to be first minister, but he was older than Rilsin had been when she first took the position in her cousin's reign.

"I know it, my friend, but I am afraid there will be no choice. We must prepare."

On that note she dismissed the meeting. Sola fell into step beside her and opened his mouth to continue the discussion, but Rilsin forestalled him.

"Not now," she said. "Save it until later, when we are alone." She was not referring as much to the guard who walked with them as she was to being in a more private, more quiet place. Ever since she became SaeKet, Rilsin had found herself at the center of things, with far too little privacy.

Her personal suite was at the far end of the palace from the formal suite that had been Sithli's. Sithli's rooms had too many memories. She had not even wanted to live in the palace, preferring her own modest house, but for the SaeKet to live anywhere but the palace was too great a breach of tradition. Rilsin wondered if she would ever get used to it. She still kept her house and dreamed of moving back to it. The guard outside the door saluted, and Rilsin returned the salute. No sooner had she set one foot into the room than she was greeted by a shriek, and something hit her hard at knee height.

"Mama! Mama!"

"Reni!" Rilsin laughed, tossing aside the dignity of the SaeKet, despite the fact that the door to the corridor was still open, with the guard standing there, and Sola behind her, half in and half out of the room. She grabbed up her daughter and tossed the little girl up in her arms and caught her again, both of them shrieking with delight.

"I am sorry, SaeKet! I don't know how she knew, but she did! She knew you were coming, and she got away from me. I've never seen such a little child move so fast!" Meffa was out of breath.

Rilsin grinned at Meffa, her friend and chief servant. It wasn't the first time little Reniat had almost escaped her nurse.

"It's all right." Rilsin put the child down and rubbed at her back. "You are getting bigger by the minute," she told her daughter, who giggled.

Reniat would be two years old at the upcoming Winter Solstice. She had been born in a cave after her mother had defeated the invading Runchot army. She should never have been born at all, if the drugs Rilsin had been forced to take in childhood had worked as they should. For these reasons, Reniat was known to the people as the sun-child, and she lived up to her name by her sunny disposition. She was blonde, as her father had been, but without his golden skin.

She was pale skinned like her dark-haired mother. Now she giggled again and held up her chubby little arms.

"More!" she demanded.

"Later," Rilsin promised. She glanced behind her and realized the door to the corridor was still open, with Sola standing in it. "Come in," she said to him.

Sola hesitated. He wanted more than anything to be part of the family scene, but he could not bring himself to it. The truth was that he resented little Reniat. He resented her not for who she was—how could he hate a small, beautiful child?—but for what she was. She was not his daughter, she was the child of Sifuat, Rilsin's executed husband. She would never be his, and she would always remind Rilsin of Sifuat by her very existence. He found it hard to admit even to himself, but she reminded him of how much he had hated Sifuat. Sola found his relationship with Rilsin difficult enough without this.

"I can't, Rilsin. I have to go, I have—" He couldn't think of a plausible pressing errand, but Rilsin didn't notice.

"Later, then," she said, distracted by the child, and he stepped out and watched the guard shut the door on the laughter inside.

Outside it was cold, with the smell of snow. The guards passed him through without comment, knowing him. *So many guards,* he thought with a frown. He knew it was necessary; the land was under threat of war, and Rilsin SaeKet was under threat even from within the land, as SaeKets were always subject to assassination, and there were still a few nobles who would not hesitate to kill her.

He thought of going to his workshop, but he decided against it. It was the best workshop in Saeditin; the SaeKet had spared no expense to see that he had anything he wanted or needed. That was not the point. He knew he would feel alone there, even in the midst of apprentices. He decided instead to visit Kerida. Although his mother had partially retired, she still lived in the back of the apartment set aside for the keeper of the cats.

Lost in thought, he ignored or failed to notice the stares

and nods of people on the streets, just as he failed to notice those who crossed the street to avoid him, afraid of his reputation for wizardry. By the time he reached the cat pens, the snow had started, and fat flakes drifted down across the palace and the city of Petipal.

In her suite at the palace, Rilsin belatedly noticed that Sola was gone. She remembered that she had dismissed him, and she wished she had not, as it seemed now, in retrospect, that there was something bothering him. She doubted that it was just the threat of war. Their relationship had been uncertain since she came to power, and even before. She regretted this, but she never seemed to know quite what to do about it. Under her cousin Sithli's rule, being close to Rilsin had carried a certain amount of peril. Love, and even friendship, had always been dangerous territory for her.

She thought of sending for him, but SaeKet or not, that was too high-handed. She would go to find him herself. She had just decided to do this, when another distraction presented itself in the form of a huge silver hunting cat. He was an enormous animal, whose big, blunt head came up to Rilsin's waist. The noise of Rilsin's arrival had interrupted his nap, and he yawned, showing impressive canines. He butted his huge head against Rilsin's hand and gave a meow, incongruously high-pitched for such a large animal.

"Mama!" said Reniat. "Chilsa hungry!"

"Yes, you can feed Chilsa." Rilsin wasn't even remotely concerned over the sight of her tiny daughter near the giant cat. Although the cats were trained for hunting and attack, Chilsa loved Reniat and had saved her life, as well as Rilsin's. Rilsin decided that Sola could wait.

2

"THEY OWE ME! THEY WOULD NOT BE AS WEALTHY IF IT were not for me! And they will be so much wealthier when I am back in Saeditin where I belong, back in the SaeKet's chair! They owe me!" Sithli sae Melisin, formerly Sithli SaeKet of Saeditin, now deposed, was flushed with fury. Her golden skin was dark with rage, and her green eyes, as green as the emeralds she loved, flashed. She strode across the room and back.

"Calm yourself, SaeKet. There is nothing to be gained should the prince's envoys see you in this temper. Nothing to be gained and much to lose." Kepit sae Lisim held up a hand to forestall the younger woman. She was more than twice Sithli's age, and in her forty-nine years she had schemed and fought and manipulated her way into power. She had lost almost everything when Rilsin forced Sithli to flee Saeditin, lost it because Sithli had refused to listen to good advice. Kepit was heartily tired of youngsters who ignored the voice of experience. Her own niece Jullka had died by staying with Sithli as Rilsin's army advanced on the capital.

"Prince Raphat was wealthy before you sold him slaves. His family has ruled Runchot for a very long time." *Longer than the Melisins ruled Saeditin,* she thought. She knew better than to say it.

"He profited from me," said Sithli, stubbornly but more quietly. "He needed me to secure his power in the south of this repulsive land."

Kepit swallowed the reply that leaped to her tongue. "We are the ones who need him now, SaeKet. If you wish, I can make an excuse, and we can see the envoy later. I can say that you have one of your headaches—"

"Not again, Kepit; I cannot claim it again. And you will *not* see the envoys alone." Sithli didn't entirely trust Kepit, but she didn't want it to be obvious. No one had a more well-deserved reputation for manipulation than the head of the Lisim clan, as Sithli had good reason to know. "I can handle this, Kepit, so you can have them sent in." She waved her hand to silence her advisor. "Now."

Kepit didn't like it, but there was nothing else to be said or done. If Sithli commanded her, she must obey, at least outwardly. It was likely that Sithli would behave herself now. All traces of temper seemed to have vanished, and Sithli could be as charming as she was beautiful, when she had a mind to it. She watched as Sithli settled herself in the most ornate chair in the richly appointed room, and smoothed her green winter silks, and adjusted the huge emerald cuff bracelet on her wrist, and checked her hand mirror to be sure the powder covered the scar on her face and the emeralds entwined in her hair were perfectly placed. However badly her cause needed funds, Sithli herself lacked for no luxury.

"The SaeKet will receive her visitors," Kepit told the Runchot servant outside the door. She wondered how much the man had overheard. She had wanted only Saeditin servants in their immediate quarters, but there were few of them who had come into exile with them. Sithli was not

willing to skimp on servants, so she had accepted the offer
of the Runchot prince, the highest-ranking merchant in this
nation of merchants, to supply her with some. Kepit did not
have the resources here to investigate them, as she would
have had at home, and she had no choice but to accept them
or face Sithli's wrath. Kepit tried to pick her battles.

"Prince Raphat of House Merri, hereditary prince of the
Five Provinces, first lord of Runchot!" trumpeted a tall man
in the burgundy and yellow colors of House Merri. Kepit
was forced backward by the strength of his voice, overwhelming in the small room.

"We did not expect you personally, my lord," she told
the tall man who followed his herald. "Welcome." Why had
she not been informed? Kepit kept a bland smile on her
face, but someone would pay for this.

"I wanted this to be an informal visit. . . . Sae Kepit, I assume." The ruler of northern Runchot, and of most of the
south, was a man just entering middle age, tall and still
strong, with a head of thick, wavy chestnut-brown hair just
beginning to gray at the temples. He wore it in a bun at the
nape of his neck, as did most Runchot nobles. He had the
presence of one accustomed to power and the obedience it
commanded and the charm of a man who knew his attractiveness to women. Both of these were wasted on Kepit.

"Wait outside," he told his personal guard, and they
obeyed, ranging themselves just outside the room, hands on
their swords.

Sithli rose from her chair but did not step forward. She
held out one slender, emerald-ringed hand, and Raphat,
smiling, strode forward and clasped it between his own.
Kepit, watching this with a critical eye, noted that his hands
were big and rough, as large and powerful as Raphat himself. It was worthy of note that Raphat had finally made a
visit to his notorious guest. For months he had ignored
Sithli, not responding to requests for an audience. Now he
was here, without warning and without invitation, or at
least without official invitation.

"You are as beautiful as they say, Sithli SaeKet." Raphat

spoke in Saeditin. He had not relinquished her hand, and did not seem about to. "My apologies that business kept me from this meeting for so long. Had I known what a truly glorious sight I was missing, I would have put business aside." He gazed at Sithli as if he were starving and she were food.

Only Kepit's long experience in politics kept her from rolling her eyes. As far as Sithli was concerned, however, there was no such thing as excessive flattery. She smiled back at Raphat and made no attempt to extricate her hand from his.

"The loss has been equally mine," she said. "Now that I have met you at last, I see how much we have in common, and how well we can work together."

Nothing like getting right to the point, Kepit thought. She leaned back against a wall, the better to observe this meeting comfortably. She was temporarily forgotten, which was just how she wanted it.

"Indeed we can. Working together," Raphat paused and lowered his voice, giving the words another meaning, "would give me the greatest pleasure." Still holding Sithli's hand, he took a step closer to her. A slow blush darkened Sithli's golden skin.

Raphat knew better than to smile in triumph, but he was all but certain of this particular victory. He had come, in fact, not necessarily to offer Sithli any aid in regaining the throne of Saeditin but because he was curious. He was not entirely convinced that his best interests lay with Sithli sae Melisin, however profitable her reign had been for him. Her instability was famous. Rilsin sae Becha, currently on the throne of her ancestors, might prove better for him in the long run. Sithli's beauty was as famous as her mercurial temper, however, and Raphat was a man with an eye for beauty in women. He had a reputation as a lover that was well deserved, some would have said too well deserved. Others would have said that his successes between the sheets threatened his success in other areas. Those who thought so did not know him well enough. Two of his mistresses had at-

tempted to use him for political gain. Both had suffered unfortunate and fatal accidents, as had his legal wife.

"Perhaps we could talk more over dinner." Sithli gently
withdrew her hand. "You will stay, will you not? I can have
something sent up."

"There is little that I would like more." Raphat's tone
made it plain that there was, perhaps, one thing that he
would like more. Sithli made a point of dragging her gaze
away from Raphat, glancing at Kepit, who still stood
against the wall. Even to Kepit, the room seemed warmer.

"Have a supper sent up to my private quarters," she said.

"Yes, SaeKet." Kepit did not complain at being treated
as a personal servant by the younger woman.

"And have wine sent, as well," commanded Raphat,
never taking his eyes from Sithli.

"Of course, my lord."

As Kepit left the room, she could see, from the corner of
her eye, that Raphat had moved up beside Sithli. Under the
pretext of admiring her bracelet, his hand had drifted gently across her breast, settling briefly. Kepit closed the door
and walked thoughtfully past the prince's guards.

Under most circumstances, with most men, Kepit would
not have been concerned about Sithli. She was aware of
Raphat's reputation, but Sithli had one of her own. While
she ruled Saeditin, Sithli had had more lovers than most
people cared to count. Despite this, she had never, as far as
anyone knew, been in love. She was an expert in the art of
using people and in getting what she wanted. So was Kepit,
although it had been some time since she had used personal
attractiveness as a weapon, or had needed to. At first, despite the prince's confidence and hasty advances, she had
felt a certain amount of amusement and even pity. The poor
man, she was sure, had no idea what he was up against.
Now, she wasn't quite so convinced. She hoped her SaeKet
knew what she was doing. If she didn't, it was going to be
up to Kepit to pick up the pieces. Kepit had been doing far
too much of that lately.

*   *   *

THE SNOW HAÐ melted by morning, as a warm wind, or warm by late autumn standards, at least, blew up from the southwest. Rilsin wanted to sneak out before dawn with Chilsa for a run in the woods, just as she had done in the old days, when she was Sithli's first minister. Reniat was still asleep, as was Meffa. The guard in the baby's room was awake, but all other staff had been dismissed the previous night. It should have been easier, now that she was SaeKet, but it was not. If anything, it was harder. There were even more people watching her than previously, alert for the slightest opportunity to gain her ear about any matter important to them. She lived in the palace now, not in her own beloved house, and the place was crawling with guards and servants. She was reminded of when she and Sithli had snuck out of the palace when they were children, but even that had been easier than it was for her now. Not only were those times long past, but their formerly secret tunnel had been blocked. Rilsin deliberately pushed the thought away. She had no desire to revisit the matter of Sithli and Kepit's escape through the passage, which had been due to her own oversight. She took a deep breath. It was ridiculous to fear leaving her own apartments.

"Stay close," she told the big silver cat at her side. She stepped from her quarters into the palace corridor.

The guard at the door saluted, putting hand to heart. Rilsin nodded at him, and as soon as she was only a few feet away, she drew her cloak around her, hoping to pass unnoticed, as if that were possible with Chilsa at her side. The hour was too early for most ministers or nobles to be out yet, even though they knew their SaeKet was an early riser, and she had made it almost to the door to the main gardens.

"Rilsin! Rilsin!"

It was Sola. Despite herself, she was pleased. She had wanted time to herself, but she trusted Sola more than anyone, and she had wanted to talk to him. He was her oldest friend, her dearest friend, and her almost more than friend. Almost.

"I see you nearly made it but for me, Rils." Now that he was close enough not to be overheard, Sola reverted to informality. "I thought I might catch you."

"You were right; you did. But if you want to talk to me, you have to come along. Chilsa and I are going for a run."

"I thought that, too." He looked prepared, dressed in thick woolen trousers and heavy boots. He looked around. "A run or a ride? It's a little wet for a run."

"A ride," she decided. "We can go and be back before my first meeting, and no one the wiser." She grinned, reminding him of the girl he had first met in his workshop years ago. He grinned back. "Race you to the stables!" she said and was off.

If the stable hand on duty thought there was anything odd about seeing his SaeKet and her minister of mines appear mud-spattered and laughing, he was wise enough not to remark on it. One of the commoners who had risen in revolt against Sithli sae Melisin, he was filled with pride that Rilsin SaeKet Becha helped to saddle her own horse and then thanked him. He firmly believed that all was right with the world, now that Rilsin was SaeKet.

They rode through the palace fields at a rapid canter, with Rilsin in the lead, avoiding the streets of Petipal. Sola was hard-pressed to catch up with her, although Chilsa was a silver streak beside her horse. When eventually she slowed, it was near the SaeKet's woods, the woods in which Sola had had his first workshop. She turned to look at him, her cheeks flushed with the cold and the exercise. Her brown hair was still cut short, a captive's cut, not the long braid of the free Saeditin, noble or not. She had continued to cut it since her victory, and as a result, the style was spreading among the free commoners. It looked good on her. She seemed happy, as if she had forgotten all her concerns, at least for the moment. It made him reluctant to speak. Something in his face alerted her.

"What is it?" Rilsin reined her horse around, the better to see him, while Chilsa took off after a rabbit. "Tell me, Sola. There is something on your mind, and there is no use hiding it." She tried to ignore the way her stomach plummeted, the way some of the light went out of the morning. She could not have even a little time away from duty, it seemed, not even with her dearest friend. She was afraid it was politics, and then suddenly she was just as afraid it was not.

Sola saw the way her face changed. "I'm sorry, Rils. It's just that this is important." He hesitated but only for a moment. "Have you made a decision on the Lisim prisoners?"

So it was politics after all. She realized she was disappointed, and she hoped she didn't look as sour as she now felt. Politics had been in their way from the very start, when she had met him in the woods as a child, before he even knew who she was. Politics had been in their way all their lives, but she resented it now more than ever.

"You cannot keep to the old ways, Rilsin; you know it. You cannot sentence a whole clan to death because they stood against you in the war."

"They did more than that, as you well know. They kidnapped Saeditin, free Saeditin, and sold them over the border to the Runchot." She remembered Cilla, the commoner she had rescued, the commoner whom Sithli had taken away from her and sold, despite her. "They worked with Sithli's blessing, but no one was safe. No one. You know that as well as I." Her horse caught her agitation and tossed his head, and she took a moment to calm the animal. "The Lisims are responsible for much more than that. Kepit and Jullka," she paused for a moment, remembering Jullka's affair with her husband, and how the young Lisim had betrayed him.

"Jullka is dead. I killed her—or you did—when we took the palace." He knew she blamed Jullka, and rightly, for the capture of her husband, but it was one thing for which he was grateful. "And Kepit is gone, in Runchot with Sithli. None of the Lisims you have now are guilty of the crimes of Jullka and Kepit."

"They are guilty of crimes of their own," said Rilsin grimly. "And they are Lisims."

"Rilsin, the people expect more of you than this!"

"You know what they expect, do you?" Her voice was dangerously soft and cold, barely audible over the rising wind. She did not stop to examine her feelings. She did not want to admit that her anger had little to do with the Lisim prisoners and not even much to do with Sola's request.

He stared at her in dismay. This was not what he had envisioned. He knew the people loved her. She had rescued them from Sithli SaeKet, she was teaching the commoners to read, and she had stopped the sale of citizens across the border. But this was not what he cared about most. This was not what he had thought about when he said he had wanted to talk to her. As he struggled for words, she held up a hand to forestall him.

"The Lisims are mine," she said. "I will deal with them." She had to raise her voice to be heard over the wind. Another storm was blowing up, and she hadn't even noticed. She whistled for Chilsa, turned her horse, and rode for Petipal and the palace, leaving Sola to follow as he could.

Sola watched her ride away. "Rilsin, I love you, damn it. That's what I really wanted to say." He whispered the words because it didn't matter. There was no one there to hear him.

3

THE FORMAL AUDIENCE WAS THAT SAME MORNING. RILSIN
sat in the SaeKet's chair in the audience chamber. She sat
where Sithli had sat, and Essit sae Tillit, her first minister,
stood beside her, in her old place. Rilsin had to remind herself that her ancestors had held the SaeKet's chair long before Sithli, and that the chair, and the land it represented,
were rightfully in her care, and not Sithli sae Melisin's. She
didn't know why it was necessary to remind herself of this.

Despite the fact that she had been in power for a little
over a year, she had passed sentence on few. She had spent
some months traveling through Saeditin, settling disputes,
putting down the few pockets of resistance, securing her
power. Most of those who had fought against her, noble and
commoner alike, had hurried to swear allegiance to her. She
had been happy to receive the pledges, knowing all too well
how the mixture of Sithli's charm and the fear she inspired
had commanded obedience, and she was as happy as her
people to see an end to the fear.

Now there was no choice. The captured Sae Lisims had

been in prison too long, and something must be done with them. They were neither commoners nor unimportant nobles; they were members of the clan that had carried out Sithli's wishes, along with their own quite substantial wishes, the clan that had been behind much of the criminal activity in Petipal and in the countryside beyond the capital. Sola was right. Jullka was beyond her justice now and in the hands of the Mother, for whatever good that would do her. Kepit, the mind behind her clan's scheming, was out of reach, for now. These two Lisims were not.

The guard at the door looked over and nodded to her. She drew herself up, just barely restraining herself from brushing at her blue trousers and overshirt. The blue was trimmed with gold, the sae Becha colors. Rilsin was only beginning to feel at home in them, preferring, and often wearing, her former black.

"Send them in," she said.

There were only two of them, two remaining chiefs of the Sae Lisims. Others had escaped, family members of lesser importance, slipping across the border to the north, if they dared, into the territory of the Confederacy, but most of them melting safely—so they thought—into the countryside and small towns of Saeditin itself. Here Rilsin's agents managed to keep track of some of them. One thing she did not permit, and that was to allow any Lisim, however young or however inconsequential, to cross the southern border into Runchot, where they might reach Kepit and Sithli. It was a risk, she knew, not capturing them all, but in this matter she agreed with Sola. She would not kill them all.

"Sae Jolass, Sae Philla," she acknowledged the two who were brought in, standing among their guards.

Jolass sae Lisim was a dark-haired woman in her thirties, Philla sae Lisim, her brother, was dark-haired, too, taller and more slender than his sister, and ten years younger. Their hair had been cut short to show their captive status, not that this meant much, as the woman they faced, who held their lives in her hands, had hair as short as theirs.

They did not speak. They did not touch hands to hearts. It was not likely that they would, of course, but they could not, either, for their hands were bound behind their backs.

"Untie them," said Rilsin. "Cut them free."

They stood rubbing their wrists, carefully not looking at each other, but she saw them glance briefly at the table with the knife and the candle. Their eyes were drawn there despite themselves. There were as yet no death warrants on the table, and the candle was unlit.

"You know," said Rilsin conversationally, "that all the charges against you have been thoroughly investigated. The charges—would you read them, please, Sae Essit—are substantiated."

Essit cleared his throat. He was dressed for this occasion in the blue and gold of the SaeKet he served, with little sparkling citrines braided into his hair, echoing the gold.

"Jolass sae Lisim and Philla sae Lisim, you are charged with treason against the land of Saeditin and against Rilsin SaeKet Becha, its lawful ruler. You are charged with kidnap and unlawful sale of citizens, with robbery, with murder—"

"Oh stop!" Jolass interrupted the reading. "Why are we wasting our time with this? We all know what is happening here, and we all know what the outcome will be." She looked now directly at the table, with its candle, still unlit.

Her brother Philla looked, too, and suddenly and without warning, burst into tears. There was a moment of startled silence. Before anyone else could react, Jolass grabbed him by one shoulder and slapped him hard across the face. He continued to sob, so she slapped him again. She would have slapped him a third time, but the guards pulled her back. They restrained her, but she still glared at him, while the tears ran down his face.

"You have always been the baby, in many more ways than one," she said with contempt. "Why can you not simply admit your guilt with courage?"

"I never wanted to do this, Jolass, never wanted any part of it, especially with the children, when we took the ba-

bies." His sobs grew stronger, and he couldn't continue. Jolass's mouth turned down, and it looked as if she had something else to say.

"Great Mother!" Rilsin decided she had no desire to hear
whatever else Jolass had in mind. "No more, Sae Jolass!"
She turned to the guard nearest the table. "Light the candle," she told him. Philla began to shudder as well as sob.

"Sae Philla," she said. "Sae Philla, look at me." Reluctantly, he did. "I believe you when you say that you wished
to have no part in what you did. I believe you, that you were
overwhelmed in this by your sisters, by your cousin Kepit
sae Lisim," the name seemed to hang harshly in the air,
"and by family loyalty." Philla had stopped sobbing. Now
he swallowed and stared at her, reminding her of a kitten
she had once seen, dragged from a stream wet and shivering. She wondered briefly if she were doing the right thing.
She had seen the reports, and even though she had met
Philla only briefly before and had never really known him,
she knew he was weak and easily led. She felt a certain pity
for him.

"Sae Philla, will you swear to me as your SaeKet? Will
you relinquish your Lisim duty?"

"I will! Oh, I will!" Philla put his hand to his heart and
dropped to his knees.

"Filth!" shouted Jolass. "Filth! I will kill you myself!
With my own hands!" There was no doubt that she would
have, but the guards were prepared now and held her
tightly.

"Then you will live," said Rilsin to Philla, "and be free."

"SaeKet, this is not wise. I warn you in the Mother's
name, this is not wise." Dremfir sae Cortin, mage to the
SaeKet, stepped forward. Rilsin had a less than completely
easy relationship with the priests and the temple, but Dremfir she trusted as a friend. He had been mage to her mother-
in-law, and he had fought beside her. His round and
pleasant face hid a quick intelligence and formidable sword
skills. "This is a dangerous path, Rilsin SaeKet, let alone
not tradition. Please do not do this."

For a moment Rilsin had wavered, and Dremfir's words seemed to echo in her mind. She looked up and saw Sola, in the shadows at the edge of the room. She had not thought he would be here, and she heard again his words that she could not keep to the old ways. That she must not.

"All things change in the Mother's time, Mage. Philla sae Lisim will go free," she repeated. "Jolass sae Lisim is another matter." She nodded at Essit.

Essit cleared his throat again. "Jolass sae Lisim, you are convicted of treason against Rilsin SaeKet Becha and the land of Saeditin. For this you are sentenced to death. Your blood will be returned to the land, that the Mother may cleanse it. On the night of the dark moon you will be taken to the Square of the Mother to give your life to the land. Jolass sae Lisim, do you admit and proclaim your guilt?"

"I do proclaim and admit it."

Jolass was defiant, and Rilsin was glad. The words of the death warrant reminded her of all the times she had read them herself, as first minister, but they also took her back to the small cold cell, not so long ago, when she had heard them read against her by a Lisim, when she was the one condemned. It would have been so much harder if Jolass had wept or pleaded. Rilsin mentally shook herself. Perhaps Dremfir was right, and not Sola. She could not afford to be too soft.

Essit lit the candle and placed the death warrant on the table beside it. He picked up the knife and ran the blade through the candle flame, and then extended it, hilt forward, to Jolass. Rilsin's guards drew closer around her, hands on their swords. It was odd, Rilsin thought, how custom armed the criminal at this crucial moment. But Jolass had no intention of doing anything but following tradition. She stepped forward and accepted the knife. With one quick motion, she sliced the blade across the ball of her left thumb. When the blood welled up, she pressed her thumb against the paper, sealing her death warrant and accepting her fate. Then she dropped the knife to the table and turned to face her guards, allowing them to grip her arms again.

She did not speak or look at Rilsin again as they led her from the room.

Philla was led away, still trembling and sobbing out his gratitude, and the room cleared. Rilsin massaged her forehead gently. She had a headache.

"I hope you will not regret this, SaeKet." Dremfir regarded her with concern. "Old ways or new, there is no Lisim who means you well. There is no Lisim who would not turn against you, even one whose life you spared. You have good reason to know them, SaeKet. You should not let them go."

"I can't kill them all, Dremfir. I have seized their holdings. They can't do much here without assets. Philla is no threat, at least. He will find shelter in Petipal overnight, and in the morning he will go east, to try to find work on some farm. We won't hear of him again. I can't kill them all," she said again. "Jolass will be a deterrent; executing her is enough."

"The Mother grant you are right," said Dremfir.

THE ÐAY OF the dark moon was windy and gray and bitterly cold. Rilsin resolved not to think about the evening, the Square of the Mother, or the first major public execution she would preside over since she became SaeKet. She took Chilsa out for morning exercise and spent the rest of the morning discussing the state of the army and the possibility of war with Runchot with Essit sae Tillit and with Pleffin sae Grisna, her commander. She discussed the harvest shortage of several villages in the eastern saedholds and authorized that stores of grain be sent to them. Then she retired to her private apartments. No one sought to keep her back with other business, and if anyone thought she was avoiding preparations for the evening, no one mentioned it.

Meffa had insisted on baking bread. It did not matter that the palace kitchens would have supplied everything they could request. When they had moved to the palace, Meffa had insisted that Rilsin's new apartments have a kitchen of their own, and Rilsin, already homesick for her own small house, had agreed.

Now the entire complex of rooms was redolent with the yeasty, mouthwatering smell. Steam pipes hissed and clanked on the wall. Chilsa, accustomed to their noise, had curled up in a corner of the big sitting room under a join of two pipes, where it was especially warm. When he saw Rilsin, he yawned hugely, showing his impressive dentition. She scratched Chilsa behind one rounded ear and then went to look for her daughter, who was sleeping in her room.

Rilsin surprised herself by missing Sithli. The chilly day and the familiar surroundings of the palace had reminded her of the times she had spent as first minister to her cousin, the times after the work for the day was done, when she and Sithli could talk and spend time together. The Sithli that Rilsin missed was not the woman who had almost brought Saeditin to ruin but the girl she had grown up with, her friend. That girl was long gone, and the friendship, closer than sisterhood, was long gone, too, but Rilsin missed it, and she wondered if Sithli ever missed it, too.

As evening approached, it was no longer possible to ignore what lay ahead. Rilsin became more and more withdrawn, and Meffa, seeing this, kept Reniat out of her way. Rilsin dressed in blue and gold, with a long, deep blue woolen cloak. She strapped on her sword. Although a SaeKet did not need to go armed, Rilsin did not feel dressed without her sword.

"Will you eat before you leave, SaeKet?"

Rilsin shook her head at Meffa. "Later, I think."

She couldn't understand why this one execution bothered her so much, when she had presided at so many as first minister. She had never liked executions, but she had schooled herself to accept the necessity. It would not be much different now that she was SaeKet, she told herself, and perhaps that was part of the problem. She had told herself that her reign would be different. Perhaps her unease came only from the conflict with Sola and his views. If the truth be told, they were views to which she was more and more drawn. She would rather see Reniat inherit a land and a people less accustomed to the spilling of blood. She wanted her daughter to inherit a land at peace and secure.

Her guard met her outside her suite, closing around her. "Send a guard to my quarters for the SaeKetti," she commanded. There was now a guard for Reniat whenever she was outside the SaeKet's apartment, and there was always a guard at the door to the suite, but on the night of an execution, Rilsin wanted more protection for her child.

"Immediately, SaeKet."

She did not recognize the guard captain; someone new, she supposed, and was about to ask his name, but saedin were meeting her in the halls and following her, many putting their hands to their hearts.

She had elected not to take a carriage to the square, but to ride. A procession formed behind her, as her council and other saedin and some dira tried to follow her to the square. It was intensely cold, with a lack of wind that seemed to accentuate the brittle chill that immediately bit through all clothing and settled straight in the bones. Even the shaggy Saeditin horses were draped with blankets under their saddles.

Evening this late in the year ended early, fading rapidly into darkness, and already stars were beginning to prick through the lavender gray of the coming night. Lamps were being lit along the up-city streets, and torches lined her route. So did the people. They began to cheer as soon as her procession came in sight, and even before.

"True SaeKet!" "Rilsin SaeKet!" "Becha!"

Rilsin smiled and waved and leaned forward occasionally, through her guards, to touch hands with someone in the crowd. Whatever the divisions among the nobles, the commoners loved her as one of their own, someone who had suffered with them under the rule of Sithli.

Under the flare of torches, Rilsin climbed the saedin platform. She walked to the SaeKet's chair, but before she took her seat, she looked up at the bulk of the prison, once the palace of her ancestors, that towered over the square. She could clearly see the tiny, high window that had been her only outlook on the world not that long ago. From that window she had seen her husband Sifuat executed. She looked down at the platform beneath her feet, feeling the land below, the land that had soaked up her husband's blood and the blood of so many more, the land that had almost soaked up her own blood. She stared but saw nothing, feeling and hearing instead the song of the land, as it thrummed up through the soles of her feet, as it sang in her blood and fitted itself to her heartbeat. The land was content. The true SaeKet had returned, and the land was content and trusted in her guidance. Rilsin wondered if she could keep that trust.

She looked up to find the square hushed. Around her on the royal platform, the saedin watched her. Nearby on the platform of the dira, the honoreds looked on in silence. Below the platforms, in the sea of darkness, the commoners were quiet. The torches lit an occasional upturned face, eyes wide with awe. They knew what she was doing. They knew what she was remembering, but they knew, too, that she listened to the song, which saedin heard before they died, but which the SaeKet could hear at any time. Rilsin nodded to them and took her seat, and the crowd sighed.

From the shadows at the back of the platform the death priest stepped forward. Dedicated to the Mother's third aspect, he was dressed in heavy gray wool, thick and soft as clouds, but his overtunic was a maroon red so deep it was almost black. He carried the long knife of execution before him on a pillow. Beside him, an apprentice priest carried the velvet case that held the crystal goblet, an object so old and sacred that only priests, the SaeKet, and her appointed minister were permitted to touch it. It was an object that had always filled Rilsin with loathing.

The death priest stopped before her and bowed slightly. Rilsin nodded back, avoiding his eyes. Behind her she could sense Dremfir sae Cortin, her own mage, whom she trusted, his presence lending her support.

Jolass sae Lisim was brought out from the prison under heavy guard. She walked without help, defiantly, and stopped before Rilsin. She did not bow.

Essit sae Tillit stepped forward. He wore the blue and gold of the house he served as first minister, but over it he wore a heavy scarlet vest. He cleared his throat.

"Jolass sae Lisim, you are convicted of treason against the land of Saeditin and against Rilsin SaeKet Becha, its ruler. You are convicted of kidnap and murder against the citizens of Saeditin." There was a hiss from someone in the crowd, hastily hushed. "You have admitted your guilt. Will you proclaim it now to the land?"

"I admit it." Jolass did not sound afraid. She sounded, if anything, contemptuous. "I admit it! You," she twisted in the grip of her guards to look across the sea of commoners below the platform, "will get what you deserve with this Becha SaeKet! At least for a time, but not for long! She will not reign long!" She turned back to look at Rilsin, acknowledging her for the first time.

"This is far from over, Rilsin. The best thing for you would be to die now! To die with me, die in my place! It will be better, and it will be easier for you than what is to be. I curse you, Rilsin sae Becha, in the Mother's name and with my dying breath! I curse you and any child of your line—" A guard had slapped his hand across her mouth to silence her, and was bitten for his effort. He swore and pulled back. Jolass drew breath to shout again, but the death priest stepped forward. He said nothing immediately, merely looked at her first, but Jolass shut her mouth and drew back slightly.

"You cannot curse in the Mother's name, Jolass sae Lisim." His voice was quiet, but it carried across the square. Jolass was not the only one who shivered slightly. The priest's voice was like steel coated in ice. "I can."

The words seemed to hang in the bitter air. Jolass looked up at him and seemed unable to look away. Rilsin was reminded of a rabbit that had once crouched quivering before

Chilsa. Jolass swallowed so loudly that all on the saedin platform, at least, heard.

"I will not curse you, Jolass sae Lisim. I have no need. You have cursed yourself. I leave you to the mercy of the Mother of Justice." He stepped back and nodded at Essit.

"In the name of the Mother," said Essit, reciting the formula, "and the land of Saeditin, and of Rilsin SaeKet Becha, you must return your life and your blood to the land. SaeKet, will you receive this gift?"

"I will," said Rilsin. She did not speak loudly, but her voice carried across the square.

The novice priest unwrapped the crystal goblet from its velvet cover. It was just as old and ugly now as ever, but the young priest held it with reverence. The death priest grasped his knife and stepped forward, toward Jolass. He began to sing in a rich, musical voice. Rilsin wondered fleetingly if a good singing voice were a requirement for a death priest. All the death priests she had known, although thankfully she had not known many, had beautiful voices. He sang the liturgy of the sacrifice. Rilsin listened, waiting. Jolass's guards gripped her arms tightly and forced her to her knees.

"We send you to the land of light, not into darkness, but into light," sang the priest, and Rilsin braced herself.

The novice had given the goblet to Essit. Now he stepped behind Jolass and grasped her short hair, pulling her head back. The death priest was still singing. Rilsin's hands, beneath her cloak, grew clammy, and she felt the prick of cold sweat along the back of her neck, but she looked straight at Jolass. She had been through this enough times. However much she hated it, she had schooled herself not to look away.

The death priest stepped to the side of Jolass and drew the long knife across her throat. She thrashed briefly in the grip of her guards, drenching them with her blood. The death priest took the sacred goblet and caught some of this crimson river. He held the goblet up above his head, where it glittered blackly in the torchlight. Essit stepped forward and took the goblet from him.

"The blood of the criminal has been purified," said Essit loudly. This close to him, Rilsin could see that he looked a little waxy. Essit had witnessed many executions and had killed more than his share of soldiers in battle, but this was his first execution as first minister, the first time he had touched the ancient goblet and performed this ritual.

"Her blood returns to the land, to strengthen it. May the land be strengthened!"

"May the land be strengthened!" echoed the crowd.

"May the SaeKet be strengthened!"

"May the SaeKet be strengthened!" The crowd bellowed out the traditional response, and somewhere in the crowd, cheering started and spread. Essit looked pleased, but the death priest looked shocked at this breach. He lifted his head and stared out at the crowd, and the cheers died. Essit approached Rilsin, put one hand to his heart, bowed, and held out the goblet.

Rilsin stared at the loathsome thing. She remembered Sithli's first sacrifice, when she had almost dropped the goblet, and she remembered Sifuat's execution, when she had watched Sithli drink her husband's blood. Sithli had been the first SaeKet in memory to revive the ancient custom and actually drink the blood of the sacrifice. Rilsin reached out and took the goblet from Essit. She stood and raised the goblet to her eye level, making no pretense of touching it to her lips. The blood swirled darkly in the ancient glass.

"Jolass sae Lisim is purified." Her voice rang out across the square. "The land accepts her blood." She held the goblet away from her and overturned it. The blood, congealing already in the intense cold, fell in a slow stream onto the platform, where Rilsin could see it beginning to freeze already. Jolass's blood would remain here until thaw.

The crowd cheered in earnest now, the commoners beginning it, but soon the cheers had spread to the dira platform, and then even to some of the saedin. Rilsin did not smile. A traitor had been dispatched, but she did not feel celebratory. She heard the last words of Jolass sae Lisim again, echoing in her mind. The death priest had said she had no power to curse, and Rilsin did not believe in curses. Nonetheless, it bothered her more than she cared to admit, and she was uneasy on her ride home through the streets of her cheering citizens.

4

KEPIT HATED THE COLD. SHE HAD NEVER HATED IT BEFORE, so she supposed it was part of growing older. She resented it, just as she resented having to spend her days catering to Sithli sae Melisin. She should be ensconced in Petipal, the power behind the throne. She would have been, if it were not for her stupid niece Jullka and for Sithli herself. It was disturbing to find Sithli more and more unreliable every day. She seemed to take very little interest in the actual work required to get her back to Saeditin and the SaeKet's chair. She left all the work to Kepit, while at the same time demanding that her every whim be met. Kepit frowned sourly. When they did get back to Petipal, perhaps she could find a way to take the SaeKet's chair from Sithli. The Mother knew Sithli didn't deserve it. The Lisim, or more accurately, she, Kepit sae Lisim, had worked for it and should have it. Her family was almost as old as the Melisins, not that it made much difference.

Kepit pulled the wool shawl more tightly around her. Never in her strangest dreams could she have imagined herself wearing such an article, but here she was, wrapped in a shawl like an old woman. Damned Runchot manor houses; they were all as cold as the proverbial Runchot hells. Sithli didn't seem to suffer, but then she had been spending the last week cuddled warmly in the bedchamber with Raphat, Prince of House Merri, the primary merchant in this land of merchants. He thought he had found himself a good bargain with Sithli, the poor fool.

She poured herself some of the strong Runchot tea, wishing it were good strong Runchot wine instead, but she could not afford to be less than sharp for the coming interview. She moved to the chair nearest the fire; this house did not have steam pipes, the new Saeditin invention. No Runchot house did. Not yet. She rang the little bell on the table beside her and frowned at the servant who appeared.

"Send her in," she said. Her voice sounded like a snarl even to herself, and she made an effort to present a more pleasant disposition. This interview had possibilities and might prove useful.

Her visitor was swathed in an ankle-length fur-lined cloak with a deep hood, making it impossible to get a good look at the wearer. Keeping the cloak on indoors was a dramatic gesture intended to impress her, and Kepit repressed a smile.

"Would you care for some tea?" she asked. "The weather is brutal, and I'm sure you could use something warm."

"I did not come for tea." The visitor tossed back the cloak and dropped the hood.

Kepit blinked. The visitor was a young woman of incredible beauty. A fall of loose strawberry-blonde hair reached almost to her waist, setting off skin as pale as that of any of the old saedin stock in Saeditin. Bright blue eyes set in a delicate, childlike face regarded Kepit with cold assessment.

"Of course you did not. What can I offer you?" There were times when it was best to come straight to the point. Kepit decided this was one. "If you have information for

me," she held up a hand to forestall comment, "and if your
information is as good as you claim," again she held up her
hand, "why would you part with it? You should know that
Sithli SaeKet cannot afford much."

"She can afford our price. We do not ask much."

"Our?" Kepit had a good idea with whom she was dealing, but she wanted it out in the open.

The visitor took a seat near the fire, settling herself. "I
represent Kirra. As you know."

The one name was supposed to be enough to tell Kepit
all she needed to know. In fact, it told her much of what she
needed to know, and it confirmed her understanding. Kirra
was a very recent power in Saeditin, in the way that wealth
conferred power. Kirra had come blazing out of nowhere,
accumulating amazing wealth in an amazingly short time.
No one seemed to know where she came from, but she had
been found working in one of the pleasure houses near the
border. The next anyone knew, she owned the house, and
then, somehow, several such houses. She serviced no
clients herself, not anymore. She had no need to. She had
immense wealth, but she had never turned her hand to in-
trigue, at least not of the political kind, until now. Kepit
would have known if she had. No one seemed to even know
what she looked like. Since the earliest days, few had laid
eyes on her, although rumors abounded. For all Kepit knew,
this could be Kirra herself, sitting in the chair by the fire.
The visitor seemed to guess what she was thinking and
smiled slightly.

"I am Phara, daughter of House Qit."

Kepit blinked. A merchant noble's child? She did have
noble manners and a good accent, but there could be many
reasons for that.

"You may investigate me. You will find it is true. My father cast me out when I refused the marriage he arranged
for me. Kirra took me in. She had use for a woman with an
education, as well as beauty." Some of this was true, at least
to a certain extent, and Phara regretted saying it; she re-

membered too late the rule to volunteer nothing. She did
not let the regret show.

No false modesty there, thought Kepit. "That does not
explain why Kirra would wish to give information to Sithli
SaeKet. Especially since we cannot afford to pay much." It
couldn't hurt to emphasize their relative poverty. At the
very least, it was a beginning to the bargaining.

"Kirra has her reasons. As I am sure you understand, we
have access to much information about Runchot troops,
their arms and supplies, and even their battle plans. And we
have access to certain Saeditin information as well. Some
of our houses are near the border, and Saeditin deserters
have been known to visit us, and sometimes troops from the
border saedholds."

Kepit opened her mouth to ask again just why Kirra
would offer this information to them, but she never got the
words out. The same servant who had brought Phara in now
ran into the room.

"I beg pardon, Sae Kepit, but there is someone demanding to see you! He looks like a beggar, but he somehow got
in! Should I send for the city guards? He says it is urgent.
He says you know him. He says—"

"I can speak for myself! Aunt Kepit!" Philla half-ran,
half-staggered into the room. He looked terrible. His shorn
hair stood out in spikes from his head, his clothes were
more like rags. His nose had been frostbitten. The tip was a
dull gray and would probably rot off if it were not immediately tended to. He looked only at Kepit. She rose to her
feet.

"Excuse us, Mistress Phara. Please, remain as my guest
until we can continue our conversation."

"I will be glad to wait," Phara said. "I understand too
well that accident and misfortune never come at a good
time."

No, thought Kepit, *they don't, especially when they make
themselves obvious even to strangers.* Once Phara was out
of the room, Kepit closed the door before turning to her
nephew.

"Philla, what in the Mother's name has happened to you?"

"I came over the mountains. I bribed my way through. I didn't think I would make it out of Saeditin. Rilsin SaeKet has troops on the lookout for all Lisims! I almost died!"

Kepit strode forward, grasped her nephew by the shoulders, and slapped him once across the face with an open palm, exactly as Jolass had done, had she known it. "Fool! We need you in Saeditin! What good can you do us in Runchot?" She was furious; this young idiot had disobeyed her explicit instructions. Jolass was supposed to keep him under control. She had always been able to trust Jolass before. The suspicion that something truly dire had taken place began to dawn on Kepit.

"I couldn't, Aunt, I couldn't! How would I live? They would be watching me!" He drew back, seeing the fire in her eyes. His instructions had been to stay in Saeditin, to do as much harm as possible to the Becha SaeKet, to wait for orders. But he had been captured, almost killed! Didn't Kepit realize that? Didn't she care?

"Jolass is dead," he said. He wanted it to sound artless, but instead it came out in a whine, and sounded spiteful. It had the effect he wanted, however. Kepit froze, all color leaving her face, and she actually sagged, catching herself on the back of a chair.

"They cut her throat in the square."

"Rilsin was to let her go," Kepit whispered. "The Becha was supposed to let her go, as she did you, if you were captured. All the reports said she had gone soft." Jolass had been the person she most trusted, most relied on, of those remaining in her clan. Since her own children had gone long ago to the embrace of the Mother, Jolass had been most like her own child. Jolass and Jullka, both of them, and both now dead at the hands of the Becha SaeKet. The room blurred in front of her.

Philla watched his aunt with something that was almost pity. She looked suddenly old. Old and shaken and sick, something he had never thought to see. Since his own mother had died when he and Jolass were small, they had been in the care of Kepit. She had never shown much interest in him, only in Jolass. Maybe now she would give him the favors that had always gone to others. He took a hesitant step toward her.

"You are going back to Saeditin." Kepit straightened before he could reach her. "Today."

Philla drew back. He looked as if he would burst into tears.

Kepit regarded him coldly, as if from a great distance. She had sensed his weakness, even when he was a child. He was a flawed tool, but he was all she had.

"I need you, Philla." Her voice softened, her face changed. There was no real affection behind the shift, but Kepit was a consummate master of deception. "The Sae Lisims need you." The truth was, she did need him. She had little to choose from now. There were plenty of those who took Lisim money and Lisim orders, and there were lesser members of the Lisim clan in Petipal and scattered throughout Saeditin, but Philla was all that was left of the clan's core. The war and Rilsin sae Becha had seen to that.

Kepit stepped toward Philla, her arms out, trying to radiate warmth and affection. For a fraction of a second he drew back, but then he let himself be enfolded in her embrace. He began to cry.

"I miss her," he gasped finally. He had to lean down to rest his head on Kepit's shoulder. "I miss Jolass." His sister had had no patience with him, but she had always taken care of him, no matter his mistakes. He had loved her, the one person who was a constant in his life.

"I miss her, too." Kepit surprised herself by wiping away a tear of her own. "And no, you don't have to go back to Saeditin today, or even tomorrow." *No later than the day after, though,* she added silently. "You have been through much, and you were resourceful to escape and come here. You can rest first, but you do have to go back. I need you to help me get the Becha out of power. And to pay her back for Jolass." She drew away from Philla so she could look at

him. "Do you understand me? I want revenge for Jolass."
He nodded, still shaken. "And I want you to do it."

He sniffed and drew himself up straighter. "I will do it,"
he said. "I will do whatever you want."

"Good. I never doubted it."

She sent him away with the servants, with orders for a
hot meal, a hot bath, good clothes, a good bed. She asked
for a Runchot physician to see to his frostbite. She wanted
him well and strong enough to be her arm in Saeditin, at
least until she could find someone better. Kepit smiled to
herself. One lesson she had learned early in life was never
to underestimate the power of affection and care. Or at
least, of seeming to care. She had cared in truth about Jolass. She could not bring herself to feel much of anything
for Philla, but she would never let him know that again.

Lost in her thoughts, she left the room and came face-to-
face with Phara. Kepit was taken aback. She was growing
old, indeed, if she could forget so easily something of so
much importance. Phara was standing right beside the door,
where she had apparently been for quite a while. It was obvious that Kirra's agent had overheard every word that was
said. To her credit, she made no attempt to look innocent of
eavesdropping.

"You asked why Kirra would help your cause," she said
bluntly. "This is why: She has a grudge against certain
saedin."

"What grudge?" Kepit thought she knew which saedin.

"That you must ask her yourself."

"I will indeed," said Kepit. "In the meantime, my
thanks, and the thanks of Sithli SaeKet, to you, Lady Phara,
and to Lady Kirra."

"Kirra is no lady." Phara smiled, a cold, sharp smile, a
brittle smile. "Nor am I, any longer. And information from
her is never free. It will cost you less than it might have, Sae
Kepit, but it will cost you."

"We understand each other," said Kepit.

*　　*　　*

IT WAS THREE days before Phara returned home. She rode through the beginning of one of the worst early winter blizzards in living Runchot memory. She was told she was a fool to travel, but her horse was one of Saeditin stock, with a heavy, shaggy coat, bred for winters. She made it back before the worst of the storm descended.

The House at the Edge was ablaze with lights. Most people assumed its name came from its situation near the border. The Runchot town of Forrz was as close to the Saeditin border as it could be without actually being in the mountains. It had grown up in the steep foothills, originally built on trade between the two lands, but more recently heavily fortified, the headquarters for Runchot troops, and a breeding ground of spies.

The House at the Edge had once been called, more simply, the House of Joy. It was here that Kirra had first become noticed, and it was the first house she had purchased. She had renamed it immediately. Only a few knew that Kirra had given it its name because she had felt close to the edge of reason, of losing her sanity, when she had worked there as a slave.

Now the lights blazed out into the falling snow. Kirra never skimped on lamp oil, candles, or torches, and the house was open for business in any weather. Phara left her horse with a stable hand and stood in the entrance hall, shaking snow from her cloak. She was wet, she was tired, and she was hungry.

"She's waiting for you. She said to bring you to her as soon as you arrived." A girl of about twelve years took Phara's cloak from her. There were a number of such very young girls in the house, whom Kirra had purchased outright. Most of them were commoners from Saeditin, kidnapped and sold over the border in the reign of Sithli SaeKet. Kirra purchased every one she could, but they were not available to patrons at any of her houses. It was bad business to keep such assets from her clients, and many speculated on what Kirra could want with those girls. The prevalent theory was that she used them herself. This was not true, but the rumors suited Kirra's purpose.

Phara wasted no time. She took the private corridor at the back of the house to Kirra's office. From elsewhere in the house came the sound of laughter. Despite the storm, there were some patrons.

Although the rest of the house was luxurious, Kirra's private office was austere but comfortable. Phara knocked twice and let herself in.

"Phara, my friend! The Mother be thanked that you have returned safely. Have a little spiced wine to warm you. I had a late supper brought in for you. I know you haven't paused since Ruda's Ford, trying to beat the storm."

It was true, but Phara did not ask how Kirra knew. It was whispered that her sources of information included the supernatural. Phara gratefully took the comfortable chair offered her and helped herself to the roast duck and fresh bread, while her employer poured her a mug of fine, heated Runchot wine.

The mysterious Kirra was neither a fabulous beauty nor exotic. She was still reasonably young, in her late twenties, and reasonably attractive, but her face bore lines of care and sorrow more suited to an older woman. Her hair was long, braided back in the Saeditin fashion, a nondescript light brown. She wore no jewels in it. Her eyes were sharp, and not much escaped that piercing blue gaze. She had reached her current position not through beauty but through intelligence and sheer, dauntless, patient persistence. She reminded many of a hunting cat waiting at the burrow of a springfox family. She was willing to wait as long as it took for the prey to come out. Now she waited for Phara to drink some of the wine and eat at least a little.

"Tell me. Did you come to an agreement?" There was a slight accent to Kirra's speech.

"Yes. It wasn't as hard as we thought." Phara wiped her mouth and sat back in the chair. "The gods came to our aid in the form of Sae Kepit's nephew, bringing news of his sister's execution. She had had no word of it before, so it was a shock. It was no difficulty at all to let her believe that we share an enemy in common. She asked why, but there was no trouble at all in putting her off."

"She is slipping. Or she believes she can discover the reason on her own." Kirra smiled faintly. "Did you see Sithli sae Melisin?"

"No." Phara regarded her employer with a certain trepidation. The venom in the tone of the question made her cautious. "Sithli sae Melisin was still with Prince Raphat. It seems they have rarely come out of the bedchamber for the past week."

"Fortunate indeed. I had misgivings about sending you on this errand at all. I heard that you did not use a disguise. You even used your own name. You were lucky that Sae Kepit did not question it. And it would have been disaster had your father seen you."

Phara shuddered slightly. She repressed her reaction at once, but she knew it had not escaped Kirra's notice. "He has no idea where I am. I want to keep it that way."

Kirra let it pass. Since Phara recognized how close she had come to losing everything, Kirra had no need to say more on the subject. Instead she asked, "Did you look?"

"I looked myself, and I had others look. There was no girl child fitting the description." Phara saw the expression on Kirra's face. She leaned forward and gently put her hand on the other woman's arm. "There were no girl children at all, fitting the description or not, who had been sold or purchased in the town during the past two years. It is an out-of-the-way place. It wasn't likely she would be there."

Kirra stared into the fire, not seeing it. Just what it was she saw, Phara did not really want to know.

"I will find her," said Kirra. "I must."

5

"PRINCE RAPHAT is still not certain that Sithli sae Melisin is even within Runchot. He does, naturally, have agents looking for her, and for her companion, Kepit sae Lisim. If he can find them, of course he will detain them and notify you immediately."

Jitta of Kiprin, supreme trade delegate of Runchot, was not happy. His delegation was staying in a fine house in Petipal, but they did not appreciate being summoned to the palace for this audience with the SaeKet during a blizzard. They had not even been permitted to shake all the snow from their cloaks, nor were they offered mugs of heated cider. If he had been ambassador, he would have had quarters in the palace itself. But there was no ambassador. He was the closest thing to one, and if he failed here, there might be war. If he were honest with himself, he would have to admit that war was inevitable. His prince was playing a dangerous game. Personally, he wished Raphat would hand over the two Saeditin fugitives. He understood that his prince was currently enjoying the young one, but what was so different about her? From the reports, she was a great beauty, but she couldn't be worth it. Runchot was full of beautiful women who came with fewer entanglements.

It was the second bad blizzard of the season, and Rilsin had already ordered the oxen teams to start clearing the Petipal roads. Saeditin were accustomed to harsh weather and were prepared for and expected to be snowbound for days or sometimes even weeks at a time, but Rilsin did not mean for weather to shut down her capital. She smiled blandly at the Runchot. She had not invited them to sit, and they stood uncomfortably, dripping melting puddles on the carpet of her audience room.

"I look forward to hearing this news from my friend the prince. Until that time, I am afraid we have nothing to discuss, Supreme Delegate Jitta. Good day to you."

Jitta stared at her. "But SaeKet, we have not discussed the trade issue! Surely we are not finished!" It had not escaped him that she had omitted "Trade" from his title. "My lord the prince has asked—"

"I am sorry, perhaps you did not understand me. This audience is concluded." Rilsin rose to her feet. Guards, hands on their swords, stepped between her and the Runchot delegation. Dumbstruck, with the snow from their arrival not yet completely melted from their clothes, Jitta and his company were escorted from the chamber, through the palace, and back out into the storm.

In the audience room, Rilsin sighed and sank back into her chair. The scar at her throat itched, something it hadn't done in a long time. It reminded her of Sifuat, of how he had almost killed her in a duel, before they had married. Before they had been forced to marry. It was odd, but she hadn't thought of Sifuat in days.

"Well done, SaeKet." Essit fairly radiated his approval. "We know Raphat has given them shelter. We should strike now, before they know it's coming."

"This is not the best of times for war, First Minister." She looked pointedly out the window, where outlines of trees in the palace garden seemed insubstantial through the thick white snow. "But they know it's coming, and they are planning for it, and we may not have much choice. Nonetheless, we will not strike yet."

Essit had been one of her captains in the winter campaign, which had stopped the previous Runchot invasion, and she knew he was remembering that war.

"I would not have chosen a winter campaign before, Sae Essit, and if I have a choice, I will not do so now."

"No one would," said Dremfir. "Rilsin SaeKet was blessed by the Mother, and called to defend our land—"

"Which she is again," Essit interrupted.

"No one disputes that, Sae Essit," said Dremfir mildly. "It is merely—"

"I dispute it," said Sola. "Or at least I question it. If war comes, then it does, but perhaps we can avert it."

Rilsin saw that Dremfir was about to object.

"This is not a council meeting," she said. "I value the opinions of all of you." She looked pointedly around the room. Aside from Essit, Dremfir, and Sola, there were other saedin present. She knew she had enemies among the nobles, and she did not want to present anything less than a united front outside of a full council meeting. She rose from the chair. "The audience is ended for today."

There was, in fact, no one left to see her. The snow had kept most commoners and nobles alike at home. She wanted to talk to Sola, but he was engaged in conversation with some earnest young saedin involved with him in the project of educating commoners. He left the room without looking back.

It was only much later in the day that she finally talked to him. She had been too busy to take time for herself, even for a meal. She had met with Essit on the matter of supply wagons stuck in the drifts to the east of the city, and she had met with a saedin who wished to request a city-trained physician for his saedhold.

When she saw Sola again, it was in the meeting over the matter of a school for the commoners. Never before in the history of Saeditin had there been such a thing, and Rilsin was amazed at the complexity of detail and the problems involved with starting one. Should only basic letters be taught, or should numbers? Which children would be qualified to attend, and how much would it cost? The priests would support it, Dremfir told her, if the teaching texts were simple prayers. The commoners whom she had invited for their opinions, Palma ria Settin and Chosi ria Zet, both of them fairly well-to-do, were so intimidated at being in the palace among saedin, and in the presence of the SaeKet, that at first they were reluctant to speak at all. She had appointed Sola to this work without understanding how involved it would be.

"I fear this takes too much of your time," she told him when at last they sat alone in one of the small meeting chambers. There was a fire burning, as the steam pipes could not completely ward off the bitter winter cold. "I had thought to solve the problem with a simple decree. From the arguments, it seems it will take a whole new ministry."

"I am glad to give the time, Rils. It will get easier, I know it." Education for the commoners had been Sola's idea, and he was proud of it. He had been afraid she would forget, once she came to power, but he should have known better. He smiled at her.

His smile crinkled the corners of his eyes and accentuated their blue color. It had done this always, from the time she had first met him when they were children. Some of his hair had escaped his long, plain braid, and it danced in fine, flyaway strands around his face. Sola rarely braided jewels into his hair as was the fashion among both noble classes. He had as little regard for ostentation as she did. His use of her childhood nickname reminded her of what she had wanted to say.

"I want to apologize, Sola. For what I said when we went riding. I was angry, I am angry with Sithli, and with the saedin that support her still, not with you."

"I know. I have something to say, too." Sola looked out the window. "What I wanted to say then, what I want to say to you now, has nothing to do with politics, Rilsin." He drew a deep breath and refused to look at her. "I loved you when we were children. I loved you when you married Sifuat, I loved you when you had no thought for me, and when you were in prison, and when you were in hiding. I have never thought about anyone else, even though my mother has urged me to marry." He had never admitted that to anyone. Kerida wanted grandchildren and was afraid she would never get them. Thinking of children made him think of Reniat and, inevitably, of Sifuat.

"I know you needed time after Sifuat died. But Rilsin, it's been more than a year. I still love you." He looked at her now. "I don't know if you can love me, I don't know if we are truly meant to be together, but I believe we are. Can we at least try? Can you love me?" He looked away again, afraid of her answer.

"Don't you know?" There was hurt in her voice, as if everything should have been plain, as if he shouldn't need to be told. But of course he couldn't know, since she had never admitted it fully, even to herself. "I have always loved you. Yes, I loved Sifuat. I will always love Sifuat in some way, but we were never right for each other, never meant for each other." She wanted to say that she hadn't been able to talk to him as she could to Sola, but she was watching the way the firelight moved across his face, the way his hair curled. Suddenly she very much wanted to see how his hair would look out of the braid, spread across his shoulders.

"I don't want you to have any doubts about what I feel." She rose to her feet and went to the door. "See that I am not disturbed," she told the guard, closing the door even as he was putting hand to heart.

She had hesitated before, when it was dangerous to show her friendship for anyone, let alone love. She had ignored her feelings for Sola as best she could when she was married to Sifuat. But now there was no Sithli to fear, to punish those she loved, just because she loved them. Now there was no husband to whom she felt a loyalty, however misplaced. They had no need to fear, no need to hide. They would be safe.

Rilsin walked over to Sola, watching the shadows shift across his face, watching the light dawning in his eyes, and the hope. She reached forward and began to undo his braid. At first he jumped, startled, but then let her do it, sighing as she ran her hands through his hair. She slid her hands down, under his shirt, and then began to undo the buttons. Her fingers were clumsy in the thick wool, and she felt unaccountably shy. She had never had many lovers, but she was not inexperienced. It was just that she had never been with anyone she cared about more. For reasons she didn't understand, she was suddenly afraid. She froze, unable to continue.

Sola reached up and gently took her hands from the buttons of his shirt. He finished undoing it himself and then pulled it up over his head and dropped it to the floor. The firelight played along his body. He was as unlike her husband as it was possible to be. Where Sifuat had been tall and brawny, Sola was slender and wiry but strong. His skin was pale, not the golden hue of Sifuat and many of the saedin, and his hair was as brown as Rilsin's, not the honey blond that had been Sifuat's. Sola was of the old Saeditin stock, the same stock as Rilsin.

Rilsin, watching him, found her breath coming short. She began to undo the buttons on her own shirt. They were silver, thick and clumsy, and they resisted her fingers until Sola came to help her with them, too. She ceased her own attempts and let him do the work while she ran her hands down his back. Eventually, her shirt joined his on the floor. He leaned forward to kiss her, his hair falling around them like a brown mist. She pushed him backward, returning the kiss with passion. There was a moment of confusion as they tried to remove each other's trousers, and they both began to laugh. Rilsin stopped the laughter by pressing her lips over Sola's again.

Later, they lay in each other's arms, watching the fire while the snow still fell outside the window. Rilsin thought she had never been so happy. Sithli, the Runchot, the storm, the nobles, everything but the present faded to the back of her mind.

"I waited a long time for this." Sola ran his hand along the curve of her bare hip.

"Too long," she said. "But the wait is over. We can be together now, and no one can stop us." Rilsin propped herself on her elbows and ran her tongue down the line of his jaw to his throat. Somewhere at the back of her mind was an uneasiness, as if by allowing herself to be happy she was invoking misfortune. The notion was ridiculous, and she banished it.

"YOU WANT it done in this weather, you do it yourself. I don't owe you this."

"You do owe me." Philla sae Lisim glared at the man across the scarred wooden table from him. "You owe everything to the Lisim, Nacrit! If it weren't for us, you would be across the border, coughing your lungs out in some Runchot mine, or worse."

"I owe your sister, the Mother rest her, and I owe that sly cat Kepit."

The firelight played over Nacrit's face, over the scar on one cheek, a reminder of pain overcome, a struggle survived. What was not visible was just as important, the sign of a different struggle survived: a brand on one shoulder beneath his shirt, remnant of a time when the agents of Kepit sae Lisim had taken him for his gambling debts and would have sold him into slavery in Runchot. Would have, if Kepit hadn't seen that he might be of value to her and kept him in Saeditin to do whatever the Lisim demanded of him.

He was not the smartest, as he would have been the first to admit, but he was strong, and he didn't mind killing if he needed to. He felt a mild contempt for this youngster of the Lisim line, this Lisim son who had wept at the feet of the Becha SaeKet, begging for his life. Philla sae Lisim was nothing like his sister Jolass had been.

"I owe them," he repeated, "but I don't owe you. And

I'm not going anywhere in this weather. When it clears, I'll do what Sae Kepit wants."

Nacrit turned away, as if dismissing Philla from his thoughts. In truth, he was far more interested in the fact that his mug was almost empty. The mug was suddenly knocked from his hand, to smash against the floor. He started to lunge to his feet, but Philla had him by the throat, and half-threw, half-heaved the larger man against the wall. Philla was nowhere near the size of the other man, but he was younger, he had been trained by his family, and he had something to prove. He had learned the hard way to never let a challenge go by.

"You decide if you owe me or not." He held his knife across Nacrit's throat. When Nacrit attempted to move, he felt the steel nick him.

"If you owe the Lisim, you owe me. I am the Lisim here, and you do what I say. If you think your debt is canceled, fine. I'll cancel it. Now." Philla increased the pressure with the knife blade.

Nacrit knew with a sudden clarity that Philla would kill him with no more hesitation than he would crush an insect, and with as little regret. He felt a cold sweat drip into his eyes.

"Gah. Stop." Just speaking moved the blade against his throat, and a trickle of blood ran down. "Please."

"Well?" Philla eased the pressure slightly. "What is it?"

"I'll do it! I'll do it!"

"Now?"

"Yes, now, the Mother curse you! Aaah, stop! I said I would do it!"

"Good." Philla abruptly withdrew the knife. He righted the fallen chair, took his own mug, went to the keg, and drew from the last of the ale.

Nacrit sagged weakly against the wall and then managed to sit down again. His hand trembled as he wiped it across his face.

"It's good we understand each other." Philla drank

deeply from the mug, then slid it across the table to Nacrit, who picked it up shakily and drained it.

"Everything is in place, and no one will be expecting anything during the storm. Now is the best time. Some of the guards are ours, and if you meet one I couldn't buy, well, let's just say it won't be a problem. Will it?"

Nacrit found he was clutching the mug, and put it down. His respect for this Lisim brat had increased dramatically. Philla saw this and smiled. It was about time he got a little respect for his own efforts rather than his sister's or his famous aunt's.

"Why," it came out more as a squeak than a word, and Nacrit tried again. "Why," he said, "don't you kill Rilsin SaeKet? If you can get into the palace and get out again. Why go through all this and not just kill her?"

"You are the one getting into the palace. As for why you won't kill her—" Philla frowned. He wanted to know, too. He couldn't tell this thug that he couldn't kill the SaeKet because his aunt Kepit said he couldn't. "It's part of the plan. You don't need to know everything." He had a sudden flash of insight. "If we kill her, it won't get Sithli SaeKet back for us now; it won't help. This will distract the Becha and will hurt her far worse." He smiled, thinking of how Rilsin would suffer. He owed her for killing his sister, for humiliating him.

"So don't kill her. Not even if you get the chance. I don't care if she lies down in front of you and offers you her throat." His smile grew broader.

Nacrit saw the smile and suppressed a shudder. He didn't care about Rilsin SaeKet one way or the other; he just cared about keeping this nasty Lisim brat away from him now. He needed more ale. He got to his feet and headed for the keg, but Philla was there before him, pulling the mug from his hands.

"Afterward you can have all the ale you want. Now, I need you thinking clearly. Or as clearly as it's possible for you to think. I want you out and back before the storm is over. The snow will cover your tracks if you play it right.

They won't know what happened. They can blame it on the winter demons."

Some of the more traditional saedin in Rilsin's court might do just that, Philla thought. He didn't think Rilsin would. She was modern. Modern enough to keep the city open during the storm, modern enough to have the ox plows out even now, clearing the roads. *The better for me to get out of Petipal,* he thought and grinned again.

6

EVERYONE IN THE PALACE KNEW. AS SOON AS THE STORM
was over, first all Petipal and then all Saeditin would know
that the SaeKet had taken a lover. Rilsin didn't care. Traditionally and in theory the SaeKet, like all other women, was
allowed as many lovers as she wished. In practice the
SaeKet, like all other women, could not have too many
without causing gossip. Rilsin planned on having only one.
She was happy, and she didn't care that it showed.

Dinner that night was informal. Because of the storm,
there were few saedin in attendance in the palace, but Rilsin
had always preferred informal meals, in contrast to Sithli's
elaborate banquets. Sola was there, and they could not keep
their eyes from each other. Rilsin had wanted to eat in her
private quarters with only Sola, Reniat, and Meffa. Her
family, she thought. But Sola still seemed a little unsettled
around her daughter, and she wasn't willing to spoil things
by having a confrontation over the issue yet. She found that
she was ravenous, and she ate more than she had planned
and drank a little more good Runchot wine than she usually

did. When at last she left for her own quarters, she was pleasantly full and pleasantly exhausted. Sola walked with her. Outside, the world had grown dark, and storm winds battered against the windows.

"Everyone knows," he said.

"Do you care?" She smiled at him. "People will talk for a time, but they will get accustomed to it." She was wondering whether to ask him to move into the palace. He had always valued his privacy, so perhaps this was too soon.

Wrapped in her thoughts, it was a moment before she realized there was something wrong. There was no guard outside her private quarters. She dropped Sola's hand.

"What is it? What's wrong?"

She heard him as if from a distance; everything around her grew as cold as the storm outside.

"Go get the guards." She was unarmed except for a slender knife she wore at her waist, a gift from the Iron Guild, more ornament than weapon. She drew this and opened the door to her quarters. She was peripherally aware that Sola was still beside her, that he had not gone to get the guards, and that he had drawn his sword.

The first thing she saw was Chilsa. The big cat was limp, half curled up on the floor right inside the door. He lay in a pool of blood, and his silver fur was matted. Rilsin dropped to her knees beside him. He was warm, still breathing. It became obvious as she moved him that it was not his own blood he lay in, or not much of it. It was also obvious that he had been drugged. The dart was still in his side. Whoever had done this to him had paid with his own blood and had been too hurt or too pressed for time to remove the dart or to finish off the cat. Rilsin removed the dart herself, dropping it to the floor, and stood.

Sola had moved ahead into the other rooms. She heard him say something, more a strangled noise than a word, and she ran forward to Reniat's room.

Sola stood in the doorway, his sword hanging loosely in his hand. Rilsin pushed by him. On the floor by the crib was Reniat's guard. The young woman had tried to defend the little SaeKetti, and she had put up quite a fight. The room and the little bed were splashed with blood, much of it still wet. She sprawled, graceless in death, partially across Reniat's crib. Meffa herself lay in a corner. Sola strode over to her, felt for a pulse.

"She's alive," he said.

Rilsin barely heard him. She was pulling the sheets from the crib, tossing them aside. She looked in the clothing alcove. She looked in Reniat's carved toy bin. She looked behind the chair.

"Reniat," she whispered, then louder, "Reni!" She turned to run from the room; there were other rooms to search. In the big parlor she was met by a blast of winter wind and snow. The big window and the adjacent door were open. They opened out to the SaeKet's private garden. It was normally locked, in this season, against the winter cold. In summer, there would have been guards outside the garden entrance, but not in this storm. Without hesitation, Rilsin strode out into the thickly falling snow.

"Reni! Reniat! Reniat!"

The snow muffled her shouts. She looked down and saw footprints of at least two people, but they were being filled in rapidly by the falling snow. Soon it would be impossible to follow them. She needed Chilsa; Chilsa could track anything, in any weather, but the big cat was wounded and ill. Rilsin followed the tracks out into the blizzard, moving farther and farther from the palace. Some distance from the palace was a body: one of the Petipal Guard. He had lost his life to the kidnapper. Rilsin followed the remaining set of tracks. Soon she wasn't following the tracks at all, but something else. She began to shiver but didn't notice. Her feet, in plain leather shoes, began to freeze.

"SaeKet! SaeKet! Stop, please!" It seemed that Sola had called the guards after all, and here they were. She ignored them to continue searching through the waist-deep snow of the garden.

"SaeKet! Commander!"Someone had her by the shoulders. The sound of her old rank made her stop searching for a moment. Rilsin blinked snow from her eyes and looked up. It was Pleffin sae Grisna. He was commander now, the commander of her forces.

"Pleffin." Her teeth chattered.

Without hesitation, Pleffin pulled off his cloak and slung it around her. "Come inside, SaeKet. You aren't dressed for this. We will search. With your permission, I will call out the cats. Whoever did this," he hesitated, "whoever took the SaeKetti can't have gone far. Not in this storm."

This reminded her of something. "Send out the cats," she said, "and have Kerida dira Mudrin come to the palace with her medical supplies. She can bring a veterinary surgeon, but I want her, for Chilsa."

"Immediately, SaeKet." Pleffin gave the order. "Come in, please. You can't track them in this. Leave it for the cats."

"Please, Rilsin." Sola was there, somehow, and he took her hands. "Great Mother, you're cold! Please come in, Rils."

She allowed herself to be drawn back toward the palace; how did it get so far away? She was far out at the edge of the grounds, and the palace lights shone like a distant beacon through the snow.

Inside it was so warm. Maltia the physician was there; she heard him say something low-voiced to Sola about "shock." Maltia was senior physician, and one of his apprentices was bending over Meffa. How could she have forgotten Meffa? With an effort, Rilsin concentrated her thoughts.

"How is she?" Her voice was weak, but it cut through the concerned hum around her. "Meffa, how is Meffa? Will she live?"

"She will be fine, SaeKet. She is drugged."

Like Chilsa, Rilsin thought. She must have said it aloud.

"Chilsa will recover, SaeKet; it won't be long. Only a few days, I believe." It was Kerida dira Mudrin, the keeper of the cats, Sola's mother. She had come as Rilsin had asked—no, commanded, Rilsin remembered. It hadn't taken her long to arrive. Had it? How long had Rilsin been out in the snow?

"Drink this, Rils. Sae Maltia says to drink this. Rilsin SaeKet, please." Sola was trying to give her a mug of something.

His use of her title reminded her that there were others around. Why did she keep forgetting things? Her feet were beginning to hurt, and she realized that she had the beginnings of frostbite. She took the mug from Sola and drank. It was mulled wine. The warmth helped. She heard conversation behind her, something about "blood" and "the SaeKetti." As the wine and the warmth flowed through her, she found her mind beginning to function again.

"The SaeKetti is not dead." This time her voice was strong. "That is not her blood in the crib. It is the guard's and someone else's. The kidnapper's. Reniat is alive and unharmed. I know it."

She had been aware of it outside in the snow, sensing Reniat somewhere in her mind, in her soul, like a faint star. It was this starlight she had been following outside in the storm more than any tracks. She rose to her feet. She was in her private parlor, which was jammed with people now. The window and the door to the garden had been closed, and outside the snow still fell in a blanket of white.

"I can feel my child," she said. "She's alive."

Silence rippled out from her words, and she caught Essit exchanging a concerned glance with Sola. They thought she was in that chilled state that distorted the mind. This happened to people caught out in storms or lost in the cold of a Saeditin winter. She had seen people die of this, of being so chilled that life never returned, even after the victim was brought into the warmth.

"It is possible that the SaeKet can sense her child. The Mother has been known to give such a blessing before, on occasion."

When had Dremfir arrived? Rilsin had not called for him.

"I came as soon as I heard, SaeKet, on the chance that I

could assist in any way. I wish I could alter weather as well as read it, but I don't have that gift." Dremfir had the capacity to feel and foretell weather. Unfortunately, it was not a reliable talent.

"Can you feel when this storm will end?"

"I can, SaeKet. It will end by dawn."

Rilsin stared out at the snow again. If anything, the storm seemed worse. She did not trust mystical powers. She knew Dremfir had his unreliable talent, and she knew that she herself had heard the song of the land, that rich blend of impressions that seemed to well up from the soil itself, that came, according to legend, from the Mother of all life. Saedin heard the song before they died, the legends said, but the SaeKet could hear it any time. Rilsin knew this last to be true, but she did not believe it was mystical. It had, she was certain, a rational explanation, which had yet to be found.

As she thought this, Rilsin felt the faint beacon connecting her to Reniat falter and fade. She sat up straighter, straining after it, but it was gone. She looked up and found Dremfir watching her. She wanted to say, *It's gone,* but she wasn't sure now that she had felt it to begin with.

A guard captain was at the door to her suite, reporting to Pleffin on the progress of the search. Rilsin called him in.

"I am sorry, SaeKet. The cats have lost the trail. The snow is too deep and falling too fast." The captain saluted with his hand to his heart, but he looked uneasy, as if he expected blame.

"Understandable. Continue the search nonetheless. Wait a moment."

Rilsin went to Reniat's room. The blood was still spattered everywhere, but the guard's body had been removed. She felt a pang of sorrow for the young woman who had died in defense of her daughter. She knew who was behind this, if not yet whose hand had struck the blows.

"They will pay," she promised the empty room and the guard's spirit, if it listened.

She found one of Reniat's little overshirts, one that had

not yet been taken to the washerwomen. She buried her face in it, inhaling her daughter's scent. There was no time for this. She took the shirt out to the waiting captain.

"For the hunting cats," she said. "To give them the SaeKetti's scent." She turned to everyone in the room. "I want the southern border closed," she said. Her voice was cold, an echo of the storm. "I know who is behind this, and I know why. Sithli sae Melisin will not have my child. Storm or no storm, I want nothing to get into Runchot that does not belong there."

"As you command, SaeKet." Pleffin knew that messengers would have to go out immediately.

"Search all night, and in the morning I will join you."

They had the sense not to argue with her. Only when they had all left, all but Sola, did Rilsin sink back in the chair again. Meffa had been taken to the physician's quarters, as Maltia wanted to watch her closely. Servants had come to clean Reniat's room, but Rilsin ignored them. Kerida and her staff had taken Chilsa into the private dining area to treat him, so Rilsin and Sola were alone.

"You need to rest, Rils. Can you sleep? Sae Maltia will give you a potion."

"I can't sleep." Rilsin was exhausted, but the thought of sleep, while her daughter was still missing, was unbearable. She looked at Sola. If she had not taken time with him, if they had not been together so long, ignoring the world, if she had not been so wrapped in her false dream of safety, if she had not been with him at the small dinner, if she had only come back to her own apartments as she had intended, when she had intended, if only she had thought to put guards in the garden, in the storm, if only she had been here when they came . . .

"Stop, Rilsin. I can feel what you are thinking. It does no good. If you had been here when they came—" He paused and shuddered.

"Do you think I would have let them take my child? Do you think they could have?" Rilsin looked at him as if she had never seen him before. "You think I would not have defended Reni, and myself, and Meffa—"

"You don't go armed in your own rooms," he said. "That poor guard was armed, and look what it got her."

"I am not a guard," she said and stalked from the room to check on Chilsa.

Sola watched her go. He knew she was hurt, and he knew she was unbearably frightened for her child, but he had the feeling of something slipping away, something dying before it was truly born. He wanted to reach to her, to comfort her, but he could not touch her across the sudden distance that had opened between them.

THE MORNING DAWNED clear. Just as Dremfir had promised, the storm had broken. Clouds streamed away to the west, chased by a bright wind that came all the way from the steppe lands far to the east. The late rising sun of a winter day rose blindingly over the new white of the fresh, deep snow. The SaeKet's Road, connecting Petipal both north and south with the surrounding saedholds of Saeditin, was already clear for miles, due to the efforts of the ox teams with their plows, who kept working all throughout the storm. Down this road came riding an emissary from the far north, urgently seeking audience with the SaeKet.

Rilsin, anxious to join the search for her lost child, was in no mood to greet an emissary, no matter how urgent the message. Saedhold business could wait.

"They aren't saedin," Essit told her. "They are Confederacy, from First Man Bilt. They have been on the road for weeks, and they were delayed by the weather."

She had to see them. Her assistance to Bilt of the Wilfrisin had been in part responsible for the Confederacy's birth. The Confederacy's aid had helped her win back the SaeKet's chair. For the sake of the land she must see what had brought them south in the worst season, and urgently. The search would have to go on without her. The land needed her as much as her child did, and she knew where her duty lay.

The emissaries looked as tired as she felt. They stood in the audience chamber still flushed with the cold. She realized she knew one of them.

"Chif, my friend! Please, you and your delegation be seated." At her gesture, chairs were brought forward for the three men. Two of them immediately sat, but Chif did not.

"We have urgent message, SaeKet," he said, his Wilfrisin accent strong but understandable.

There were few in attendance that morning: Essit, Dremfir, and some guards at the chamber's periphery. Most saedin and dira were still home, digging out from the storm, and those in the palace saw no need to concern themselves with a barbarian delegation.

"You may speak freely, my friend."

"We travel south from Confederacy for many days now. We keep off big roads so few notice us, and we blend into countryside, even though this delay our travel." The big man had been a Wilfrisin fore-fighter and still kept his hair dyed blue, as was fore-fighter custom, and he still kept his bushy red beard. Combined with his great height and massive frame, this made him noticeable under any circumstances. Rilsin had had no reports of this group, and she couldn't understand why not, unless her countrymen had suddenly all been stricken blind.

"I wear hat most of time." Chif grinned at her, his blue eyes twinkling. He pulled out a knit cap of the kind common in the Saeditin north as well as the Confederacy, and held it in his huge hands. "All my hair fit under this."

One of his compatriots cleared his throat, and Chif's smile faded.

"Bad news, SaeKet," he said bluntly. "There is division in Confederacy. First Man hears much from Clinsi, some Clinsi, about how they no longer like Confederacy and want to be on own again. If they do this," he gestured, an abrupt chopping motion, "no Confederacy."

Rilsin frowned. "Is it many Clinsi?" If the Confederacy broke down, there could be trouble to Saeditin's north again, instead of a stable alliance.

"Not many. Confederacy remain strong, truly."

"Then why are you here?" Rilsin could feel herself losing patience and willed herself not to show it. The search for her daughter would continue without her.

"Because in dealing with this small problem First Man Bilt find something bad. He find," Chif lowered his voice so that Rilsin and Essit, standing at her right hand, leaned forward, even though they could still hear him perfectly. "He find," said Chif again, "that some Clinsi want to raid Saeditin farms again. That they are, how do you say, helped, encouraged?"

"Yes. Encouraged." Rilsin tried not to fidget.

"Encouraged, thank you, encouraged in this by outsiders. By Sae Melisin. By Sae Lisim. That Sae Kepit, she send money, too, to Clinsi, so they attack over border, attack Saeditin farms, without First Man knowing. But he knows now, and he send us to warn you. That way you know, if he cannot stop all raids, that this is not his fault."

Raiding across the border had been a spring tradition of the tribes before Bilt had united them and forged an alliance with Rilsin. It had been a rite of passage for many young barbarian men. It was a custom she was glad to have seen the last of.

"Thank the first man for me, Chif. When spring comes, we will be prepared."

"Not in spring, SaeKet. Raids are to start now. By Sunreturn, even. First Man Bilt cannot stop them all."

7

"THEY HAVE NOT BROUGHT THE CHILD INTO RUNCHOT. WE would know it if they tried, and so would Rilsin SaeKet. She has closed the border. It is almost impossible for anyone to slip through."

"'Almost' is not the same thing as 'impossible,' as we both know." Kirra looked intently at her lieutenant, but Phara just shook her head.

The afternoon light lay long and red across the table between the two women. Bread and cider sat on the table, untouched. A fire crackled nearby in the fireplace, but the room was still too cold, and Phara was glad of her thick woolen overshirt. The sooner the Runchot got around to learning the Saeditin magic of steam, the better.

"She has not been brought south. I am sure of it. Our network would know."

"What could they be doing with her? Where can they be hiding her? Sithli sae Melisin had Reniat once, took her from Rilsin sae Becha." There was a certain amount of grim satisfaction in Kirra's voice. "The Melisin said she was adopting Reniat."

Phara knew this: Anyone who followed the events in Saeditin knew this and knew also that Sithli had used the baby for a shield to help her escape Rilsin's army. If it hadn't been for Rilsin's hunting cat Chilsa, the baby would have died when Sithli flung her from a balcony. Chilsa had caught the baby in his mouth.

"Sithli wants the child for revenge on Rilsin," said Phara, "or for a hostage. Or for some purpose of her own."

"That's what the Melisin wants with everyone," said Kirra dryly. "She always has a purpose of her own, and the purpose is always Sithli sae Melisin." She leaned over, took a mug, and poured herself some cider.

"Are we sure Sithli sae Melisin took the child?" asked Phara.

"Her agents, or Kepit sae Lisim's, which is the same thing. There are still members of the Lisim clan alive. Rilsin SaeKet did not kill them all. She always had a soft streak." Kirra looked at Phara but did not see her. She saw the past instead, saw a slightly younger Rilsin, still Sithli's first minister, still trying to uphold her cousin's reign, no matter what the cost.

Kirra shook herself from the past. Phara was patiently waiting, accustomed to the dark memories of her friend and patron.

"What do we do now?" Phara asked. "We can't get the child if we don't know where she is. If my father gets her—"

"That we must prevent at all costs. We need to know just how much support he will give to Sithli sae Melisin. We need Sithli to move before she is ready, and that will be hard with Kepit sae Lisim in control. Sithli is easy to fool; Kepit is another matter."

"We can have Kepit removed." Phara showed no expression. They both knew what she meant by "removed."

"No. I doubt we could, and we do not want to try. We want the Melisin woman to think she is proceeding at her own pace and that she is in control. The best would be for

Rilsin sae Becha to attack now, before Sithli gets what she needs."

"I pray with all my heart there will be no war. I will light candles to the gods for this. They may, out of justice, grant my prayers."

Kirra snorted indelicately. "The gods are not just; they never have been. Not even the Mother Herself is just, let alone those you Runchot worship. How can you be so pious? You know from your own experience that no god cares. They don't listen to us, Princess of Merri."

"They brought me to you when I had nowhere else to go," said Phara calmly. She knew why her mentor had lost her faith, and she knew why this matter of a stolen Saeditin child was almost unbearably painful for her. She understood the impulse Kirra had to take out her anger on someone else, but she refused to rise to the bait. "What are the chances that the SaeKet will come over the border in winter?"

"Slim. Rilsin is good at war, but she does not love it. Another softness."

"Your Saeditin might be better off without her," Phara commented.

There was a crack as Kirra set her mug down on the table so hard that it chipped. "Rilsin SaeKet Becha is the true SaeKet. The land itself cried out for her! I wish only that she had acted far sooner."

Phara did not flinch. "I wonder for whom Runchot cries out," she murmured.

"Not for you, I fear. For your brother, perhaps." Kirra had regained her calm. "A woman has never ruled in Runchot, at least not in her own name. You should have been born in Saeditin."

The two women exchanged rueful smiles. There was silence for a moment as both were lost in thought. During their conversation, the sun had set. The room was bathed in dusk and firelight. Phara thought of her brother Tonar, whom she missed terribly.

"What will it take to get Rilsin to act?" said Phara at last.

"Wrong question, my friend. You should ask instead what it will take to bring Sithli to act. Unless Rilsin can prove that Sithli has her child, or unless there is an imminent threat to Saeditin, she will not cross the border in winter. Every moment she delays is a moment the Sae Melisin will use. We must make Sithli—and Kepit—in a fever to move, in a fever to cross the border northward and attack Saeditin."

"There will be raids; we know they are planning raids. Perhaps that will be enough—"

"Not just raids, Phara. They must think they have the forces to invade Saeditin, to take Petipal, but they must not have them. When they cross the border they will find that the Saeditin army will have them, instead," she smiled, "for an easy meal."

Phara stared at her. "How can that be accomplished, Kirra? Surely Kepit sae Lisim knows what troops are committed to their cause."

"It can be done. Surely your father taught you that people believe what they want to believe with very little encouragement. A merchant of northern Runchot wishes to support Sithli. Wishes to supply not just information but troops. Enough troops to make a good showing, with a promise of more to be raised when they are needed."

"What merchant? Kepit sae Lisim will investigate."

"I am the merchant. We don't hide that. Surely your father also taught you to tell as much truth as possible when you are engaged in deception. We let it be known that I wish many substantial rewards in return for this aid. Rewards of plunder from Petipal, but also young and attractive Saeditin captives, female and male, to be used for my business. Sithli sae Melisin will not question this. It was her practice as SaeKet to sell prisoners, as I personally know, and it costs her nothing." She paused, looking into the distance again. "I am, in fact, thinking of bringing in some young men." Kirra tapped a finger thoughtfully against the table. "I have had enough patrons request them. I should have at least a few to offer."

Phara swallowed. There were times when her benefactor and employer frightened her. She knew what Kirra had been before she was Kirra the pleasure merchant, even before she was Kirra the Saeditin slave. She had been a washerwoman in the Saeditin capital of Petipal. If a hard fate had not brought Kirra to Runchot, would all her talents have been lost, or would she have found another outlet?

"Kepit sae Lisim has already investigated you, were you aware? Or rather, she has investigated one Phara of House Qit. Luckily, Phara is a common name. Even should she, for some reason, mention your name to Raphat, it will not arouse his suspicion. It is Raphat I am concerned about. Your father sees more clearly than many. I do not know what he thinks of Sithli sae Melisin, and I do not know what his plans are in regard to her. I need to know."

From somewhere in the house came deep male laughter and the lighter chiming laugh of women. It was after dark now, and the House at the Edge was entering the busiest part of its day. Kirra rose, lit one of the lamps, and straightened her overshirt.

"I need to make the rounds, see some of the guests. It's good for business. How do we find out what your father thinks of Sithli sae Melisin, Phara?"

Phara knew this wasn't really a question, that Kirra already knew the answer.

"We cannot send a pleasure woman. My father has Sithli sae Melisin in his bed now. Whatever his faults, he has never had more than one woman at a time, or at least more than one mistress." She heard the bitterness in her own voice. "We need someone in the household who will not be noticed, someone who has access to the rooms and who knows what to listen for and what to look for. We need a servant, I think. A native Runchot who can read and write both Runchot and Saeditin."

"Yes, indeed. And there will be one, not just a servant, but a slave carefully trained in quiet but useful arts. A charming and beautiful slave, not as beautiful as the Melisin woman herself, of course. This servant will be my personal gift to Sithli sae Melisin, to wait on her every need, to fulfill her every wish. This slave will be a token of my very great esteem for Sithli sae Melisin and a promise of a profitable relationship, should she choose to accept and use this gift. And she will accept and use it."

"Perfect." Phara quickly ran through a mental list of potential candidates for this position. There were a number of Runchot women who came close to having the qualifications, but all were commoners, and none could read and write.

"Who will fill this post of slave, Kirra?"

Kirra smiled faintly. "You will," she said.

Phara opened her mouth, shut it with a snap, then opened it again. "You told me to stay away from my father," she said. "What if he should see me?"

"You will stay away from him, and he will see you, both. Don't you think we can disguise you so he will never recognize you? You will be Sithli's property. She will not want you to have much to do with the prince, you can be sure. You will not be alone in that household. I will place some help for you there, perhaps in the kitchens, or perhaps," she smiled, "a washerwoman. Someone to help you get the information out and to help you get out, should the situation become dangerous. More dangerous. Too dangerous." She smiled again. "Clever I know you are. Can you be careful? Can you be careful enough not to jeopardize our work? And your life?"

"I can."

"Will you do this, Phara? Of your own will, I mean. You are a free woman and not property, after all." Kirra looked down for a moment and then looked directly into Phara's eyes. "You are my friend."

Despite herself, Phara was touched. She wasn't sure that Kirra really knew what friendship was. Nonetheless, she knew she was the closest thing Kirra had to a friend.

"I will do it," she said. "Of my free will."

"Why?"

Kirra's eyes had locked onto hers, and Phara couldn't look away. The question hung in the air between them.

"You know why," Phara began, but she stopped. "It's my father," she said slowly. "I needed to get away from him, to escape what he wanted for me, and I did that.

"Now I want to pay my father back. In part for what he did to me, but more for what he did to my mother. I want him to suffer as she did!" Phara's voice wasn't as cold or as steady as she would have liked. "And he will ruin Runchot, especially now that he has taken in Sithli sae Melisin. He will bring us to war with Saeditin, and he will destroy this land. I will kill him if I must!"

"Well, that's honest. But you shouldn't have to kill him, and I would much prefer that you not. Stay away from him. Spoiling his alliance with Sithli will keep him from another power base in Saeditin. It will ruin his plans, and that should be enough." Kirra wondered if Phara realized that she loved her father as well as hated him. It was unfortunate that she had no one else to send.

"But that doesn't really answer my question. After you have taken whatever revenge you need to take on your father, Phara, what do you want for yourself?"

"I don't know," said Phara slowly. "I had not thought that far."

"Honest again," said Kirra. "That is all I can ask."

She needed to ask the same question of herself, she realized. All of her energies had been focused on her lost and stolen child and bringing down the woman responsible for her loss. She had not thought beyond this. It was an odd twist of fate that she and the rightful ruler of Saeditin shared the same loss and the same enemy.

KIRRA HAD BEEΠ right; Phara's disguise was excellent. She had already come into contact with servants of her father who would have remembered the Princess Phara but who did not look twice at the soft-spoken, shy, and gentle slave who was given into their temporary custody while Kirra's official emissary spoke with Kepit sae Lisim. Phara's stunning strawberry blonde hair had been cut short, as was the custom for captives and slaves in Runchot as well as Saeditin. It had also been dyed a very dark brown, and her eyebrows had been tinted to match. Phara had inserted a pebble into her left shoe, which gave her a slight limp.

Most convincing was the scar across her right wrist, a feature neither the princess nor Phara of the minor house of Qit, Kirra's first emissary, had shown. The scar was real. Phara had made the cut herself, and Kirra's house physician had rubbed ashes into it to make it heal more slowly and become permanent. It still hurt, and it was red, raised, and ugly, but in truth she regretted it less than the loss of her hair.

The scar was part of the story of Kirra's gift to Sithli. The slave Barrit had displeased the pleasure merchant, the story went, and Kirra had punished her by cutting her with her own knife and then sending her to Sithli as a gift.

"You, Barrit, come. Sae Kepit wants to see you before you are given to your new mistress."

Luckily, Phara remembered her new name just in time, before the servant could notice her distraction. She had been engaged in a surreptitious examination of the back kitchen of this house, one of her father's. She had never been in a back kitchen before, and she was amazed at the quantities of pots and utensils, knives, cutting boards, and dishes stored there. She jumped to her feet, realizing that she needed to focus now. The servants were one thing, but if her disguise could withstand Kepit's scrutiny, then she was on her way to success.

Kepit sae Lisim was waiting in the same room Phara had seen before. A fire crackled in the fireplace, and Kepit had pulled her chair close to its warmth. Sithli sae Melisin was not present. Phara entered the room and immediately crossed her arms over her chest and bowed like a good Runchot slave.

"So you are Barrit. Come closer and stand up straight."

Phara did as she was commanded, but she kept her eyes downcast. She could feel the intense scrutiny of the older

woman, and she was careful to keep herself completely
still. Suddenly Kepit reached out and grasped her right
wrist, just above the inflamed scar. Phara tried to suppress
a soft mew of pain.

"Tell me about this, Barrit."

"I displeased my mistress Kirra, and she punished me."
Phara kept her eyes down.

"So they told me. I want to know what happened."

"It was one of my duties to keep track of traders bringing in new stocks of captives and slaves. My lady Kirra
wants to know about all children for sale. I neglected to talk
to one trader. He had three girls. By the time I remembered
and spoke to him, the girls had all been sold. My lady was
furious. She said she wanted me out of her sight."

This was the tale Kirra and Phara had cooked up between them. If anything would anger her, it would be an
oversight such as the one Barrit had supposedly committed.
Her desire for young girl slaves was well-known.

"It is good you told me the truth." Kepit drew her shawl
closer around her. "A lie would have gotten you whipped
and sold. So you see, you must always tell me the truth."

It occurred to Phara that she had not considered all the
possible dangers of her mission and how completely pow-
erless she would feel. If Kepit had sold her, especially to a
slave merchant headed south or east, it might be a long
time, if ever, before Kirra could rescue her. She began to
shiver.

"I see you understand me. Tell me, do you resent the
lady Kirra for what she has done to you? Look at me when
you answer!" Kepit's voice cracked with command, and
Phara looked Kepit in the eyes for the first time.

"No. I don't resent her." Phara let her eyes fill with tears.
The ability to cry on command was a talent she had discovered when she was very young. It had helped her in the
past both with her father and with her beloved older brother
Tonar. "I am sorry I failed Kirra. I am so sorry. She was so
kind to me. I thought she would forgive me for this, but I
failed her trust. She trusted me, and—" Phara began to cry

harder, her sobs choking off her words. She glanced at Kepit from under her lashes. Perhaps this was too much. She reined in her sobs. "I will never fail again," she said earnestly.

"I hope not." Kepit seemed relieved that Phara's tears were ending. "Lady Swiffa has assured me that you know how to dress hair and care for clothing, that you know how to apply makeup." Swiffa was Kirra's current emissary.

"I do." Phara sniffed.

"And you can also read and write."

Phara tensed, then forced herself to relax. Why did Kepit ask this? None of the information she had been given about Barrit would have suggested this. It was an arrow shot in the dark, a leading question. Phara was tempted to lie, but she remembered Kirra's advice to tell at least some truth when possible.

"I can," she said proudly.

Kepit went to a table, picked up a piece of paper, and handed it to her. "Read this to me," she said.

Phara looked at the paper, which she was holding upside down. It was an invitation, written in Saeditin, from her father to Sithli sae Melisin, asking her to attend a Sunreturn festivity in this house. As a member of the ruling family, Phara had been taught to speak Saeditin fluently and to read it. "I cannot," she whispered, letting the tears build up in her eyes again. "It is not in words I know."

Kepit took the paper from her and handed her another. This one was written in Runchot.

"Five, no five-ty, fifty! loaves of new, ah, bread." It was a list for the kitchens, for a feast. She had often made up such lists herself in the past. Kepit took it from her.

"That will do. You will serve Sithli SaeKet, Barrit. You will sleep on a bed in the changing closet, and you will eat your meals in the servants' kitchen." Kepit rang a bell, summoning a servant. "Go with Rudfa here and get something to eat. Rudfa will show you around the house." Rudfa was the first among servants, a free man. Phara would be under his supervision.

"Thank you, my lady."

"Sae Kepit. You may as well start learning Saeditin forms of address." Kepit turned her back, dismissing Phara.

She did not see the smile of triumph that Phara could not repress. Kepit, the brilliant saedin who noticed everything, had not recognized her. She was in.

8

"SURELY YOU WON'T GO, YOURSELF. SAEDITIN NEEDS YOU here, Rilsin SaeKet. In Petipal." Sola was worried. He had managed to obtain this audience with her, and the fact that it was an audience, in the formal audience chamber, and that others were present added to his concern. Since her daughter had been stolen, Rilsin had found every opportunity to avoid seeing him privately.

The room was filled with nobles, with saedin and some dira who had heard of the Wilfrisin delegation's warning, and who had been murmuring among themselves about the continued threat from Sithli and her probable Runchot allies. Essit sae Tillit was there, in his capacity as first minister, and Sae Dremfir the mage, and Pleffin sae Grisna, the SaeKet's commander.

"Someone has to go north to protect the border farms. Chif said the raids will start now. In winter. And someone must be prepared to go south, to the Runchot border." Rilsin looked out the window. The sun on the whiteness of the new snow was blinding. "You don't need to say it, Dira

Sola; I should not go myself; it isn't safe, and I'm the SaeKet." Rilsin's frown made clear how little she thought of that argument. "Don't worry, I'm not going north to deal with a few raids. We still have no news of Reniat, and I intend to search for the SaeKetti. Sae Pleffin will go north to insure the safety of the border farms. You should not need many troops for this job, Sae Pleffin, as you will be able to rely on the aid of the Wilfrisin and the Confederacy."

"As you command, SaeKet." Pleffin put his hand to his heart. He was no stranger to campaigns in any season.

"Some of the troops must stay in Petipal to protect the capital. Sae Essit, they will be under your command."

Her first minister looked happy. Essit was a good captain.

"Some of the Petipal guards will go south, to patrol the roads and continue the patrol of the border." *Searching for Reniat.* Rilsin didn't say it, but they heard it as clearly as if she had. She planned to join them when she could. She didn't say this, either.

Sola looked as if he wanted to argue with her, but she held up a hand to ward off dissent.

"This will wait." Rilsin motioned him to silence as one of the guards entered the room and nodded to her. This was what she had been waiting for. "Send them in," she said.

It was the Runchot trade delegation, and a murmur of anger from the assembled nobles greeted them. Sola could see from their bewilderment that Rilsin had summoned them, and they didn't know why. He glanced at Rilsin, and suddenly he understood. Her face was tight, and her eyes were very cold. The supreme trade delegate, a short, round man with a pink face and fair hair—his name was Jitta, Sola remembered—had seen Rilsin's expression. He bowed to Rilsin, trying not to look as worried as he obviously was.

"Delegate Jitta, you have heard that my daughter, Reniat SaeKetti Becha, was kidnapped several days ago."

Jitta's pink face paled. "I was devastated to hear of this, SaeKet."

"Were you, indeed."

Something about the way she looked at him made the trade delegate step backward, bumping into others of his delegation.

"Surely you don't think we had anything to do with it, SaeKet!" He glanced around the room again in search of support from some of the Saeditin, not finding any. "We are here only as trade delegates! Nothing more!"

Rilsin let his words fall into silence. "No, I don't believe you had anything to do with it," she said and waited for the relief to show on his face. "Nor do I believe your prince was behind it." She paused again and was rewarded by seeing the dawn of understanding in Jitta's eyes.

"Then perhaps we can talk of the trade agreement again." Jitta's words were belied by his hopeless tone.

"We will not talk of trade until my daughter is returned and until the criminals Sithli sae Melisin and Kepit sae Lisim are given over to me. I know Prince Raphat did not have my daughter abducted. Sithli sae Melisin did, and she is his guest. As long as he harbors her, and Kepit sae Lisim with her, and as long as my enemies have the SaeKetti, neither you nor any official of Runchot is welcome within the land of Saeditin. You, Jitta, and your delegation with you, will leave Petipal within the hour."

"But SaeKet—"

"Guard, have them escorted until they cross the border safely into Runchot."

The protesting Runchot were taken from the room, and Rilsin sank back in her chair. She felt tired, although it was still morning. She looked around at the saedin and the few dira in the room.

All of them looked stunned.

"You have all but declared war, Rilsin SaeKet," said Sola.

"Not yet," she said, "but we are ready if the Runchot so choose."

The room erupted into cheers. Saedin whistled and stomped like commoners at a horse race, and two of the dira were slapping each other on the back. Her guards were grinning.

"They have it coming," she heard someone say, and someone else said, "At last."

"Clear the room," said Rilsin. She knew the commoners would support her, as they remembered all too well how their children had been kidnapped and sold across the border, but she was warmed by the support of the nobles and honoreds. Some of the dira had lost children, too, during Sithli's reign. Although they and the saedin had much to gain from trade with Runchot, it seemed that the old injuries were not forgotten, nor was the long history of enmity and insults from their southern neighbor. She wondered if Prince Raphat would really let Sithli bring about a war or if he would choose the wiser and, in the long run, more profitable course.

Essit left, and Dremfir. Pleffin left to begin preparations for his northern campaign, which he hoped to conclude quickly. He was anxious to come south again to help if war should break out with Runchot.

"Although I could use your help in the north, SaeKet," he said, only half in jest. "You have a way with the barbarians."

"As do you," she replied, but it was true, the northerners held her in great esteem, and First Man Bilt was her personal friend. "And they are Confederates now, Commander. Dira Sola, stay, please," she said.

When everyone had left but the guards outside the audience chamber, Rilsin leaned back in the SaeKet's formal chair, running her hands through her short hair. There were gray strands mixed with the brown, even though she was only twenty-four.

"Sit down, Sola, there's no one else here." Rilsin swung her feet up and propped them on the arm of the SaeKet's chair, her boots leaving smudges on the gold. She was dressed in the dark blue and gold of her family colors, formal for the meeting with the Runchot. "Tell me why you want me to stay in Petipal, as you so obviously do."

Sola perched on one of the chairs at the side of the room, ill at ease. The room was empty now but for the two of them, yet it was still the audience chamber, and he felt very keenly the authority and formality of the place. He wished Rilsin would see him truly in private. "Your people need to see you here, in the capital, at the center of things," he said. "When the Runchot invaded last, you would not let Sithli leave Petipal."

"If Sithli had left, she would have left in a panic, and caused a panic. There was no time to send her anywhere else, and nowhere else for her to go. Sithli has never been a warrior. She could not defend Saeditin, but I can."

"The people need you here, Rilsin—"

"Say what you mean, Sola. You want me in Petipal where you believe I will be safe."

She was right. "I couldn't stand it if you were hurt or— Rils, you almost died in the last Runchot campaign."

"Not from the Runchot but from giving birth in a cave in a blizzard," she said with a slight chuckle. Her smile faded. The child born in that blizzard, whose second birthday was almost upon them, was still missing.

"The Runchot are not invading, and they are not going to invade. I need to do what is right for Saeditin, Sola, not what is right for you. Or even," she paused, and then made herself say it, "what is right for me."

She felt a stab of pain in her heart as she said this. How could she tell the difference? She wanted her daughter back, but for the almost two weeks since the abduction she had remained in Petipal, dealing with other urgent matters. She wanted to ride for the border and Runchot right now. She wanted to find Sithli and take Reniat back from her. She wanted to find Sithli and kill her. Rilsin looked up to find Sola watching her.

"Rilsin, you will get her back." He went to put his arms around her, and for a moment, she let him. It felt good to rest her head against his shoulder, to feel him stroking her hair, but as she rested against him, she felt his doubt.

"You don't think Reni is still alive, do you." Something

about the way he held her, about the tension in his hands gave him away. There was a moment's silence, and she could feel him debating whether or not to lie.

"No," he said. "I'm sorry, Rilsin, but I don't think so."

She pushed away from him. "You're wrong." Her voice had gone hard, but her eyes were wounded.

"Rils, I'm sorry, but you would have found her, or heard; Sithli would be using her now as a bargaining point. But there has been no word, nothing."

"You're wrong! She's alive, Sola, I know it." She didn't know it. She was afraid he was right. That strange, bright connection she had felt with her daughter when Reniat was taken had faded. Rilsin felt tears prick somewhere behind her eyes, but she couldn't cry, she would not. "You don't want her alive because it would make it so much easier for you. You are happier with her gone."

As soon as she said it, she saw Sola's stricken look. Too late, she regretted it, but she could tell that she had also hit on the truth. She clamped her lips shut on the apology that she almost blurted out. Instead, she turned on her heel and left.

Sola stood alone in the empty audience chamber. He had told the truth because she had asked him, and he didn't want to lie to her. In return, she had not lied to him. Somewhere at the very back of his soul, he had believed that it would be so much easier without the little girl. What would be so much easier? His relationship with Rilsin, whatever that was? Apparently and obviously not. Sola was ashamed of himself. How could he ever have felt this, with any portion of his soul, no matter how dark? How could he make it up to Rilsin? Sola left the audience chamber and hurried out of the palace.

The streets of the city were buzzing with rumors and speculation. Word had gone out already about the expulsion of the Runchot delegates, and the excitement was spreading. A crowd had collected near the palace's formal entrance in the hope of seeing the Runchot expelled. The Petipal Guards assigned to the palace had their hands full keeping order, and they had already sent for reinforcements to prepare for when the Runchot delegation left.

Anyone leaving the palace was immediately accosted, assaulted with questions. It did not help that Sola dira Mudrin was well-known, a friend of the SaeKet and a member of the council.

"Dira Sola! Will there be war?"

"What did the SaeKet say? Did she really kick the Runchot trader in the backside?"

"Rilsin SaeKet kicked no one. I really do not know any more. Please, let me through!"

"Dira Sola! Are you really the SaeKet's lover?"

This last came from a big man with greasy brown hair, bundled into a commoner's thick gray wool overshirt, with the hood thrown back. He grinned at Sola, showing off an incomplete set of front teeth. Sola noticed a well-healed scar down the side of his face, and turned away, planning to take a side street away from the palace. Even the side streets were more heavily trafficked today, however, as the news spread.

Sola dodged into an empty alley that ran along the back of several shops, one of them a tannery, from the smell of it. He glanced behind him and saw the same brown-haired man with the scar. Sola stopped, threw back his heavy cloak, and put his hand on his sword hilt. He was only a passable swordsman, but he hoped this man did not know that.

"Are you following me?" he said.

He never heard the answer. There was a rush of footsteps behind him. Sola whirled, trying to draw his sword, but the big man with the scar was on him, pinning his arms to his sides. He struggled and kicked and then began to shout, and the big man cursed.

"What is keeping you, you Mother-forgotten Lisim filth? Hit him!" the big man said.

Something hard came down on the back of Sola's head, and he dropped to the ground like a stone.

*　　*　　*

Iᴛ ᴡᴀꜱ ᴅᴀʀᴋ, and it was cold. Sola had the most terrible headache. He groaned and tried to raise a hand to his head but found his hands were bound behind him. He had been lying on them, and they were numb. When he tried to move, he found that his ankles were bound together, too. He could tell without looking that his sword was gone. With a little effort he remembered the man who had followed him into the alley and the resulting ambush. He groaned again. What he could not understand was why he still lived. Once the thieves had stripped him of anything valuable, they should have killed him.

In fact, he had not been stripped of all his valuables. He still had his cloak, which was wool lined with fox fur. It had been wrapped around him by whoever had left him here, and its warmth had helped to keep him alive. He lay back, waiting for the pounding in his head to ease. When it did slightly, he began to try to work his hands. The effort sent pains shooting up his arms and made his head pound again, and he groaned.

There was a sound of a door opening and footsteps. Even in the near darkness Sola could see the darker bulk of his visitor.

"You're awake." It was the voice of the man outside the palace. "You don't look so good."

Sola felt his head lifted up, and fought down a wave of nausea. His vision seemed blurry, too. He groaned again.

"You've been bleeding back here on your head, and you've got one Mother-blessed lump. Philla hit you too hard. I don't care if you're a magician like they say, you hit a man that hard, it's lucky he don't die on you, magic or not."

Whoever it was propped Sola up, and began to gently wipe the back of his head with a wet rag. The pain from this was so unexpected that Sola began to shiver. Just in time, his attacker turned him to the side, and Sola vomited until there was nothing left in his stomach. When he was done, he felt weak and wrung out but oddly better.

"I'm cutting these ropes now. Then I'll get you some water. You don't try anything, you understand me?"

"I understand," Sola whispered.

There was a chuckle. "You say you understand, but I don't hear no promise not to try anything. Don't matter. You couldn't get farther than a newborn babe, the state you're in right now."

Sola's arms were yanked and pulled as his jailer sawed at his bonds with what had to be the dullest knife in Saeditin. He set his teeth so as not to cry out or moan again. Eventually the task was completed, and Sola's arms were free. They fell limply, like dead weights, to his sides.

"It'll be awhile before the feeling comes back, and they'll hurt like the demons got you when it does. Here. Take a drink of this."

A waterskin was held to his mouth. Sola stopped trying to lift his hands to take it and let himself simply drink. The water, which smelled slightly musty from its sojourn in the skin, tasted wonderful, and he gulped it down until the skin was removed while he was still gulping.

"That's enough. You can have more later, but you don't want to spew again."

Sola sighed. He felt very tired and suddenly wanted nothing more than to sleep again. Even the floor, vile and wet and cold, didn't seem so bad.

"Hey there, no, none of that! Sit up! Stay awake! You don't want to sleep after that hit on your head. You might never wake up again."

Sola recalled hearing something along those lines once, back when he was with Rilsin's army. Back when they were fighting Sithli's forces, back when Rilsin was on the run—

"I mean it, sit up! Damned brat Philla, why'd he have to hit so hard, what good will you be if you die on us, and he calls me stupid, damned saedin don't understand nothing, nobody wants to ransom a dead man."

There was something in this mumbled stream of discourse that seemed important to Sola, but he couldn't quite figure out what it was. Suddenly something cold hit him in the face. It was a stream of water from the waterskin, and it left him gasping but more alert. Feeling was starting to come back to his arms, too, and it hurt like demons were prodding him with hot needles, just as promised. At least the pain would help him stay awake. Sola looked up at the big man, who was sitting back on his heels, regarding him with concern.

"I'm awake now," Sola said. He rubbed his arms. "And I'll stay awake. What's your name?"

For a moment the big man just looked at him. Then he sighed. "I guess it don't matter much," he said, "not where you're going. My name's Nacrit."

CHILSA WAS LYING across Rilsin's bed. After her argument with Sola, Rilsin had wanted only to go back to her own suite, to lie on her bed for a few moments, and to think. It had been hours, however, as she attended to other matters, before she had been able to come home. Now she was more tired than ever, but she did not have the heart to make the big cat move, as he was still not completely recovered from the poison. Chilsa had always lived in her quarters since his first days as a kitten, and never in the cattery with the other hunting cats. Rilsin looked down at him for a few moments. Kerida had told her that it might take some time for the full effects of the poison to wear off, and she felt another surge of anger against whoever had done this. She let the big silver cat sleep and went to find Meffa.

Her friend and chief servant was also still recovering from the attempt on her life. She had insisted on returning to work, however. Her beloved charge, the sun-child, had been taken, and she blamed herself. She blamed herself still more because she had not gotten a good look at the attackers and could not identify them should she see them again.

"I really saw only one, SaeKet," she had said miserably, shortly after regaining consciousness in the physician's chambers. "And he had a scarf over his lower face. He was big, though. And he had a scar like this," her finger had traced a shaky line down her left cheek. "I think the scarf came off later, but I can't remember." Meffa was completely miserable. "He grabbed me, and when I went to scream, he forced a waterskin into my mouth. I tried to fight him, but he squeezed the skin, and I had to swallow. I'm sorry, SaeKet. I don't know why he didn't just kill me."

There was little progress being made in the search. It was obvious that some of the Petipal Guards had been bribed. Two had never reported for their duty and later had been found dead. There was only one noble family that could be behind this. Rilsin thought she had confiscated all the significant Lisim assets, but obviously she had not. She thought she had removed the Lisim leadership in Saeditin when she had had Jolass executed. Obviously she had not. Her regret and her guilt were more than the equal of Meffa's.

Rilsin put her arms around the older woman. "It isn't your fault, Meffa," she began, but Meffa pulled away.

"I want vengeance," she said.

"What?" Rilsin stared at her.

"I want vengeance, SaeKet. Against those who took my little Reni. The SaeKetti. I want to bring them as much sorrow as they have brought me. Us. I know I am not trained to fight, but I want to do more than wait. Promise me that I can, SaeKet. I have never asked anything of you before, but I ask this now. Promise me, Rilsin SaeKet."

"I promise," said Rilsin. She had no idea how she would keep her promise.

Someone was banging on the door. It was one of the Petipal Guards, with Dremfir the mage beside him. Rilsin felt her heart plummet, and something seemed to be stuck in her throat. She knew that something had just gone from bad to even worse, and all she could think was that someone had found Reniat's body. It was a moment before what the guard said made sense to her.

"Perhaps Dira Sola went to his workshop," she said.

Dremfir shook his head. "No, SaeKet," he said. "He intended to visit his mother, Dira Kerida, but he never arrived. The last he was seen was leaving the palace just before the Runchot delegation was expelled. Several people remember seeing him followed by a big man, as he went to take some side streets away from the crowd. In an alley they found this."

The guard held out something: a cloak brooch. It was silver, not gold, a rather plain item. Sola had never cared much for ostentation, and it was the only brooch Rilsin had ever seen him wear. She looked up at Dremfir.

"In an alley," she said. Her voice sounded strange. "It was found in an alley?"

"There were signs of a struggle, and this must have been torn off, SaeKet," said the guard. "I am the one who found it. There was nothing else."

"The man who followed Dira Sola, who was he?"

The guard shrugged slightly. "I don't know much, SaeKet. He was big, they said. Brown hair. A scar on his left cheek."

Behind her, Rilsin heard Meffa gasp.

"He can't have gone far." Rilsin said. "I want the city turned inside out. I want every house searched!"

"SaeKet, we have just done that for the SaeKetti—"

"Do it again."

"I doubt he is still in Petipal," said Dremfir. "It's been hours. Whoever took him is probably out of the city by now, if he's smart. The roads have been open for days. But they can't get across the border."

Rilsin stared at him. "Don't be a fool, Dremfir," she said shortly. "I may have closed the border, but there are always ways across it. We know where he is going. The same place the SaeKetti went. Sithli will have them both. She just won't have them for long." She didn't say what they all knew, that Sithli wanted Sola not just for bargaining power but for the plans for fire-tubes and for whatever else she could get from him.

"I am taking troops and going south," said Rilsin. "I will take this war to Sithli and to the Runchot myself." She saw the guard's eyes go wide. At the same moment, Dremfir stepped forward.

"Say nothing of this," he commanded the guard. "SaeKet, let me speak to you alone." He didn't wait for her approval but stepped inside and shut the door. "Rilsin SaeKet," he began.

"Are you going to tell me, as Sola did, that my place is in Petipal?" Rilsin cut him off. "Are you going to tell me to wait for an answer from Prince Raphat? My patience is ended."

"I will not tell you what course of action to follow. I will tell you one thing, since I have known you for so long."

Rilsin looked at him sharply, remembering how he had cleared a curse from her once, how he had fought beside her, how he had never let her down.

"This is the one thing, Rilsin SaeKet. The land will tell you what you need to know. Listen to the song of the land, Rilsin. Listen to the song."

Rilsin looked at him. It was true that she had not listened to the song of the land for some time now. Dremfir was too good a friend, and a priest besides, for her to say what she wanted to say. She could listen to the song of the land all day and it would do no good. It would tell her nothing, nothing at all.

9

It was both harder and easier than she had imagined, working in her father's house as the slave of Sithli sae Melisin. Phara had never realized just how hard servants worked until she became one. But her real work as a spy looked at first to be easy, for the simple reason that no one expected her to do anything of the kind.

Sithli was pleased with the attention that Phara gave her and with Phara's skill at applying makeup. Sithli was especially pleased with Phara's ability to cover the scar on her face, the remnant of a failed assassination attempt. This Phara understood, but Sithli's vanity seemed to have no end, and she seemed unable or unwilling to do many of the simplest tasks for herself. Phara was required to dress her new mistress and to undress her, except when Raphat did this last task himself.

Sithli had slapped Phara a few times for tardiness in responding to a command or for inadvertently pulling her hair in combing, but in general Sithli was pleased, and she treated Phara as another useful possession. Phara kept her eyes downcast whenever possible and her voice melodious and soft. The art of soft and musical speech was one she had learned as a princess, and she put it to good use now, both soothing her Saeditin mistress and directing attention away from herself. It never occurred to Sithli, apparently, that Phara might have wishes or desires beyond her service, or that she might have capabilities beyond what she showed.

This suited Phara perfectly. The less notice she attracted, the better. She was expected to care for Sithli's clothes, an enormous task in and of itself, and this required her to be in the rooms when her mistress was not present. She used these opportunities to look around and to read whatever correspondence or papers were left nearby. She had to be extremely careful, however. Other servants, both slave and free, were in and out of the rooms frequently, and more worrisome than this, Kepit sae Lisim was apt to appear without warning, either looking for Sae Sithli or leaving something off in Sithli's rooms.

Phara had been there for two weeks already without finding anything of significance. The longer she stayed, the more chance there was of being discovered and the more danger there was that Sithli sae Melisin would forge a true political alliance with Raphat, one that would require Phara's father to commit resources and troops to her. If Raphat did this, he would be sending good men to a cold and certain death in Saeditin. More importantly, he would be sending her older brother into danger. There was only one member of her family whom Phara still loved, and that was her brother Tonar, who commanded their father's troops. Raphat would think all the risks worth it, as nothing was more important to the man than his own ambition.

She had seen her father, of course, and had seen him at close quarters. She took great care never to draw his attention to herself. However good her disguise, and it was obviously very good, she didn't know that it would stand close scrutiny from someone who knew her well. She was surprised at how little real attention the nobles, Runchot or

Saeditin, paid to the servants. That her father did not recognize her was due in part to this tendency to simply not
see those he perceived as social inferiors. Had she herself
been like this? Phara wondered.

She was in Sithli's bedchamber this evening, brushing
out the saedin's emerald-green velvet dressing gown, one
of several Sithli owned. As she brushed, Phara considered
what course of action to take. She needed information to
send back to Kirra, and she needed it badly. It might be necessary to try to eavesdrop on Sithli's conversations with
Raphat.

No sooner had she made this decision than she heard
laughter in the outer room. It was Sithli. Phara did not have
long to wonder who was with her; Raphat's voice could be
heard saying something unclear. Normally, Phara would
have hung up the robe immediately and exited the bedchamber, keeping her eyes downcast, hoping not to be noticed. Now, without a second's hesitation, Phara hung the
robe in the closet and then went in after it, pushing her way
to the very back, where there were blankets folded. She
moved some of these aside and crawled into them, pulling
them around her. She forgot to close the closet door behind
her.

"No one is here; they have all left for the evening. I have
found that servants will slack off if you give them the
chance." Despite her words, Sithli did not sound annoyed.

"One less obstacle in our way," said Raphat. There was
silence, then the sound of scuffling, and Sithli's laugh.

"Look," said Sithli, suddenly. "That stupid slave girl has
left my closet open. I should have her whipped for negli-
gence. That might be amusing, don't you think?"

Peeking from a slit in the pile of blankets, Phara could
see the Saeditin woman, her long blonde hair lit from behind into a golden halo, before Sithli closed the closet door.

"Forget the slave," said Raphat. "I have something more
amusing for you here."

In the closet Phara gritted her teeth, listening to the
sounds of her father and Sithli sae Melisin together. They

were not making love; Phara knew better than that. She wondered if her father had ever made love with anyone, even her mother, or if it was all only sex. It seemed to be the same with Sithli. Phara put her hands over her ears and sank down as far as she could into the nest of blankets. She withdrew so far into herself that it was some moments before she realized that time had passed, and Raphat and Sithli were conversing again. Phara took her hands from her ears.

"Well done, my beautiful prince," said Sithli. She sounded tired, languorous, and extremely pleased. Phara blinked. She had only heard that slightly condescending, proprietary tone used before by men to women or of them, never the reverse. She remembered again that Sithli sae Melisin had been a head of state, someone with the power of life and death over her people. That absolute command had given her an arrogance that remained, even after her power was gone.

"I hate to do this, my sweet," Sithli continued, "but I must ask you now, as we never seem to have the time to discuss it. In truth, there are always things I would rather do with you."

There was a moment of silence, and then Raphat's protest of "Sithli!" But he did not sound displeased. "If you want to talk, you can't do that."

Phara closed her eyes again.

"Well then, let's talk." All traces of the coquette had vanished from Sithli's voice. "I want a minimum of twenty thousand troops, and I want them immediately. I don't want to wait for Rilsin to organize, and she will be organizing, you know."

Phara opened her eyes, staring at the thin beam of light under the closet door.

"Twenty thousand! Sithli, you can't be serious." Something rustled: Raphat either sitting up or getting out of the bed.

"If you want a stake in Saeditin, if you want that northern base, it will cost you. Anything that valuable must be paid for."

"But twenty thousand troops! I can't give you my whole army!"

"It's not your whole army. Not nearly."

There was more rustling.

"True. But I won't give you twenty thousand. You have a promise from Kirra, or so Sae Kepit tells me. Someday I want to meet that woman." There was a pause, and more rustling, and then Raphat laughed. "Although I think I understand a little bit about her now. She holds a powerful grudge, to have promised you fifteen thousand troops. Sae Kepit tells me you have not closed the deal."

"That is because I want twenty-five thousand from her."

Raphat laughed again. "You won't get them!"

"No, but I will get twenty."

"And you still want twenty from me. I will give you fifteen. Sithli, don't complain." There was a sudden edge to Raphat's voice, one that Phara had heard frequently. It made her shiver. "I am going to give you an advantage that Rilsin SaeKet—"

"Don't call her that!"

"That Rilsin SaeKet Becha will never have. I am going to give you my son, the Prince Tonar, to insure our victory. I know Sae Kepit is good, Sithli, but Tonar is better."

"And younger, and he owes his allegiance to you and you only," said Sithli, dryly. "You are right, he is better than Kepit, from what I hear, but I thought you would command your own troops, Raphat. You wouldn't even have to leave the capital, you could do it from Tressig."

Almost nothing was more important to Sithli than her comfort. She hated being in a small out-of-the-way town, and she wanted with a desperate intensity to be in Tressig, the Runchot capital, until she could return to Saeditin. Phara knew her father, and she knew he would keep Sithli away from his capital and from his own power base.

"I would think you know nothing of war, Sithli. I would

not command my troops from a distance!" Raphat was disgusted.

Phara could hear him getting dressed, stomping around the room. Phara winced, but Sithli didn't seem to have any fear of the Runchot ruler. Obviously, she did not know him well enough, Phara thought. *Pray to your Saeditin goddess that you never know him well enough.*

"I suppose we could go to a town nearer the front, nearer the border." Sithli's reluctance was obvious. It would not only be more dangerous, it would not have the luxuries of even this manor house.

"The battle will not be fought near the border," said Raphat, "or not the decisive one, at any rate. Rilsin thinks it will be. She thinks you have her daughter, do you know that?"

"I should have her. Something went wrong; I don't know what. What do you mean, the battle will not be fought near the border?" Sithli refused to be distracted.

"Because we are not invading across the border, or rather, not across this border only. Tonar will take my troops north and come down through the Confederacy, through Clinsi territory. First Man Bilt won't find out until it's too late to stop us." He was smiling. Phara could hear it in his voice. "Tonar will get as close to your Saeditin capital as he can and lay waste to the city. Don't look at me like that; what he burns, we can rebuild. It's already in motion. I have sent troops across the steppe lands, heading northeast."

"Raphat! The steppes in winter! There are barbarian tribes there, not just in the Confederacy. And they will have to cross the mountains to get into Clinsi territory!"

"They can do it. Tonar can make them build roads out of snow; the troops love him. Those are your fifteen thousand, Sithli. They are already committed."

For a moment Sithli said nothing. She would be stunned, Phara thought, just as Phara herself was stunned. Her father meant to have Saeditin for himself, under the guise of help-

ing Sithli sae Melisin to regain the throne. She wondered if
Sithli realized this.

"Sae Kepit will want to know about this," said Sithli at
last.

"Oh, she knows. She agrees with the plan, and she is
happy to have Tonar in command and have him to brave the
snows as well as the enemy. She has no desire to do either,
at her age."

Phara sat up suddenly. Raphat did not have in mind that
Sithli should take back the SaeKet's chair at all, or if she
did, it would not be for long. Kepit sae Lisim was plotting
with Raphat. In her surprise and agitation, Phara jerked
against the blankets. One of them slid, and pulled against a
wooden box containing some of Sithli's scarves. The box
toppled from its perch.

Just in time, Phara caught it, before it fell to the floor in
a clatter. She hugged the box against her, struggling to control her breathing.

"What was that?" said Sithli. "Did you hear something,
Raphat?"

"No. Don't change the subject, Sithli. You wanted to talk
about this; let us talk it out now and be agreed. Our plan re-
quires that we have Kirra's promised forces. Some of our
troops, a surprise force, will come from the north, yes,
where Rilsin least expects it, but we need a force to move
north over our border and catch the Becha between us."

"We have the rest of your army—"

"I am not using the rest of my army for that, Sithli. I
need my troops in my own capital and at my own southern
border."

Phara shifted uneasily. That was more, undoubtedly,
than her father wanted to admit. He ruled northern Runchot
and supposedly the south, but the south was not entirely
happy with the arrangement.

"Then we will use Kirra's troops." Sithli dismissed the
problem suddenly. "Now, about Sunreturn, my sweet. You
have invited me only to the festivities here, but not in Tressig. I thought surely you would ask me to the capital."

"No, Sithli, you are not coming to Tressig. You Saeditin have your own rites. You can celebrate in your own way here. I will see you have what you need."

There was the sound of a door closing forcefully. Raphat had left.

"Damn it!" There was a crash, and Phara jumped. Sithli had thrown something at the closet door.

"Damn it! I should be in Petipal, you Mother-forsaken fool! When I *am* back in Petipal, you will pay for this—" Sithli stopped.

"Where is that fool slave? Barrit! Barrit!"

Phara hunched down in the closet and closed her eyes again. She had for all of her seventeen years been religious, and now she wanted to pray.

"Barrit!" Sithli was losing the tiny amount of patience remaining to her. She stormed out of the room. There was another crash as something in the small parlor was overturned.

Cautiously, Phara crept out of the closet. She could see Sithli, her back turned to the bedchamber door, in the parlor. Phara hurried out, scurrying behind Sithli as quickly as she could. She reached the door of the suite and stepped out, turning back just as Sithli herself turned.

"I am sorry, Sithli SaeKet," she gasped, breathless. "I came as soon as I heard you."

"Well, you are here now." Sithli seemed mollified by Phara's obvious terror of her. "Come in and brush my hair."

With relief, Phara went in to do as she was told. She took a last glance behind her into the hall outside the suite. Rudfa stood there watching. He held a long-spouted oil jar, as if he had been refilling the oil lamps in the corridor. Phara had the sinking, horrible suspicion that he had seen her leave Sithli's quarters before pretending to enter them. He continued to watch her as she hastened in to Sithli.

Sithli wanted her hair brushed, and she wanted Phara to sing to her. Phara obliged, hiding her own nervous anxiety. It was several hours before Sithli fell asleep at last and Phara could leave.

The oil lamps had burned down in the corridor now, and as she left the guest quarters she found herself in darker portions of the house. Although it was dark, Phara had memorized her way around as one of her first acts in the household. She wanted to find her contact now, as quietly as possible. It was urgent that she get a message out.

Her contact was the kitchen maid, Greffa, who slept beside the hearth in the same back kitchen that had been Phara's introduction to the servants' quarters. She knew Kirra expected her to bring the message herself, but she intended to go north, to find her brother and warn him. If he invaded Saeditin from the north, he was lost. The support he would need from Runchot troops in the south would never come. Her father had said that he was already committed and ready to act. That meant either that Tonar was out on the steppes or that he had already crossed the mountains into the Confederacy, into Clinsi territory. Phara meant to give her message to Greffa and then go to her father's rooms to search his documents.

Phara hated the thought of war, but worse was the thought of Runchot losing a war, and worst was the thought of losing her brother. If her brother lost his battle, the border with Saeditin would be open. Rilsin SaeKet Becha could invade Runchot. Phara was no longer Princess of Merri, but she did not intend to let that happen.

Wrapped in her thoughts, she rounded the corner that led from the dining hall to the kitchens. The rooms were steeped in shadows, and she didn't notice when one shadow detached itself from the others and followed her.

"Wake up! Greffa!" Phara had found the kitchen maid wrapped in a dirty cloak, asleep in a cot near the back kitchen's hearth. She shook Greffa but kept one hand clamped over the woman's mouth until she saw Greffa was awake.

"Barrit! Do you need to get out? What is it?" To her credit, Greffa seemed to need almost no time to come fully awake.

"I'm not going to Kirra. I want you to get a message to her. Can you do that?"

"Of course. Will you tell me what it is, or write it?" Greffa could neither read nor write. She was a brown-haired woman in her thirties, old for a commoner, and older still, considering her former trade as a street prostitute. Kirra had taken her in, and then, realizing her intelligence, had given her different work.

"I will write it," Phara said.

The fire in the hearth was banked to embers, but it was only a moment's work to stir the flames a little higher. Finding paper and ink would not have been as easy, but Phara had hidden a little cache for just this purpose in a corner of the kitchen, under a stack of little-used roast pans. By the flickering firelight Phara wrote Kirra of Raphat's plans and that Sithli sae Melisin, and Raphat, too, had bought the false promise of Kirra's nonexistent troops.

"Is it safe for you to stay, Barrit? Kirra said to let no harm befall you and to get you back to her safely as soon as it could be done." Greffa took the message and folded it into a pocket in her apron. In the firelight, she looked haggard. "Sithli SaeKet is dangerous. Prince Raphat is dangerous, and so is the Lisim woman. Do not risk yourself among them, Barrit, unless you must." Greffa leaned forward and took Phara's face in one hand, turning her to the light.

"You are a beautiful young woman," she said. "Get out of this house, let your hair grow, wear clothes as beautiful as you can afford. Go back to Kirra's place and find a rich client who will marry you. Bear him a child, or more, if you can, to seal the marriage. Then by law he must care for you for the rest of your days." Greffa dropped her hand and stared into the fire. "It is what I should have done." She turned back to Phara. "Take your own message south to Kirra." She held out the paper, but Phara pushed it back into Greffa's hand.

"I am indeed leaving tonight," she said, "as soon as I have found out a little more that I need to know. I am not going back to Kirra, not yet. There is something I must do first. An errand to the north. Take care of yourself, Greffa."

She left the kitchen hastily, not wanting to answer any questions and knowing that Greffa would not call after her for fear of waking the household. She took the stairs up to the guest quarters two at a time, unaware of the shadow still behind her.

Sithli still slept, and Phara walked softly to the smaller closet, the one that had been remade into her bedchamber, if so small a space could be called a chamber. She took her cloak, a thick wool one with a hood, and her boots, which she had not worn since she had been brought to the household. She tied these into her cloak and then reached under the straw mattress, which lay on the floor. There was a tiny supply of silver coins hidden there. On her way out, she took a heavy silver candlestick from a table.

Once back in the corridor, she turned to the right, heading for her father's rooms. She had never been there as Barrit the slave, but she knew where they were, and she knew how they would be laid out. Her father always had everything arranged in the same manner, no matter where he was. All his houses were on the same plan.

There was a guard at the door to Raphat's suite. She smiled at him timidly but met his gaze with her own. Her eyes were an intense blue, and when she wanted it to, her gaze could be melting. She wanted it to.

"Sithli SaeKet sent me," she said, smiling, her voice so musical it was almost a song. "She has a gift for the prince, a gift I am to take him."

The guard smiled at her. He had seen the Saeditin woman's slave before but had never paid her much attention. Who would have guessed she was this beautiful?

"The prince is asleep," said the guard, "although it is almost dawn, and he rises then. You could leave the gift with me." He glanced down at the bundle in Phara's arms. All he could see was the cloak.

"No, I must not. Sithli SaeKet would not like it." Phara's eyes got bigger, and her lip trembled slightly.

"I can't let you in there alone—what is your name?—I can't, or the prince would not like it." He had not stopped smiling at her. She was no threat, anyone could see that, and perhaps he could see more of her when he was off duty.

"Perhaps you could help me to take it in, then. My mistress Sithli told me to put it where Prince Raphat would find it in the morning. It is a surprise gift from her."

"Oh well, yes, I suppose we could take it in together. Here, give it to me. What *is* your name?"

"Barrit," said Phara. "My name is Barrit."

She handed him her cloak, wrapped around her boots, and brushed against him as she gave it to him. He took it from her with a slightly confused expression, already sensing there was something wrong. He turned to precede her into the room, and Phara took the heavy candlestick from under her thick overshirt and brought it down hard against the back of his head. The guard fell to the floor without a cry, and Phara managed to partially break his fall by catching him as best she could.

"I'm sorry," she whispered. She felt the side of his neck. There was a pulse, so he would probably live. She dragged him out of the doorway and onto the rug, taking a cushion from a chair to place under his injured head. She wondered briefly if her father would punish him for his failure.

She went right to the small room that she knew would be the prince's study. It was so cold it was almost icy, for the fire had been allowed to die and had not yet been relit. The oil lamps were out. Frost flowers were blooming on the windowpanes, but Phara could see that the midwinter darkness was beginning to ease with just the first pale hint of dawn. She would need to hurry.

Phara went straight to her father's desk and began to sort through the papers there. Her father did most of his paperwork himself and did not rely quite as frequently on a scribe as most nobles. Luck was with her; in moments she found a copy, in her father's hand, of orders to her brother Tonar. Tonar was to take his troops northeast across the fringe of the steppe lands. If the gods were with them, they

would avoid the nomad tribes, who tended to stay in the
southern part of their range for the coldest months. Tonar
was to cross the mountains and be in Clinsi territory by
Sunreturn. This was dangerous. Although Raphat had been
stirring up trouble among the Clinsi and had allies there, the
Clinsi were still part of the new Confederacy and had no
desire to incur the wrath of their powerful Saeditin neighbor by aiding an enemy force. Once he was over the mountains, Tonar needed to move fast, because First Man Bilt of
the Confederacy would move against him as soon as he
knew.

Phara frowned down at the paper. Sunreturn was less
than two weeks away. Although the weather had been terrible, Phara knew that her brother was probably in Clinsi
lands now, trying to elude detection by the loyal Confederates of First Man Bilt.

Phara stared out the window at the slowly increasing
light. She hated Raphat for making her brother risk his life
not just in war but against the elements. She hated him for
putting Runchot at risk, and she hated him for making her
go north into storms and enemy lands to look for Tonar. She
already had plenty of reasons to hate him, even before this.
She found a map of Saeditin and the Confederacy on the
desk and rolled this to put under her shirt.

"Well, well, what have we here? So the young slave can
in fact read."

Phara whirled. "Rudfa!" She stared at the chief servant,
noting that he blocked the doorway, her escape route.
"What are you doing here?"

"That's my question of you, Barrit. But it isn't really
Barrit, is it?" Rudfa smiled at her.

Phara backed up, her mind whirling. Unless she could
find some way to keep Rudfa silent and to induce him to let
her go, all was lost. She felt the edge of the desk hit her
thighs. There was nowhere to go. Rudfa had advanced until
he stood right in front of her, and she could feel his body
heat.

"What were you looking for, Barrit? If you had merely

wanted to steal something and try to escape, you could have taken any number of things." He glanced toward the silver candlestick, which Phara had dropped after she hit the guard. "What is it you really want?"

He smiled again, and now Phara could smell his breath. He had eaten sausage recently, she thought incongruously.

"I could be persuaded to say nothing. You came from Kirra, and everyone knows what Kirra's slaves are for. You were trained in those arts. Share them with me, whatever your name is, and I will say nothing to the prince." Rudfa leaned over her, grasping her by the shoulder with his left hand. His right hand went up under her shirt to cup her breast.

Phara felt an icy shock go through her. She had, in fact, never been one of Kirra's girls. She had never even had a lover. She had been too closely guarded for that. All she knew of the arts to which Rudfa referred was what she had read in books.

Rudfa's breathing was getting faster. He jammed his right knee between her legs, forcing them apart. His left hand went from her shoulder to the back of her head, bracing her, and he brought his mouth down over hers and pushed his tongue between her lips. *Definitely sausage,* Phara thought. His right hand still held her breast, but now he squeezed it.

Phara tried to cry out, but the sound was muffled as he forced his tongue deeper, almost into her throat. She began to struggle, but he had her pinned, and her attempts to squirm seemed to excite him more. His hand left her breast, and he thrust it down her wool trousers between her legs, his fingers probing.

Phara's initial panic left to be replaced by a strange calm. She seemed to see the scene from a distance. She saw, as if from outside herself, when Rudfa yanked at her trousers, pulling them down from her hips. She heard a button pop as he did so. He began to push her back on the desk. Phara put a hand back on the desk to brace herself and felt a paper knife under her fingers.

She closed her hand around the hilt of the knife and in one smooth motion brought it up and stabbed Rudfa in the back of the neck. His eyes bugged out with surprise but his shriek was muffled as Phara kept her mouth clamped over his. He tried to pull away, but she drew the knife out in a sawing motion so she could stab him again. There was no need. With a twitch and an odd gurgling noise, Rudfa slid down onto the floor.

Panting, Phara stared down at him. His eyes were open, and a red stain spread from the back of his neck onto her father's thick wool carpet. His legs kicked briefly, thrashing, and then stopped. Rudfa was dead.

With trembling hands, Phara pulled up her trousers, doing up the remaining buttons. She stepped away from the body and ran her hands through her hair. She saw the map on the floor near Rudfa and snatched it up just before the spreading red reached it. She found her cloak and boots and managed to get the cloak around her, although her hands were still shaking. She clutched her boots, knowing she couldn't find the coordination to put them on, and looked around. Her father's desk was now a mess.

The guard seemed to be waking up. Hastily, Phara crossed the floor to him and unbuckled his sword. She had only the vaguest idea how to use a sword. Maybe she should go back to the kitchen and ask for Greffa's help. Maybe—

"What in the name of all the gods!"

Phara whirled, still clutching boots and sword. Her father was standing in the door that connected to his bedchamber. Raphat's glance swept from Phara to Rudfa, sprawled on the floor, to the guard, who was now groaning and putting his hand to his head.

Phara began to back away toward the door that led out to the corridor. As she edged away, she saw her father look at her, really look at her, and he started with surprise.

"Phara?" he said.

Phara turned and ran. She ran through the corridor and down the stairs, out through the servants' quarters, bumping into several servants starting their morning duties. She ran out of a servants' entrance into the kitchen garden and dashed out into a side alley. She could hear shouts behind her, but she kept running, in only her house shoes, still clutching her boots and the sword.

10

THE ANSWER HAD COME FROM PRINCE RAPHAT OF RUN-chot, and it had come much sooner than expected. His emissary had come back under a flag of truce, with only a small escort. Sunreturn was only a few days away, and it was bitterly cold. It was the time of year usually given over to celebration. Despite the threat of war, the citizens of Petipal were decorating their houses, but Rilsin was not feeling celebratory. Over the past days a certain numbness had set in, relieved by occasional flashes of something that was perilously close to panic.

"The prince regrets that he does not have your daughter, the SaeKetti," said the emissary. He was Rerran of Sophrin, a noble in his middle years, an accomplished diplomat and a friend of the prince. "If he had her, or even if he knew where she were, rest assured he would do everything in his power to restore her to you, SaeKet."

Rilsin was not surprised. Of course Raphat would not give Reniat up; he was saving her as a bargaining chip for

Sithli and for himself. Nonetheless, she had hoped, and despite herself, she was disappointed.

Her entire council was present for this audience, along with as many saedin and dira as could manage to cram themselves into the audience chamber. The only council member missing was her commander, Pleffin, who had departed for the north to deal with the possibility of border raids. The air was thick with smells of old food, damp wool, bodies left too long unwashed in the cold weather, and the perfume that many of the nobles and honoreds used instead of bathing. The combined odors and her lack of sleep made Rilsin slightly ill.

There was a fire in the big hearth, but the steam pipes occasionally clanged, eliciting jumps and nervous twitches from those unaccustomed to the invention. At least the room was warm, almost uncomfortably so. Rerran was clearly overdressed. A trickle of perspiration ran down the side of his face.

"Will your lord the prince give me the criminals Sithli sae Melisin and Kepit sae Lisim?" Rilsin asked. She knew the answer to this question, too. Of course Raphat would not.

"He will," said the ambassador.

There was a stunned silence, and then a sudden buzz of murmurs and conversation throughout the room.

"Silence!" Rilsin's voice cut through the noise.

All talk immediately ceased.

"When will he give them to me?" She thought she knew the answer.

"There are a few matters, details, you understand, that must first be decided. When those have been resolved to the satisfaction of Saeditin and Runchot both, and when the roads to the south have been cleared, for you must understand, Rilsin SaeKet, that we have had abominable weather in the south, when those matters have been resolved, at that point, my prince will have those saedin escorted to you."

"Will he, indeed," said Rilsin sourly. It was not a question. "That could take well into the summer and beyond.

Well beyond, I would imagine. I am not prepared to wait so long, Lord Emissary. I want Sithli sae Melisin and Kepit sae Lisim now. And I want the SaeKetti returned to me, and also Sola dira Mudrin, a well-known citizen of this land."

"I have said, SaeKet, that the prince does not know the whereabouts of your daughter. As to the whereabouts of any other citizens of yours who are missing, surely you do not think he would know where they are."

"I think he knows very well where this particular citizen is," said Rilsin.

"I will ask him, then, SaeKet. Of course everyone knows of Sola dira Mudrin," Rerran glanced at the steam pipes on the wall, which clanged again, as if to underscore his words, "and I am very sorry to hear that he, too, is missing. This is the first I have heard of it, but I will ask the prince. I feel certain that he knows nothing of this, however, and will be as shocked as I. I will, with your permission, SaeKet, take this news and your answer back to the prince. I would like some time to first recover from my journey here, if this pleases you. It was a very grueling journey. The roads are bad—"

"So you said, Ambassador," Rilsin cut in. "You need not leave for some time. There will be ample opportunity for you to recover from the rigors of your journey and for Runchot to get its roads cleared of the snow. You and your party will be comfortable here; we will see to it." She smiled cooly at the emissary. She waited until the Runchot had been shown out and then looked at the throng who still remained, all Saeditin.

"We will have peace at Sunreturn," Rilsin said, "but not perhaps for much longer."

When the audience chamber had cleared, she asked Essit and Dremfir to accompany her to her private study. The big windows looked out on the formal palace gardens. Snow-covered bushes made fantastic shapes, looming out of the early twilight, all of it made more fantastic by being seen through frost-glazed windows.

"We are almost at Sunreturn," said Rilsin. "The Runchot

celebrate for two weeks. I don't know if they will attack us during this time. Perhaps it is unlikely, but I do know that we cannot afford to wait." She turned from the window. "I want to move now, across the border, as soon as possible, and go all the way to Tressig if I can."

"Have you thought this through completely, SaeKet?" Dremfir was a warrior priest, but Rilsin didn't think he was questioning only her military wisdom. She chose to answer him as if he were, however.

"I know it will be difficult at this season, but you heard the emissary, Sae Dremfir. Raphat will not meet our demands, no matter what he says. He will talk and talk until he is in position to strangle us. He will move as soon as he is ready, and that, I fear, will be soon. I cannot let that happen."

"No," agreed Dremfir, "you cannot." His round, pleasant face was set in lines of concern.

"What message will the ambassador take back?" asked Essit.

"None," said Rilsin. "He is not going back." When she saw how Essit looked at her and realized how it sounded, she laughed. "The emissary will be quite safe, Sae Essit. I am simply not sending him back to Runchot. Let Raphat and Sithli think he is enjoying the Sunreturn holiday here— as well he may. I can play the same game they play. I will appear to delay and delay, but in reality, I will move."

"Are you certain that invading Runchot, and invading now, is really the best course?" asked Dremfir.

Rilsin looked at him curiously. "If you know a better way, Sae Dremfir, please tell me."

"I don't know a better way. I am not the SaeKet." Dremfir smiled slightly. "But Rilsin, please, be certain before you act. Are you even certain that Reniat and Sola have crossed the border?" His gentle question gave her pause the way a forceful statement would not.

Rilsin sat looking out the window long after they had left, watching darkness fall, hiding the snow-covered garden. She knew what Dremfir meant. He wanted her to listen to the song of the land. Rilsin frowned. What possible use could the song be to her? It was the connection of the land to its SaeKet, but that was all. She could feel, if she wished, the pulse of the earth and the tide of the seasons, the strange connected hum of all the inhabitants of the land, animal and human, that made up Saeditin. But what did that have to do with a decision to invade Runchot? What could that possibly have to do with her daughter's kidnapping, with Sola's disappearance?

What she needed was more information, she decided. Dremfir had asked if she were certain that Reniat and Sola had been taken to Runchot. For some reason he thought they might still be in Saeditin, even in Petipal itself, despite the searches.

Abruptly, Rilsin rose and went to her private quarters, nodding at the guard who was ever present now. She could hear Meffa somewhere in the apartment, but Rilsin avoided her, moving quietly to her bedchamber. Chilsa, who had been sleeping on her bed again, jumped off and came to give her a massive head butt, which, had she not been prepared, would have knocked her backward. He was obviously almost fully recovered from his run-in with the kidnapper, and Rilsin was pleased. He gave a loud and happy meow. She wanted to attract no attention, however, not even from Meffa, so she gave the big cat the hand sign for silence. Chilsa sank down to the floor, flattening his ears back, confused by her imposition of hunting protocol indoors.

"You can't go with me tonight," she whispered into one of the rounded ears. She scratched gently around his whisker pads, and the big silver animal closed his eyes and gave a barely audible purr.

She found a pair of heavy wool trousers and a heavy woolen shirt, both black, from her days as first minister, when she could not safely wear Sae Becha colors. She put these on and belted on her sword. Next came a pair of heavy leather boots lined with thick fleece and a heavy black wool cloak with a hood. A long knife went down the top of the left boot, and another knife into her belt. She wanted very much to take one of the fire-tubes with her, but she knew that would make her too noticeable. At the last moment she thought to take a small pouch filled with some copper coins and a few of silver. As first minister she had rarely needed to carry her own funds, and as SaeKet she never needed to, but she would have use for coins tonight.

"Stay, Chilsa," she whispered, and slipped from the room.

It was not difficult to keep to the sides of the rooms, to slip from shadow to shadow. She was only avoiding Meffa, after all. She had intended to leave through her parlor doors, the same doors through which the kidnapper had entered. At the last moment she remembered that they were guarded. She could not leave her own quarters in secrecy. Rilsin straightened and sighed. There was no help for it, then. She opened the door to the garden and came face-to-face with the Petipal guard on duty.

"SaeKet!" said the guard, putting her hand to her heart.

"Not tonight," said Rilsin. "Tell no one you have seen me leave." She paused and frowned, thinking that this might cause a problem for the guard. "How long is your duty?" she asked the guard.

"Until dawn, SaeKet."

"A long time, in the cold."

"They bring me hot cider." The guard was flushed not just with the cold but with the pleasure of being noticed by the SaeKet. And, Rilsin realized, with being on the inside of something secret.

"I will be back before dawn," Rilsin assured her. "If I am not, then you must tell your captain."

Rilsin drifted back through her garden. There were other guards, but she managed to avoid them. She had always been good at avoiding detection, a result of a childhood in her cousin's shadow.

It was growing darker by the second, and the cold was increasing. Rilsin drew her cloak more tightly around her, drew up her hood, and headed in the direction of down-city, the seedy part of town.

First she had to traverse the better sections of the city where saedin and wealthier dira had their residences, and the streets of the better-off commoners and lower-ranked dira. There were shops, many still open despite the early darkness, and she passed through streets that were filled with people, despite the cold. Sunreturn was just around the corner, and the citizens of Petipal were out bringing gifts of baked goods and small items to their neighbors and friends, and there were vendors in the commoner streets selling hot apple cakes and roasted nuts, standing by their brazier fires. Rilsin thought of the muted preparations at the palace for the festivities. She had just come to power at the previous Sunreturn, which had as a result been a somewhat muted affair. She owed it to her people to have something a little more lavish this year, but she had not planned for it, nor was her heart in it, not with Reniat and Sola both gone missing.

Wrapped in these thoughts, she entered down-city. There were some residences here, and some shops and a few inns, but all were of poor quality, and many were downright shabby. There were alleys that snaked in and out among the buildings without apparent plan. Rilsin had entered an area that had been under Lisim control.

There were also taverns of the less reputable sort. Rilsin knew several of these fairly well. She had frequented them in what seemed like another lifetime now, when she had been first minister. Even then, she had not come as who she really was but in an assumed persona. It had been safe enough. Rilsin was arguably the best swordsman in the land, and she was utterly unremarkable in her dress. If no one had expected the first minister to be in such places, even less would anyone expect the SaeKet.

Rilsin found one tavern she remembered. Its sign was painted with a sheaf of wheat. There was no lettering. In this part of Petipal few could read. Rilsin hesitated for a second and then pushed open the heavy door and entered.

She was greeted with a blast of noise. Many of The Sheaf's patrons were well on their way into celebrating an early Sunreturn. There was a split second of silence when Rilsin entered, but the noise resumed almost immediately, as Rilsin was examined and then dismissed as being no immediate threat. She looked like a somewhat rough customer, but in that she was perfectly ordinary for this part of town. Even her short hair drew no particular attention. Prisoners still had their hair cropped short, but so now did some commoners, following the fashion set by the SaeKet.

There was no empty table, so Rilsin took a portion of a bench that ran along one wall, and leaned against it. She caught the eye of a young boy bustling by with a tray of mugs.

"Mulled wine," she told him. Rilsin glanced around. What she wanted could be had here, if she were lucky.

When the boy came with her wine, Rilsin motioned him closer for a moment. He looked irritated, but the look vanished when Rilsin gave him a glimpse of the copper in the palm of her hand.

"I am looking for someone," she said, "and I want it kept quiet."

"What's her name?" asked the boy.

"I don't know. It's a man, tall, big, with a scar down his face," she illustrated by drawing her finger along her cheek. "Brown hair, tied back."

"Greasy hair?" asked the boy.

Rilsin nodded, although she wondered what constituted greasy to this not very clean child.

"I think you mean Nacrit. He's got a scar like that. Comes in all the time, buys ale from the owner in short barrels when he can."

Rilsin blinked. Was it possible that she had succeeded in her search so soon, on the first try? Her hopes were dashed with the next thing the boy said.

"He hasn't been in for a while now. Not for more than a week." He frowned. "Maybe he finally drank himself to death."

"Do you know where he lives?"

The boy hesitated for a moment, looking uneasy. Rilsin opened her hand, showing him the coin. When he made no move to take it, she pressed it into his hand.

"There's another one like this for you if you show me where he lives," she said. "Can you get away from work?"

The boy nodded. "I can get Jephet to fill in for me," he said. "Let me see the other coin."

Rilsin slipped her hand beneath her cloak, under her shirt and into her pouch. In the process, the boy got a glimpse of her sword, and the hilt of the first knife. Rather than alarming him, the knowledge that she was well-armed seemed to reassure him. Rilsin showed him two copper coins. "Both for you," she said, "if we find this Nacrit. There's another smaller one for Jephet, so you don't have to give him any of your share. What's your name?"

"Porit," the boy said. He was grinning broadly now, his mind on his coming wealth. "Wait here," he added unnecessarily.

Rilsin leaned back, sipping her wine, which was just this side of vile. Without seeming to, she examined the other customers of The Sheaf. They were a rough bunch, commoners from the neighborhoods nearby. Many of them worked at the local market square, unloading produce from the wagons that came in. She could guess at the various trades of others. Some worked in kitchens of the local inns or hauled wood. One small but garishly dressed group of both women and men, with no cloaks and with thin overshirts and trousers, either worked in a local whorehouse or paid The Sheaf's owner for a room in which to work.

"I got Jephet." Porit was back. "He said he'd do it, but he wants a big copper."

"Then you give him one of yours," said Rilsin. "I told you, two for you, a small one for Jephet. That's all I'm paying. If Jephet wants more, that's your business." She didn't want this boy to think her funds were endless, which in fact they were not. She had not brought much with her.

Porit shrugged. "Follow me," he said, throwing an undyed short wool cloak over his shoulders.

The bitter cold hit Rilsin again as they stepped out the door, dispelling the slight warm glow from the wine. Porit set off through an alley at a brisk pace.

"Slow down," said Rilsin. "Tell me what you can about the neighborhood of this Nacrit. What's the house like, what neighbors does he have, does anyone live with him?"

"It's just a house." Porit dropped back to talk with her. "An old one. No one lives in the top of it; it's falling down. Nacrit lives in the bottom. Across the street there's Jellillit; he's got cockfights every week. He's got a hunting cat to guard the birds, can you imagine?" Porit grinned at the joke. "A cat to guard the birds! It won't eat them, though, I've seen it. It's one mean cat! He got it from some dira who couldn't pay his debts. You don't want to mess with Jellil-lit."

"Mmm," said Rilsin, taking it all in. "Anyone live with Nacrit? He married?"

"Don't think so. He did have a roommate the last few weeks, though. A young man." Porit looked at her out of the corner of his eye, and then apparently decided she had paid enough to know. "I think he's saedin."

Rilsin felt the hair rise along the back of her neck. She had come to the right place. "What makes you think so?" she asked.

They were walking through an alley that looked to be used only for garbage disposal. The only reason it did not smell now was because the garbage was frozen. In the summer, it would be unbearable. Rilsin made a mental note. Down-city needed more garbage removal and cleanup.

"Well," said Porit shrewdly, "he talks like you, like he had some education. And the way he carries himself, and he gives orders to Nacrit. But I think he's on the run."

Rilsin stopped dead in the street. "Philla," she said. "Philla sae Lisim."

"That was the name. You're looking for him, aren't you?

Just as much as for Nacrit. That should be worth more than
a couple of big coppers."

Rilsin looked at him. "Yes," she said, "it should be. How
old are you, Porit?"

"Thirteen winters," said Porit.

"You are very smart, Porit, for thirteen or for any age.
Can you read?"

"Read?" Porit burst into laughter. "Why would I be able
to read?"

"Do you want to?" Rilsin asked curiously. "What do you
want to do, Porit?"

"If I could do anything, you mean?" For all of Porit's
worldly knowledge and attitude, he was still a boy with
dreams. "I would own the tavern. No, I would have an inn.
A really good one. Much better than The Sheaf. I would
hire someone to just cook, you know, not do everything?
And I'd have someone else to wait the patrons. And I would
have my inn in a good neighborhood, with stables! I love
horses!" Porit stopped suddenly.

Rilsin could see him pulling back, remembering where
he was and what they were doing. He wasn't used to re-
vealing so much about himself, and certainly not to a
stranger.

"Reading will help you with that. There are schools
opening, you know, well, one anyway, for commoners. You
should go." She was going to continue, but Porit took her
arm.

"That's it," he said. "The house over there."

The house Porit designated was even more run down
than Rilsin had imagined. They had left the street corner
lantern behind, but even in the available light from the stars
and a few lit windows in other buildings, Rilsin could see
that the roof of Nacrit's house was missing more than it was
present. It looked as though the upper half of what had been
a two-story dwelling had partially collapsed on itself. There
was no light from the house, not from any room that Rilsin
could see. Porit pulled a small unlit torch from within his
cloak. Rilsin grabbed his hand.

"Don't light that!" she hissed.

Startled, Porit put the torch away. Rilsin, without taking her eyes from the house and the shadows around it, reached into her pouch and drew out by feel alone one big copper piece and one small, and one of the silver coins. She gave these to Porit. Then she drew her gloves on again and threw back her cloak, freeing her sword.

"Thank you, Porit," she said. "You have helped more than you know."

"I'm not leaving," said Porit.

"What?" She glanced at him.

"I said, I'm not leaving. I'm going in with you."

Rilsin snapped her glance away from the house and gave all her attention to the boy. "You have shown me the house," she said, "and you gave me information. I paid you. Now go home."

"No. You need me, sae. I know my way around that house. I delivered short barrels here sometimes, and kegs, whenever Nacrit got the money for them. And I'm armed, sae." He threw back his own short cloak to reveal a long dagger.

"What makes you think I'm saedin?" Rilsin was momentarily distracted.

"You have to be. I said before, you talk like you're educated. And that sword," he nodded toward the weapon on her belt, "it cost a lot. And besides, only a saedin would care about me learning to read."

Rilsin stared at him, not inclined to argue the point. She watched as Porit drew his long dagger, flipped it end over end, and caught it again, sheathing it in one fluid movement, then drawing it again.

"I know how to use this, sae," he said. "I know it's dangerous, but I'm not leaving you."

Rilsin wondered what she had done to elicit such loyalty and then decided it was probably a youthful taste for adventure.

"All right," she said.

Porit led the way to the house. They did not approach by

what passed for the front entrance but went around to a boarded-up window at the side. One of the boards had pulled away from the window, leaving a gaping dark hole. In one swift motion, before she could even think to stop him, Porit pulled away from Rilsin and boosted himself up into the dark space. A moment later his head reappeared in the opening.

"The house is empty," he said. "Come to the front, if you want, and I'll open the door."

"No need," said Rilsin.

She boosted herself in the way he had, swinging her sword to keep it free. Once down on the ground again, she drew it in a scrape of steel.

The room had once been a bedchamber. There was an old bedstead in one corner, but it obviously had not been used in a long time. There was a chamber pot near the bed, crusted with something half-frozen. Rilsin wrinkled her nose and moved out of the room.

What had been a parlor was empty, but Rilsin went to the hearth. There was a half-burned log there, and it looked fairly recent. She kept her sword in her hand, and she was alert for any hint of movement. There was none.

"In here," half-whispered Porit.

"Here" was an inner room with a cold dirt floor. It was empty but for a child's small bed. In two strides Rilsin was at the bed. There was a heavily stitched quilt on the bed, which Rilsin drew aside. Under the quilt was a child's little overshirt trimmed in blue and gold. Rilsin felt her breath freeze in her throat and her heart almost stop. Gently she picked up the overshirt and turned it in her hands. There were no bloodstains. She held the little shirt to her face, suddenly blinking back tears. She was too late. How long since Reniat had been here?

"Sae!" Porit's cry snapped her from her reverie.

Rilsin whirled. Behind her was a dark figure, but the light, what there was of it, glinted from a sword. She realized she had placed her own sword on the bed. She dropped the shirt and grabbed it up. Even as Rilsin engaged her assailant, she saw two other figures in the room. One was in hand-to-hand combat with Porit, but she had no time to assess his danger. The other figure came straight for her.

Both her opponents had swords, and it was obvious that both knew the house, knew the layout of the room, knew the unevenness in the floor, and were familiar with all the little irregularities that Rilsin did not know. It was also obvious that they had some training and some sword skill. Rilsin went after her first attacker without hesitation and seemingly without caution. She wanted him to have no time to think. She came in low and tried to move to her opponent's left, to get through his guard, but he was ready for her. He parried and went back on the attack. At the same time, her second opponent came in from the other side.

Without a pause Rilsin drew the dagger from her belt, aimed, and threw, left-handed. She aimed for the center of the widest part of the dark figure. Luck was with her. The figure gave a high scream and doubled over, sliding to the floor.

It was just in time. Rilsin's first opponent had taken advantage of her momentary distraction to come in close and under her guard. Holding his sword low, he came up from below, trying to run her through the heart.

Rilsin had been told again and again as a girl in arms training to keep her weapon, but now she ignored the rule. She dropped her sword and with her left hand whirled her woolen cloak forward to entangle her opponent's sword. At the same time she twisted aside and bent down, drawing the second knife from her boot. Using the dangerous closeness to her own advantage, she trapped the sword in her cloak, lunged forward, and slid the knife into her assailant's abdomen. She yanked upward on the hilt, at the same time drawing him in closer by pulling on the cloak. He gave a short, hoarse scream and then began to breathe in little grunting, coughing cries. He dropped to the floor, almost pulling her down with him, as she drew her knife free. Rilsin let him go and grabbed up her sword again, looking for the third assailant.

The third assailant was on the floor with a knife in his eye. He was very definitely dead. Standing over him, panting, was Porit.

"Great freezing Runchot hells," gasped Rilsin. She was slightly winded.

"I told you I was good in a fight," Porit reminded her. "Good thing I was here, sae," he said.

"A very good thing," Rilsin agreed. It was plain that even at thirteen winters, he had killed before. She took the sword from the man at her feet, who was now mewling with pain, and went to look at the man who had her knife in him.

It was not a man; it was a woman, a young woman, and a dead one. Rilsin's knife had pinned her right through the heart, a very lucky throw. Rilsin bent down, put her foot on the dead woman, and dragged her knife free. She wiped the knife on the dead woman's cloak and resheathed it.

"Are you hurt?" she asked Porit.

"No, sae. Well, a scratch. He got me on the shoulder."

Rilsin went to look. Even in the almost-dark she could see blood, black in the dim light, welling from a deep cut.

"Great freezing Runchot hells!" she said again, bundling the boy's shirt to put pressure on the wound.

"Really, sae, it isn't bad," he protested.

"Hold that down," she said, ignoring his protest, "until we get you to a physician. That needs stitching."

"I can't afford a physician! But Jephet's pretty good with the doctoring. This will be his first time stitching, though."

"You will see a physician," said Rilsin shortly. "But first I want some answers."

She went to the man she had knifed, who was still moaning on the floor. She knelt beside him and pulled his clothing away from the wound. It was hard to see, and she dragged him to the doorway and more light. As the light fell on his face, she thought he looked familiar.

"Who are you?" she demanded.

When there was no answer but another moan, she looked at his wound again. He was slick with blood, and where the clothing had been pulled away, she could she a loop of intestine. From the smell, the intestine had been punctured by her blade.

"You will not live," she told him. "Who are you?"

"Whiffit sae Lisim." His voice was faint. "I am so cold."

"Tell me where they went, Sae Whiffit. Tell me now, and I will make your death a little easier, a little faster."

"I don't think so," he whispered. He coughed and sighed. Then there was silence. Rilsin leaned down, but he was no longer breathing.

"Damn it," Rilsin said softly. She had obviously punctured something more immediately fatal than his intestines. "Damn all Lisim to a Runchot hell. How could I have been so foolish as to let any of them go!" She sat back on her heels, staring blindly into the dark room. "Why couldn't I get here sooner?"

She stood slowly, looking around her. Porit had gone to the bed and was standing there, holding something in his hands. It was the little child's overshirt. Rilsin took this from him and tucked it into her own belt. She pulled the quilt from the bed and ripped it as best she could into strips, making a bandage for Porit's shoulder.

"I told you to hold this," she said. "Hold it tightly. It will stop the bleeding until we get to a physician."

Outside the house, nothing much had changed, except that any lights from nearby buildings were now gone. The fight had made noise, and any residents wanted nothing to do with the source of the disturbance. Rilsin glanced at Porit. He seemed to be doing reasonably well, but she wanted to get him to a physician as soon as possible. The best and quickest thing would be to take him to the palace and have Maltia care for him.

Rilsin did not want to go back to the palace. She wanted to find out why there were still Lisim in the neighborhood, and she wanted to find out where they had taken her daughter. To have come so close to finding her child was almost more than she could bear. As they left the street, Porit turned in the direction of The Sheaf.

"No," said Rilsin, putting out a hand to stop him. "You

will come with me and see my own physician. We can send a message to your tavern."

Porit opened his mouth to say something, but whatever it was, Rilsin did not hear him. Overhead, an aurora had begun to flicker, great banners and streamers of light, gold and green and rose. There was a popping and crackling sound as if someone were shaking out and snapping great sheets of cloth above their heads. Rilsin and Porit both looked up at it.

It was not an unusual sight in winter, but now Rilsin seemed to feel it, the colors and the sounds, flowing through her and down into the hard, frozen soil beneath her feet. Rilsin felt something welling up to meet them: the layered impressions of everything alive in Saeditin, in the land under her care. It was the song of the land. She stood in the street and listened to the aurora and felt the song. Some things were in harmony, as they should be, and some were not. She realized that she had made a mistake, and it was almost too late to correct it. Dremfir had been right. She had needed to listen.

Rilsin became aware of the street again, and of Porit beside her. He was staring at her with something like fear.

"What were you doing, sae?" he asked. His eyes were big in his small face.

"Listening," she said.

"To the aurora?" Porit looked confused. Surely a mere aurora, no matter how spectacular, would not bring on such a trance.

"To the song," said Rilsin. "The song of the land."

Porit's eyes seemed to get even larger. He made a noise sort of like a squeak and put his right hand over his heart.

"SaeKet," he said.

The wad of quilt began to slip from his shoulder. Rilsin reached out and caught it before it fell. She took the boy's hand from over his heart and placed it back firmly on the cloth on his shoulder.

"Great freezing Runchot hells!" she said. "I told you to hold that!"

11

THEY HAD BEEN KEEPING HIM DRUGGED. THEY WOULD force his mouth open and pour some liquid in, something that smelled even worse than it tasted. No matter how Sola tried not to swallow, tried to spit it out, some always went down his throat. Once even a little of it was in him, doing its work, it was easy for them to force more down him. Once they were late in dosing him, and he began to think again, slowly and painfully. He wondered how long he had been captive and where he was and why they were holding him and who they were. He thought he heard a child crying. Then they came back and made him drink again.

He had dreams. He dreamed that several people bundled him into his cloak and wrapped a blanket around him as well. They bound him and gagged him and put him in the back of a wagon, under mounds of hay, wedged between barrels of something. He rode this way, and when they stopped they were outside of Petipal. In the dream they unbound him and forced some thin soup into him, which was hot and good but made him feel sick. They laughed and

joked about how the Becha SaeKet kept the roads open, and
how this made it easier for them. Then they bound him
again but did not gag him, and they put him back in the
wagon. He dreamed that the hay and the blankets kept him
from freezing. He dreamed he heard a child crying.

He woke from dreaming to find himself in the wagon.
He was lying on hay, with hay spread around him, and over
him, and over his cloak and several blankets. His hood was
up over his head, and his hands were bound and were very
cold. The sun, a pale, thin winter sun, was rising on his
right. He twisted to see better where he was, and saw the
wagon was actually moving, on a road. The motion made
him feel sick, and he lay back again.

After some time, thought began to come back to him and
to make sense. If they no longer saw a need to drug him,
then perhaps he was beyond the reach of help. This thought
was so depressing that tears came to his eyes. He was afraid
his tears would freeze, so he closed his eyes, and then he
was asleep again.

When he woke again, he felt weak, but also hungry,
which he took as a good sign. It was dark, and he was still
in the wagon, but someone, during the time he had slept,
had unbound his hands and tucked them down under the
blankets and the hay to keep them warm. He was now
chained around the waist, and the chain was attached to the
side of the wagon. He was able to determine that he could
not easily free himself, as the chain was looped through the
side of the wagon boards and locked.

Sola looked to the front of the wagon. There was a small
raised and covered cab there. Whoever was driving the
wagon at least had some protection from the weather. Just
as Sola thought this, it began to snow in big, fat flakes.

He hunched down under his coverings again, only peering over the side of the wagon once to look up ahead. He
tried to imagine where they could be going, but he could
not force his mind much beyond food, and the almost overwhelming need to relieve himself. He couldn't even remember how exactly he had come to be here. He had

thought that agents of Sithli sae Melisin had him, or perhaps Runchot agents. If either of those parties held him, however, they should be heading south, toward the Runchot border. They were not. They were going north.

The wagon turned down a side road. This road had not been plowed as cleanly as the road they just left. Sola wondered if they had just left the SaeKet's Road, the main north-south artery that ran most of the length of Saeditin, flowing into the Petipal Road as it neared the capital. If so, he should be able to find his way home, if he could escape.

Sola peered over the side of the wagon, hoping to see landmarks, something to mark his way out again. The wagon jounced up to a farmhouse that loomed suddenly out of the snow. As it pulled to a stop, he lay back again and pretended to be asleep.

There were sounds of people alighting from the covered cab. The horses were stomping and snorting, and someone came out of the farmhouse to help with them. Then a child cried.

"It took long enough for you to get here," someone grumbled.

"We couldn't leave the city right away. The Becha SaeKet had a search out. And we had to keep the magician drugged; no telling what would have happened if he came to." This last was said in a low tone.

The child cried harder, drowning out whatever was said next. There was the sound of a door slamming. Then there was a woman's voice.

"What's wrong with her? Have you hurt her? Give her to me. Are you sure this is the sun-child? She looks just like any baby."

Sola stopped breathing.

"I'm not a baby!" said a clear, small voice. "I'm Reniat! I want my mama!" She began to cry again.

"Well, that won't happen," said a man's voice. "You won't ever see her again, you little brat, unless you see her throat cut in the Mother's Square."

Reniat began to cry harder.

"There's no need for that talk!" said the woman sharply. "Little one, come inside and get warm. I have nice porridge for you." There was the sound of packed snow crunching beneath boots, and Reniat's crying faded.

"You might as well open your eyes," said a voice right above Sola. "I know you're awake. No one could sleep through that racket, drugged or not."

Sola opened his eyes and looked up through the snow, which was coming down harder now. He saw a man's broad face, with a scar down one cheek. "Nacrit." He remembered the name. Now he remembered being followed into the alley and being ambushed.

The big man grinned. It was not a pleasant sight. "You got a good memory," he said. He pulled an iron key from under his cloak, and with a little grunting and swearing, unlocked Sola's chains. He did not remove the chains from around Sola's waist. During this process, Nacrit's sleeve was pushed back, and Sola caught a glimpse of healing claw marks on his arm.

"Get out," Nacrit said, "but don't try anything."

He kept hold of the chain, and when Sola, stiff from inaction and the aftereffects of the drug, had trouble climbing over the side of the wagon, he yanked on the chain, half dragging Sola out. Sola stumbled and slid, tripping, to land in the snow at Nacrit's feet. Nacrit snickered. He helped Sola to his feet again and let him relieve himself in the snow before they entered the farmhouse. Nacrit had to half-support Sola up the steps to the farmhouse door.

The warmth hit Sola like a physical force, and he stood blinking, dripping melting snow onto the floor. It was an ordinary farmhouse parlor, sparsely furnished, with a fire roaring in the fireplace. From the kitchen, which Sola could see through an open doorway, came the smell of hot porridge and of freshly baked bread. The smells made him suddenly nauseous.

"If you're going to be sick, go back outside! Nacrit, take him out before he vomits!"

Nacrit gave a tug on his chain, but Sola resisted, wobbling. "I won't be sick," he promised. He looked toward the speaker. "Philla sae Lisim," he said before he could stop himself.

"I'm glad to see you remember me, Dira Sola."

Things were clicking together in Sola's mind. He knew he didn't have all the information yet, but he took a chance. "Of course I remember you," he said. "I'm the reason you are still alive."

In what seemed the blink of an eye Philla was in front of him. Philla grabbed his face in one hand, tipping his head back. Sola swayed, off balance.

"What do you mean? The Becha SaeKet let me go!"

"Because I talked her into it ahead of time. Which was more than I could do for your sister Jolass, although I tried." It was true enough in a way. Sola fought back another wave of nausea and dizziness and looked Philla in the eye.

"Why would she listen to you?"

"I'm her lover, remember?" Sola remembered Nacrit asking about this, outside the palace. If Nacrit knew, all Petipal knew. "Let me go, Sae Philla, before I puke in your face."

"Why would you ask her to spare me?" Philla asked, but he released Sola.

"Get these chains off me. Let me get cleaned up, and get warm, and get something to drink, for the Mother's sake. We can talk later."

"We'll talk when I say!"

"Have it your way, Sae Philla." Sola added a wobble to his sway and turned his face aside, as if to be sick. Philla hastily stepped back.

"Do it!" Philla said to Nacrit and to another man who lingered at the edge of Sola's vision. "Get him cleaned up. Get the chains off him. If he tries to run, kill him."

Nacrit and another man took him into the kitchen. There was another large fireplace here and a stone oven. There was a big pot of stew and another of porridge on hooks over the fire, and there was a loaf of bread sitting beside the oven.

There was a woman in the kitchen, too, sitting at a scarred wooden table. She was spooning up some porridge with a small wooden spoon and feeding it to a child in her lap: Reniat. Reniat looked well, although dirty.

"Come now, sweet cake, eat another spoonful," said the woman. Reniat turned her head at the noise and saw Sola.

The little girl's eyes widened as she recognized him. Sola caught her glance and gave his head a tiny shake. Reniat saw this, gave a little sniff, and turned back to her porridge. Sola felt a wash of amazement and a strange sort of pride. Reniat had always been precocious for such a little girl, but of course she would be. She was Rilsin's child.

There was a pail of cold water, and Sola was permitted to wash his face with some of it. Nacrit then took him and shoved him down forcibly onto a stool at the wooden table. The woman had finished feeding Reniat, and picked her up and took her away into another room. Sola was given some porridge, but no stew, and a hefty slice of the bread. He ate ravenously. When he asked for something to drink, they gave him water from the same pail in which he had washed. He hesitated, but his thirst was overbearing. He drank it.

As he was finishing, Philla came into the kitchen. He drew up a stool and sat at the table within reach of Sola. Nacrit and his companion had been joined by two more men, who positioned themselves casually but purposefully around the kitchen. One blocked the door, another was right behind Sola. Sola felt his heart plummet into his newly filled stomach. He was about to be interrogated, and it did not look as though his captors were expecting to be gentle about it.

"Where am I?" asked Sola. "And why have you kidnapped me? My mother is my only close relative, and she cannot afford much ransom." Taking the initiative was the best strategy he could think of at the moment.

"Surely you know you are worth much to others, including Rilsin SaeKet," said Philla. He grinned. "But first tell me about saving my life. Why would you do that, Dira Sola?"

"I couldn't see any reason for more bloodshed," said Sola truthfully. "I also must admit, Sae Philla, that I have certain admiration for your aunt, Sae Kepit. I hoped that I could persuade Sae Kepit to leave Sithli sae Melisin, and I hoped to persuade Rilsin SaeKet to accept Sae Kepit back in Petipal."

"Why?" Philla stared at Sola in complete astonishment.

"Because your aunt, Sae Philla, is one of the most astute political minds I've ever known. Rilsin SaeKet has need of her." It was true, Kepit sae Lisim had one of the most astute minds of their time, but Rilsin would never accept her service or let her back into Saeditin alive. Sola was betting that Philla was too stupid to know this.

"Saving your life, and I had hoped to save your sister's, also, was the first step. I wanted to find you, to get you to take a message to Sae Kepit. But I could not." Philla seemed to be buying this, so Sola took a chance. "If you are expecting Rilsin SaeKet to pay for me, she will not. Kidnapping me will not help bring your family back into favor, Sae Philla. Sending me back to Petipal might help."

It was a mistake, and Sola knew it as soon as he said it. He did not know whether or not Rilsin would ransom him, but it wasn't smart to tell his captors she wouldn't. And it wasn't smart to put Philla's actions in a bad light, especially not in front of his men.

Philla leaned over the table and grabbed the front of Sola's overshirt. He pulled, half-dragging Sola across the table. Sola found it hard to breathe and put his hands over Philla's to try to loosen his grip. Suddenly his arms were grabbed and twisted behind him. He was held in this uncomfortable position across the table, with Philla half choking him.

"I am not even going to offer you to the Becha," snarled Philla. "I have other plans for you." Philla released him with a suddenness that left Sola gasping.

"What plans?" Sola's voice was husky. He was back on

his stool, but his arms were still twisted behind him by one of Philla's men. It was suddenly too much. Sola took a chance and rammed his head backward. He felt the back of his head connect with something soft, possibly the solar plexus of the man behind him. The man swore, Sola's arms were free, and he turned, diving sideways off the stool, pulling the man down with him.

That was the signal for all of Philla's men to get into the act. Sola was kicked and punched, but his anger and fear lent him some strength. By the time Philla got them to stop, one of the men was bleeding from his nose, another had a swollen eye, and Nacrit had a deep bite on his wrist. One of Sola's eyes was swelling shut, his head rang from being punched, and his ribs hurt fiercely. He knew he had not behaved rationally, and he prided himself on rationality, but for once he was not sorry.

"Get him out of here," said Philla. "No, wait. Drug him again first."

Sola was held down by several men now, as the drug was prepared and then forced down his throat. He was held so tightly that he could not even struggle. After they had made him swallow the repulsive mixture, they hauled him to his feet and pulled him, stumbling, down a short hallway into another room. Sola could see a certain amount of respect in their eyes.

They did not bind him again but pushed him down, almost gently, onto a cot with several blankets. There was a candle burning in the room, and Sola could see a chamber pot in a corner. The door was pulled closed, and Sola could hear a key turn in a lock. As soon as he knew himself alone, he dragged himself to the chamber pot in the corner. He was dizzy and his hands and feet were cold again. The drug was already taking effect, and soon he would be unconscious.

Sola leaned over the chamber pot, and after several tries with muscles already uncoordinated, he managed to get his finger down his throat. It helped that the drug made him dizzy, and the dizziness made him slightly nauseous. After a moment, his efforts were successful. His dinner came back up, but so, he hoped, did most of the drug. Sola staggered back to the cot and half-lay, half-fell onto the blankets. He did not have the ability to pull one over himself. He closed his eyes and dozed.

He did not know how much time had passed when he heard the key in the lock, and the door opened. He kept his eyes closed.

"He's out, Sae Philla," said Nacrit's voice.

"That stuff really does the job," said another voice. "Gaah, look here, he puked in the corner first! Do you think we gave him too much? It's a wonder he's not dead."

"He may be yet," said Philla. "If the drug doesn't kill him, we may have to. That would be a waste of all my effort." There was a creak, and the cot depressed as Philla sat on it beside Sola. He shoved Sola slightly to move him over and give himself a bit more room. Sola remained completely inert.

"I don't know why you brought him," said the woman's voice. Apparently Sola's captors had such faith in their drug that it never occurred to them that he might hear them.

"You do know why I brought him. He's valuable. Sithli SaeKet can use him—"

"For what?" said the woman's voice. "You think Rilsin sae Becha will pay for him? That isn't like her. She will either try to take him back by force, or take revenge for him, or most likely both."

"But he's a magician! It's his magic that is valuable!"

"If you mean the fire-tubes and the steam machines, cousin, we have that magic already. The Runchot want steam, and they are already building steam machines. It is not that hard once you have the idea. The genius of Dira Sola was in seeing something obvious. It is the same with the fire-tubes. A little work, and Sithli SaeKet will have them for her army. I would bet the Runchot have some already."

"She won't have them soon enough," said Philla, sounding petulant.

"No, she won't, but Dira Sola here won't make them magically appear."

"You don't know what he can do, Wennit. He's a magician! I thought Aunt Kepit could use him, so I took him."

"Nobody asked you to think," muttered Wennit. Sola did not recognize the name, but he knew she must be one of the enormous extended Lisim clan. Not only had she called Philla "cousin," but she had the Lisim edgy belligerence. *A delightful family,* thought Sola.

"What I want to know," put in a male voice, "is how we are going to get safely into Clinsi territory. The barbarians make sacrifices you know, at Sunreturn. Human sacrifice. They take travelers." The voice held a shudder in it, and Sola thought it was the man he overheard outside the farmhouse, the one who had called him a magician.

"If the Clinsi warriors demand payment in a sacrifice, we are in no position to deny them. We will have to give them someone for their rites."

Footsteps came up to the side of the cot. Sola could feel someone looking down, but still he kept his eyes closed. He could feel Philla shift beside him on the cot.

"We can always give this one to the Clinsi," said Wennit. Something poked Sola sharply in the side. He did not wince, did not respond at all. "We cannot give them the little Becha brat, and I would hate to give them any of our loyal partisans." There was a sarcastic edge to Wennit's voice.

Not good, thought Sola. *Sae Kepit would never let anyone hear anything but sincerity unless she meant them to. Wennit is no Sae Kepit.*

"So maybe you did well to take him, Philla, after all." Wennit's hand brushed Sola's hair back from his eyes, which he kept closed. It was difficult not to alter his breathing.

He lay still, without opening his eyes for some time after he was sure they had left. The truth was that he was still sick. Some of the drug was in him and doing its work. He wished he had been able to purge the drug and not the food, and especially not the water. Of course that was not possible, but now his thirst was so intense that it almost drove back his fear. It did not drive back reason, however. Sola prided himself on reason, and now he put it to use.

It was obvious they were not taking him south to the Runchot border. Apparently they did not trust themselves to evade Rilsin's border patrols. They were not only taking him north but east, if they were going toward Clinsi lands. This meant they had already left the SaeKet's Road, most likely. But why were they heading into Clinsi territory? The Clinsi were members of Bilt's Confederation, and the Confederation had, under Rilsin's generalship, signed a treaty with Saeditin.

Sola missed Rilsin terribly, and he wished he had been able to tell her he was sorry for what he had said about Reniat. But no. She had said it. She had said what he secretly thought and felt. He wondered if he would ever see Rilsin again. Despite his desire to think rationally, he wasn't doing it. Thinking about Rilsin made him so very sad.

Sometimes he drifted into sleep, where the drug gave him strange dreams. After one of these episodes he awoke with a clearer head. He realized that he had been approaching the problem the wrong way. He had been wondering why they were taking him into Clinsi territory, but his presence was unplanned, a last-minute addition by Philla. They were taking Reniat into Clinsi territory. With the new clarity that he found vaguely surprising, Sola realized something or that someone was in Clinsi territory that posed a grave threat to Saeditin. It was up to him to find out what this threat was and to get a warning back to Rilsin.

Sola sat up. The candle had burned almost all the way down. He could see a little gray light under the door. He rubbed his sore ribs and winced. He would somehow have to find a way to avoid being drugged again, and he would also have to get his captors to stop thinking of him as any sort of threat. That goal would be more difficult to achieve after the fracas of the previous night. He needed to remem-

ber to use his head, he told himself, and not just for ram-
ming someone in the stomach.

They came for him not much later and began to prepare
him for travel. He pretended to be more groggy than he
was, but he asked for water, and they gave it to him. To his
intense relief they did not force more of the drug on him.
They wrapped his cloak around him, grabbed his arms, and
pulled him out to the wagon.

It had snowed for most of the night, something Philla
and his party had apparently not taken into their calcula-
tions. They could not take the wagon over the roads. They
would have to go on horseback. There was a short debate as
to whether or not to wait for the roads to be plowed, but
they could not afford to wait, it seemed.

Packs were made up quickly, and horses were saddled.
The chain was again wrapped around Sola's waist. The man
who did this sported an amazing black eye. He gave Sola a
respectful and not entirely unfriendly glance.

"Mount up, magician," said the man. When Sola did,
with some effort, the chain was secured to the saddle.

"I should chain your horse to mine," said Philla, from
where he stood watching the proceedings. "I should, but I
won't. The snow is too deep, and the horses will have heavy
enough going without that. But mark me well, Dira Sola. If
you try to escape, I will have you shot." He nodded at two
of his men, who carried bows. "If we meet anyone on the
road, keep your mouth shut. If you say anything, anything
at all that I don't like," Philla paused and drew a wicked-
looking long dagger from under his cloak, "I will cut out
your tongue. It would give me great pleasure to do it. Do
you understand me?"

"I do," said Sola.

"Good." Philla mounted his own horse but did not
sheath his dagger. He sidestepped his horse until he was
right beside Sola's horse. "Do not move, Dira Sola," he
said. With a quickness that surprised Sola, Philla reached
out and pushed back his hood. Sola flinched away.

"I said, don't move. I don't want to cut you. Yet." Philla

grinned. He grabbed Sola's long braid, which was rather disheveled from recent events. With one quick swipe of the knife, he severed the braid, and Sola's now-short hair swung raggedly around his ears.

"You are a thief," said Philla conversationally. "You stole from me and were caught and sentenced to a term of service with me. A term of twenty years." Philla grinned again. "I have a small holding near the northern border, and I am taking you there to begin your service. This explains the chain, should anyone ask." He dropped Sola's braid into the snow and rode to the head of the little column, grinning.

Sola watched as Reniat was brought out, bundled into several long cloaks, and tied into the saddle in front of Wennit, who was coming with them. Reniat's ropes were less for restraint and more to keep her from falling out of the saddle, if Wennit failed to hold on to her. In less time than Sola would have believed possible, they were heading out.

It was very tough going, but Philla pushed them relentlessly. It was obvious that he was concerned with being in Clinsi territory by a certain date. They ate in the saddle. Sola was given some bread, which he ate hungrily. Their water bottles had frozen, but Sola managed to scoop a little snow from a tree they passed under. It was not enough to satisfy him, but there was nothing he could do about it. They did not stop until well past midday and into the afternoon, when Reniat began to cry.

"Can't you shut the brat up?" demanded Philla irritably.

"She needs to stop, Philla. She's hungry, and she wet herself, and she's shivering."

Philla wrinkled his face in disgust, but he found a heavy stand of pine trees not far ahead. Their thick boughs had kept the ground beneath them relatively free of snow. Here they stopped. Wennit fed Reniat and cleaned her while the others ate and stretched their muscles. Sola had to be helped from the saddle, not only because of the chain but because he was so stiff and weak. When he saw Philla watching him, he made the most of it, staggering and half-falling.

They were back in the saddle again all too soon. The ter-

rain was hilly and wooded, and Sola realized that they were
far from the SaeKet's Road, heading into the steep country
of the northeastern saedholds. He had been drugged for
longer than he knew, and they had traveled far in that time.
They were near the border of Saeditin and the edge of barbarian lands.

Sola knew they were not really barbarians. He had
fought with them, and he had accepted the hospitality of
Bilt, their first man, but it was hard to overcome longstand-
ing Saeditin tradition. Besides, Bilt was Wilfrisin, and they
were heading into Clinsi territory. The Clinsi had a reputation all their own.

The midwinter day was short. By the time the evening
darkness began to gather, they were in the middle of the
woods, and the road was barely a trail beneath the trees.
Sola wondered how much farther they had to go before they
reached whatever destination Philla and Wennit had in
mind. He decided that as soon as the first opportunity presented itself, he had to escape, whether he knew what they
were doing or not.

Philla found a small clearing for them to camp in. They
had not intended to spend a night in the open, but they had
made far less progress than they had planned. It was a clear
evening, promising to be a clear night, and bitterly cold.
Two of the men managed to come up with some dry wood
from the forest, and Philla set others to stamping down and
packing some of the snow in the clearing. The only reason
Sola was not set to this work was that he could scarcely
move. Hunger, thirst, the aftereffects of the drug, and stiff-
ness from a day in the saddle caused him to collapse in the
snow.

"I suppose there is no reason to chain you," said Philla.

Once the fire was started, Sola crept as close as he could
to it. They all did. Tree branches cracked from the cold in
the nearby woods, and as the early darkness fell, an aurora
began to play in the sky overhead, lighting everyone's features with a strange and shifting glow. Huddled in his cloak
and three blankets beside the fire, eating the bread and cold

meat that he had been given, Sola began to consider the possibility that he might not make it home. He glanced toward Reniat, bundled up beside Wennit, and wondered if she would ever see her mother again. Perhaps all of them, captors and captives alike, would die out here in this bitter wilderness.

From the forest, which was all too nearby, came strange sounds. There were bears in the forest, but they would now be in their winter dens, asleep. Not so the wild cat prides, the feral relatives of Saeditin's hunting cats, and not so the wolf packs that had only recently begun to enter the territories west of the mountains. The forest was also home to slipe, small furred animals with a vicious temper, which hunted in hordes that more than made up for their small size.

What came out of the forest was none of these animals. It was a group of men and deer. At first Sola could not understand what he was seeing, but as the group approached, very rapidly, he realized what it was. The deer were harnessed to a sled, which moved easily across the snow. Tiny bells on the harnesses tinkled prettily.

Philla's men had stood up, encircling the horses. Wennit slung Reniat under one arm and drew a knife, and Sola stood staring. One of the men on the sled called out a command to the deer. The sled slowed and then halted. One man leaped from the sled and fearlessly approached the group in the clearing. He was bundled in furs, and he carried a spear.

"Hey, Philla Lisim, that you?" he called, in accented Saeditin.

"Pellefik!" said Philla. "Welcome. We were coming to meet you."

"You late. We come south to meet you. I see the girl," he was looking at Reniat, still bundled into Wennit's cloak. "You got payment?"

"I got," said Philla shortly.

This was the signal for others of Pellefik's party to come to the fire. It was a group of seven men altogether, all of

them with thick beards and wearing heavy furs. Clinsi.
Philla dragged a saddlebag from one of the horses and
opened it. Gold glinted under firelight and aurora.

"Good," said Pellefik. "Good start on payment. For this,
we take girl to Runchot prince." Sola, listening unremarked
by the fire, started violently. No one noticed.

"Runchot warriors are in my lands now," Pellefik went
on. "I want them south soon. Before Bilt and Wilfrisin can
stop them. Besides, Runchot eat a lot. So we take girl. Now.
We leave now."

He waved commandingly at Wennit, who walked forward, and he tried to pull Reniat away from her. Reniat
clung to Wennit and started to cry. Pellefik leaned down
and grabbed her firmly. Reniat began to scream. Pellefik
pulled one glove from a massive hand and slapped the
child's face. It was a slight blow, but the crack of flesh on
flesh was loud in the clearing. Reniat stopped screaming.
Before she could draw breath to continue, Pellefik spoke.

"You make no noise," he said. "Noise will bring animals. Big cats. Who eat you. You stay quiet." Reniat sub-
sided. "Good," said Pellefik again, replacing his glove. He
handed the child off to one of his men.

"Now," he said, "more of our payment."

"What do you mean, more payment?" Philla took a
stance, and his men lined up behind him. "The gold was
agreed on."

"Yes," said Pellefik, "but you are late. If you make us
late to Sunreturn rites, it is very bad. We have to give gift to
winter demons. Gift of human life."

"I told you," muttered one of Philla's men. "I warned
you."

"We take one of you. Maybe woman." Pellefik moved
toward Wennit. Wennit slung back her cloak. She was still
holding her dagger, and she dropped into a fighting stance.

"We'll give you someone," said Philla hastily. "We were
going to give him to the Runchot, but you can have him."
He grabbed up the end of Sola's chain, which lay in the

snow, and pulled on it, dragging Sola forward. "He is yours. Do what you want with him."

Pellefik walked over and looked down at Sola. *The man is huge,* Sola thought. *What is it that makes barbarians so big?*

"What kind of man is he?" asked Pellefik. "He does not look like warrior."

"He's a magician," said Philla. "He is Sola dira Mudrin, of Saeditin."

"Ah!" Pellefik took a step back. "Man who magic steam!" He squinted at Sola. "Are you?" he asked.

"Yes," said Sola. He saw no point in lying.

"Good. We take him. Demons will like."

Pellefik took the end of the chain and wrapped it around his massive fist. He tugged on the chain, pulling Sola after him to the sled. He pushed Sola up onto this and then wrapped the chain around one of the restraining bars on the side of the sled. He carefully tucked a fur robe around Sola. Apparently the demons wanted their gift to be alive and not frozen. Reniat was already bundled under several furs, held by a Clinsi as massive as Pellefik. When everyone was settled, Pellefik called something in Clinsi, and the deer took off at a trot.

Looking back, Sola saw Philla, Wennit, Nacrit, all the men and horses, gathered by the fire in the clearing. The aurora streamed overhead as the figures grew smaller with distance. Then they were in the forest again, heading north.

12

"NORTH," SAID RILSIN. "THE DANGER IS FROM THE NORTH."
She was looking over the last-minute supply list for her
troops. "Well, not all the danger, Sae Essit, which is why I
need you here in Petipal. If Kepit sae Lisim or Raphat himself tries to come over the border from Runchot, you need
to be prepared to ride south in our defense. It shouldn't happen before I get back from the northern border; I did not
sense anything immediate from the south. But we have to
be prepared."

"I will be ready, SaeKet." Essit wanted to ask if Rilsin
was completely certain about going north in the middle of
the winter with more troops.

"I am completely certain this is the right thing to do,
First Minister," said Rilsin. "Don't look like that, Sae Essit;
I'm not reading your mind. Your thoughts were written on
your face."

They were seated in the audience chamber, but it had
been transformed into a temporary staging area. Cold-
weather gear was heaped in piles, and there were captains

in corners poring over lists. Rilsin was taking more of the army north to meet up with Pleffin, if possible.

She was in a fever to start, afraid that she had wasted too much time. A search of the down-city neighborhood had brought no further information and no other signs of Lisim agents. Rilsin found it hard to forgive herself for not taking Dremfir's advice sooner. She should not have needed his advice. She should have followed her instinct, but she had always been reluctant to give credence to what she thought of as magic.

A commotion near the huge doors of the room caused her to look up. Her guards were trying to eject someone who refused to be turned away, a young boy in plain, commoner dress who had literally dug in his heels, making scrapes in the wooden floor, and who was hanging onto the edge of the doorframe.

"Just let me see her, please! The SaeKet knows me! Really, she does!"

"Porit? What are you doing here? Let him go," she said to her guards. "What is it, Porit? How is your shoulder?"

"It's healing well, SaeKet." Porit was out of breath from his struggle, and a little disheveled. Rilsin noticed that his hair, which had been long, the standard for free citizens, was now cut short, as hers was.

"I want to come with you, SaeKet! I would join the army, but they say I'm too young!"

Rilsin blinked at him, surprised. "What about your work? The Sheaf? And your family?"

"I have no family. They all died in the lung sickness three years ago."

Rilsin remembered that epidemic; she had almost died in it herself. "But Porit," she said, "surely you have some family left, and what about The Sheaf? And you promised you would learn to read."

"I have no one, SaeKet." The boy's jaw was set stubbornly. "And Jephet will take care of The Sheaf. Besides, I will never learn to read if barbarians and Runchot and the Sae Lisims and Sae Sithli take Petipal. And the rest of

Saeditin," he added as an afterthought. A true Petipalian, he barely recognized the existence of anything outside the city. "You need me, SaeKet. You do!"

Rilsin tried not to smile. "We may be able to stem the tide, Porit," she said gravely. "Besides which, you are wounded. Go home and let your shoulder heal."

"Please let me come with you! You need me, SaeKet!"

If he were younger, he might have cried. She knew he did still have family and that Jephet was his cousin, who had taken him in after his parents died. The problem was that Porit reminded Rilsin of herself. Beyond that, she felt something strange, in the brief moments of silence that followed his plea. He had said that she needed him, and she felt a faint tingle that she knew better now than to disregard.

"All right, Ria Porit," she said formally. "You may come with me." She watched as his face was transformed with joy.

"But you must see Sae Maltia, the physician, again, about your shoulder. Every day." Rilsin frowned. She was not sure just what a thirteen-year-old boy might need, and she was now responsible for him on a personal level.

"I will see that he eats right, SaeKet, and I will see that he cares for his shoulder. I can even start teaching him to read."

"Meffa!" When had her chief servant appeared?

"I am coming with you also, SaeKet. You promised me."

"I have not forgotten." Rilsin turned from watching Meffa take the boy away to find Dremfir waiting.

"I hope you will allow me to accompany you also, Rilsin SaeKet," he said formally.

"Of course, Sae Dremfir, my friend." She must have a priest with her. And Dremfir was trained as a warrior.

"May I speak to you as a friend, then, SaeKet?" When she nodded her consent, he continued. "I know you blame yourself for not rescuing your daughter before she was taken from the city and for the fact that she was taken at all. I think you also blame yourself for Dira Sola's disappearance." He paused for a moment, regarding her. Her face was grim and thunderous. The air itself seemed to crackle around her. Most people would not have continued. But Dremfir was not a warrior priest and the SaeKet's mage for nothing.

"It is possible that nothing could have prevented the kidnappings. There may be a purpose in this, a working of the Mother." Rilsin turned away from him, saying nothing. Dremfir knew what she thought of pious platitudes, and that was not what he had meant to convey. "Wait, Rilsin. I have to tell you this, although I know you will discount it. I promised the seer of the temple. He has had a seeing."

Rilsin turned back to him. There were few seers anywhere in Saeditin, a fact for which she was grateful. She considered their prophecies to be ambiguous, manufactured, and frequently self-serving. "Why does the seer not come to me himself?"

"Because he knows what you think of his gift," said Dremfir bluntly. "Fontir has never used his gift for gain, and he has never fabricated his prophecies. True, much of what he says is foggy and dream-bound and makes little sense, but sometimes he does see true.

"Fontir has seen you beneath the earth, wrapped within the Mother's song, the song of the land."

Rilsin felt the hair rise on the back of her neck. "Is he foretelling my death, Dremfir?" Even though she did not believe in portents and signs, she did not want an ill omen from her own priests.

"I asked him the same, SaeKet. He said not. But he said that you will walk the halls beneath the earth, and that you must trust yourself if you are to save Saeditin." Dremfir shrugged slightly. "I'm sorry, Rilsin, but that's all he could say. I think he is right that you must trust yourself, at least, and also I would add that you must not blame yourself."

She knew that he meant well. She even believed him, as far as it went, which was not far.

Because she couldn't wait, not for a moment longer than necessary, they set out at night, a day before midwinter day, on Sunreturn eve. Rilsin could not help thinking that this was the anniversary of her child's birth and the anniversary of her betrothal to her child's father. She had been at war on both occasions. At her betrothal, she was at war with herself and her own feelings. When Reniat was born, she had been at war with the Runchot. *Nothing has changed,* she thought sourly. When she had won back the SaeKet's chair, she had thought there would be peace.

Dremfir reminded her of another duty, as they rode northward on the SaeKet's Road, with the gates of Petipal behind them.

"We must celebrate the dawn rites, SaeKet," he said. "The army needs this, and the land needs this."

"As you say, Sae Dremfir. But we will march through the night. We will stop before dawn for the rites and rest then. We must get north quickly. I feel it."

Dremfir put his hand to his heart and wheeled his horse away.

As the sky began to pale, the army stopped. Tents were pitched in the snow, and an altar was set up in the east. The troops were assembled. Rilsin stood in the front, just before the altar. She looked impatiently at the braziers filled with scented woods, the unlit fires of Sunreturn, waiting for the torches that carried the flame of the previous year.

Dremfir came to stand by the altar, nodded at her, and motioned. Down through the lines of the waiting Saeditin army came the lesser priests, carrying the lit torches of the old sun. They came in silence but for a low hum, the hum that encouraged the Mother Sun, waiting to rise. In ancient times the SaeKet herself would have been the priestess waiting at the altar to perform the rites. Rilsin was glad that times had changed, for behind the torches came the sacrifice, chosen to give his life's blood on the altar as the sun rose on the shortest day of the year. He was the living incarnation of the Evil One, over whom the Mother triumphed, and who took with him into death all the sins and sorrows of the people. In reality, the sacrifice was always an enemy captive or a criminal. The chosen sacrifice this year was a man condemned to die for the murder of his

family. Rilsin wondered if he believed that the gift of his
blood would in truth help the land.

He came between two death priests, who held his arms
tightly, although he was bound. The predawn air was bitterly cold, but sweat stood out on his face, and his eyes
darted in panic from one face to the next, seeking a way of
escape. He met only the hard, intent, or curious eyes of the
soldiers of Saeditin. In the temples of Petipal, the sacrifices
were often given a drug to calm them, but that had not been
done here. The prisoner's eyes rested for a moment on the
altar, and he gave a short cry, deep in his throat, and tried to
pull back. The priests were ready for him, and their grip
tightened on his arms as they dragged him forward. The
prisoner began to sob.

With an effort, Rilsin suppressed a frown of distaste. Apparently, he did not believe his blood would help the land,
or at least he did not wish it to. It did not matter. The rites
must be accomplished. Glancing at the faces around her,
Rilsin could see many of her soldiers concentrating, trying
to will their hatreds and fears out of themselves and onto
the prisoner, as tradition said they should. Rilsin wondered
if it would help if she imagined Sithli in place of the condemned criminal. For a moment she tried. All she could see
was Sithli as a girl, Sithli laughing, Sithli whispering se-
crets to her. Even when she replaced this picture with one
of Sithli tossing Reniat from the palace balcony, tossing
Rilsin's own child to what Sithli hoped would be her death,
Rilsin did not feel hatred. What she felt, suddenly and surprisingly, was pity.

She looked up from her thoughts and caught the eye of
the condemned prisoner. His hoarse "No please no please
no," said without pause even for breath, made a harsh coun-
terpoint to the humming of the priests. When he caught
Rilsin's eye, his pleading stopped, frozen in his throat. For
what seemed like an eternity, prisoner and SaeKet stared
into each other's eyes. Rilsin's pity for Sithli overflowed
into pity for this man, a condemned murderer. Whatever he
had done, he was paying the price now. She wished she

could tell him to be brave, that it would soon be over, that perhaps the Mother would forgive him now, but she did not speak. He had been someone's child, and Rilsin found herself wanting to comfort him.

The prisoner straightened up between the two priests, no longer fighting against them. He stared at Rilsin with wonder and something like a dawning and surprised hope. Unable to put hand to heart, he bowed his head to her, and then calmly walked slightly ahead of the priests to the altar. He needed assistance mounting the altar, where he was spread-eagled and bound again, but now he seemed no longer afraid but at peace.

When the rim of the sun touched the horizon, the new torches were lit, the old were extinguished, and the blood of the sacrifice stained the altar. If he cried out at all, Rilsin did not hear it over the suddenly loud chanting of the priests. She listened to the victorious shouts of the priests and the exchange of good wishes among the troops with a curious sense of distance. She seemed to see another altar in a different place, and she felt the heartbeat of a different sacrifice. She swayed slightly, blindly putting out a hand for support, only half aware that Dremfir took her hand and steadied her.

"Sola," she whispered. "Reniat."

PHARA WAS TIRED of traveling, and she had not been traveling all that long. It was very different traveling as a commoner than as a princess, and it was difficult traveling as a fugitive. It was not simply a matter of hiding, finding help, and going to ground; it was a matter of staying on the move.

After a day of hiding in alleys and dodging her father's patrols, freezing and hungry, Phara had gone to the edge of town to her only other contact, another of Kirra's people. Actually, two of Kirra's people, a husband and wife, respectable middle-aged tradespeople, both smiths and ironworkers. They had taken her in, fed her, and hidden her. They were going to send her back to Kirra, like it or not, but after some deliberation, Phara had told them her real identity and what she had discovered. She could see no other way, and she hoped she was not endangering her benefactors.

"Don't worry about us, child." The smith-wife was not awed by Phara's identity, but she and her husband were good Runchot, willing to do what they could to aid their country, if not their prince. If Prince Raphat were endangering Runchot by his dalliance with the Saeditin woman, then something must be done about it.

It was with their help and provisioning that she had made it northward over the mountains, through the infamous Arm Pass, where the Runchot had been defeated three winters before, and into Saeditin. Phara was traveling with associates of the smiths, a large and untidy family of tinkers and peddlers who regularly crossed the border. They spoke both Runchot and Saeditin fluently and had ties on both sides of the border with other traveling families.

All they knew about Phara was that she needed a safe and quick way out of Runchot and into northern Saeditin. They assumed she was fleeing marriage trouble. They had accepted a fair payment for their trouble, and they would not cheat their friends the smiths. Phara found herself accepted, almost as one of the family, and put to work at the daily chores of cooking, wood gathering, and mending.

They managed to cheerfully avoid both Runchot and Saeditin patrols, crossing the border in one of the hardest places, where patrols would not be frequent because of the difficulty of the terrain. This meant two days of hiding in the rocks, with no fires, huddling together with the horses for warmth, until they knew the Saeditin patrol was gone. Then they had to lead the horses carefully through rocks, ice, and snow, unable to ride for fear of injuring the animals. They had made it, however, and were soon heading northward. They were lucky in that the weather, after one more big snow, remained clear, if bitterly cold.

"We have made a decision, Barrit." Fredert, the patriarch of the little clan, informed her. It was evening, and the clan was gathered around a roaring campfire. "There is a town a little to the north, Mills Crossing, in Tillit Saedhold. We are going to stop there, settle in for the rest of the winter. Blancha and Krofa," he nodded toward his two teenage sons, who had ridden to some of the farms along the way, collecting news, "report there is unease to the north. A contingent of the Saeditin army came through not long ago, heading for Hoptrin. We want to stay clear of that. You are welcome to stay with us this winter or as long as you wish," said Fredert kindly. He saw how Phara paled when she heard they were stopping. So did his sons.

"You didn't say who you're running from, Barrit," said Blancha, "but whoever he is, he won't follow you this far. Even if he did, even if he could find you, he couldn't take you away from us. We will fight for you." He looked at his father for support, and Fredert nodded. So did Krofa, and so did the women.

Phara felt tears come to her eyes. She barely knew these people, yet they took her on face value and had accepted her, and they would defend her as if she were one of their own. They were kinder than her own family.

"Don't cry, Barrit sweet." Lufran, Fredert's wife, came and put a motherly arm around her. "You can stay with us as long as you want, not just through the winter. You're a good worker, good with the horses, good at chopping firewood. We can always use you. If you want, we can make sure the man you're running from has no claim on you."

She meant that Phara could marry into her clan. Touched beyond measure, Phara swallowed hard and then began to cry for real. Her tears prompted most of the group to come to comfort her, all of them giving her hugs or pats on the shoulder. One old woman, Auntie Nostin, brought her a mug of hot broth from an iron pot over the fire. Sipping this gave Phara the chance to get control of her emotions. She wondered how to tell them she couldn't stay. She didn't need to. Looking up from the broth, she found Fredert watching her.

"She can't stay with us," he said. There was a murmur of surprise, but he held up a hand before it could become indignation. "What I mean is, she won't. She won't of her own choice. She may be running, and I think she is," he looked at Phara shrewdly. "I haven't been alive as long as I have without knowing the look of a runner, but there's a bit more to it than Barrit told us, I'm thinking. She's running, but she needs to get somewhere, too. You don't have to tell us, girl." He shook his head at Phara. "I'm sure there's a good reason for us not to know. Am I right?"

Phara nodded. "Yes," she said at last, finding her voice. "I wish I could tell you, but I can't. I am sorry." She looked over Fredert's shoulder at the night sky, twinkling with brilliant stars. Had Sunreturn already come and gone? She didn't know. The traveling clans didn't seem to celebrate it the way either Runchot or Saeditin did. All she knew was that her brother would be leading his troops southward. He might well be in Clinsi territory already. Did he know that there were Saeditin troops nearby, just across the border? Obviously the Saeditin had been tipped off to something. The thought of striking off northward on her own frightened her more than it had back in Runchot, now she had some idea of just how difficult it was to travel alone. She wanted nothing more right now than to stay with Fredert's big family.

"I have to go," she said softly. "I have to go north. Over the border, I think. Into the Confederacy." She looked up now, half-hoping that one of the family's men would offer to go with her. No one did. Letting her stay with them was one thing; leaving the clan to go with her, someone with whom they had no ties of blood or marriage, was a totally different matter. She wished now that she had the authority of her own family behind her; then they could not refuse. It was a fleeting thought, and it made her ashamed of herself.

"At least stay until morning," said Lufran. "The weather should stay clear. You can get a good night's sleep, and we will give you a good breakfast, and some food for the road."

Phara accepted the offer, but long after all but the camp sentries were asleep, she was still awake. She lay in the

heavy skin tent that she shared with two of the young, un-
married girls of the family. She listened to them snore and
watched the faint flicker of firelight through a crack in the
tent flap. There was a sense of family here that she had not
found in her own home. She wondered what it was that itin-
erant peddlers had that was lacking among the rulers of
Runchot and also, if Sithli sae Melisin was any example,
among the rulers of Saeditin. Why was it that those in
power seemed to care only for themselves? Was that true of
all who had wealth and power? Eventually, she slept.

When she woke, it was well after dawn. The tent was
empty, but she could hear activity outside, the laughter and
soft conversation of the family loading up the horses or still
eating breakfast. Before she left the tent, Phara filled her
own pack. Thanks to the smiths, she had two extra wool
overshirts and one extra pair of trousers. She pulled on one
of the overshirts over the one she already wore. She put two
pairs of thick stockings over her feet and legs and then
pulled on her fur-lined boots. She wrapped her thick cloak
around her and picked up the pack and the sword she had
taken from the guard. She still did not know how to use the
sword well, despite a few lessons from Blancha and Krofa.
They had given her a long knife, smaller than the sword and
easier for her to use, and this she strapped to her leg under
the top of her boot, as they had shown her how to do. Phara
looked around her and then rolled up the fur sleeping robe
and tucked it beneath her arm. She had delayed as long as
she could.

Not much later she was on her way. The family had fed
her breakfast, as promised, and Lufran had given her a large
parcel of food. They had also given her a horse. When
Phara had protested, Fredert insisted.

"We took good money to help you, back in Runchot," he
told her gruffly.

Phara knew it hadn't been that much money. Horses
were prized possessions, especially the heavy, winter-bred
horses of Saeditin. She had felt close to tears again.

The entire family stayed with her until the road turned

and split. The right-hand branch went to Mills Crossing. The main road ran straight north. Phara kept turning in the saddle to look back. For a while, someone would wave back at her—one of the old women on horseback or one of the children—but then they were out of sight beyond a turn in the road, and Phara was alone. She continued straight north.

She met no one at all during her first two days of travel. She had no idea how to find her brother now; she had been counting on the peddler family to get her into the Confederacy and then to be able to glean intelligence when they stopped at villages or hunting camps. Lying beside her small fire, off the road in a clearing, she pondered the problem before she fell asleep, rolled into her fur sleeping robe.

On her third day she wondered how close she was to the border. She had left the main road, urging the horse carefully over frozen meadows and through the woods. She did not want to be stopped at the northern border any more than at the southern, and by dint of poring over her map, she concluded that the best thing to do was to leave the road, use the sun for a guide, and cross the border that way. Unfortunately, she was now lost. The wooded hills were not clearly marked the way the map was. To make things worse, it had started to snow. Frustrated, Phara stopped under a low branch in a grove of fir trees. She didn't know whether or not to make camp and wait for the snow to stop or to try to find the road again. She wasn't sure she *could* find the road again.

She was hungry, and the food package she had been given was almost gone. The horse was hungry, too, as there wasn't much for him to forage in the forest. The shaggy horses had long upper canine teeth, which gave them a predatory look. They were not predators at all; the teeth were used for scraping away snow to find whatever vegetation lay beneath. Unfortunately, in a pine grove there wasn't much beneath the snow except pine needles.

While Phara stood indecisively, stroking her horse's muzzle, the snow came down harder. It seemed she would have to camp, and camp now, while she could still see what she was doing. Phara tethered the horse and then began to rummage through her pack. She planned to use the sleeping robe as a roof to keep off the snow, and she was trying to determine how best to do this, when the nervous stamping of the horse caught her attention. It took a moment to see that there was a pattern in the snow, a moving one, and then she saw the yellow eyes.

It was a wolf, and there was more than one. Even as Phara realized this, one of the animals raised its head and howled. A long, wavering cry drifted out into the snow and was answered after a moment by several more howls. Phara shivered. The wolf song sounded as if the storm itself were speaking. The horse began to whicker and tug at his tether. The wolves were big animals, as high as her waist, but rangy and thin, and with a shock Phara realized that they were all around her. This was their strategy. There were more howls, coming nearer. It was a big pack, and they were closing in.

Phara tugged the sword from where she had secured it to the saddle. She debated jumping back into the saddle and trying to ride out, but discarded the idea. She had no idea where she was going, she couldn't see, and the wolves would be on her in a flash. She wanted to get the horse to safety, but if she tried to back him up against the trees, the wolves could simply come in under the trees. She stood in front of the horse and drew the sword.

One of the wolves was very close now. She hadn't seen him move, but he was suddenly there, so close to her that she could see the saliva when he opened his mouth and snarled. She drew on her background of privilege and stared him in the eye.

"Get away from me, you filthy animal!" she commanded, in the haughtiest tone she could manage. "You and your equally filthy friends are not going to have me for dinner! Me, or my horse, either!"

The wolf flicked his ears, looking confused, and stopped

his forward glide. Encouraged, Phara took a step forward and waved her sword.

"Go back in the forest where you came from," she shouted. "Find something else to eat!"

The wolf actually backed up a step and put his ears down. Phara began to think this odd strategy might work, until a frightened neigh from the horse made her look back. One of the wolves had taken advantage of her distraction to come in close. As Phara gasped in surprise, the wolf lunged at the horse.

Phara screamed and brandished the sword. The horse reared back, the whites of its eyes showing clearly. His hooves flashed down toward the attacking wolf, and Phara just barely managed to jump out of the way. It was then she saw the wolf on the other side of her horse, and the wolf that had come around behind her. Screaming, Phara swung the sword around. By sheer good luck, the flat of the sword connected with the head of the wolf nearest the horse. It yelped and leaped back. Phara was about to go after it when something heavy and huge landed on her back.

She fell hard on her face in the soft snow, the sword flying from her hand. Immediately, she tucked her head down to protect her face. Reaching back, she grasped fur; she had part of the wolf, just what part she didn't know. But the wolf also had her. Only the thick wool of her hood, which had fallen back from her head, saved her life. There was a snap as the wolf's teeth closed in the bunched fabric instead of the back of her neck. Phara tried desperately to get her dagger free, but she couldn't reach it. The wolf was heavy, and she was pinned in the snow.

When the body of the wolf sagged and went limp on her, it took a moment before she realized it. Over the hiss of the snow and the growls of the wolves and the frightened neighing of the horse there was another sound. It wasn't until she actually saw the arrow sticking out of the neck of one of the wolves and heard the *thunk* of another arrow hitting home that she knew what it was. Phara managed to squirm out from under the dead wolf and looked up.

Out of the swirling snow loomed several huge, vaguely human shapes. One of these was inspecting the carcass of the wolf that almost killed her. Another was chasing off the rest of the pack, who apparently decided that this was not, in fact, any easy meal, and they should try elsewhere. The third form leaned over Phara and extended a massive hand to help her up.

She got to her feet in the increasing darkness of the storm. Her rescuer was indeed a man, although a big one, bundled into heavy furs. Looking at him more closely, she started with surprise. His beard, which was matted with snow, was fiery red, but his hair, what she could see of it under his hood, was bright blue. He called something to his two companions, who left off what they were doing and came to his side. He then said something unintelligible to Phara in a voice that was rich and beautifully musical. Phara spoke excellent Saeditin as well as her native Runchot, but she had never learned the tongues of any of the northern barbarians.

"Are you—are you Clinsi?" she asked in Saeditin. She did not expect an answer she could understand, so she was surprised when the big man answered her in passable Saeditin.

"I am Chif, of Wilfrisin, captain to First Man Bilt. What you want with Clinsi?"

13

SOLA TOOK A LONG DRINK FROM THE WATERSKIN. THAT THE skin was slightly musty didn't matter to him, especially since it held not water but ale. He swallowed a good bit of this before handing the skin to the Clinsi beside him. Then Sola moved slightly closer to the fire, accepting a thick slab of roast deer meat as he did so. He ate it with the juices running down his chin, just as the Clinsi did. He was no longer chained or bound in any way, although he was under constant guard. The Clinsi believed in treating their sacrifice well, so he would have nothing to complain of when they sent him to the afterworld.

"There is another reason, too. We give you a good time now," Pellefik told him, "because demons will have you for slave forever. Winter demons do not give good times. So you enjoy now."

Sola appeared to take this advice. He ate well, and he appeared to drink whenever they passed him the skin. He grinned when they spoke to him in Saeditin, and he grinned insanely when they said anything in Clinsi, anything at all,

so they would think he did not understand. He wanted them
to think he was drunk.

They had taken him to a Clinsi camp in the east. It was
a big one, and it was bustling with activity. Unknown to his
captors, Sola did speak some Clinsi, and he understood it
better than he spoke it. By dint of listening carefully and
piecing together what he heard, Sola was able to learn
things that left him cold. It appeared that some Clinsi clans
had no wish to remain in the newly formed Confederacy
and had formed an alliance with the Runchot. In return for
letting Runchot troops through their territory to attack
Saeditin from the north, they expected Runchot help to
overturn the Confederacy. This was far more serious than a
few minor Clinsi raids across the border into Saeditin, and
Sola wondered if First Man Bilt knew.

What was worse was that a portion of the Runchot army
was not far away. Somehow they had made it across the
mountains in winter, and they were poised to strike south
soon. Sola knew that Rilsin had not sent enough troops
northward. Pleffin sae Grisna, her commander, was expecting to stop Clinsi raids, not a Runchot army.

Kidnapping Reniat was just insurance. They had meant
to take the child over the southern border into Runchot, to
Sithli sae Melisin, just as Rilsin had thought. When Rilsin
had sealed the southern border, Philla sae Lisim had made
arrangements to send Reniat north. If the SaeKetti were in
the hands of the Runchot army, she could still be used for
leverage.

He grinned at the Clinsi nearest him and pantomimed for
the ale skin again. When it was forthcoming, he pretended
to take another deep drink. As he did, he let his eyes roam
around the campsite.

There were probably close to two hundred large,
rounded skin tents, of the kind favored by the northern
tribes. There were whole families here, but mostly there
were warriors, Clinsi men and women who had fought
against Bilt's Wilfrisin in the unification two years past. So
many Clinsi together was unusual, especially in winter. Just

the hunting necessary to keep such a group provisioned would strain the local resources. It was Sola's best guess that the camp would soon break apart so that the individual groups could mount their distracting raids across the border on Saeditin farms. They were staying together to make a good showing to the Runchot, who would not be far off. And also, Sola thought, to celebrate Sunreturn.

In the center of the untidy camp was a large earthen mound. It had been swept clear of snow, a project that various Clinsi undertook on a daily basis. The top was flattened, and there were unlit torches at the four corners of this earthen platform. Except for the flat top, its shape echoed the mountains that loomed to the east, and deliberately so. It represented the first land, the primal mountain. It was the Clinsi altar. At the precise center of the flat top was a huge, flat stone. It would have taken considerable effort to bring this stone through the forest and into this camp, but the effort had been necessary to the spiritual well-being of the Clinsi in this camp. The stone was their sacrificial table. Just before dawn, Sola would be taken there, and, just at dawn, his beating heart would be ripped from his chest.

Sola speculated briefly on the widespread belief in the winter demons. It was common among the northern barbarians as well as the Saeditin and the Runchot, despite their various and differing gods.

Sola looked down from the altar to find his Clinsi guards watching him. One caught his eye and nodded, unsmiling, with some considerable respect. The sacrifice was appreciated for his gift, willing or not. Unless they were provided with a human soul, the winter demons could ravage the Clinsi clans. Sola nodded back, equally unsmiling, and then took the ale skin and pretended to drink. This time he let the skin almost fall from his hand, to be rescued by the quick reaction of one of his guards. Sola grinned idiotically, tried to rise, and fell back, almost into the fire. It was uncomfortably hot where he was, but he let his eyes begin to close. One of the Clinsi grabbed his arm and tried to pull him up.

"Get up!" said the Clinsi, but Sola remained dead

weight. "Help me here," said the Clinsi to his friend. "He's drunk himself stupid."

"Wouldn't you?" was the reply, but the second guard came over to help the first.

Between them they got Sola to his feet. He opened his eyes partway, looked at them, and snickered. He made them work hard to get him to the tent set aside for the sacrifice. It was a large tent, with an actual oil lamp in it as well as a fire already lit beneath the smoke hole. There was a wolf-skin rug on the ground, and the bed was a heap of slipe furs, blinding white. Nothing was too good for the sacrifice. Sola staggered to the bed, collapsed onto the pile of furs, and began to snore. His guards stood above him for a moment, breathing hard.

"He doesn't look that heavy," panted one of them.

"I hope we don't have to drag him back out again, come dawn," said the other. "Poor fool. If he'd had the sense not to drink so much, he could have had any woman in camp tonight."

"Or all of them."

"He doesn't look the type."

They both laughed. "At least he makes our job a little easier. He's not going anywhere before dawn."

Sola had hoped they would leave him in the tent, and he was dismayed when the two of them sat down together on the wolfskin rug near the fire. Perhaps if he waited just a little longer, at least one of them would leave. He must have had more ale than he thought, because instead of staying awake until they left, he fell asleep. When he woke again, it was almost dawn. The guards were gone, and in their place was Pellefik, putting more wood on the fire.

"Good morning," said Pellefik. "It is almost time."

Sola sat up abruptly. The sudden rush of adrenaline helped to banish the lingering effects of the ale. He wondered if he leapt up and charged Pellefik if he could make it out of the tent, and out of the camp. Pellefik smiled at him, seemingly reading his thoughts. It was obviously a pathetic hope. He *was* pathetic, Sola told himself. How could he have fallen asleep?

"Drugged." Once again Pellefik seemed to know his thoughts. Sola actually bit his tongue, wondering if he had spoken aloud.

"Drugs not in drink," Pellefik mimed drinking from the skin. "Drugs—plants—herbs?—I think you say? Herbs were sprinkled on meat. You eat meat, then later—" He pantomimed falling asleep. "I take no chances with Saeditin magician." He smiled but nodded warily at Sola.

"I see. Well, congratulations." Sola rubbed his hand over his face. He was growing a beard. Soon he would look like the barbarians. Except there wouldn't be a soon, he reminded himself.

"Do not look unhappy." Pellefik seemed to mean it, and Sola laughed abruptly.

"I suppose I should be grateful," he said, "for having the chance to go to the winter demons."

"It is we who are grateful." Pellefik was completely serious. Sola would be performing a service to Clinsi society.

Pellefik reached into the coals at the edge of the fire and drew something out. It turned out to be a flat stone on which he had been warming bread. He tore off a piece and handed it to Sola, who took it warily.

"Eat, my friend. We have a little time. I must tell you about what you do for us, what will happen."

Sola was pretty sure he knew what would happen. In just a little while they would rip his heart out. He was surprised that the thought did not dampen his appetite, but he was ravenous, so he took the bread, which was very good, with a sort of spicy taste.

"You will be offered to winter demons. You know this. Perhaps you do not know that you have chance to fight demons first."

Sola sat up suddenly and winced. It seemed that the effects of the drug and the ale were not completely overcome, after all. "What do you mean, fight the demons?" he asked, his mouth full of bread.

"It is four Clinsi priests. They are warriors and priests, and now, at Sunreturn, they become for one time priests of the winter demons. They will be armed. You will not be. You fight them. If you win, you go free. You have won victory over demons for all Clinsi, for one year. You become Solstice Warrior. Then you must stay with Clinsi, as good luck, for whole year. If you lose, demons take your life, your soul becomes their slave, and Clinsi will be free of demons for one year." Pellefik sat back and looked at Sola. "Understand?"

"You want me to fight four warrior priests for my life," said Sola. "Armed warriors."

"Yes. You do nothing like this in Saeditin?"

"Not exactly. The Mother defeated the demons at Sunreturn and gave birth to the Sun-Child. We sacrifice a prisoner in the dawn rites."

"Ah. Prisoner get chance to fight?"

"No."

"No?" echoed Pellefik, looking dubious. "Saeditin say they are civilized, and we are not. Perhaps you are glad that we are not so civilized, magician."

"You have a point, barbarian," said Sola, smiling. Pellefik laughed uproariously and slapped Sola on the back, making him choke.

"You do not have to kill priests to win," Pellefik said. "Just make them not able to fight, that is all. You can use magic, if you want, magician. I would do this," he advised seriously. "Our priests are good magicians, but not so good as man who make magic steam."

If only it were that easy, Sola thought.

"If you win," said Pellefik, "perhaps the Suncat will bless you. Suncat accompanies warrior as sign of peace, as sign of prosperity. Then we keep you extra happy during year you stay with us." He did not explain this remark, and Sola was too concerned with the thought of facing four armed men to ask.

When breakfast was over, two Clinsi women appeared. They carefully brushed Sola's hair, clucking over its short length. They brushed out his clothes, and they washed him with water heated in the fire, despite his protests that he could do it himself. They spoke no Saeditin, and he didn't want to use his Clinsi, limited though it was. When they had finished, and he was dressed to their satisfaction, he was escorted from the tent. Sola couldn't help but notice, during the dressing process, that they made certain that he had no weapons of any sort. They draped him in a short but gorgeous cloak of furs and purple velvet, sewn with little coins that jangled.

Outside it was clear and bitterly cold. The stars were beginning to fade as the sky paled in the east, but an aurora was flickering faintly overhead. The Clinsi camp was awake and buzzing with activity. Fires were being stoked up and food was being prepared: for a solstice feast, Sola thought, after the demons were defeated or placated.

When people saw him emerge from the tent, they bowed to him. A few actually thumped him on the back and wished him good luck, at which he smiled vaguely, pretending not to understand, and several women flung their arms around him and kissed him. And then, amazingly, there was a moment when no one was there beside him, and no one was paying him the slightest attention. All eyes had gone to a huge buck that was being spitted for roasting and to several young women who were carrying swords and bright metal shields for the warrior priests.

Sola looked around the camp and saw that the horses were penned just where he remembered. He would take a horse. He didn't need to go far. He had never been here in his life, yet he knew the area. He had read the reports of naturalists who had found coal near these mountains, and he had read reports of the strange creatures frozen in the rock when the Mother brought the time of the Great Cold. He had studied the maps. He knew where there were caves to be found and where the rivers flowed that would be frozen now, making passage easy. He knew where he could hide to wait for pursuit to pass him by.

He almost ran for it. What stopped him was the sight of

a child in the arms of a Clinsi woman. He could not leave
without Reniat. He knew Rilsin needed to be warned of the
Runchot army to the north. He knew, too, that no matter
what, she would not forgive him if he left her child behind.
She would say she was grateful, and she would thank him
for bringing his information, but her heart would grieve.
She might never look at him the same way again, and he
couldn't bear the thought of losing her love. She might
never look at him again, in any case, but if he left her child
behind, he was lost. Even as he thought this, he knew it was
too late. He had only that brief moment for action, and now
it had passed.

As Pellefik turned back toward him, Sola looked down.
On a stone beside a campfire was a piece of roasted meat
on someone's knife, left for just a moment, as the owner
was distracted and called away. Sola tripped and fell, amid
murmurs of dismay. The beautiful, jangling cloak swirled
across the stones of the campfire ring as Sola rose to his
feet, shaking his head at his own clumsiness. No one noticed the piece of roast meat beside the fire, with no knife.

Two Clinsi came to take his arms and guide him to the
central altar. The march became a procession. Clinsi lined
the way. They cheered him, women blew him kisses. Someone shoved an infant in his face. Sola placed his hand,
briefly, on the uncovered head, feeling the soft baby hair,
and looked up to find the mother bright with gratitude for
the blessing. People knelt to kiss the footprints he left behind in the snow.

"Blessed!" they shouted. "Blessed!"

"Blessed sacrifice!" shouted someone else.

The eastern sky was lighter now; dawn would come
soon. At the foot of the altar mound his two guards took the
jangling fur and velvet cloak from his shoulders. He was
afraid for a moment that they would search him again for
weapons, but they did not.

There were earthen steps that led to the top of the
mound. When Sola hesitated, one of his guards gave him a

slight push. Sola looked down. The man held a knife, and would use it, Sola was sure, to force him up the steps.

"Brave," said the Clinsi, in halting Saeditin. "Be brave. Fight well."

"I will do my best," said Sola in Clinsi. As the man's eyes widened in surprise, he turned and ran up the steps, taking them two at a time. The crowd cheered.

The four priests waited for him at the top, beneath the flaring torches. They were dressed in thick leather, and they had shields of bronze, polished to a brilliant gleam. Their swords were already drawn. Sola stopped. He had no idea what was supposed to happen. Would they rush him all at once? It seemed not. One of them stepped forward.

"Welcome, sacrifice!" he said in a deep voice calculated to carry over the crowd, which quieted.

"When the sun rises," continued the priest, "we will give your life to the winter demons, that you may serve them and we may be free. We honor you for your gift." He bowed, and his fellow priests bowed.

Sola stood straight, at the edge of the altar space, not acknowledging them. He looked around at the altar, taking in the details. The sacrificial stone was placed right in the middle, a hazard in any battle, even a battle as one-sided as the one he faced. Four torches blazed at the four corners of the earthen platform. The four priests were lined up with their backs to the east and the coming sun.

"Sola dira Mudrin." One of the priests knew Saeditin, it seemed, and knew who Sola was. "You know you may fight for your life, but you will die here this morning. I am sorry we cannot send a message back to your family that you died in such a good cause. If you want to pray to your gods, to your Mother, you have a moment to do so. Do not take long. We must have your soul as the sun rises."

Sola swallowed. He had not thought to pray for help once during this ordeal. He nodded his thanks to the priest and went down on one knee, lowering his eyes, bowing low to the ground. He hoped the priest who spoke Saeditin did not realize that this was not the customary attitude for

Saeditin prayer. The priest turned his gaze aside, giving Sola a moment of semiprivacy. As Sola drew the dagger from his boot, he thought that perhaps he should pray. *I wish I were a real magician,* he prayed. *I need this to work.* He rose from his crouch and, in an extension of the same movement, he rushed the first priest.

He took the priest by complete surprise. Sola was in and under his guard almost before he could blink. Without thinking twice about it, Sola rammed his dagger upward into the man's abdomen. As the priest fell, Sola rolled, pulling his knife back with him. He had wanted the sword but could not get it in time, but he did yank the shield free and raised it.

He was barely fast enough. A sword clanged down on his raised shield. Sola tried to roll again, but the shield weighed him down, and besides, he was right at the edge of the altar space. He would go off the side. He managed to come up in a crouch, but not before one of the three priests had given him a nasty cut on the arm. Dimly, Sola was aware of noise. The priest he had wounded was moaning, and the crowd was cheering. They were cheering for him, Sola realized. He wondered how long it had been since the sacrifice had fought back.

Heartened, he thrust forward with his dagger and managed to wound one of the priests on the leg. The man shouted and jumped back, taking the dagger with him. Sola had a moment to wish he were not such an indifferent swordsman. Interested though he had always been in how things worked, he had never given the rules of swordsmanship much attention. *This is not a fight by the rules,* said a voice in his head, which sounded surprisingly like Rilsin's.

Right, thought Sola. He reached out, still crouching under the cover of his shield. As one priest battered the shield with his sword, Sola pulled hard at the trousers of the man and then heaved. With a cry, the priest lost his balance and went over the edge of the altar. Sola couldn't afford the time to look down. There were still two priests left.

Both now looked at him warily. Sola had just enough

time to get to his feet. As he did, he reached up and pulled hard at one of the torch supports. The torch came away in his hand, and Sola swung it at the two remaining priests. The flames caught the beard of one of his opponents. The man screamed and dropped his sword and shield to put out the fire. Sola pushed him off the altar, too, and grabbed his sword.

The remaining priest gave a shout and rushed toward Sola. Just then the sun rose on the shortest day of the year. The priest had his back to it. As its rim flared above the horizon, Sola raised his shield. The shield was bronze, burnished to a high and brilliant polish for this ceremony. The rising sun reflected blindingly into the eyes of the one priest left, and he screamed and dropped both sword and shield. When he was able to see again, he found Sola standing above him. The crowd, which had been cheering madly, had gone silent.

"We have failed," said the priest in a husky voice that carried over the silent camp. "This warrior has won his freedom. But the demons must have a soul." He looked up at Sola. "Kill me, warrior," he whispered in Saeditin. "Make it quick." He grabbed his woolen overshirt with both hands and tore it, ripping it down the middle.

Sola stared at him. What kind of strength was necessary to tear the fabric like that? And had he really managed to defeat four men? Fleetingly, he thought that they must be worse fighters even than he, unless, somehow, he had been protected.

"Kill him!" shouted a voice from the crowd. Sola looked down and saw one of the priests he had pushed over. "Send his soul to serve the demons!"

"Kill him!" echoed the crowd.

Sola looked down at the priest at his feet. The man nodded. Sola ran him through the heart.

He had no time for regrets or to wonder if there were any other way off the altar for him. One of the surviving priests was limping back up to the altar now.

"Suncat!" someone cried, and the priest looked up into

the sky. Then he dropped to his knees and held up his arms, turning his head aside. Sola looked up in the direction the crowd was gazing.

There was something in the sky beside the sun. It was a rainbow that glittered, a sort of oval rainbow that sparkled the way rainbows usually did not. Sola frowned. He remembered Pellefik saying something about a Suncat. Was it a trick of the light, here in the north? Obviously, to them, it was far more. All of them, all the Clinsi, priests and hunters and warriors, men and women, were falling to their knees, holding out their arms.

"Suncat!" One of the priests was calling out. "Golden child of the winter sun!"

All of the Clinsi had their attention on the phenomenon in the sky. Sola actually hesitated, his curiosity was so strong, but then he recognized his opportunity. Perhaps he really didn't need to know more about the Suncat after all.

Sola bent down and stripped the sword from the priest he had killed. This one was clean. He sheathed it and strapped it around his waist. He found one of the priests' cloaks at the far edge of the altar and took it. Below him, the crowd was still kneeling, looking at the Suncat.

Sola ran down the steps from the altar. No one stopped him. He ran through the crowd. When a woman with a child glanced up at him, he grabbed her shoulder.

"Where is child?" he shouted at her. She gaped at him, clutching her own infant closer.

"Saeditin baby!" He was rewarded by her sudden look of understanding and relief. She pointed toward a tent.

He crashed through the tent flaps to find Reniat in the arms of a hefty Clinsi woman. She cowered back from him as he snatched the child from her. He grabbed up two heavy fur robes and wrapped one around Reniat as he ran back out again. Just before he left the tent, he saw a Clinsi pack near the door. With no idea what it contained, he grabbed it, too. Clutching child, pack, and robes awkwardly, he ran toward the horse pen. Again, no one stopped him.

Several horses were saddled. He did not question his

luck but mounted one, hauling Reniat up into the saddle in front of him. As he tucked her in, wrapping the robe around her and around him, he really looked at her for the first time. She had not cried or screamed when he grabbed her up, and now he saw that she was smiling.

"Dada Sola," she said.

Sola drew a deep breath. "Hold on tight," he said.

They thundered out of the pen and through the Clinsi camp. He saw faces upturned to them, and he was aware of the Suncat, still spinning in the sky. Then they were out of the camp and riding into the forest.

14

Sola headed into the steeper foothills in the east. He could see the map in his mind's eye: a whole area near the Clinsi Mountains that a Saeditin explorer and naturalist had marked "the caves and deep caverns." Caves sounded good to Sola; of the caverns, especially deep ones, he was less certain.

It was difficult going through the deep snow. The horse plodded ahead, much slower than Sola liked, but he knew he could not hurry without risking injury to the animal. His own injury, the cut he had taken to his left arm, burned like fire and ached. He bound it as best he could while still in the saddle, but he did not dare to stop. He expected pursuit, Clinsi warriors on the backs of their swift deer. He had no desire to be kept a prisoner, even an honored one, in some Clinsi camp for a year.

Reniat had fallen asleep on the saddle in front of him, wrapped in her furs. Her fine golden hair fluffed out around her tiny, pale, heart-shaped face. The pale skin marked her as Rilsin's, and the golden hair was a reminder of her father

Sifuat, but Sola no longer saw her in this way. Now he saw only Reniat, baby Reni, the little girl who had called him "Dada Sola."

He had only the sun and the hills for directional guides. Toward midday the sun clouded over, and the forest helped to obscure the lay of the land. The air was dead still below the treetops, but there was a heavy, brooding feeling, and the temperature seemed to rise slightly. It would snow before long. If he wanted to go to ground somewhere, he needed to do it soon. If he could find the right place, the snow might cover his tracks from any pursuers.

The ground was rough and broken, and in places some of the earth's limestone bones had broken through the soil. They were making their way across the side of a limestone hill as the first fat snowflakes began to fall. At first he thought it was just a dark, discolored crack in the stony hillside. Numbed by travel, worry, and cold, he almost rode by it.

He had to dismount and force his way past some bushes that obscured the cave mouth. Once he had done that, he found that what he could see of the cave was big enough even for the horse. He led it inside and tethered it to a bush just inside the entrance. Then he took Reniat from the saddle. She had been awake for a while, peering out of her furs at the monotonous forest, sometimes giggling and trying to point at trees or at the big crows that occasionally flew overhead. Now she was asleep again, and he put her down gently on the cave floor, still wrapped in her furs.

He wanted to check out the cave to be sure it was safe. To do so, he needed light, for this cave stretched back farther than he could easily see. Rummaging in the stolen Clinsi pack produced some useful items. There was a package of dried deer meat and a package of dried berries, both wrapped in oiled, stitched hides. There was a bundle of dried, soft grass, which Sola puzzled over. It looked too fine and soft for animal fodder, and there wasn't all that much of it. There was also a child's parka, folded, and two pairs of child's trousers. He had, it seemed, grabbed the traveling pack for a child, maybe for Reniat herself. There was a small metal bowl, a small spoon made out of horn. There was also, incredibly, a partially burned torch and a fire-stone.

By now the fat snowflakes had given way to smaller flakes, which were hissing down beyond the cave mouth. This looked to be a big storm, or at least big enough to hide their tracks. Sola went back out into the snow to drag in some firewood. He debated whether or not to make a fire and decided to wait. He also dug beneath the snow in an open space, looking for dried grasses for the horse. He pulled some up and brought it in for the animal, who began to placidly munch.

He had just decided it was time to light the torch and ex-amine the rest of the cave when Reniat awoke. The little girl began to cry, but noiselessly. Apparently, her brief time with the Clinsi had taught her the value of silence. Sola went to her immediately.

"What is it, Reni, what's wrong?" He expected to hear that she was afraid, or missed her mother, or that she was cold or hungry.

"Wet," said Reniat, with little quiet sobbing gulps. "Wet!"

Sola discovered what the soft, dry grass in the pack was for.

PHARA FOLLOWED HER rescuers. They knew the country, after all, as she did not.

"Do we have to go in there?" she had asked, when Chif led them to a cave.

"No, Princess," Chif had replied politely. "You may stay outside. The rest of us, we go in."

She had not stayed outside, of course. She hadn't wanted to leave her horse, either, but Chif had insisted that there was no way to take animals through the cave system, and she had to trust him on that. He had sent the horses off with one of his men, "to find First Man," he told her.

At first Phara was astonished that they believed her

story. She had told them the truth about who she was and why she was looking to find her brother. She had not told them that her brother had actually brought a Runchot army into the Confederation. From her urgency to reach him, however, she suspected that Chif guessed something of the truth. And as for believing her, well, perhaps he did not, but he was acting as if he did. She found that she believed everything he said, implicitly. She surprised herself in this. She had never expected to believe anyone's word again, except Kirra's.

"Caves can bring us out deep in Clinsi land, Princess," he told her. "They bring us near your brother and his— mission."

The thought of being under the earth bothered Phara so much that she couldn't sleep the night before they planned to go into the caves. She lay awake under the brilliant stars, wrapped in her traveling furs. They had made camp but pitched no shelters. Phara found herself uncharacteristically nervous at the thought of the men nearby. Even though her father and her brother had forged an alliance with some of the northerners, she retained the common Runchot and Saeditin view: These were barbarians. They did not act like it, however. They all spoke Saeditin, of a sort, although Chif spoke it the best. All were unfailingly courteous to her, sharing food and fire, so much so that she was ashamed to doubt them. After a bad night thinking about the caves, she helped them break camp in the morning.

"Do not worry," Chif said to her reassuringly, when he found her fidgeting nervously beside her horse. "If you stay with me, you be safe. There is some danger, yes, but I know way through caves well. Caves go under Clinsi lands here, for very long way. Nobody knows how deep they go, how far. So you stay with me and not get lost, yes?"

"Yes," Phara agreed in a small voice, trying not to shiver.

The entrance to the cave system must have been just over the border from Saeditin, as Phara figured it. She wondered how many people knew of its existence. It was an unprepossessing split in a rocky hillside, something she would have ignored under any other circumstance.

Just as she was reluctantly saying farewell to her horse, the men began to talk excitedly in their native Wilfrisin. Turning, Phara saw a strange sight in the sky: a spinning rainbow beside the sun.

"A Suncat, Phara Princess," Chif told her. "A sacred sign. This is Midwinter Day, Sunreturn, and the Suncat is sign of big change. In Northern tales the man who is blessed by Suncat is the change-bringer. The Suncat is companion to the Solstice Warrior. The Suncat is the bringer of peace and prosperity. Suncat can be actual cat, or sometimes small child. Solstice Warrior is—" Chif broke off his explanation when he saw that Phara was not listening.

Sunreturn. It was the solstice, and Phara hadn't known. The men with her did not seem inclined to celebrate in any way. At home in Runchot there would be celebrations and gifts. In her father's house there had always been a feast. Phara felt tears coming. She couldn't understand why. She had no right to miss what she had forsworn. She fought down the tears and looked up to find Chif watching her.

"You will manage, Phara Princess," he said. "You will manage well. You do brave thing."

"Going into the caves isn't so brave," said Phara, still struggling for control. Actually, she thought that going into the caves was very brave indeed, but she would not admit it.

"It is, perhaps," said Chif, "but that's not what I meant. Giving up family is hard. I know. To choose to give it up, that is brave."

Without any further discussion, the men filed into the split in the rock. Phara was left alone outside with her pack. She stared around her for a moment, feeling the cold of the snowy hillside, the whip of the wind, wondering if she would ever feel these things again. Then she drew a breath and went after the men.

It wasn't bad inside, not at first. They didn't really need the torches they had lit, as daylight spilled in from the cave entrance. The wind was cut off, but there was a drift of leaves on the cave floor, and some scraggly grasses and plants, winter-killed, right inside the cave mouth. There was a little shelf of rock along one side of the cave. It was obvious that people had been here before. There was a charred fire pit near the entrance, and someone had painted things on the wall of the cave: suns and moons and little stick figures of people, like a child's drawing.

"Very old," Chif said, when he saw her looking. "Made by first ancestors. There is more, and better, when we go deeper."

At the back of this cave a damp breeze blew, but not from outside. It came from somewhere beneath the earth. There was a sort of passageway leading down, and Chif and his men went into this without hesitation. Their torches had wind shields on the front of them, a good thing, as the breeze blew stronger. A sudden shaft of gray light showed why: above them was an opening, a chimney, to the outside world. Air blew down through this, and also snowflakes. Outside, a storm had begun. Shortly after this, the passage narrowed, and the ceiling closed in. The party had to get down on hands and knees and crawl through the passage downward into darkness. Chif went first, holding a torch, and Phara followed close behind him. Behind her came the other men, only the last in line holding another lit torch. Conversation ended, and they crawled in silence.

RILSIN MET UP with Pleffin near Hoptrin, the capital of the northern saedhold of Sudit, the territory of her former husband. Pleffin had made Hoptrin his base of operations, and much of his small force was quartered in the city.

"No raids," Pleffin told her as they sat at dinner in what had been her mother-in-law's manor house. "No raids at all, and no signs of any barbar—ah, Northerners, Confederates wanting to come across the border. It's been boring, SaeKet. There is a message from First Man Bilt for you, though. He seemed to know you would come north yourself."

"Let me see it."

Bilt had written the message himself, in Saeditin. As a result, the language was less than perfect, but its tone was urgent.

"Sae Becha, my friend, I have big problem. Some Clinsi fight against Confederacy. This you know. But these Clinsi get offer of help from south, from Runchot. I fear that Runchot troops will come, in Clinsi lands. I have not found them, but I look for them. They come through eastern lands, and over mountains. My spies tell me Runchot say they will help Clinsi to conquer north, after they conquer Saeditin. I warn you now, Sae Becha, my friend, so that we make sure these things never happen. If I find Runchot troops, I send word."

When she looked up, Pleffin said, "It sounds preposterous that any troops could cross the mountains in winter. But we can't take the chance. We need to find these troops, if they exist, and stop them before they reach Saeditin."

"No, Sae Pleffin, we don't have to do any such thing. We know they will come across the border. I think I know where. When they come, we will be waiting for them. All we have to do is know where to meet them and to make sure they do not know that we are waiting. And we need to know when."

"How do we find out these things, SaeKet? We are relying on what the barb—ah, the Confederates can tell us."

"I already know where, Sae Pleffin. The Demon Bridge."

Pleffin stared at her.

The Demon Bridge had a legend behind its name. It was a natural bridge of slender stone, arching across a deep ravine through which a river tumbled, thousands of feet below. It had been magically built, so the legend claimed, by the winter demons fleeing the Mother's wrath. She had allowed a few to escape from Saeditin into the wilderness beyond, where they had remained ever since. It was a route that bypassed both the dangerous marshes and the better-

traveled forest roads, a dangerous but a quick and more secret way to Saeditin's border.

"It makes sense, but do you think a Runchot army can
cross there?" Pleffin was dubious, and with good reason.
Even during warm weather, the bridge could be dangerous.
It was wide enough for perhaps fifteen people to walk
abreast on it, but the winds could be strong, and many people were afraid of the great fall into the chasm below. In
winter, it could be icy.

"It is risky, yes, but we already know their commander
does not mind risk. Think, Sae Pleffin. How did the Runchot enter the North?"

"Across the steppes and mountains," said Pleffin slowly.
"In winter."

"A stone bridge, no matter how high and windy, would
not daunt such a commander."

"Especially since he will not expect anyone to be fore-
warned and waiting."

"Exactly," said Rilsin, reaching for the wine. It came
from Runchot, and there wasn't much of it left now, she
thought regretfully. Saeditin wines were good but could not
match the wines of southern Runchot's milder climate.

Beneath the table, Chilsa stirred, and Rilsin reached
down absently to scratch behind the huge cat's ears. Since
Reniat had been taken, Chilsa had become extremely atten-
tive to Rilsin. Now Chilsa seemed edgy. Rilsin was debating sending him out of the room or taking him out herself,
when a servant burst in.

"SaeKet! Commander! Barbarian warriors! Just to the
north of the city! They have burned farms!"

Rilsin was on her feet at once. These were the Clinsi
raids they had been waiting for, but closer to a Saeditin city
than they had expected.

"How far from Hoptrin?" asked Rilsin.

Simultaneously, Pleffin asked, "How close are they?"
He exchanged a glance with his SaeKet. "I cannot believe
the barbarians had the nerve to come this far into Saeditin."

"That is because they are not Confederates or any sort of

barbarian, SaeKet." A soldier had come on the heels of the
servant and now stood blinking in the light and the warmth,
snow still melting from his boots.

"What are they, then?" Rilsin asked, although she knew
the answer before he spoke it.

"Runchot, SaeKet," said the soldier. "At least some of
them. We were on patrol and found one of the farmhouses
still burning, so we fanned out and found them. Most of
them were Clinsi, but some were Runchot. There was no
mistaking it."

"Did you kill them all?" Pleffin asked urgently.

"Some, but a few escaped. Unfortunately, they know we
have recognized them as Runchot."

"What of our farmers?"

"None left alive, SaeKet. Two families dead, even the
children."

"Damn it all to a Runchot hell!" said Rilsin. "It is no
longer boring here, unfortunately, Sae Pleffin." She swung
away from the table. "We had best find what's left of these
raiding Runchot before they get back to their commander
with the news that we know of them."

"I will ride out immediately, SaeKet!" Pleffin was on his
feet and moving.

"We will ride out," said Rilsin. When Pleffin looked as
though he might object, Chilsa gave a low growl. Rilsin felt
she needed to go, and Chilsa, it would seem, felt the same.

By the time Rilsin had her cloak and sword and a traveling pack, a small troop was ready. They mounted their
horses in the bitter cold. Although they looked to her to lead
them, Rilsin left this task for Pleffin, but she rode with him
at the head of the little column. Chilsa loped beside her
horse. Looking down the line of flickering torches, Rilsin
saw that several troops had drawn woolen mufflers across
their faces and pulled down the hoods of their army cloaks
almost to their eyes against the bitter wind.

They were guided by the messenger from the troop that
had surprised the raiders. They rode through the night and
stopped after dawn to briefly rest the horses and to eat.

Toward midday they skirted the burned farms. Rilsin felt the start of a slow rage. These were her people, who had trusted in the force of the SaeKet to protect them. They should have been safe. It was surprising, too, that the raiders had ventured this far into Saeditin to do their damage. It meant two things: They were scouting Saeditin defenses, and they were certain they would meet no resistance. By evening, a messenger from Pleffin's troops met them, reporting that her small contingent had pursued the fleeing raiders and had cut off their line of retreat just across the border.

"They are between the marshes and the hills, SaeKet, Commander," she said. "The marshes are partly frozen, but they are unsafe. I do not think they will take that way. There are four still alive, three Runchot, we think, and one Clinsi. My captain thinks they will try to hide in the forest until morning."

"I want the Runchot alive," said Rilsin. "I have questions for them. I don't care about the Clinsi."

They met up with their border squad just as the early darkness was falling. The Saeditin troops had lit a fire, and most of the small group was clustered near it, although lookouts and sentries patrolled well into the trees. If the raiders were in the dark of the nearby woods, they dared to light no fire that might guide their enemies to them.

Rilsin hated to stop the pursuit, even for the rest they all needed. She hoped the patrol captain, Clerin sae Tillit, was correct when he said the raiders were pinned down until first light. Clerin was Essit's younger brother, eager to distinguish himself in the service of the SaeKet and somewhat awed at finding himself in her presence. Pleffin, in whose experience she had more trust, was in agreement with his young officer.

They set up lean-to shelters of blankets to keep off the worst of the wind. These were much easier to take down than tents. It would be only a matter of moments to strike camp in the morning. As Rilsin lay in her sleeping furs that night, with Chilsa sprawled across the entrance to her shelter, she watched the sentries in front of the fire and the soldiers who occasionally left their own shelters to warm themselves.

One rather small soldier went to the fire to warm his hands. There was something familiar about him, but Rilsin could not see his features, only his shape against the brilliance of the fire. Another soldier, female from the shape of her against the flames, came and pulled the small one away. There was something familiar about this soldier, too. Rilsin struggled for a moment to place just what it was, but she was too tired to keep her thoughts together, and she drifted into sleep.

She was awakened just before dawn by Chilsa growling softly. Rilsin sat up abruptly, but it was only Clerin sae Tillit, come to wake her himself, so they could resume the hunt.

Breakfast was a little heated bread and some warm cider. The sky was still dark, although the stars were fading, and the cold was intense. As Clerin was about to order the fire extinguished, Rilsin held up a hand to forestall him.

"Leave the fire, Sae Clerin. Let our quarry think that we tarry here for the warmth. We can leave a few behind to make noise, and also to cut off the raiders, if they think to escape this way." She saw that Pleffin was nodding at her in agreement and approval.

"How far off are they, Sae Clerin?"

"Not far, SaeKet. The scouts did not hear them move during the night."

Several small parties went quietly forward on foot, fanning out around the place where they thought the raiders were hidden. Behind these troops were soldiers on horseback, ready to cut off any raiders that might break through.

"This is a lot of work for a few renegades," she heard one man mutter.

"These few renegades could prove the undoing of all of Saeditin," she told him, "if they return to the Runchot army with the news that we are ready for them."

Rilsin insisted on going with one of the foot parties to

try to flush out the enemy. Pleffin made a point of assigning himself to her group, and Rilsin suspected that he meant to take it on himself, if necessary, to insure her safety.

They made their way through the brushy ground cover before the sun rose, and they soon gave up any attempt at silence. The crunchy snow and the ice coating the low branches made it impossible to move in secret. Whenever one of them brushed against a branch, tinkling shards of ice hit the packed snow crust like shattering glass.

There were twelve in Rilsin's small party: Rilsin herself, Pleffin, and ten soldiers, all carrying fire-tubes. The new invention had won Rilsin back her throne, but she did not know how useful it would be here. It took time to prepare and fire the new weapon, and more time to aim it and wait for it to fire. Not only that, but it was cold, and all of the scouting troops were wearing thick gloves. To use the fire-tubes they would have to remove their gloves.

At the back of the little group were the small soldier and his larger female companion. Although both kept their faces muffled against the cold, their appearance tickled at the edges of Rilsin's thought. She seized an opportunity, as they were pushing their way through an ice-crusted briar thicket, to drop back near the mismatched pair. As the small soldier grunted slightly and tried to edge sideways through the thorns without ripping his cloak, Rilsin realized that his gloves were neither thick nor regulation. She reached out with her own heavily gloved hand and pulled the briar to the side.

"Let me help you, Porit," she said, "since you joined this troop without suitable equipment. Next time you do something clandestine, make sure you are completely prepared. How did you manage it, anyway?"

Porit stared up at her, as frozen as the landscape. "Meh—meh—someone helped me," he stuttered.

"Meffa," said Rilsin quietly, looking back at the muffled female soldier right behind her. She saw a flush spread up across the soldier's face, what she could see of it.

"Ria Meffa," said Rilsin, carefully looking away from

the flushed soldier, "of course has the influence to arrange something like this. I wonder where she is now. Back in Hoptrin, I suppose, leaving you by yourself out here in the wilderness."

"I would never do that, SaeKet! You know I would not let the boy come out here alone and unprotected!"

"I do not need protection!" said Porit hotly. "I can protect myself! And I came to protect you, SaeKet!"

"I'm grateful," said Rilsin dryly. "I still want to know how you managed it." She looked pointedly at Meffa, who had pulled the muffler down from her face.

"It wasn't hard, SaeKet. Troop orders are always coming through your quarters. I simply copied some of them, and I got us assigned to go with you."

"You forged them. With my signature?" As Meffa looked down in shame, Rilsin began to laugh. She was quite certain that she was the first to discover this particular drawback to educating the commoners. "You have many talents, Meffa." Then she grew serious again.

"You have no training in war, either of you," she said. "This was a dangerous thing to do."

"I may have no training in war, SaeKet, but I know how to fight," said Porit stubbornly, "and you know I do. I had to be here with you. I just had to!"

Rilsin frowned. She felt the peculiar resonance that she had felt before, when Porit had insisted on coming north to Hoptrin with her.

"Well," she said, "here you are. I suppose we must make the best of it." She grinned at him, seeing the look of concern that had spread across his face vanish. Whatever she might have said next was cut off by a whistling sound.

Rilsin grabbed Porit and pulled him down partly into the brambles. Meffa cried out and dropped beside them. All around them were whistles and thunks. Arrows seemed to suddenly sprout from the tree trunks. One jutted from the snow in front of Rilsin's face.

"Ambush!" shouted Pleffin from the head of the little troop.

"Only four of them," muttered Rilsin, "and they can do this to us."

She glanced around and saw the other members of her troop crouched amid the brambles. One particular non-human member blended in so well that he was hard to see. Chilsa regarded her with an inscrutable gaze. Rilsin gave him a hand sign, and the big cat vanished into the underbrush.

The Saeditin troops were craning to see their enemy. A few were also struggling to bring out and load their firetubes, in the hope of getting a good aim at their attackers. Rilsin did not reach for hers. She had no faith that there would be time enough for a clear shot.

She saw a flash of movement just uphill of the brambles where her troops crouched. Others saw it, too. Pleffin looked at her, and she nodded. Silently, Pleffin waved at his troops to begin inching forward.

It was hard going through the brambles, staying down on the ground. Despite the snow and the cold, Rilsin felt sweat break out on her face. There was the whine of more arrows. Then, suddenly, there was a scream. It was a high scream, full of agony and surprise, and it was cut off almost immediately. As soon as she heard it, Rilsin was on her feet.

Something was thrashing in the brush uphill. Someone was down on the ground, and two other people were attempting to get out of the way. As she ran closer, she saw Chilsa standing over the fallen man, his lip curled back, exposing his impressive fangs.

Behind her, Rilsin heard the rest of her troop. Somehow she had surged ahead of all of them, even Pleffin. Even as she saw one of the Runchot draw his sword to attack her cat, Chilsa picked up the fallen enemy soldier in his jaws, backed up, and vanished into the undergrowth. There were shouts of surprise and also relief from the remaining enemy, and then other sounds: the cries of Saeditin soldiers coming from uphill as well as from below them. The sounds of the encounter had drawn the rest of the Saeditin hunting parties, who were closing in. There was a cheer from Rilsin's troop, who ran forward with renewed energy.

Now that they were close enough, Rilsin could see the three enemies. One was the Clinsi they had been told of. His identity was obvious from his furs and hide clothing. The other two were obviously Runchot, dressed in the thick russet wool of the Runchot winter army uniform.

"Take them alive!" Rilsin cried, her voice carrying over the shouts and calls. She drew her sword, trying to separate one of the Runchot from his companions. Even as she heard her order repeated, an arrow whined and buried itself in the throat of her chosen Runchot.

"Alive, damn it!" she shouted. "I said, alive!"

At the sound of her voice, Chilsa appeared, dragging his victim by the throat. The big cat proudly deposited his trophy at her feet. Chilsa's prize was one of the Runchot, and he was most thoroughly dead. Rilsin sighed in disappointment.

"Good cat," she said, pausing to give Chilsa a rueful scratch behind one round ear.

The remaining two enemy, the Clinsi and the one Runchot still alive, were running, but Saeditin parties were approaching them from all sides. The brush was thick, however, and Rilsin did not intend to let them out of her sight. Panting slightly, she followed them. Chilsa kept pace beside her, and she glanced back and saw Porit and Meffa keeping close to her, although Meffa's face ran with sweat and she looked glassy-eyed. Close on their heels was Pleffin sae Grisna.

Because she glanced back, she did not see the enemy disappear. No one was near enough to see what happened to them. Rilsin stopped and stared around: They were definitely not there.

"Chilsa," she said, "find them."

The big cat began to hunt through the brush and then stopped, whining. Rilsin came up beside him, but she saw only the snow-crusted rock of the hillside.

"Sorcery and magic!" said Pleffin, coming up beside her.

"They were here," said Rilsin, "and Chilsa thinks they are still here. Somehow."

As she spoke, Porit and Meffa caught up with them. Meffa was breathing heavily, leaning on the boy's shoulder for support. Rilsin saw that Meffa's cloak was thrown back, and her left sleeve was dark and sticky with blood.

"Oh Meffa!" Rilsin took a step toward her friend. One moment she was on the hillside, under the cold midwinter sun, with her commander and her friends beside her. The next moment, the earth gave way beneath her feet and she was falling into darkness.

At first she closed her eyes, as dirt and stones fell with her. So did Chilsa; she could feel him beside her, his legs tangled with hers. She bounced against the earthen walls, and then, with a bone-jarring thud, her fall was broken. She lay stunned. Something landed on top of her: Chilsa. She moaned and felt the big cat move. He grabbed the back of her cloak gently but firmly in his teeth and dragged her a little distance. It was just in time. There was the sound of more bodies hitting the earth and more moans.

Rilsin sat up, spat dirt from her mouth, and opened her eyes. There was a very faint light from far above. By its aid she could see she was lying on dirt, not far from a pile of fallen and drifted leaves on soft sand, which had broken her fall. She was incredibly sore, but by carefully moving her arms and legs and swiveling her neck, she determined that nothing was broken: a minor miracle. Chilsa was washing himself with a disgusted air, with no injury except an offense to his sense of cleanliness. She could see that others sprawled on the leaves that had broken her fall. Pleffin, Porit, and Meffa lay in a tangled heap. Rilsin made her way to them.

Pleffin sat up first, grunting and rubbing his hand across his face.

"Are you hurt, SaeKet?" he asked.

"No," she said. "Are you?"

None of them were hurt except Meffa, who had taken an arrow below her left shoulder. The fall seemed to have aggravated her wound. Pleffin himself bound this as best he could in the poor light, with material torn from the edge of his cloak. He was grim and silent as he worked, embarrassed at finding that the chief servant of the SaeKet had come on this mission without his knowledge.

While he worked, Rilsin stared upward at the light. They had fallen a long distance, perhaps the height of eight or nine tall men, and she was amazed that they were not hurt by the fall. She listened hard but could hear nothing from above. There was no way to climb up. The last few feet of the shaft were solid rock, and above that, the earth crumbled.

"Down here!" Rilsin shouted. "We are down here!"

There was no response from above, but her voice boomed and echoed hollowly. Rilsin drew in her breath and looked around her. The others stared back, and she could see the whites of their eyes reflecting the small amount of light there was. Chilsa pressed up against her. Pleffin recovered first and strode to directly beneath the open chimney through which they had fallen. He shouted, his voice at parade-ground bellow.

"Hello above! We are down here! The SaeKet is down here!"

"Here!" cried hollow voices from deep below the earth. "SaeKet . . . here . . . here . . ."

Meffa began to sob, and Chilsa whined.

"It's a cave system," said Rilsin in what she hoped was a calm and rational voice. "It's a system of caverns that runs deep beneath the earth. I have read of this. What you hear is merely echoes, our voices rebounding from the stone."

They huddled beneath the shaft of sunlight, occasionally calling out, trying to ignore the echoes, through the rest of the short winter day. There was no answer from above, and eventually the light began to fade.

"Why don't they come?" said Porit. He wanted to sound brave, but his voice wavered slightly.

"They did not hear us," said Pleffin grimly. "I don't know why, except for magic our enemies laid upon us. Our enemies who are also down here somewhere."

"We had best see what we have with us," said Rilsin, "in the way of supplies." She was in no mood to argue Pleffin's explanation of magic, and she was shocked to realize that she had forgotten the surviving Clinsi and Runchot, who were almost certainly, as Pleffin said, down here with them.

As the last of the light faded, they determined that they had among them six waterskins, ten packages of bread and dried meat in their packs, several overshirts and thick trousers, extra gloves, and, miraculously, three partially used torches, as well as firestones. Rilsin insisted that they all eat and drink a little before setting out, even Chilsa.

"At night?" whispered Porit. "We will go at night?"

"It makes no difference down here," said Rilsin.

15

"SO SHE HAS COME HERSELF." Sithli looked so satisfied that Kepit had a difficult time concealing her disdain. "I knew she would not forgo the opportunity. It is not often that a poor Runchot merchant has an invitation to an audience with the SaeKet of Saeditin."

Kepit couldn't resist any longer. She could feel her temper snap so suddenly that she was surprised it was not audible.

"Kirra is here not because you invited her, SaeKet. You invited her many times previously, and she declined to accept. Nor is she a 'poor Runchot merchant.' We need her. She is here because she is embarrassed. She did not realize that her gift, the slave girl Barrit, was in reality—" Kepit stopped abruptly. Sithli's face was flushing, always a dangerous sign. It was never wise to condescend to Sithli. "Was who she was," she finished. "The important thing, SaeKet, is that there is gain to be had from this situation. It would be best if, ah, perhaps you would allow me, SaeKet, to handle the negotiations."

Sithli now looked intrigued, if greedy. At least that was an improvement over self-satisfaction or petulance, Kepit thought. Sithli's petulance had never been an endearing trait, and now it could cost them their chance to retake Saeditin. Kepit could not afford to let that happen.

"Well then, bring her in," said Sithli, waving her hand. "I want to meet this mysterious Kirra." She sat down in the large, overstuffed chair near the fire and carefully smoothed her green silk trousers and overshirt. "Wait, Kepit! Is my powder smooth?" Since Barrit had left under such odd circumstances, Sithli had not found a suitable replacement as good with clothes and makeup.

"It is perfect, SaeKet." Kepit hid her impatience. Personally, she saw scars as badges of honor, but she knew the scar on Sithli's cheek reminded her of the time Rilsin had saved her life. One of the times Rilsin had saved her life, Kepit corrected herself, and therefore something Sithli would rather not remember. Before Sithli could say anything else to delay the interview, Kepit left the room.

In the chamber outside were several people, all members of Kirra's party. Three women sat in chairs near the fire, while four men, obviously Kirra's guards, stood nearby. One of the women was elegantly dressed in finely brushed wool trousers of a deep maroon hue with the newly fashionable slit that allowed the deep blue wool of her undertrousers to show through. Her hair was long, blonde, and elegantly dressed into curls. The other two women were nicely dressed but less fashionably so. If they wore undertrousers, there was no guessing their color. When Kepit entered the room, the conversation among the three women ceased.

Kepit stood and regarded them. Her glance lingered on the finely dressed woman and then moved on, eventually coming to rest on one of the less fashionable, a woman whose light brown hair was pulled back in a plain braid. Her clothing was as plain as her hairstyle but of good quality, and there was an indefinable air of control about her that was apparent to Kepit, who had studied power all her life.

"Lady Kirra," Kepit inclined her head slightly. "Permit me to welcome you. I am Kepit sae Lisim, and I ask you on behalf of Sithli SaeKet Melisin to honor her with your presence."

"It is I who am honored." Kirra rose from her chair with a slight smile. She did not seem surprised that Kepit had picked her out, although her companions looked impressed. As she moved toward Kepit and the doorway to Sithli's room, the other women took places behind her, and the men formed a silent but solid presence around them.

"There is no need to bring your guard," said Kepit. "You are quite safe in the presence of Sithli SaeKet." *And certainly in the house of Prince Raphat,* she thought.

At her words, the men closed in more tightly around the women, but backed away when Kirra merely flicked her hand. They looked uncomfortable and edgy, but they obeyed promptly.

There was something vaguely familiar about Kirra, but Kepit could not place it. Perhaps it was the sheer ordinariness of this immensely wealthy woman that made her seem familiar. Preoccupied with trying to solve this puzzle, Kepit almost missed Kirra's reaction when she saw Sithli.

Kirra hesitated for a moment in the doorway, her gaze fixed on Sithli, who was seated in her green splendor in the big chair. Her reaction could have been taken for awe, for nervousness, or even for surprise at Sithli's beauty, but it was none of those things. It was hatred. Hatred and something else Kepit could not identify. It was there, and then in a flash it was gone, as if it had never been.

"Lady Kirra, welcome. I have so looked forward to meeting you, and at last here you are." Sithli had decided to be charming. Although she did not rise from her chair, her smile was brilliant. Her command of the Runchot language had improved enough for her to converse in it easily, and she used it now to honor her guest. "Please do sit. Your companions may wait for you outside. Sae Kepit, see them out." Unfortunately, Sithli had made the mistake that Kepit had not. She had addressed herself to the fashionable member of Kirra's party, the woman whose name Kepit did not know.

"I am sorry, SaeKet. If I am welcome here, then my companions are also." Kirra smiled faintly at Sithli's surprise, but she still did not introduce her companions.

"I will have more chairs brought in, SaeKet," Kepit put in hastily before Sithli could decide to dispute the arrangement.

The chairs were brought in quickly, but Kirra did not sit until there were enough for her whole party. When she sat, she smiled and stretched out her hands toward the fire, as if to warm them. Or as if to show them off, Kepit thought. Why would she want to show off her hands? They were not especially beautiful. They were square, blunt hands, as if Kirra had once used them for some sort of rough work. They were, in fact, ugly hands. Kirra saw Kepit watching her and withdrew her hands slowly.

She wanted me to see that, thought Kepit. Kirra had had no need to warm her hands. It was a piece of a puzzle, deliberately handed to her, given to her as a challenge. She had no idea where the piece fit, but she did have one other piece of the puzzle. Kirra spoke Runchot well, and her grammar was perfect, but she had a slight accent. However slight the accent, however unnoticed it was by others, even by Sithli, it would seem, Kepit knew it. Kirra was not a native Runchot. She spoke Runchot with a Saeditin accent. Standing to the side of Sithli's chair, Kepit turned her head slightly, so that her revelation could not be read on her face.

"It was my fault entirely, SaeKet," Kirra was saying. "I purchased Barrit from a reputable dealer, one whom I had no reason to doubt. In fact, I believe that he was duped. Beyond this, there is a very strong possibility that this slave merely resembled the prince's lost daughter. Be that as it may—"

"You take in a lot of young women," interrupted Sithli,

"do you not? Runaways, strays, petty criminals, and perhaps some not quite so petty."

Kepit started and stared in horror at Sithli, urgently willing her to be more diplomatic. Kirra seemed unperturbed.

"I take in no one justly accused under Runchot law," she said. "And I attempt to check backgrounds as best I can, although when I buy from a slave dealer, I assume that has already been done. If you have any question regarding me in this matter, I am sure it will not take long for you to verify my claim."

"We have no reason to doubt you," put in Kepit hastily, hoping Sithli would not contradict her. "Prince Raphat thinks most highly of you." This was true, despite the recent incident. Raphat apparently believed Kirra's explanation completely. Kepit had checked. "As you say, it is possible that Barrit was merely like the missing princess and not the princess herself."

"And be that as it may," said Kirra again, "I am still devastated that my gift to you, SaeKet, should have failed and should have caused you any upset."

"I can't find anyone now who can do my hair and makeup as well," said Sithli. There was a trace of a pout in her voice.

"I would like to offer you another gift, SaeKet, to replace what was lost."

"That is most generous," said Sithli. She rang a little bell on the table by her elbow, and a servant appeared with a tray of glasses and another with bottles of wine and cider. There was a momentary pause while the guests were served. Sithli took none herself. Kepit accepted cider, not because she wished any, but to reassure their guests that the refreshment was safe. All the same, she noted that Kirra merely touched the glass to her lips and did not drink.

"I am offering you several personal slaves, trained in various arts, in compensation for this unfortunate incident." Kirra set her glass down, and her companions followed her lead, as if they had been rehearsed and choreographed.

"I had in mind more than just a few slaves." Sithli sat upright in her chair. "I had in mind much more than that."

When Kirra opened her mouth to reply, Sithli's eyes flashed, and she held up her hand. She appeared suddenly much more than a pampered exile. She looked every inch the SaeKet, of noble saedin blood, inheritor of the Mother's grace and authority. Kepit drew herself up straighter, surprised and gratified. If only Sithli would call upon this aspect of herself more often, success would be assured.

"You must realize, Kirra, that you have insulted Saeditin, and you have insulted your own prince. That this was not deliberate on your part does not make it less so. I have nothing to say about whatever amends you must make to Prince Raphat, but you owe me more than mere servants."

Whatever Kirra thought, she looked abashed. She picked up her glass again and twirled it in her fingers. If it was an act, it was a very good one.

"What is it you would ask of me, SaeKet?"

"Not more than you can give." Sithli leaned forward, and her eyes glittered. She looked predatory. "I want funding for troops to help me retake what is mine. To help me retake Saeditin."

There was a moment of silence as Kirra put down her glass and leaned forward. Her eyes bored into Sithli.

"I can do better than that," she said. "I know where trained troops can be hired, and I will give them to you."

If Sithli had looked predatory, Kirra looked more so. Threat seemed to roll off her in waves, so much so that Kepit put a hand to her sword. The movement caught Kirra's eye, and her smile lost some of its edge.

"I know you wonder why I will do this. The reason is simple: profit. I expect a return on my investment, SaeKet."

"The reason is not entirely that simple, Ria Kirra," said Kepit, stepping forward from behind Sithli's chair. She had heard the slight taunt in the word "SaeKet." However good Kirra was at dissembling, she had not had quite enough practice at it to fool Kepit. It was time to get a few answers.

The use of the Saeditin respectful title for commoners drew an astounded glance from Sithli, but Kirra herself only smiled.

"No," said Kirra, "I suppose nothing is ever simple. As you have realized, my family was Saeditin. I spent my early years there."

Kirra had spent far more than her early years there, but she did not mention this. She was almost certain that Kepit did not know who she really was, for she had taken great care to guard this knowledge.

"I have a reason other than profit for offering you what I do." Kirra leaned forward again, willing sincerity into her voice. "There are certain Saeditin whom I hate. Whom I will do what I can to bring down. I now have the means to accomplish this. Or rather, to help you accomplish this, Sithli SaeKet."

"We are of one mind in this," said Sithli. She believed herself a good judge of character. Hadn't she known, after all, when her cousin Rilsin turned faithless? Sithli believed herself to be the Mother's chosen, the true SaeKet, and the Mother protected Her own. She heard the sincerity in Kirra's voice, and she believed it. "I want twenty-five thousand troops."

"I cannot do that, SaeKet. Even I do not have that much money."

"Oh, I think you do." Sithli was intent. "I believe you can afford even more."

"I can give you ten thousand, SaeKet. Surely that will insure success."

"I will accept twenty thousand," said Sithli. "Twenty thousand and no fewer."

"I will give fifteen, SaeKet, and that will strain me."

"Twenty thousand," said Sithli. "Twenty will wipe out the insult to me and to Saeditin. Twenty thousand will insure our success. Twenty thousand will insure your profit, Ria Kirra, Lady Kirra. When I am back in Petipal, you will be rewarded in more ways than you can imagine. You can, if you wish, return to Saeditin, and not as a commoner."

Sithli smiled. "You can have an estate in Saeditin and expand your enterprises in the capital itself and all throughout Saeditin, if you wish."

Kirra was silent for so long that Kepit was afraid she would refuse the offer. She need not have worried.

"That would suit me very well, SaeKet. You will have your troops. I will see to it personally that you have them within weeks."

Kirra was shown out, and Kepit felt an equal mixture of relief and satisfaction. She believed she now knew more about what motivated this prominent merchant, and knowing someone's motivation always made Kepit feel better. Nonetheless, there was still something disturbing about Kirra. Someone of Kirra's background, and in her business, would have taken some stringent and quite possibly shady means to achieve such success, but it bothered Kepit that her investigations continued to draw some blanks. How was it possible for Kirra to obtain and ready so many troops in a matter of weeks? Had she been prepared to offer them all along? For the moment, Kepit dismissed the matter, intending to return to it later. Sithli wanted to celebrate. Kepit, for once, agreed with her. This was a victory that deserved a celebration.

"THIS IS DISTURBING, although not entirely unexpected." Essit strode nervously across the room to stare out the window again, as if still hoping to see Rilsin, his SaeKet and his friend, ride up to the palace. He turned back to the spy, who sat comfortably on the bench near the fire. They were in one of the SaeKet's private audience chambers, off the big public audience chamber.

Essit had discovered the need for intelligence and the uses of spies during the siege of Hoptrin, when he had been shut up in that city until Rilsin had relieved the siege. He suspected that he might not have been trapped if his spies had been better, and he had learned the lesson well. Now, as first minister, he had spies throughout Runchot and informants within Saeditin itself. This spy was from Runchot, but he was Saeditin born. He was a young man in the household of Prince Raphat. He was one of the prince's secretaries.

"When will these troops be ready, Gigrat?"

"Within only a few weeks, supposedly, although the prince isn't certain. He doesn't believe Kirra can prepare so many men so quickly. Although she does have a reputation where men are concerned." Gigrat grinned at his own joke but sobered when Essit did not respond. "Prince Raphat is pleased. He has his own ambitions regarding Saeditin, and he is just as happy to use someone else's troops to achieve them. Many of Kirra's troops are mercenaries from southern Runchot, so that means they will be unavailable to Raphat's enemies there. I will send word as soon as I hear that the troops are indeed ready to move."

"I don't want you going back, Gigrat. It's too dangerous for you."

"I have to go back." Gigrat had wanted to see the first minister's reaction to this nasty surprise, but unfortunately, Essit wasn't giving him one. One of the things Gigrat liked about his spying was the sense of power it gave him. It was his reward, far more than the money he received, far more than the abstract satisfaction of aiding his birthland. When Essit did not react more strongly to his news, he felt cheated. "The prince expects me back. He believes I left only to see my sister, not far from Tressig. I can't stay away too long."

"I don't like it; I don't want you going back. It's too dangerous."

"If I don't go back, Prince Raphat might take my sister and her family hostage. And he will guess where I am." Gigrat was gratified to see the realization of the truth of this dawn on Essit's face. He smiled to himself, pleased. The first minister of Saeditin would have to let him return, despite his misgivings. Gigrat, only a secretary, controlled the doings of the mighty.

"I suppose you will," said Essit slowly. "When you know that the troops are ready, find some excuse to leave, an excuse that will give you plenty of time before the prince questions why you have not returned. Then take your sister and her family, and come north, back to Saeditin. Bring me word yourself; do not send a message."

"I will," said Gigrat.

Essit did not know whether or not to believe him. He did not understand that sort of stubbornness, or dedication, or perhaps it was simply a love of risk. Whichever it was, it seemed to have made Gigrat a good and reliable funnel for information.

"If you are going back, you had best leave soon." Essit stared out the window toward the east, where the afternoon sky was darkening early. "Another storm looks to be coming up. You don't want to get caught on this side of the border."

Gigrat left in a hurry. Essit saw him out personally. The fewer people who knew the identity of his visitor, the better.

Outside, the air was bitter cold. Essit stood in the palace garden and looked northward. Where was Rilsin? Where was Pleffin sae Grisna? The news had recently made its way south, by messenger, far slower than sun-flash, which was not reliable at this time of year. Even had it come faster, Essit did not know what difference it would have made. The SaeKet and her commander had both vanished. Disappeared in broad daylight from a hillside where they had been chasing barbarians. That the barbarians had also vanished was no consolation, none at all.

Essit had not wanted the news to get out, but it had anyway. Many saedin knew, and some dira, and soon everyone would know. There were whispers of magic. Essit had called in the priests, none of whom had been the least bit helpful. They had muttered and wafted incense, but no amount of chanting had produced the SaeKet.

Dremfir, Mage to the SaeKet, had sent word that he was on his way south, back to the capital, but Essit was doubtful that he had anything useful to offer. He had been nowhere near Rilsin when she had disappeared, and if there was anything he could do, he would have done it already. It appeared that Essit was truly holding the reins of Saeditin government, all alone, until Rilsin should come back. Essit refused to consider the possibility that she might not come back.

16

SOLA KNEW HE WAS LOST. HE WAS LUCKY HE HAD THE pack with him, and the meager supplies it contained, but unless he found a way out soon, they would not be enough. He shifted Reniat, who was asleep in his arms, struggling to find a more comfortable position in which to carry her. It was hard. She was heavy, and his arms ached, but the little girl couldn't walk for long without tiring.

If only he had thought to note more carefully how the passages turned. At first he hadn't even realized that the passages had branched. There had been noise outside the cave, the unmistakable sounds of people and horses, awakening him from a sound sleep. They had been followed. Hastily, he grabbed up Reniat in one hand and the pack in the other, and retreated back into the cave. Reniat hadn't made a sound, but the fool horse had whinnied. There had been shouts from outside. Whispering to Reniat to stay quiet, he had hoisted her on his hip and fled deeper into the cave. He had not lit a torch. There had been no time to do so, and he had no desire to give his pursuers such a clear sign to follow.

Down toward the back of the cave there had been a low sort of tunnel. Into this he had crawled, with Reniat. He heard their pursuers enter the cave, so he had crawled deeper. After a while, he could feel the tunnel open up a bit. There was the sense of space around him, so he stood, still holding on to the child, afraid to set her down where he couldn't see. It had been dark, and he had not even been aware that the passageway branched, and then branched again. He had not been aware until much later when he had lit one of the torch stubs and attempted to find his way back. That was when he had become hopelessly lost. He had wasted far too much time, and more important, he had wasted torchlight, trying to find his way back to that first cave. The torch was burning dangerously low before he realized that he needed to find some other way out, and he blew it out to save it.

He tried to remember what he had read. There had been a diagram of the known caves in the little book. That was one problem: the known caves. He knew with uneasy certainty that the explorer who had written his little book had not known the extent of the cave system. The other problem was equally severe. Even had he remembered the diagram, and even had the diagram been accurate, Sola had no idea where he was within the cave system. He no longer knew, nor could he guess, compass points, as all directions seemed the same in the dark. For a time he clutched Reniat to him and crawled, like some three-legged animal, in the direction he thought was back the way they had come. Then he thought how foolish this was and froze.

Then they simply sat in the dark. Sola was afraid to move. He was afraid to light one of the torches again because burning it meant losing it, and being that much closer to being in the dark forever. He kept one hand on Reniat at all times. The child sat close to him, on the cold stone floor. She slept. Sola may have slept, too, but he didn't know for sure. At one point he realized that he could not tell whether or not he was awake or asleep. It was dark, he was in the caves, Reniat was with him, but these things did not alter, awake or asleep. Then he felt Reniat stir.

"Dada Sola. Dada Sola. I'm hungry! I want to go home!"

Sola knew suddenly that she wasn't afraid because he was there. She trusted him to get her out. He couldn't let her down.

"We'll go home, sweetheart," he said. He made himself believe it. "I'll make some light," he told her, "and we'll have some food. Then we'll get out."

"Find Mama?"

"Then find Mama," he said.

Fumbling in the darkness, he found the torch stub, the last one he had used. He found the strike-stone, and fumbled with that, too, but he was extra careful not to drop it forever into the darkness that swam around them like a sea. Eventually, the torch flared into life. Sola held it up and gasped.

Jewels dripped down like long icicles from the roof of the cavern high above. Jewels grew up from the floor like reverse icicles. The colors were incredible: azures and lavenders, glowing greens and ruby reds. By sheer luck, he and Reniat were standing in a clear space. Sola, breathing carefully as if somehow even his breath might disturb the wonder around them, lifted the torch to see better. The light bounced from sparkling surfaces, reflecting back again and again, until it seemed that all the stone jewels were blazing.

"Oh!" said Reniat. "Pretty!"

Sola swallowed, unable to speak. As if in a trance, he held up the torch and walked among the glittering stones, the jeweled icicles. After a time of doing this, he looked for Reniat and found that she was some distance away, sitting on the cave floor where he had left her. He had wandered away from her, and had he not come to his senses in time, he could have left her behind.

Deciding that his strange behavior was in part the result of not having eaten in an unguessed amount of time, Sola

took out food and water. He found that he was desperately
thirsty, as was Reniat. He tried to ration their water, knowing that they could go longer without food than without
water if they had to. He had filled their two waterskins at a
stream before they settled into the cave at the onset of the
storm. He didn't know how long it would last them now or
when they might find more water.

When they had finished eating, Sola picked up Reniat
and slung her across his hip. He was becoming accustomed
to her weight and to her presence. He discovered that he
loved her sunny little smile, and he liked the way she chattered at him. He found it comforting. Much of what she said
made no sense at all, in the way of babies, but being
Rilsin's daughter, and precocious, she did have things to
say. For the most part they were comments on the "pretty
rocks." Sometimes she said, with great authority, that she
would "see Mama soon." Sola always agreed with her
when she said this.

When the torch burned too low, he lit the next one. He
wondered how far this cavern extended. He could see the
roof of it, high above him under its dripping stone icicles,
but he could not see the sides of it, or any end to it. He was
afraid that he was becoming resigned to walking endlessly
in this place of wonders until the light ran out.

"Water," said Reniat, clearly.

"No, Reni," he said patiently. "No water. Only stone.
Stone that shines as if it's wet, but stone." He tried to walk
on, but Reniat was squirming on his hip now, trying to get
down.

"Water!" she said again, more urgently.

Thinking now that she wanted a drink, Sola braced himself to try to explain to a baby that she could not have more
water yet. He stopped and set her down, the better to look
at her while he made his poor and sad explanation. As soon
as her feet touched the stone floor, Reniat was off, running,
dodging among the stone columns. Shocked, Sola ran after
her, his torch casting jumping and wavering light as he ran.
Because his legs were longer, he caught up quickly and

scooped her up, but his heart was pounding. If she decided to hide among the stone formations, or if she fell and was knocked unconscious, he might never find her.

"Don't you ever do that again!" He was tempted to shake her, but instead he clutched her to him, and to his horror, began to sob. He buried his face in her little shirt, but the harder he tried to control himself, the worse it was.

"Don't cry. Dada Sola, don't cry. Come see water!"

Sola gulped and swallowed. He put her down and knelt down beside her. Now he desperately wanted a drink, too. "There is no water, Reni," he said again.

"Is too! There!" One stubby finger pointed.

Sola glanced in the direction she pointed, but all he could see was shadows and stone. He sighed and prepared to pick her up, but she danced back. At least she did not run again, and he was grateful.

"Water is there!" She pointed again, her eyes flashing. In that moment she looked very much her mother's daughter. "Feel it! I feel it! Like a big fountain! Out of the ground!"

Sola stared at her. She was Rilsin's child, her daughter, the SaeKetti. Could she hear the song of the land, could she feel water?

"Listen, Dada Sola! Listen to the water."

Sola listened. Now that he stilled his thoughts and he listened, he heard it. It sounded like a river, and it was not that far away.

"I hear it, Reni," he whispered. "I hear it." He gripped the little girl's hand. "Let's go find it," he said, and was rewarded with her brilliant smile.

They picked their way carefully through the forest of stone, in the wavering light of the torch. The sound of water running through stone, chuckling and singing to itself, became louder in the vast silence of the caves. Eventually they saw it.

The river ran between smooth stone banks, in a channel it had cut for itself over the ages. Sola had a sudden vision of the river carving out the vast caverns themselves. The amount of time that would have been necessary for such an event made him dizzy, and he swiftly put the thought from his mind. The priests would have told him that the Mother made these caverns all at once, which was by far a more comfortable theory. What was more immediately important, however, was that he was able to kneel on one stone bank, holding the torch in one hand, and with the other hand, leaning over with care, he was able to scoop up some water. It was cold and clear, and he drank it gratefully. He propped the torch carefully against a stone formation and refilled their waterskins. Both he and Reniat drank deeply. As he was restoppering the waterskins, Reniat came and sat beside him.

"Big fountain," she said. She had never seen a river, Sola realized.

"It's a river," he said, and smiled when her eyes grew big.

"River fountain water goes out," she said.

In the act of replacing the waterskins in the pack, Sola froze. She was right, of course. The river came in from somewhere, and undoubtedly it went out again, too. If they could follow the river, they, too, would come out, if they could reach the exit before their torches were completely burned out.

"We will follow the river, Reni," he said.

"Good. River go to Mama."

Sola was finishing with the pack and didn't answer.

ΠEFFA'S WOUΠDED ARΠ was quite obviously bothering her, although she did not complain. Rilsin was worried about her, especially when she saw, in the torchlight when they stopped for a rest, that her friend's face was gray and wet with perspiration. Rilsin felt her forehead, over Meffa's protests.

"You have a fever," said Rilsin, trying not to sound grim. "We need to keep infection out of the wound." She was very much afraid that infection was already in the wound and causing the fever, and she was afraid to look. "Do we have any willow bark?" She was sure she knew the answer to that, too.

"No, SaeKet," said Pleffin. "Nothing to bring down the fever but water, and not a lot of that. If the wound is infected, I can try to burn it out, cauterize it. I have done this before; it's battlefield surgery, SaeKet, and not pleasant."

"We'll do it if we must," she said. "We need to get Meffa out of here, to a physician."

"Your pardon, SaeKet, but that won't happen in time. Look." Pleffin pointed at Meffa's arm, which he had unwrapped, and Rilsin saw red streaks beginning to spread outward from the wound.

"If we wait, she will die. The poison will go to her heart. I need to do it now. If I don't, it is possible that we will have to take off the arm. We may have to do so in any event."

Rilsin drew a deep breath, suppressing the wave of nausea that threatened her. "Meffa," she said, "what do you want to do?" Rilsin hoped that her fear was not obvious. Meffa had been her friend for so long; losing her now was unthinkable, but Meffa must make the decision herself.

"Let Sae Pleffin do what he can," said Meffa. Her voice was thin and whispery. She sat in a boneless heap on the stone floor of the cave, looking as if she had melted. "How big are these caves, anyway? Will we ever get out?"

"We will get out," Rilsin assured her, "but I don't know how big these caves are, or how far they run."

Even as she spoke, she knew she was wrong. She *could* tell how big the caves were. She could feel them. The land sang to her even here, encased in stone. In a way it made more sense, for she was now within the land. If she stopped and listened the way she had learned to, she could sense the drip of water through limestone, sense the slow movement of air, and sense the flow of water. She was within the song of the land, just as the seer had foretold. She looked up sharply and found the others watching her.

"I can get us out," she said. "I can feel where the caves run deep, and where they come near the skin. The surface."

"Is it near?" asked Porit. His voice trembled slightly.

"Near enough. I can feel it, but I do not know what lies in the way. There may be walls of stone, there may be tunnels—" She frowned, concentrating, and then shook her head. "I cannot tell. I can get us out, but it may take a day. It may take two." It might take more, and she refrained from pointing out that they had no way to measure time down here. They were not even certain how long they had been down here already.

"We cannot wait even a day for Meffa's arm. If I am to do anything for her, I had best do it now." Pleffin knelt and took Meffa by the shoulders. "I don't know if this will work, but it is the best chance you have now. What do you say, Meffa? It is your decision, not mine or even the SaeKet's."

"Do it," said Meffa.

Pleffin reached beneath his overshirt, drew out a small waterskin, and unstopped it. Rilsin knew immediately that it did not contain water. When they had inventoried their supplies when they first found themselves in the caves, Pleffin had not volunteered this skin. Pleffin glanced up and caught her eye.

"I thought it might be needed later," he told her without the slightest embarrassment. "Drink as much as you can," he advised Meffa.

While Meffa drank, Rilsin set Porit to arranging Meffa's cloak on the hard floor of the cave to make her as comfortable as possible. The boy looked as ill as Rilsin felt. Chilsa stretched out behind Meffa so that she could lean against him, and when she did, he poked his big head forward and snuffled her ear comfortingly. Pleffin stood to one side, running the blade of his sword through the flame of the torch. Rilsin blinked, seeing for a moment the tower prison cell, hearing Jullka read her death sentence, and watching Jullka cleanse her knife with fire. She shook her head slightly to clear away the memory. Pleffin took a drop of wine from the waterskin and dropped it on the sword. It sizzled.

"It's time," he said.

"Wait!" Porit darted forward. He pulled off his overshirt

in one rapid jerk. He wadded it up and rolled the sleeve into a tight tube. "Bite on this, Meffa," he said. "It will help."

Obligingly, Meffa gripped the shirt with one hand and bit down on the rolled sleeve. Rilsin took her by the shoulders, wedging herself between her friend and Chilsa, and tried to hold the wounded arm immobile. Nonetheless, when Pleffin brought the hot metal against her wound, Meffa screamed. Rilsin gripped her tightly as she thrashed. Then suddenly Meffa fell still. The smell was incredible. First it was foul, and then it was like meat roasting. Rilsin felt intense hunger pangs, followed by a revulsion so overpowering she was afraid she might vomit. She fought to control her nausea and found herself breathing heavily through her mouth. She closed her eyes and held her friend tightly. When she opened her eyes again, Pleffin was ripping strips of bandage from a shirt and cleaning the wound with what was left of the wine.

"I realize she must be moved, but we need to let her rest as long as we can here," he told Rilsin. "It is well that she is no longer conscious."

Rilsin nodded in agreement, unable to find her voice. It was then she noticed that Porit was gone. Pleffin noticed the absence as well.

"You had best go find the boy," he told her. "I will care for Meffa."

Rilsin got shakily to her feet, lit a torch stub after several tries, and took a few steps away from the group. Her teeth were chattering, and she drew her cloak around her. She realized that Pleffin had not addressed her as "SaeKet" and had, in fact, given her a command. She was grateful for it, she found, and grateful for Pleffin's experience. She swallowed hard, blinking away tears she had not realized were in her eyes. After a brief try, she found her voice.

"Will she be all right?"

"I don't know." Pleffin was still calm. "The poison had not spread far, so it is probable that she will live, especially if you can get us out quickly and we can find a good army physician. Whether or not her arm can be saved, I do not yet know."

"I see." Rilsin was gratified to find that her voice sounded normal again and was back under her control. "I don't know how to thank you for this."

"No thanks are necessary." Pleffin smiled slightly. "She is a credit to Saeditin and to you, SaeKet. I remember how I felt, the first time I witnessed field surgery. It is harder when you assist, and harder still when it is a friend whose life is at stake."

"Nonetheless, thank you." Rilsin turned away, holding up the torch, hoping to see Porit.

"SaeKet."

She turned back to see Pleffin kneeling above the still-motionless Meffa.

"I vomited my guts out, SaeKet, the first time I saw anything like this." He turned his attention back to Meffa.

Rilsin continued to watch him for a moment, and then she turned back to the darkness of the cave. She walked some paces across the stone floor and held up the torch. The cavern they were currently in was made of smooth and sculpted stone. Smooth and rounded by what? Rilsin had a sudden insight, a visceral knowledge of water, water and time. She shivered. The caves were not nearly as cold as the land above them, but they were cool. She remembered that Porit had taken off his overshirt to give to Meffa. He would be feeling the cold soon. She held the torch higher but saw only dancing shadows. Her worry was overlain by a sudden flash of anger. Running off as Porit had done was both foolish and dangerous. Who knew what lived in these caverns? Without thinking, one hand dropped to her sword.

"Porit!" she called. Her voice was soft, but she pitched it to carry.

The cave echoed it back: "Porit Porit Porit." Right on the heels of her own voice came the answer, in a half shout.

"Here!"

The cave flung this word back again from all directions. Rilsin had no idea where he was, and now she was certain that he was in trouble. Why else would he call out but not come to her light? Apparently the echoes had shocked him to silence again. As the sound died, Rilsin listened. From a short distance away came a soft scrabbling sound, and then a sniff. She shifted the torch to her left hand and drew her sword. Advancing cautiously, she found the boy behind an outcrop of rock that looked as if waves had been turned to stone. No one was with him, but he was crouched down with his face in his hands.

"I'm sorry. SaeKet, I'm sorry." He had been crying, and the face he turned up to her was tearstained. "It's all my fault." He began to sob again, and sure enough, he was shivering.

"What's your fault?" Rilsin had done a quick check of the area. She saw no one else and nothing else nearby. "Are you hurt?" she asked again.

"I'm not hurt, SaeKet. I wish I were! I wish it had been me instead of Meffa."

"You should be glad it was not!" Rilsin snapped. Now that she knew he was safe, relief transformed her worry to annoyance.

"But it's my fault," he said again, miserably. "I insisted on following you here. If it weren't for me, Meffa wouldn't have come."

"Yes, she would have." Rilsin propped the torch as best she could against the stony wave formation and resheathed her sword. Then she knelt beside Porit. In the face of his obvious misery, her annoyance vanished. "Meffa would have done anything to stay near me, whether or not you came along."

"She didn't know how to fight. She didn't know how to protect herself."

"She knew more than you give her credit for." Rilsin took off her cloak and wrapped it around the boy. It was true, Meffa was nothing if not resourceful. "You could not have stopped her, and you could not protect her. What happened to her could have happened to any of us." *Protecting her was my job,* Rilsin thought. Over the past days she had come to the conclusion that both her child and her lover were dead. That any more of those close to her should die for her now was not to be contemplated.

"Come back now, Porit. You have no blame in this, and you do no good here. Meffa needs you." Rilsin paused. "And so do I." It was true, she realized. She was gratified to see him straighten up. He wiped his eyes and then pulled her cloak around him. She saw him realize the cloak was hers and begin to shrug it off again.

"Keep it for now," she told him, "until you reclaim yours." His was currently keeping Meffa warm. She reached out a hand to help him up, and he took it.

"So Meffa lives?"

She felt a pang as she realized that he hadn't known. "She lives, yes, and Sae Pleffin thinks she will continue to do so." She was rewarded by his faint smile.

"What about her arm? Will she lose it?"

"Sae Pleffin doesn't know, but he thinks there is a good chance her arm can be saved, especially if we can get her to an army physician soon."

"Which we can do, because you will get us out of the caves, SaeKet." Porit's confidence in himself had returned full force, as well as his confidence in her.

"I will do what I can," she assured him, "but first let's go back and see how Meffa is. Sae Pleffin says she should rest awhile before we try to move her."

She retrieved the torch and put her arm around Porit, drawing him back with her toward the glow from Pleffin's torch, which was farther away than she realized. She was surprised that Porit had gone so far in the darkness. They picked their way carefully by the light of her torch, saying nothing for a moment. It was in this silence that they heard it: a sharp sound like something breaking or something dropped. The sound echoed around them, rebounding from everywhere at once. Rilsin and Porit stopped and stared at each other. Despite the echoes, Rilsin was completely certain that it had come from behind them. Looking into Porit's eyes, she saw that he shared the same certainty.

"What is it?" breathed Porit softly.

"I think there is someone behind us," Rilsin breathed back, equally softly. She took his hand and blew out their torch.

In front of them the light from Pleffin's torch suddenly vanished. They stood in the darkness of the caves, senses straining, listening for something. It came again more clearly, now that they knew to listen for it. It was the sound of a footstep on stone, from behind them. Someone was moving toward them in the dark.

PHARA WATCHED AS her companions filled their waterskins from the underground river. Although she was still fascinated by the underground landscape, she wished they were through it and back out into the open. The knowledge of so much stone and earth pressing over their heads made her uneasy, as did the breathing darkness of the caves themselves.

She was also unhappy that there was nothing she could do to help. Chif knew where he was going, so she followed him. They brought their food with them, and although she had contributed her small supplies, most of it was supplied by the Northerners. She could not even volunteer to cook it for them, as they did not light fires other than their torches. Their food was cold and dried, and she couldn't wait for a hot meal again.

It was cold and damp in the caves. Phara huddled within her cloak, and at night they all slept together in a pile, for warmth. Her father would have been shocked beyond measure to find his daughter sleeping in a heap with three barbarians, and that thought gave her a certain satisfaction. He would not have believed that these same barbarians were acting with perfect gentility toward her. The only thing that made Phara uncomfortable about her situation was being so completely dependent upon these strangers.

In truth, they were becoming less strange the longer she was with them. Even Chif's blue hair began to seem normal. She had always been a quick study, and she was beginning to pick up bits of the Wilfrisin language. She did not reveal her dawning understanding, however. She had learned young never to completely trust anyone, and she was not going to give up her advantage.

One night, she could not sleep. They did not post a guard, a precaution they would have taken anywhere else, one that Chif had explained to her was unnecessary in the caves.

"No one but Confederation people knows the caves are here, Phara Princess," he had said. "So we are quite safe."

She did feel safe with them, but tonight, for some reason, she was uneasy. They kept one torch burning at all times, and by the light of this she rose and quietly made her way a short distance from their camp.

They were not far from the underground river, which sang softly to itself in the near distance. She did not dare go all the way to the river, as that would have taken her out of the farthest perimeter of the torchlight, but she went as far as she could. She sat down behind a tower of stone that tapered toward the bottom rather than the top. It was still broad enough for her to rest against, and she drew her cloak around her and tried to make herself as comfortable as possible.

She was not sure just what it was that had awakened her or why she felt such unease. Perhaps it was that they were nearing the end of their underground journey, something that made her realize that she would be faced again with all the urgent problems of the world above ground. She knew that Chif guessed more about her urgency to reach her brother than she had revealed. Eventually she would have to tell Chif the truth, that her brother had brought a Runchot force secretly into Confederation territory.

"What is it that steals your sleep, Phara Princess? Is it thoughts of the world above, thoughts of your brother?"

Phara started and barely stifled a scream. Chif's words, so closely echoing her thoughts, as well as the eeriness of the place, were almost too much for her.

"I apologize, Phara Princess. I had no meaning to

frighten you." He looked truly repentant. "In this place fear is too easy."

"I'm not frightened now." It was true, now that he was there. Phara did not stop to think about this. "Sit down, Chif. Please. And do not call me 'Princess.' I am no longer a princess."

"No?" Chif sat comfortably beside her, stretching out his long legs. "Are you not daughter of your father, the prince of Runchot? The would-be ruler of Saeditin and yes, Confederation, too?"

"I am no longer his daughter." Phara ignored the rest of Chif's question.

"He has disowned you?"

"I don't know," said Phara honestly. "I would assume he has. But I have disowned him."

"Ah." Chif took her statement seriously. He did not comment, as many Runchot would have done, that a child, especially a daughter, could not disown a father. "Can you tell me why you have done this so drastic thing?"

Phara looked at him. It was hard to see his face in the shadows, but she knew he truly wanted to know. For reasons she could not have explained to herself, she decided to tell him.

"He killed my mother," she said. "They all said it was a suicide, but it wasn't. I heard him talking about it when he didn't know I could hear. He didn't even kill her for politics, which is his usual reason for doing anything." Phara made no attempt to keep the scorn out of her voice. "He killed her because she objected to his mistresses. Finally, after all those years, she objected. So he killed her. It was poison, and he put it out that she took her own life."

"Why not divorce?"

"She is—was—the daughter of a southern noble. He could not risk her father's anger. Her death was easier to explain. I sent a message to my grandfather." Phara realized she was clenching her hands, and she took a deep breath, relaxing them. "I told him the truth. You know what he wrote back? He said I was overcome with grief. Understandably distressed, he said. In that way very like his daughter, my mother."

"I am sorry."

Chif held something out to her. With surprise, Phara saw it was a handkerchief of pure soft cotton, as fine as anything she would have had at home. She realized that tears had been streaming unchecked down her cheeks.

"Thank you," she said, taking it. "You know, I don't think Grandfather would have minded if my father had divorced her. It was all for nothing."

"He would have cared. At least he would have to say he did." Chif's voice was gentle, belying the harshness of his words. "It was his honor at stake, if your father divorced your mother. Not so when your mother died. Then it is sad, only. That is more politics, Phara Prin—Phara." Something in his tone made Phara strain to see him more clearly in the dim light.

"What do you know of politics?"

"Enough. And I know what honor can make people do." Phara did not fail to notice the edge of sarcasm he gave to the word "honor." "I am captain to First Man Bilt. And I know of grief, too. Do you know why my hair is blue, Phara?"

"Because you are a fore-fighter."

"I was one. No longer. I fought at the front of every battle. I fought without shield. I fought to regain favor of battle goddess and favor of tribe, because I had killed. Killed in peacetime. Killed my own tribe, my own family. I fought so I could forgive myself. I hoped then to die for what I did."

When the silence grew long, broken only by the gentle song of the river in its stone banks, Phara asked, "Why? Whom did you kill, that you wanted to die for it?"

"My brother. My own brother, two years older." The answer came back in a whisper, harsh and painful. "He took my Luthin, the girl I was to marry. He did it on challenge from friend of his. When her father find out—found out— he say Luthin can never marry me. When Luthin found she carry child of my brother, she kill herself. She kill herself for honor. So one night I get very drunk thinking of my Luthin. I drink and become angry. Then I see my brother. I kill him. I kill his friend with him. I kill Nofa, my brother, whom I love. My Luthin is gone. My brother is gone. My father he tell me to run, to leave Wilfrisin lands before he kill me himself, so he can restore family's honor. But I don't run. I go to fore-fighters, and they take me."

Chif had his face turned away from her, but Phara saw something glisten on his cheek. She had long known, in an abstract way, that she and her family did not have a monopoly on horror and grief but she had known it in the way of the young and protected and privileged. Even when she ran from her father's house and had seen more of the world than the palaces of her family, she had been too wrapped in her own emotions to feel much for anyone else.

"I am so sorry," she whispered. She found a clean corner of the handkerchief he had given her. She leaned over and touched his face with gentle fingertips, finding the tears and softly wiping them away. After an initial start of surprise, Chif allowed her to do this.

"Well," said Chif after a moment, "I redeem myself. I save tribe. I help form federation. I become important man, friend to first man. I gain all sorts of *honor*. But I never speak to Father again. My mother die before I see her again. I never forget my brother Nofa, or my Luthin. I never have another sweetheart. And I keep hair blue, so I never forget."

In the darkness Phara took Chif's hand and held it. After a moment, he reached over with his other hand and covered hers. They sat that way together, in the shadows, in silence.

17

Raphat glanced over the top of the report he was reading to look at his secretary. Gigrat was an excellent worker, smart and motivated. He was also uncannily aware of everything that went on around him, even though he tried to project the opposite impression. Raphat never let on that he wasn't fooled.

"Gigrat, I want that report from Lord Frult."

"I have it here, my lord, somewhere." Gigrat knew exactly where it was, but he made a pretense of searching for it. He had been aware of Raphat's scrutiny, and it disturbed him. Raphat had always scrutinized everything in his reach; the man was addicted to detail. It seemed to Gigrat, however, that Raphat had been paying him extra attention since he had returned from Saeditin. Perhaps First Minister Essit had been right, and it was time for him to consider leaving Runchot, and leaving this dangerous game he played. The thought disturbed him so much that he was truly flustered as he finally handed the report to the prince.

"Here it is, Lord Prince," he said.

Raphat took the proffered paper without a word, leaving Gigrat to go back to his work making two copies each of the prince's recent letters to Lord Frult of the south, requesting payment on a loan, with interest. As he copied, Gigrat committed details to memory. He was certain Sae Essit would be interested that Raphat needed money. Raphat wanted to pay for troops, troops to commit to the cause, not of Sithli sae Melisin but of Kepit sae Lisim. Gigrat had overheard a certain conversation. He was aware that Raphat watched him as he worked, but he decided that there was nothing unusual about the scrutiny after all.

"Gigrat, have you seen the report on Kirra? I cannot find it."

"It's right here." Gigrat made no pretense of having misplaced this.

"It is unfortunate that she had the Princess Phara in her hands without having the remotest idea who she was."

"Can that really be true?" Raphat had seemed to be talking to himself, but Gigrat could not let this interesting tidbit go.

"If I thought otherwise, even for the briefest of moments, Lady Kirra would no longer walk with the living."

Despite himself, Gigrat shuddered. Raphat's tone gave no doubt that he meant exactly what he said. Gigrat tried to hide his reaction from the prince, but he saw the slight smile on Raphat's face and knew he had failed. Although usually charming, at least outwardly, Raphat enjoyed inspiring fear.

"I believe Kirra completely," the prince continued. "I know my daughter. She is capable of the greatest subterfuge and artifice." There was a note of distinct pride in Raphat's voice. "Kirra knew only what Phara wanted her to know. I wish I knew what game my daughter thought she was playing with me."

Gigrat said nothing. He knew a lot more than Raphat thought he did about the prince's relationship with his daughter. He knew Phara had run away and not gone to visit an aunt in the south, as her father gave out. He knew the prince had sent spies out to find her, with no result. Her trail had gone cold immediately. He realized that Raphat was awaiting a response from him, and he struggled to remember just what the prince had been saying.

"Undoubtedly, my lord, but who knows what she was doing?" he said. "The Princess Phara has your intelligence."

"She does, indeed, but she is not quite as clever as I am, do you think, Gigrat?"

"Of course not." Gigrat had no idea what the prince was getting at.

"Because I know where she has gone now. It's only a matter of time until she's found and brought back."

Gigrat waited, but the prince did not elaborate. At last he couldn't stand it. "I'm glad of it, my lord."

"You will never imagine where she is," Raphat said, and then without waiting for Gigrat to comment, he continued. "She has taken it into her head to cross the border into Saeditin. Yes," he said, seeing Gigrat's surprise, "she was seen with a band of travelers in the southern part of that land. Rilsin SaeKet believes that I have her daughter. She does not realize that she has mine." He smiled grimly. "I will have Phara back before the SaeKet realizes she is there, and if I do not get her back, then it will not matter."

Gigrat did not even attempt to hide his astonishment. "Why is that, my lord?"

"I will have Saeditin itself," said Raphat meditatively. "The troops are ready. We will go over the border from the south and catch Rilsin between my troops and Tonar's, from the north. We will have Petipal itself within weeks." Raphat was watching Gigrat carefully. "Do you not believe me?"

"Of course! I am simply amazed, my lord."

"As so you should be." Raphat smiled, full of charm and self-satisfaction. "It is a very good thing that I can trust you, Gigrat. A very good thing. Here."

Raphat reached into his long burgundy overshirt and pulled forth something, which he held out to Gigrat. It was a money pouch, and it clinked. Not jingled, but clinked, as with heavy gold.

"You deserve a reward. I like to let my servants know when I am pleased with them."

"Thank you, my lord! Thank you!"

Gigrat felt the hair rise along the back of his neck. He took the pouch, looking suitably grateful, he hoped. His skill at dissembling was excellent, but he wasn't sure it was up to this challenge. Raphat was making him unaccountably nervous, more nervous than was normal for the prince, and every sense in Gigrat's system was suddenly shrieking. He was going to leave Runchot immediately. It was suitably ironic that Raphat's latest gift would help him.

Raphat kept him at work for another few hours. When he left the prince at last, it was getting dark. Gigrat left the mansion with a brief nod at the guard on duty. They knew him and were accustomed to letting him go unchallenged. If he wanted to look for amusement after dark in the bitter cold, it was his business.

Gigrat went straight to the small, run-down house of his contacts. He wanted to get word out fast to Essit sae Tillit in Saeditin. He would bring word himself, but he needed to get his sister out of Runchot, which would take a little time. He wanted Essit to know that Runchot troops, large numbers of them, would be crossing the border from the south, and they would be meeting the troops of Prince Tonar, coming down in a surprise move from the north, to catch Petipal between them.

The woman who answered his knock took one quick glance at him and almost closed the door in his face. Gigrat forestalled this by the simple expedient of sticking his foot in the door. He glanced behind him nervously, but he was almost certain he had not been followed.

"You know me!" he said to the smith-wife, but he kept his voice low. "Why shut me out? It's cold, and I have business."

"We have been under watch recently, I'm sure of it."

Gigrat frowned. It was odd to see the big woman jumpy

and nervously plucking at her stained trousers. It increased his sense of unease.

"I was not followed. I took great care."

"Gods grant you are right. Well, since you are here, come in. Tell me your business and then be on your way again. There is no reason for a secretary of the prince to be visiting a smith this time of night."

"I'm sure I could think of one." Gigrat's anxiety was displaced by annoyance. His contacts had been safe and unsuspected for a very long time, while he was the one taking all the risks. He looked around. "Where is your husband?"

"Out back. The forge is not fired, but he has work to prepare for customers. Whatever it is, you can tell me."

Why did she keep glancing over her shoulder toward the door? Gigrat wondered.

"Is there a message you want to send? Give it to me quickly. I'll get it out tonight."

"I'll take the message myself. I just want what I left with you." What Gigrat had left was more funds and some supplies for a hasty getaway. He wanted them now, more urgently every minute.

"Wait here." The big woman moved surprisingly quickly, light on her feet.

While she was gone, Gigrat looked around him. He could see no sign of anything to make his hostess so anxious, but something made his neck prickle. When she returned with his bundle in her arms, he had come to a decision. It was best to take no chances.

"I will send the information with your messenger, as well as take it myself," he said. "It's important; it must get through to Sae Essit." When she nodded, looking at him alertly, he glanced around again. There was still nothing to indicate a cause for the alarm he felt.

"Prince Raphat has troops ready; he will be moving across the border within days. He means to take Petipal—"

Gigrat did not finish his warning. A number of things happened too fast for Gigrat to notice them all. The door crashed open, and someone rushed into the room. The smith's wife screamed. Gigrat started to run, but the intruder reached out and closed a hand around his throat in one continuous movement. Gigrat recognized one of Raphat's personal guards who not that long ago had seen him leave the prince's house. He opened his mouth to say that the prince would not look kindly on an attack on his secretary, but before he could form the words, the guard slammed him against the kitchen wall. It was then that Gigrat saw the long knife in his hand, and what he had meant to say turned into a scream.

The scream became a gasp as the guard slid the knife into his stomach, leaned against the handle, and drew the weapon upward. Gigrat sagged against the knife.

"That's for betraying the prince!" said the guard. "He says to tell you that your service to him is now rewarded as it should be."

In the next moment, the guard was gone, pulled away by the smith-wife. With vision that was quickly becoming blurry, Gigrat saw that she had a poker from the kitchen hearth in her hand. He blinked in disbelief as she skewered Raphat's guard with this, then pulled it free and slammed it across his throat. She actually bent the iron as she strangled him. As Gigrat blinked and struggled to find his voice, her husband came up behind her. The big man's leather apron was covered with blood.

"I took care of the others," he told his wife. "We haven't much time. The horses are saddled. Get your things, and let's be on the road." He glanced down at Gigrat and then back up at his wife. "Leave him," he said. "He's done for."

"Wait!" Gigrat tried to speak. What came out was a gurgle and a whisper, but somehow the smith-wife understood. She leaned down over him.

"I am sorry," she said. "Had I been just a little quicker, he might not have done this to you."

"Leave him!" The smith was urgent, almost frantic, but his wife shook him off.

"I will see that your message gets through," she said. "I will take it to Sae Essit myself." She knelt down beside him, and with a surprising gentleness, she smoothed the hair back from his eyes.

Gigrat tried desperately to speak. He wanted to tell her that Raphat had already sent troops down from the north to threaten Saeditin's capital. He wanted to beg her to go to his sister and help her and her family escape over the border. He heard moaning and realized the moans were his. He was dimly aware of the smith urging his wife to leave. Once again he felt the woman's gentle hands. She pushed aside his shirt, and he wondered dimly if she could stanch his wound. But she did not try. She felt through his clothing, pausing when she found Raphat's money pouch. She took this, handed it up to her husband, and then continued to search. Gigrat wanted to tell her that there was nothing else to find, but his mouth felt full of wool and his tongue would not work. He knew he had failed. Saeditin would receive no warning, and the Runchot would take over his native land. He noticed in a far-off way that the smith-wife's face was surrounded with darkness and that he was very cold. As he watched, her face vanished into the darkness.

"THEY ARE iΠSiStiΠG that they have vital information for you. They were creating such an annoyance that my captain said to bring you the message."

Essit looked at the Petipal guard, who was clearly unhappy at bringing this message to the first minister. Essit didn't know who these people were, this couple who had somehow slipped through the patrols and crossed the border from Runchot. He was tempted to have them arrested simply for evading the Saeditin patrols. They could very well be spies. Essit's nerves were enough on edge these days. The SaeKet was missing, along with Commander Pleffin. Essit was still in Petipal, but he was uneasy at simply keeping the government running. He had received no intelligence reports from within Runchot, and he was getting a very bad feeling, the same sort of feeling he got sometimes in summer, before the clouds massed and thunder broke the heat.

"They claim they were smiths in Runchot," said the guard. "They say they have a message from someone named Gigrat."

Essit heard the thunder in his mind. "Send them in," he said. "I will see them." The storm was almost on them.

Several hours later, Essit had made his decision. He would call up the troops and march south to defend the border against a Runchot invasion. He only hoped that he had enough time.

He sent the Runchot smiths to a room within the palace itself, wishing he could have done the same for Gigrat. He wondered if Gigrat's sister still lived, but there was nothing he could do for her, even if she did. The smiths had brought him other news, too, valuable news. Raphat's daughter Phara was missing, and very possibly she was within Saeditin. If Essit could only find her, she would be valuable. And if only the SaeKet would return, he need not make these decisions himself. Unfortunately, he had no choice.

In THE UTTER blackness of the cave, Rilsin drew her sword as silently as possible. She felt beside her until she found Porit again and clasped his hand. She wanted to tell him to stay near her, but she did not dare to speak. Around them the silence of the cave seemed to breathe. She saw spots and streaks in front of her eyes. In the absence of even the smallest glimmer of light, her brain played tricks on her. She wondered if whoever or whatever was behind them could see in this intense dark. If they could, then she was doomed. They were all doomed.

The silence grew around them. Beside her, Rilsin felt Porit begin to tremble. She knew, somehow, that he was about to say or do something, anything, to bring back life and end the loss of sense. Rilsin gripped his arm to silence him, but before he could cry out, another sound broke the silence. It was a cry of pain and a curse. Someone behind them had just run into one of the stone formations and was swearing in Clinsi.

Rilsin grinned. She squeezed Porit's hand, willing him not to do anything foolish. To her surprise, he gripped her hand back. Then he touched her with something: the torch. With a flash of insight, she knew what he was trying to communicate. She nodded, then realized he couldn't see the gesture. She tapped his arm: *yes*. Then she stepped away from him and waited.

There was a scraping sound and then the sudden flare of light. Porit had used a match to light the torch. The resulting light was blinding to those whose eyes had become accustomed to absolute darkness. Rilsin found herself blinking, her eyes tearing, but she had the advantage of knowing the light was coming. Those behind her did not.

Their followers were two northern barbarians, their fur and leather clothing filthy, their hair matted. Rilsin was almost certain these were the same barbarians who had disappeared from the hillside above, in what seemed like another age. Porit held the torch high, and Rilsin leaped toward the two men.

Although she had the advantage, they responded with alarming rapidity. Rilsin didn't really want to kill them. She wanted them alive, for information. She also hoped that they knew the way out. Unfortunately, they didn't seem to be in the mood to give her anything but a fight. One of them had already drawn his sword and was ready for her, and his companion was not far behind him.

Rilsin took a chance. She leaped toward the two men, trying to close the distance quickly. She vaulted a low rock formation, hoping the cave floor was level on the other side of it. It was.

She tried to come in under the Clinsi's guard, but it was difficult to judge distances in the torchlight. Rilsin nicked her opponent's wrist, but it was more by chance than by skill. She avoided his blade by luck, too, it seemed, and she was worried about his companion. She could not see the man, even with her peripheral vision. What could he be doing? The torchlight was jumping and flickering, sending the shadows dancing madly across the combatants and the stone formations of the cave. What was Porit doing? She needed a steady light. She wanted to call out to Porit, but she needed all her concentration to stay alive.

Her opponent leaned into his attack with a sudden ferocity. Rilsin backed up into the stone formation she had jumped. She beat back the Clinsi's sword, and suddenly she was under his guard. Her sword met an initial resistance in his leather overshirt, and then was through the material. He gave a scream of surprise and dropped his sword. Rilsin felt her own sword meet one of his ribs, and she pulled away, not wanting to break her weapon.

She was just in time. Whatever her opponent's companion had been doing, he was now ready to attack her, and he went at it with zeal. He came at her from the side, and Rilsin barely had time to meet him, her bloody blade scraping along his.

"Wait!" she said, in Clinsi. "I don't want to kill you. I just want—"

The torchlight wavered and jumped even more. Shadows skittered, making everything seem illusory. Her attacker reached out with one hand and grabbed her suddenly, his hand like a vise, jerking her toward him. His sword went straight for her throat.

There was an intense light and heat right near Rilsin's face. Someone was pushing between her and her opponent. The Clinsi's sword sliced downward, no longer under the control of its wielder. Rilsin pulled back just barely in time. There was a horrible smell, and someone was screaming.

"Close your eyes! SaeKet, close your eyes! Go to your right! No, I mean your left! SaeKet! Pull back! Close your eyes and grab his sword!"

She did close her eyes, just for a second, because the light was so intense. She made no attempt to follow any more of Porit's confused instructions, except to lean away and turn her head. When she opened her eyes again, she saw spots and flashes, her vision returning piecemeal.

Porit was no longer shouting instructions, but the Clinsi was screaming. His hair and beard were on fire from the

torch that Porit had shoved in his face. He flailed ineffectu-
ally, sending sparks everywhere. The fur on his clothing
caught fire and began to burn, its smell adding to the reek
of his burning hair. Rilsin coughed and moved away, staggering slightly as she tripped over a low rock formation.
Porit had grabbed up the Clinsi's fallen sword. As Rilsin
blinked, he lifted it.

"No!" she cried."Porit! Don't—"

She was too late. Porit had run the Clinsi through with
his own sword. The man gave a gurgling cry and collapsed,
ironically extinguishing most of the flames around his face
as he landed on the stone floor of the cave.

Rilsin groaned. "Porit," she said, and stopped. She
didn't know whether to thank the boy or shake him until his
teeth rattled. He looked upset and astonished but very
pleased with himself. He had saved her life, but he had also
cost them valuable information. She saw the torch from
Pleffin's position in the cave blazing again, and it began to
move. Pleffin was coming toward them, almost certainly
leaving Meffa behind.

"Porit," she said again. Another sound behind her made
her stop and turn. From the direction from which the Clinsi
had come, there was light. It was flickering and distant, but
coming closer. Rilsin drew in her breath with a little hiss.

"This place is beginning to seem like the Petipal Road,"
she said dryly. "Porit, keep that sword. You may need it
again."

She took the torch from Porit and wedged it into a stone
formation. Then she faded back into the shadows, motioning to Porit to do the same.

Pleffin had seen the light, too. He reached her torch and
then looked around. Rilsin stepped from the deep shadows
at the base of a stone formation and nodded to him. He nodded back, grounded his own torch, and stepped back into
more shadows.

Whoever was approaching was not attempting to be
stealthy about it. They were cautious, certainly, but their
familiarity with this cavern was clearly not great enough to

allow them to move without light. Rilsin wondered just how well the two dead Clinsi had known these caves, to attempt to move through them in darkness.

As she waited, Rilsin let her mind relax and flow. She felt the stone around her, and she felt more strongly now where the stone skin broke through to the surface above. It occurred to her that they might no longer be below Saeditin territory. Whatever lands they were below, she could hear the song. She could feel the stone, and the earth, and she could feel the life of the world above. She could feel the lives around her in this cavern, too, if she tried: Porit, and Sae Pleffin, beside her, Chilsa guarding Meffa back at their campsite. She could feel the four people moving toward her. *Four,* she thought. She caught Pleffin's eye, and then Porit's. She held up four fingers, nodded in the direction of the approaching party, and she saw their eyes widen as they understood. One of those approaching seemed slightly familiar to her. Rilsin concentrated harder, trying to find what it was that was familiar about this person.

There was a strange sense of standing outside herself, and then, suddenly, a feeling that there were two more people in this labyrinth below the world, and she knew them both. Her daughter Reniat shone like a star. With Reniat was Sola. They were both here, near her, and yet separated by the mystery of the caves and the heavy weight of darkness and earth.

"Reni," she whispered. "Sola." Rilsin felt her eyes filling with tears. There was a feeling of water near them, water flowing. But then it was gone. After a moment she concluded that her mind had been tricked by her desire. Reniat and Sola were both dead.

Distracted by her dream, she almost missed the arrival of the four they awaited. The approaching torch was near now, and she could see the shapes of the people: one very large, the others more normal in size. Three had drawn swords, and the fourth, whom they surrounded, carried the torch. She saw the big leader glance at their torches. He did not seem surprised to see no one with the torches, and as he motioned to his companions to fan out, Pleffin caught her eye. Rilsin nodded.

Pleffin leaped forward, his sword ready. Porit was right behind him. As the group turned, Rilsin realized what was so familiar about the big man at the front. Pleffin's sword was slicing forward in a deadly arc.

"Stop!" Rilsin shouted. "Sae Pleffin, hold! They are friends!"

Although he was already committed to the attack, Pleffin's training, experience, and control were excellent. He pulled back, barely avoiding wounding the leader of the little group.

"Chif, is that you?" Rilsin stepped forward from the shadows.

The big man turned, gaping. He had been ready to parry Pleffin's attack. His control was not quite as good as the Saeditin commander's, and he stumbled slightly as he aborted his defense.

"Who?" he cried, squinting in the torchlight. He blinked. "Rilsin SaeKet, is that you? Is you, by all gods!" Chif lowered his sword. "What you do here in caves?" The big man strode forward, and would have embraced her, had not Porit suddenly come between them.

Rilsin introduced the boy, and Chif, with all due solemnity, grasped his hands, as if Porit were a grown warrior. Pleffin he remembered from their joint campaign, when they had helped Rilsin regain the SaeKet's chair. During the greetings, Rilsin watched Chif's companions. The two men with Chif were surprised, but to Rilsin's eye it was an honest surprise, with nothing hidden. It did not escape her attention, however, that the young woman in the center of the little group, who bore the torch, started in surprise and something more when she heard Rilsin's name. She drew back slightly, and her eyes narrowed. Rilsin doubted she was Wilfrisin or Clinsi; something about her said otherwise.

"We are here by chance and not by plan," Rilsin told Chif. "We had to kill two Clinsi," she said, explaining how they had chased the raiders, fallen through the hillside, and wandered.

"Way out is near," Chif told them.

Rilsin nodded, seeing in her mind again the twists of the tunnels and passages beneath the earth. "It is that way," she nodded toward her left, "three, no, two chambers distant. There is a little crawl space upward."

"You have been here?" Chif was astonished. "Only Confederacy know these caves!"

Rilsin's eyes cleared. "No," she said, "I have never been here." She did not elaborate. "But we need to get out quickly."

A hoarse meow interrupted her. Chilsa had come up, unseen in the darkness, and was butting his head urgently against Rilsin's waist. Chif's party drew back at the sight of the big cat, and Rilsin saw the unnamed woman's eyes widen in fear. Rilsin reached down to scratch her cat behind the ears, and Chilsa meowed again, insistently.

"Meffa!"

Rilsin snatched up one of the torches she had propped in the rocks. She could hear the others behind her, following more slowly, as she hastened after Chilsa. The big cat had come for her because something was terribly wrong; she knew it.

The wavering light of the torch showed Meffa sitting up. She was holding her left arm gingerly, but she was conscious. Rilsin felt a wave of intense relief.

"Thank the Mother," whispered Meffa. "I saw the torches in the distance, but I knew you would never leave me, SaeKet."

"I would never leave you, Meffa." Rilsin felt tears sting behind her eyelids and was glad of the shadows. She knelt by her friend, but when Pleffin came up, she moved aside. Her commander had the experience that she did not. While he checked Meffa, Chif leaned forward, trying to see.

"She need doctor," the big man told Rilsin in a low voice. "Friend Sae Pleffin do good work, but she need medicine and good food and rest."

"I agree," said Rilsin. "We cannot stay here, but Meffa cannot walk."

"I can," said Meffa faintly but with determination.

"With your permission, Rilsin SaeKet, I carry."

Meffa stopped protesting after she tried to get to her feet and the pain almost caused her to faint again. Chif carried her easily in his arms, and Porit stayed beside them, refusing to let anyone come between him and his friend. Rilsin, with Chilsa pacing beside her, followed them. The way they went seemed somehow familiar to Rilsin now. Although she had never been there before, she recognized the winding side passage that narrowed and led upward.

TOΠAR, PRIΠCE OF House Merri, heir to northern Runchot, sat in his cold tent, as close to the covered fire pot as he could get without actually burning himself. Fire pots were all he would allow his troops right now. This close to the Demon Bridge, he did not want open fires. He could not risk being stopped now. He needed to get his troops across the natural bridge. The Clinsi scouts had brought them here and then left, having a superstitious fear of the landmark. Tonar did admit that it was impressive and even frightening. The passage was not something to be trifled with, and he had no desire to attempt it in the dark, and it was dusk when they came to the bridge. Once they were across, the next day, he intended to put his strategy into motion. He intended to split his forces in two and send them by differing routes. He wanted both forces to come as close to Petipal as possible before making their presence known. Then they would burn and lay waste what they could, which with any luck would include the Saeditin capital.

Tonar pulled his hood over his receding strawberry-blond hair. He was not fond of cold weather, and it was so much colder here than back home in Runchot. He wondered if it would be possible to read in what little daylight was left. He rummaged in his pack and drew out a book with great care. It had been published just this past year, in

Saeditin. It was a book on astronomy, extremely controversial, more so in Runchot than in Saeditin.

The heavens were Tonar's passion. One of the more fascinating essays in the little book had been written by Rilsin SaeKet Becha herself, one of Saeditin's foremost scholars. The piece was titled simply, "The Planets," and it proposed that those nearer stars did not circle the earth but circled the sun, as did the earth itself. Tonar found the idea audacious and excitingly plausible.

There was, unfortunately, not enough light by which to read. Tonar did not replace the book in his pack, however. Instead he held it close to him and thought about Rilsin sae Becha. She was brilliant, and it was obvious that she shared some of his own interests. Her sword skills were as formidable as his own, according to reports. He had heard, too, that she was beautiful. Tonar wished he could meet her.

Tonar had met enough beautiful women in his time, and he had taken several of them as mistresses. Despite this, he had never been at ease with them. All the women he had met had been conscious of his position as prince and had had their own advantage in mind. Tonar wanted a woman of his own rank, almost impossible to find in Runchot; he wanted a woman of intelligence equal to his, which might be impossible almost anywhere, and he did not feel at ease with sheer beauty.

He knew well enough that he was not beautiful himself. He had been cursed with a shape that was naturally rather round. Despite all his hard physical work, his practice at arms, and his work with the troops, nothing altered his shape. On top of that, he was short. And his hair, the red-blond shade that he shared with his sister, made him look rather washed out. Even worse, it was now thinning and receding away from his brow. Tonar did not trust the attentions of beautiful women, because he could not believe they would be attracted to a man as unprepossessing as he.

Despite his poor assessment of his physical charms, Tonar knew his own intelligence, and he had supreme confidence in the abilities of his mind. He could outthink anyone he had ever met, and that included his father, Prince Raphat. Tonar knew his father did not value him. It did not matter that he was his father's heir. Raphat had supreme confidence and supreme, blind self-interest, too. If Tonar should die in this endeavor, it did not matter to his father, because Raphat believed himself capable of getting another heir at will. Also, Raphat seemed not to believe that a time would ever come for an heir to be necessary.

None of this bothered Tonar. He did not intend to die on this campaign. He knew his military skills as well as his intelligence. He intended to complete his mission and to survive, and more than that, to cement his own power base in Runchot. If he could burn Petipal, his position would be unassailable. Perhaps in the course of this, he might meet Rilsin sae Becha. These circumstances, of course, would not be conducive to discussions of astronomy or other intellectual matters. In reality he knew that the only way he would meet the SaeKet would be in battle, if she captured him, or, if he were lucky, if he took her captive. Tonar knew this last was not likely, but he allowed himself the fantasy. He was not physically attractive, but he was intelligent, and he had always been one other thing. He had always been lucky.

18

THEY EMERGED INTO A WINDY WILDERNESS OF SNOW-covered scrub and a rocky hillside. Meffa was shivering almost uncontrollably in Chif's arms, and one of the Wilfrisin pulled a robe from a pack and used this to wrap her.

Rilsin drew in a deep breath. The stinging wind felt wonderful, and the gray, cloudy day seemed brilliant after the darkness of the caves. She found herself smiling, feeling as if all the weight of the earth had been lifted from her. She could feel the eyes of Chif's companion, the unnamed woman, resting on her, and when she returned the gaze, the lightness of relief began to drain from her. There was something not only troubled but troubling in that look, and in the light of day she looked much younger than she had in the caves. *She's still a girl,* thought Rilsin. She frowned, puzzled, and took a step forward, noting as she did so that the girl was far more beautiful than she had originally noticed. And there were red-blonde roots growing through her dark hair.

Phara saw the Saeditin woman step toward her with a

questioning look. *The SaeKet,* Phara told herself. Chif knew her, and Chif had called her "Rilsin SaeKet." The ruler of Saeditin, her enemy from birth. However unlikely it was that the leader of this neighbor nation should have been lost in the caves, it did not surprise Phara, especially in light of her own travels. What did surprise her was how old the SaeKet seemed. Rilsin SaeKet Becha was only a few years older than Phara, but there was gray in her hair and lines around her eyes, but more than that, there was an air of command about her. In this regard she reminded Phara of her father, and Phara took a step back.

Rilsin saw the girl back away from her, and her puzzled frown deepened. Why would she be afraid? She stepped across the rocky scree of the hillside toward the girl and then gasped, her attention torn away by a stunning sight behind the younger woman. A natural stone span arched gently, curving away from them across a vast and misty depth. It looked impossibly thin and tenuous, for all that it was stone. The snow around the base of the span was trampled and scuffed and dirty, as if a great many people had recently passed there.

"The Demon Bridge," said Pleffin, stepping up beside her. "We are on the Confederacy side."

Rilsin strode to the flat land at the edge of the cliff. The snow was dirty with more than just dust and churned-up earth. Rilsin stared at the debris: horse dung, mostly frozen now, but also other things. She picked up a piece of leather and trailed it through her hand. It was a bit of broken rein. There was a partially eaten bread crust and other trash. A large number of people had passed this way recently. *Troops,* she thought. They were not hers, not Saeditin's. She picked up a torn russet hood that someone had cast off or lost.

"The Runchot winter army," she said.

Phara heard the steel and ice in the other woman's voice and drew in her breath. Her brother had already taken his troops out of Confederate territory, across this impossible ribbon of stone, and into Saeditin. Alarm and a fierce pride blazed up simultaneously within her, and she felt blood rush up into her face. She looked up to find Chif watching her, and she knew her blush deepened.

The others were talking, milling around. Sae Pleffin, *Commander Pleffin,* Phara reminded herself, had taken out a long-glass and was examining the Demon Bridge. She heard him swear.

"Out in the middle there; look." Pleffin handed the long-glass to Rilsin. "They have done what they can to smash the stone, to destroy the bridge."

"Hard work with hammers and hands," said Rilsin, peering through the glass. "Who did they think was behind them? Not us, surely."

"Wilfrisin," said Chif. "Confederates, my people, with First Man Bilt. At least, they not want to take chance of it." Rilsin had passed him the glass, and he gazed through it briefly before handing it back. "They have destroyed bridge in middle. There is piece missing."

Rilsin snatched the long-glass from his hand and looked again. He was right. A section of the natural stone bridge, which had spanned this chasm for ages, had been smashed completely, leaving a gap in the elegant line of the stone.

"Great freezing Runchot hells!" said Rilsin, aware of the irony of her oath. "We are too late. We have to get word south fast. We can't follow the Runchot by the bridge and slip by them on the other side. We will have to go around." She slapped the long-glass against her palm in frustration. "Sae Pleffin, you must go now, as quickly as possible. Leave Meffa. We will take care of her. Get to the army. And get word to Sae Essit as fast as you can."

"You must come with me, SaeKet," said Pleffin. "Perhaps we can leave Ria Meffa with our Wilfrisin friends. You must get to the army."

"Yes," agreed Rilsin. Whatever she had lost, whomever she had lost, Saeditin remained, and her vow to the land. She would ask Chif to take Meffa to safety, and Porit—

"Runchot troops," said Chif. He spoke in Wilfrisin. Something in his voice stopped Pleffin and made Rilsin

turn to stare at him. He was not looking at her, however, but
at the girl. "Runchot troops," he said again, still in Wilfrisin. "So that was the mission. Just why did you need to
find your brother, though, I wonder?" He was speaking
more to himself than to any of them.

Rilsin understood the Wilfrisin words, but for a moment
the meaning escaped her. Looking at the girl, she could see
just the opposite. The girl obviously did not speak Wilfrisin, but she seemed to guess the gist of Chif's words. Before Rilsin could work at this puzzle, Chif repeated himself,
this time in Saeditin.

"So that is secret mission, Phara Princess," he said.
"That is mission of your brother, to bring Runchot army
through our lands, without our knowledge."

Phara stared at Chif, the color burning still higher in her
face. "Don't tell me you didn't guess!" she said. "Don't tell
me that! I told you who I was!"

"I did not guess, Phara Princess, even though I believed
who you are. I thought—" Chif stopped. In truth, he did not
know exactly what he had thought. He had no time to pursue it.

"Phara," said Rilsin. She took a step toward the girl.
"Princess Phara of House Merri, daughter of Raphat. Sister
of Prince Tonar, Raphat's commander." Without realizing
it, her hand had dropped to her sword.

Phara took a step back and then another. She saw the
way the Saeditin ruler looked at her, and she felt the men-
ace, but for the moment, it didn't matter. Even her brother
didn't matter. Runchot didn't matter, the looming war that
it seemed she could not stop was not important. What was
important was Chif and the way he was looking at her, as
though she had let him down.

She hadn't told him. She had meant to tell him. Had she
really thought he had guessed? That he knew why she was
here? No, not really, not if she were honest with herself.
She had hoped he would guess. In his eyes she saw sadness
and something else. She wanted to explain, but now she
couldn't.

"Prince Tonar thinks to come down from the north and take my capital between his forces and those of your father." Rilsin stepped toward Phara, intent on the younger woman. "I want to know what you are doing here, Princess Phara, and how you fit into this plan. I want to know it now!" Rilsin's voice cracked sharply, bouncing back from the rocky cliff. "What are you doing here?"

"If I told you, you wouldn't believe me!"

"Try me."

Phara stared at the Saeditin woman. Suddenly all of the events of the past months seemed to crash over her in waves. Her mother's death, her flight from home, her recruitment by Kirra, her discovery of her father's plans and her brother's danger, her second flight, this time into Saeditin, almost losing her life in the forest, and her rescue by Chif—wave after wave. She couldn't come up for air, and she would drown. She gave a strange, inarticulate cry and whirled. Before anyone could think to stop her, she was sprinting across the Demon Bridge.

They stared after her in shock. Chif was the first to react. He lunged forward and almost caught her, but her trailing cloak just escaped his fingers.

"Phara! Wait!" He was after her, running out onto the stone arch. His men remained on the hillside, looking confused.

"Where does she think she's going?" asked Porit. "The bridge is broken!"

"She can't go anywhere," Pleffin agreed. "Chif will bring her back."

Not so, Rilsin thought suddenly. Phara had no intention of coming back.

"Sae Pleffin," she said, "you must get to the army, whatever happens now. Send Meffa with the Wilfrisin." Before he could respond, she, too, stepped out onto the Demon Bridge.

The span was wide enough for several people to walk abreast, or even people and horses. This was, after all, how Tonar's troops had crossed. But the span didn't seem so

wide when you were on it, Rilsin thought. The wind
seemed to leap out of the depths below as well as the
heights above, and it buffeted Rilsin and tore at her cloak.
She glanced down and froze.

Below her the walls of the canyon swept down and
down, an incredible distance. Occasional, scrubby bushes
clung to the cliff sides, but then the walls became too steep
even for the tough plants, the drop too sheer. The opposite
cliff seemed as far away as a dream. Down at the very bottom of the canyon, impossibly far beneath, crawled a silver
river, made slender as a thread by the vast height. Below the
thin stone on which she stood, an eagle circled and banked
into the wind. Odd little wisps of mist floated near the
eagle. *Clouds,* Rilsin thought.

She forced herself to breathe. She wrapped her cloak
tightly around herself and looked up from the depths. She
wanted to close her eyes to erase her fear, but she did not
dare. She focused on the stone beneath her feet and the
stone of the arch directly in front of her, and took a step.
She forced herself to take another, until she was moving
steadily along the Demon Bridge.

She kept herself from thinking of anything but her
progress along the stone. She hadn't been afraid like this in
the caves, even with the knowledge of the weight of the
earth above her head, even when she saw the fear of those
with her. She hadn't been afraid like this in battle. She wondered if any of the Runchot troops had felt this way when
they crossed the bridge. Ahead of her she could see Chif
and Phara huddled together, talking. The girl made a sudden gesture, and her cloak whipped out from her shoulders,
flying across the side of the Demon Bridge and over the
chasm like a flag, until she pulled it back. Rilsin swallowed.

Behind her she could hear cries and footsteps. She was
being followed by both Pleffin and Porit; she knew their
voices. Something brushed against her legs, almost making
her lose her balance. She glanced down. It was Chilsa.
Somehow, his presence steadied her.

After what seemed an age of wind and stone, she drew

close enough to Chif and Phara to hear snatches of their conversation. They were speaking in Saeditin, but the buffeting wind tore away words and the sense that went with them.

". . . must be stopped," said Phara.

"You could have . . ." said Chif. ". . . believe you . . ." he said.

His hand was on her arm. Just beyond where they stood, the stone span of the Demon Bridge stopped. It crumbled into jagged splinters hanging out over the void. Not too far away but more than far enough, after an expanse of nothingness, the bridge began again, in more splinters and jaggedness.

Phara glanced away from Chif and back along the expanse of the Demon Bridge. Her eyes widened when she saw how close Rilsin was. Chif turned and saw her, releasing his grasp on Phara's arm.

"I can't," said Phara, clearly. "I won't." She turned to Chif. "I cannot trust her! I will not let her take me to Petipal, a captive! Whatever you believe, Chif, she will not believe me! And I must get to Tonar! This must stop! It's the only way!"

Chif opened his mouth to say something. Rilsin stepped forward. She wanted to assure Phara that she would not harm her, that there was no reason to fear her. Was it true? Rilsin felt that she had lost everything but Saeditin, and she would do anything and everything to protect her land now. Whatever she intended to say, Phara read something else in her eyes. She tied her cloak around her waist with a sudden, brisk motion. Then she ran toward Rilsin.

Astonished, Rilsin backed up a step, afraid the Runchot woman would charge straight into her. Phara did not. Before she reached where Rilsin stood, she spun, turned, and raced back toward Chif, picking up speed. Chif saw her coming and held out his hand, but Phara ignored it. She sprinted past him, running right to the edge of the jagged stone. Then she leaped.

Chif shouted and lunged for her but missed, just barely

catching himself before he lost his balance and tumbled over the edge. Rilsin heard shouts behind her, and she knew that she herself cried out. She sprinted forward, stopping beside Chif at the edge of the bridge.

"Phara!" cried Chif.

The Runchot girl had not fallen. The speed of the run had carried into the forward motion of her leap. It had flung her across the open space of the broken bridge to the other side. She clung now to the jagged stone that leaned across the gulf, and as they watched, she pulled herself up and onto the bridge itself. She paused for a moment, looking back across at them, the wind whipping her hair and clothing. She locked eyes with Chif, who reached out a hand as if he could touch her. Then she turned and walked away, down the expanse of the Demon Bridge, following the trail of her brother.

"No," said Rilsin. "She can't get to Tonar!" She turned to find Pleffin beside her.

"We can't stop her now," he said. "All we can do is try to get to the army as fast as we can, and—"

"I can stop her!" Before anyone could react, Porit leaped, flinging himself into space.

"No!" Rilsin cried.

"Great Mother!" said Pleffin.

The boy had jumped from a standstill, and they firmly expected to see him plummet down to the canyon. But he caught himself on one of the broken overhangs on the opposite side, and agilely swung himself up. He waved at them, completely at ease.

"I will get her, SaeKet!" he called across the gap, and turned to sprint after Phara.

Several things happened with such rapidity that Rilsin, thinking about it later, was not sure which came first. Chif slipped on the ragged edge of the broken Demon Bridge. Pleffin saw him slide and stepped forward, grabbing him. He pulled the Wilfrisin to safety, but the combined weight of the two big men on the shattered stone caused a piece of rock to break away. They pulled back, but Rilsin, standing toward the edge of the stone, fell forward.

She was aware of the stone cracking and then of the sudden lurch as the rock beneath her feet fell away. They told her later that she did not scream. She believed it; there wasn't time. She was aware of falling, and she leaned forward and stretched up. She felt something scrape against her legs: the side of the bridge. She kicked out against this and flung herself forward rather than back. It was this that saved her.

For an endless moment she fell forward. She was aware of the wind around her, and the river far below, and the rocky cliffs. The land sang to her even here, a song of stone and river, and the animal lives in the canyon below. She felt the great eagle circling, and for a moment it was as if she flew. Her hands reached out, and she caught herself on a shattered rocky overhang and clung tightly. She looked down. She was on the other side of the gap.

She hung precariously below the bridge. She tried to find purchase with her feet, but there was nothing below her. The exhilaration vanished. She swung there, feeling her fingers beginning to numb and slip, feeling the stone beginning to crack. Across the gap, she was peripherally aware of the shouts of Pleffin, and of Chif and the Wilfrisin. Then a boy's face appeared above her, upside down.

"SaeKet!" said Porit. "Take my hand."

The promised hand appeared, dangling just above her head. She let go with her left hand, and stretched upward. Porit's fingers closed around hers, he pulled, and her right hand slid from the stone. There was a sharp crack, and the stone under Porit gave way.

The boy scrambled back, pulling hard. Rilsin felt as though her hand would rip away from her arm. For a moment, it seemed as if he could, by strength of will, pull them both to safety. Then her hand slipped through Porit's.

Something hit Rilsin hard from behind. There was the snap of teeth closing at the neck of her shirt. Then Rilsin was lifted and scraped along the rough edge of the broken

Demon Bridge. Her sword banged against her legs, and the surface of the stone abraded her palms. She hit with a force that knocked the air from her lungs, and she lay, briefly stunned, on the far side of the Demon Bridge. Chilsa panted above her, and with a soft grunt began to lick her face. Rilsin sat up.

Chilsa sat back and chuffed at her. Rilsin drew her hand across her face. Her hand was bloody, and little bits of stone and dirt were ground into the palm. Porit was lying on the stone near her, the wind knocked out of him by the force of Chilsa's landing. Chilsa leaned forward and sniffed Rilsin's hand. She pulled it back before he could lick her palm.

"I'm fine, Chilsa," she told the cat. She began to shiver. "Porit, are you all right?"

"Fine, SaeKet." Porit sat up. It was true; he looked none the worse for almost falling off a cliff.

Rilsin stood. Across the near distance, Pleffin and Chif still stood. Both were pale, and Chif looked as if he might faint. She walked closer, but kept a fair distance from the edge.

"Sae Pleffin!" she called.

"SaeKet! Thank the Mother!"

"Yes," said Rilsin. She was more inclined to give the credit to her cat. "Listen to me. You must get between Tonar's troops and Petipal, and get word to Essit that Raphat is coming over the border. Do you hear me?"

"I hear you, SaeKet!"

"I bring First Man down with troops, if you need!" bellowed Chif.

"I need!" said Rilsin. "And take care of Meffa. Sae Pleffin, I will meet up with you, wherever you are. I will find you."

"I have no doubt, SaeKet!" Pleffin put his hand to his heart.

There was nothing else to be done. Rilsin turned away. When she glanced back, she could see the figures of the men growing smaller as they made their way back along the

Demon Bridge, back to the Confederate side. She turned and looked at Porit and Chilsa.

"Let's go," she said.

As she began to walk down the remains of the Demon Bridge into Saeditin, she almost turned back to look down at the canyon. For a moment, a brief moment, she thought she felt below her two lives tossed on the silver thread of river: Sola and Reniat. Rilsin paused. Then she shook her head. Dreams and wishes, she thought; they weren't real. Saeditin was real. Saeditin could be saved. She continued down the bridge.

SOLA HAD FOLLOWED the river through the caves as long as it was possible. He had to carry the torch, their supplies, and usually Reniat, too. This was hard enough by itself. Doing it on the stony bank of an underground river was difficult far beyond anything he had imagined. It became progressively more so as the river began to flow faster. The stone banks became steeper, and the walls of the cave closed in closer and closer to the water. At one point they had to crawl, and Sola had to push Reniat ahead of him. He was desperately afraid that she would slip and fall into the water, which was boiling over hidden rocks. He was so afraid for her that his attention wandered, and he lost his own footing, just barely catching himself in time. He almost lost the torch then, too. Reniat came back to him and threw her arms around his neck.

"Don't worry," she told him earnestly. "It gets bigger. Soon."

She was right. They inched their way precariously around a tiny ledge that hung over the river. The light of the torch illuminated the little path and not the water, but they could hear the rush of the current. Reniat wobbled along the path ahead of him, but Sola held her hand tightly. The path broadened. Reniat skipped to the side, and Sola lifted the torch, alarmed that she would fall into the dark water he heard below them.

The light of the torch illuminated a broad cavern with a

flat stone floor. Near them, the floor sloped down to the
river. Sola held the torch higher and almost cried out with
surprise. The cavern broadened, and the river broadened,
too. The current was still swift; he could see the swell of the
water over the occasional submerged rock, but it no longer
rushed with its former ferocity. And where the rock floor of
the cave came to the water's edge was something Sola did
not believe. He blinked and would have rubbed his eyes but
for the fact that his hands were filled. Beached tranquilly
beside the underground river was a boat. As Sola stared,
Reniat pulled away and toddled over to it.

"Wait!" said Sola. There was something almost supernatural about finding a boat just there. When he looked at
it, however, it was perfectly ordinary. It had oars, and it
seemed in sound condition. Sola wondered what had happened to the person who had brought the boat in, how often
this river was used, and for what.

Reniat climbed over the side and settled herself comfortably on the boat's bottom. Sola wedged the torch into a
slot on the bow that looked as if it had been made for just
such a purpose. He placed the oars in the oarlocks, pushed
the boat into the current, and jumped in. The river caught
them, pulled them out into the channel, and they were off,
rushing through the darkness of the caves.

He had to use the oars to push the boat away from the
cavern walls, as rowing served no purpose. The current
picked up speed as the caves narrowed, and Sola doubted
he could stop the boat now if he had to. There was a roaring from up ahead that grew louder by the second. They
were being borne along in the center of the current, so Sola
edged to the front of the boat. At first he saw nothing but
the bounce of torchlight on the black river, but then he saw
a glimmer, straight ahead. It grew.

"Out!" said Reniat, happily. She giggled.

The roaring grew louder. With a flash of horror, Sola realized what it was.

"Hold on, Reniat!" he cried.

He threw himself over the child, clutching her to him.

The river-flung them around a bend, and the light was right in front of them, blinding. It was the cavern's exit. Sola saw a flat riverbank, a place to pull over and beach the boat. There were stairs carved into the rock behind the little beach. But you had to know the beach was there, you had to be ready for it, if you wanted to pull out of the river. Sola saw it too late. The boat flew, straight as an arrow, past the beach and over the curving edge of the falls.

They were falling, with the rush of water around them, and the white foam and the spray. Sola had Reniat pinned beneath him, his arms outflung, clutching the sides of the boat, trying to anchor them both. He was terrified that Reniat would fall out or that he would fall out and leave Reniat alone in the boat, hurtling down the river. More likely, they would both fall out and drown in the tumult of river and rock. He saw rocks and water, and for a moment his death grip on the wooden slats of the boat was all that kept them both from flying up and out and into the churning water.

Then, suddenly, it was over. The roaring faded a little, and the boat was still upright and afloat. More miraculous, they were still in it. Sola sat up.

They were out in the open air, under a high and cloudy sky. Behind them, the waterfall tumbled down from the mouth of the cave, shouting its wild song. As a shaft of sun broke through the clouds, and rainbows danced in the falls. But more astonishing than the falls was the landscape through which the river now carried them. Soaring up on either side of their tiny boat were the red walls of a magnificent canyon.

The walls rose up and up, rusty red and orange and salmon, in jagged slabs and crumbles of stone. In some places there were what looked like thin paths, perhaps animal trails, that narrowed and vanished, and here and there scruffy bushes clung, along with patches of snow. High above, an eagle soared and banked, among wisps of cloud. Higher still, and for a moment directly above them, was a thin arch of stone, impossibly high and far: the Demon

Bridge. The slowing current carried them under and away, but as he looked up, Sola could see that a portion of the bridge had been broken. Then the river carried them on.

"Mama!" cried Reniat. The little girl was staring back and up at the broken stone arch of the bridge. Sola felt a pang. He had to get her home safely to Rilsin; he had to.

He got the oars back into the oarlocks, took his seat, and began to row. He was soaking wet from their journey through the falls. Reniat, sitting at his feet, was soaked, too. She no longer bounced or giggled, and she was shivering. Sola realized he had to get them off the river, find some shelter, and build a fire to get them dry. Thankfully, the current had lessened as the river broadened.

Just ahead, there was a small, sandy beach where the cliff wall had been eaten back by the river. Sola leaned hard on the oars, pulling them across the current. He heard the bottom of the boat scrape against the sand, and then he was out, pulling the boat up on the shore. His legs felt wobbly, and he collapsed on the sand. Reniat half-climbed, half-fell out of the boat to come up beside him. Sola reached out to pull the girl to him. He was more relieved than he could have imagined to know that she was still safely with him. He hugged her and was about to help her get out of her wet clothing, when she pulled away from him.

"Look!" she said. "Dada Sola, look!"

Sola looked. Coming toward them were several people dressed in furs and leather. Barbarians. Northerners. Confederates. Sola was unarmed, and his teeth were chattering. There was no time to find a weapon. He put Reniat behind him and rose to his feet.

19

Whatever Raphat thought, and Sithli had a good idea what he thought about bringing her along on a military action, she was not going to be left behind. She was going on this campaign. Sithli would not be without her comforts, of course; there was no reason to think otherwise, but she was not going to let Raphat take Petipal and Saeditin without her. She was not going to let Kepit sae Lisim and Raphat together go anywhere near her capital without her. She needed to stand up for her interests, as she always had.

Well, perhaps not always. Sithli remembered when she had been SaeKet and Rilsin was not only first minister but loyal to her. It seemed to her that she had been able to count on Rilsin to look after everything for her and to always put her first. She had once been able to trust Rilsin almost more than she trusted herself.

The wave of sorrow and regret that washed over her was so intense that Sithli felt suddenly dizzy. Why had Rilsin changed? She walked to the window, feeling sorry for herself, more sorry than she could have explained. Outside, it had begun to sleet, and the day was as gray and dreary as she felt. For a moment she wished again for the old times. She missed Rilsin's friendship.

"SaeKet. Are you well?"

Sithli turned. How long had Kepit been standing there, watching her?

"Quite well."

"I have Kirra's reports here, SaeKet. Her troops will be ready to cross the border within two weeks."

"I will be ready to lead them." Sithli turned to look at the woman who would be her first minister when she returned to Saeditin.

"Wonderful," said Kepit calmly. "I will make the preparations for you."

Sithli stared at her, surprised. She had expected to hear objections, put forward with all the force of Kepit's logical mind, as to why it would be best for her to stay in Runchot until all was safe in Saeditin. Maybe she was wrong to suspect that Kepit had anything other than the best for her in mind. Maybe Sithli had simply needed to take charge sooner.

"I was afraid you would not wish to cross the border until all was safely ready for you," said Kepit smoothly. "But it is very important that you be there, especially when we move on Petipal. Rest assured, SaeKet, that everything will be done to assure your safety and your comfort." Kepit had no desire to keep Sithli safe in Runchot, not when so many accidents could happen in the field or on the road.

"Good." Sithli smiled with relief. "I will want this couch to go with me; it is the most comfortable of the ones Raphat has given us. And enough furs for warmth. How will my tent be heated, Sae Kepit? This is nasty weather. I must not become ill." Sithli looked out again at the sleet.

"It is a campaign, SaeKet." By sheer will, Kepit managed to keep smiling, but she couldn't keep the acidity completely from her voice. "We cannot take with us all the luxuries of home." She saw Sithli begin to pout, and she couldn't resist digging further. "You must be willing to sacrifice a little for your people."

"I am the SaeKet! I will be treated like the SaeKet, no matter where I am!"

"Of course." *I really must control myself better,* Kepit thought. It was becoming increasingly difficult, however, the closer she came to being rid of Sithli. If she weren't careful, the former SaeKet would back out and decide to stay behind in the relative haven of Raphat's town house. Not that she couldn't deal with this contingency if she had to, but Sithli in the field would be a much easier proposition.

"I will make sure you have whatever is necessary for your comfort." Kepit turned to leave. "With your permission, SaeKet."

Sithli waved her out and watched her go with a sense of gratification. She was still able to control those around her, even saedin like Kepit sae Lisim. It was certainly time for her to return to her own land, to retake the leadership of Saeditin.

On the other side of the door, Kepit stood for a moment, getting herself under control. *Idiot,* she thought. She couldn't have said if she was thinking of Sithli or of herself.

ESSIT WAS PACING. The troops were called up, and he was ready to leave for the border, but the weather was in the way. It almost seemed as if the storm had sprung up deliberately to slow him down.

He stared out at the sleet, which had turned to snow and then back to sleet again, coating everything with ice. "We need to move! Damned weather," he muttered.

"Sometimes there is a good reason behind a seeming setback, some purpose not apparent to us right away," said Dremfir.

Essit started. He had forgotten for a moment that the little priest had come in at his request.

"Can you sense when this storm will break?" Essit came

directly to the point. He had small use for religious explanations; in that he was like his SaeKet.

"No, First Minister, I cannot, but not for lack of trying. As you know, sometimes the gift does not work."

It would have to fail now, Essit thought. *So what use is it?* He didn't say it. "Try again, if you would, Mage."

He turned from Dremfir back to the window. He would have to take the troops south in any event, as fast as was possible, however bad the weather. At least, in this weather, he need not worry about leaving more than a token force to protect Petipal. If he had trouble moving south, the invaders from Runchot could not possibly cross the border and threaten the capital before he could move against them.

Engaged in his thoughts and trying to give Dremfir the quiet for him to use his weather sense, it was a moment before he realized that one of the Petipal guards was standing in the doorway, trying to get his attention. Essit felt overburdened. He wished again, desperately, that his SaeKet were here. It made him more than a little uneasy to govern in her stead.

"It's urgent," said the guard. "This messenger says he has ridden south from Hoptrin without pause. I believe him, First Minister; he looks terrible. He says he is from Commander Pleffin."

Essit's head jerked up, and he crossed the room in three strides.

"Send him in!"

The messenger looked as bad as the guard had said, but Essit barely noticed.

"Sae Pleffin has been found?" Essit could barely contain his rising excitement. "And the SaeKet?"

"Commander Pleffin, yes," said the man, "but not the SaeKet. The commander says she is alive, but I have not seen her with my own eyes."

Essit almost ripped the dispatch from the man's hands, tearing it open, only belatedly thinking to send the messenger off for well-deserved rest and food. He read the dispatch and then stared up and out at the snow again. Without a word, he handed it to Dremfir. Dremfir read it but said nothing, and Essit appreciated his restraint.

"Some troops must stay to defend Petipal, until Commander Pleffin can get here. But I must go south. Sithli's forces *will* come over the border." He looked at Dremfir. "Sae Pleffin will try to meet Tonar's force before he can bring it south, and we must hope he can stop them. I have had no reports of enemies moving within our borders, but that is not surprising, considering the weather."

"The weather will break tonight," said Dremfir. He met Essit's surprised gaze. "I don't know, any more than you, why my gift works when it does and fails when it does. There are those brother priests in my order who say it is at the will of the Mother." Dremfir smiled slightly. "Whatever the truth of that, I can feel the winds shifting. The storm will pass tonight." He handed the message back to Essit and put his hand on the other man's arm. "She's alive, Essit. Pleffin says he saw her safe on the other side of the Demon Bridge with Chilsa and with the commoner boy."

Both men pondered this for a moment.

"How do you know she is alive and safe?" Essit hoped, ironically, that Dremfir had some magical surety on this.

"We both know the SaeKet. You know Rilsin as well as I. What do you think?"

CHIF WAS HOPING against hope to reach Wilfrisin territory and bring the news in time. First Man Bilt needed to call up his warriors. They had known the Clinsi were unhappy, but that any member of the new Confederacy should allow enemy troops passage to attack their neighbor was unthinkable. If Bilt did not act, the Confederacy was dead.

There was something else that was even more unthinkable, or at least that Chif wished to think of even less. He had no reason to expect that Phara would have trusted him with her true purpose. Nonetheless, Chif felt betrayed. He had known her such a short time; he did not understand why he felt so terrible about this, why he could not get his mind from her.

In an effort to clear his thoughts, Chif moved ahead of his companion, walking along the edge of the canyon. It was only the two of them, Chif and Olu, as the third member of their party had been sent south with Sae Pleffin, to help with Meffa. Chif did not mind. Pleffin needed the help to get her back, and Chif could travel just as fast with one companion as with two. He would have gone to Bilt by himself, but two of them gave better insurance that one would make it through alive, if trouble came. The Wilfrisin must be warned.

A flicker of motion from below drew his attention. Chif dropped flat to the ground. There were people on the bank of the river, looking small with the distance. Drawn up on the bank was a boat. Chif would have given much just then for the use of Sae Pleffin's long-glass. The boat could only be the boat from the Cavern of Waters, the boat the Wilfrisin kept there, a tradition and a safety, for a quick passage downriver to their lands. Who could have taken it, and for what purpose?

Olu had taken his cue and dropped when Chif dropped, and now he crawled up next to him. Chif pointed with his chin at the cliff edge, and Olu peered over. Chif nodded at him, and Olu nodded back. It was unlikely that they would have been overheard by the party below, but who knew what others might be lurking nearby. Both Wilfrisin reverted, automatically, to silent stalking protocol. Chif made a hand sign; Olu nodded. They moved silently back from the cliff edge.

By the time they were down the cliffside, having taken a path made by the wild goats of the canyon, the sun was sinking. The cold seemed even worse down in the canyon, and there was ice along the rocks at the river's edge, where the moving water had stilled. In front of them, under the shelter of the cliff, a fire was burning, with several people around it. They could hear snatches and drifts of words and laughter from those near the fire. The words were in Clinsi.

Olu moved to the left, Chif to the right, both of them with their large knives in their hands. The plan was to rush in from both sides, kill as many Clinsi as possible in the initial surprise, but take one of them captive, for information. There were four men, all seated close to the fire's warmth, eating and passing waterskins. There was someone else near the fire, too, Chif saw. A child, bundled into furs, only a small lump in the flickering shadows. He frowned. Why would Clinsi raiders or scouts have a child with them? Was this a stolen Saeditin child, or worse, a stolen Wilfrisin baby? Chif caught Olu's eye. They both shouted in concert and leaped forward.

Sola was in the act of taking the waterskin from one of the Clinsi when the dusk erupted with Wilfrisin battle cries, and two huge warriors charged their fire. Shocked, he dropped the waterskin and leaped to his feet. One of the charging Wilfrisin grabbed him by the shoulder; Sola tried to twist away, thinking of Reniat, afraid for her. As he twisted, he caught a glimpse of the second Wilfrisin warrior, an enormous man with blue hair and a bright red beard.

"Chif! Chif, is that you!"

The blue-haired man gaped. "Sola dira! Is that truly you?" He spoke in Wilfrisin, but Sola understood.

"Yes!" he shouted.

"Olu, stop! This man is a friend!"

Olu had already determined as much and aborted his knife attack. He still held Sola by the shoulder, however, in a tight grip.

The confusion and momentary delay had cost the Wilfrisin their advantage. Two of the Clinsi warriors had drawn their knives and were advancing, intent on Olu, while the third moved toward Chif. Chif realized First Man Bilt might not get his warning, after all. He and Olu were outnumbered, with Sola an unknown quantity. Chif prepared to fight to the death.

"Stop!" shouted Sola, in Clinsi, to the Clinsi. "Do not them kill! They friends be, and we must make them peace!"

To Chif's complete and utter astonishment, the Clinsi ceased their attack and lowered their weapons. He stared at them, tense, his own knife still at the ready.

"Please, Chif friend," said Sola, this time in Wilfrisin, "not kill, not kill, important is that—damn!" Sola pulled away from the equally astonished Olu. He frowned. "I can't think in more than one dialect at a time!" he said in Saeditin.

"Then speak in your own language, Sola dira," said Chif, also in Saeditin. "These Clinsi, do they understand it?"

"No." Sola shook his head, straightening up. He was relieved to see that no one looked ready to resume hostilities immediately. He tried to look for Reniat from the corner of his eye. He was afraid to look more directly, to draw attention to her before the situation was more settled.

"Then explain now, in your own Saeditin, what you do with these Clinsi."

"They are going to escort me over the border and see me to safety." Sola tugged at his clothes; his fur-lined parka, a gift from his new Clinsi companions, was slightly large on him and had been pulled up in the struggle. "You need to know, Chif, that Runchot troops have come through Clinsi lands into Saeditin. They are going to attack Saeditin, attack Petipal! I have to get word to Rilsin SaeKet!"

"She knows."

Sola stared. "How can she know?"

"She knows. But if Clinsi let Runchot go through, to attack your land, how is it you, Sola dira, you, a Saeditin, are with Clinsi?" said Chif. Chif liked Sola and had worked with him in the past, but he was loyal to Wilfrisin and the Confederacy. If Sola had betrayed his own land and his own SaeKet, and in doing so had harmed the Confederacy, Chif would kill him. That he himself would probably die almost immediately thereafter did not matter.

"I am with these Clinsi because they helped me from the river." Sola spoke now in Clinsi. It was the worst of his languages, but he wanted the Clinsi with him to understand completely. He knew Chif would understand, although he was not sure of Chif's companion. He also saw the way Chif still held his knife, the way Chif looked at him. He knew, without a doubt, what was on the Wilfrisin warrior's mind.

"They help me from river, give to me food, and fire make, and dry clothing." Sola glanced sideways at the Clinsi, who stood together in the flickering firelight. They still held their knives, but had let them fall to their sides. They were listening. "Not all Clinsi want to see the Confederacy fail."

Sola was right, Chif thought, but he did not take his eyes from the young Saeditin. "And these Clinsi are loyal Confederates, you say?" he asked in Clinsi.

"We are now." One of the Clinsi spoke up. "We were not, not so long ago. We are of the band of Egroji, our first man. First man no longer, not in our eyes. Not since this warrior defeated the demons and slew them on the altar at Solstice." He looked at Sola and dipped his head in respect. "Egroji will not be first man in the eyes of others, when they hear what this warrior says."

Chif stared, looking from the Clinsi to Sola and back. "Sola Dira is the Solstice Warrior Victorious?"

Sola shifted his stance a little. He wished Chif did not sound quite so incredulous.

"He is," said the Clinsi leader. "He and the Suncat fled into the earth after the battle. We followed them and found them, with the boat, on the side of the river, just as the Sun Warrior and the Suncat came from the earth in the beginning days of legend. That this warrior is Saeditin does not matter. Sola has explained to us the links between our lands and his, and the help his SaeKet will give to us, how good it is if we are Saeditin's friends, if the Confederacy is strong."

"If all Clinsi remain in the Confederacy," added a second Clinsi. "We will see to it, after we help Sola return to his own land, where he will speak for us to his first man the SaeKet."

Chif heard the ring of truth. He looked at Sola with surprise. The man had a reputation as a magician in his own land, and it seemed there was something to it. Chif had known him as brilliant and brave, but not a strong warrior. There was obviously even more to him than Chif had guessed. But something else was niggling at his mind.

"The Suncat." Olu said it first. "The Suncat accompanies the bravest of Solstice Warriors, in the form of a gold hunting cat or a little child with golden hair. Where is the Suncat you spoke of?"

"Can I come out now, Dada Sola?" asked a little voice in Saeditin. "Nobody is fighting anymore."

As one, the men turned. Reniat was sitting up, half out of the fur in which she had been bundled. The firelight glinted on her golden hair. She held out her arms to Sola, who picked her up. For a moment no one spoke. The fire spat out a shower of sparks as a log split, and the wind sighed down the cliffside. The sun had set, and the winter dark had descended.

"The Suncat is Warrior Sola's child," said one of the Clinsi.

Sola swallowed. Not all the Clinsi had known Reniat's identity, and he had not chosen to make it clear to his current companions. But now Chif moved in to look at the child more closely. Reniat looked up from Sola's arms to see the big warrior looming over her. She smiled. Then she reached up, trying to catch her fingers in his beard. Chif grinned back, the flickering shadows making a strange mask of his face and of his red beard and blue hair. Reniat was unafraid, and her smile became a giggle. Sola glanced around. He could see the men were impressed with the Suncat's lack of fear. Chif straightened and looked at Sola.

"In Saeditin they have been looking everywhere for the SaeKet's missing child." Chif continued to speak in Clinsi. "They think she was taken south, across the border to Runchot." Chif paused, not taking his eyes from Sola.

"She was not," said Sola, also in Clinsi. "She was kidnapped and brought north."

"This is not your child, Warrior Sola?" The Clinsi leader looked slightly confused.

Sola hugged the little girl closer. The thought of anything happening to her tore his heart, not because she was the future ruler of Saeditin, and not even because she was the child of Rilsin, his beloved, but because she had taken a place in his soul. He loved her, but she was not his child. He looked at the men around him.

"She is Reniat SaeKetti Becha," he said.

20

NIGHT WAS COMING ON, AND THEY STILL HAD NOT CAUGHT up to Phara. Rilsin knew they would have to stop soon. Porit, despite his youth, was tiring, and Rilsin herself was tired. They had no food and only two waterskins. Rilsin knew she could go a day or two without food, and she was sure Porit could do the same. If they had time, and if she did not find Phara soon they would have to make time, she and Chilsa could hunt. Water would not be hard to find.

The compulsion to keep moving was almost overwhelming. All she had left to her was the land, and she must save it, but she could not push on when a child in her care needed rest. He was a Saeditin child, and one of the SaeKet's titles was Mother of the Land. All of Saeditin and its people were her children.

"We should stop before it becomes too dark to see," she said. In fact, it was already too dark to see. She remembered that Porit did not think of himself as a child, and that he might resent any implication that he was tiring. "I need the rest." Rilsin made a point of stopping and of claiming the need for it herself.

"Then we should stop, SaeKet," said Porit gratefully. He sank down almost immediately, resting his back against an outcrop of rock, and drank from the waterskin when Rilsin insisted that he do so.

She decided they could not dare to make a fire. She collected some branches and made a quick shelter, a lean-to, over which she spread her cloak. Such was Porit's exhaustion that he did not protest long when Rilsin sent him into the shelter with Chilsa, and within moments, he was asleep.

The night was bitterly cold, and clear. The stars were so bright overhead that it seemed almost possible to reach up and pluck them from the sky. They had been traveling through a sparse forest that bordered the cliff lands, but it would soon merge into the tracts of thick wilderness that edged the northern parts of Saeditin. Rilsin could have found her way through to a settlement, and, she was sure, all the way to Hoptrin itself, alone. She had not forgotten the woodcraft she had learned as a child. She could certainly track the Runchot troops.

An aurora began to burn, starting as a glow among the trees to the north and then flaring in blazes of color across the sky, paling the stars. Rilsin sat watching it, her arms wrapped around herself. She wondered if both land and sky would sing to her as they had when she had won Saeditin back from her cousin Sithli, as they had just weeks ago, when she still had faith that she would find her child. That now seemed like a lifetime ago. She tried not to think of Reniat, but a sudden wave of longing for Sola swept over her. She wanted him here to comfort her. When her husband had lived, he had never been the sort of man on whom she could lean; on the contrary, she had always been Sifuat's support. But Sola was different, and she couldn't believe how much she missed him. He was like a piece of her soul, lost now. Rilsin fought back tears, surprised at herself.

She pushed the thoughts aside to concentrate on the song of the land. She could feel the presence of the Runchot

troops not far away, somber shadows that did not belong on
her land. And closer still she could feel another life, flickering dimly in the forest. It had to be Phara, another enemy
upon her land.

Rilsin's teeth began to chatter. She crawled into the shelter and under Porit's cloak with him. Chilsa moved up beside her, and eventually their combined warmth eased her
into sleep.

The cold and the increasing light woke her. Rilsin felt
stiff and tired as she emerged from their shelter to the light
of the rising sun. Chilsa yawned, showing his impressive
canines, butted his head against her waist, and stretched,
digging his claws into one of the supports of their makeshift
shelter. Porit still slept, even when Rilsin took her cloak
from over the shelter, snapping it in the frigid air to shake
out the tiny ice crystals. She looked at the area in which
they had camped and felt her breath come short.

They had camped near the edge of more broken terrain.
There were no more cliffs over which to stumble, but the
ground broke into fissures and cracks, some of them deep
and steep. Had they continued on in the darkness, disaster
would have been all but certain. Rilsin saw something else
in the earth: footprints on the light skim of snow that had
fallen some days past. Someone had passed this way before
them, and recently. Rilsin knelt to examine the tracks. One
person, not heavy, moving quickly. She smiled faintly to
herself.

"Is she far ahead of us, SaeKet?" Porit asked.

"Not far," said Rilsin, straightening.

Anxious though she was to be on the move, Rilsin first
took down their flimsy shelter, scattering the branches and
scuffing the snow. She took care to cover Chilsa's tracks,
too, as best she could, for some distance away from their
camp. She doubted anyone was following them, but she
wanted to leave no clear signs, at least until they were away
from their campsite.

They made good speed through the ever-thickening forest. Chilsa disappeared briefly to return with blood on his

whiskers, having found something for breakfast. Seeing this, Porit looked hopefully at Rilsin.

"If we eat anything now," she said, "it will be a raw breakfast, like Chilsa's." When Porit turned pale, she relented a little. "After we find Phara, Chilsa and I will hunt, and perhaps we can build a fire."

Phara's trail wandered, and they almost lost it but for Chilsa. The big silver cat led them up over a big rock outcrop. As Rilsin and Porit were negotiating the last stages of the icy descent, Chilsa whined and growled.

The cat was on the ground below the outcrop. Rilsin and Porit were exposed on the cold stone sweep of the little hillside.

"Down!" Rilsin said softly. "Now!"

She half-jumped and half-slid the remaining distance to land beside the cat. Once on the ground, she disappeared into the brush. Porit stared for a moment and then followed her, landing awkwardly. An arm appeared from behind a bush and pulled him in. Rilsin put a finger to her lips, and they crouched silently there for a moment. Rilsin pointed to the ground near where they hid. There were signs on the torn earth of many people and horses passing. Tonar's force had not traveled as quickly as they might have, and they were close now.

There was a moan from close by. Porit's eyes widened, and he opened his mouth, but snapped it shut immediately. Rilsin had her hand on her sword. The moan came again, followed by words, too fast and low and strange for him to understand whatever it was that was said, but Rilsin obviously could. She nodded and motioned for him to remain where he was. Then she left with Chilsa. He was becoming nervous again when she reappeared.

"You can come out," she said. "I think one of our problems has been solved for us."

Chilsa was crouched down in the brush nearby. As Porit got closer, he could see the big cat was at the edge of one of the deep fissures that broke this rocky land. Rilsin moved silently on the crusted snow, and the only sound was that of Porit's footsteps on the frozen earth. And then there was a sob.

Porit edged slowly up to the lip of the fissure. It was terribly deep, with a smell of old earth and damp stone rising up from below. He could not see the bottom of it. The crack in the earth widened out and then narrowed, going down into darkness, with sheer rock sides. Clinging to a scruffy little bush partway down one side was Phara. She had obviously tried to climb out, but the bush, which had saved her life, had broken. Not much remained of it now, and she clung to what there was desperately. As Porit leaned over, horrified, she looked up and sobbed again, and then made an effort to control herself.

"SaeKet, what do we do?" Porit was unable to keep his eyes away from the woman on the bush, about twenty feet below them. It was plain they could not reach her.

"Nothing." Rilsin was calm.

"We can't leave her there! She can't get out!" It occurred to Porit that he had not considered what Rilsin meant to do with Phara once they found her.

"No, she can't get out. And yes, we can leave her. She will not be able to take information to her brother to aid him in Runchot's war against us, and Saeditin is less one enemy." Rilsin looked down at the young woman below her. Phara stared back up at her, not with fear or pleading but with a certain pride. Rilsin gave her credit for that.

"I am sorry," she said in Runchot. She was not, exactly. She supposed she could have been, if she were not desperate to get to her army, if she did not have to defend her land against this woman's brother and father, if she could afford to care.

"I would give you a quick death, if I could, and not leave you to die slowly here. But that is beyond my power." It was true. Rilsin had no bow and arrows, and her fire-tube was with Pleffin. She had her sword, but that was useless here. Short of dropping rocks on Phara, she could do nothing to hasten her death.

"I am not your enemy, nor even Saeditin's." Phara's

voice was steady, but hoarse and raw. She had screamed until she lost her voice entirely, when she first fell into the crevasse during the night. Her abused throat had only recently begun to recover. She spoke in Saeditin because she wanted her listeners to make no mistake about her meaning.

"Well, I suppose I am your enemy, but not as you think it. I did not come all the way from home, tracking my brother, to help in his attack on you. What could I do that would help him?" Phara leaned back, away from the cliff wall, to see Rilsin better. It was a dangerous thing to do, and the branch she held to cracked slightly.

"I don't know," said Rilsin slowly. "I don't know why you came."

"Then let me tell you. I want you to understand this clearly. I came out of love for my land and for love of my brother." Her voice was a raspy whisper, and Phara had to pause to swallow. "I came to try to stop my brother and his troops. I came to try to prevent this war."

Rilsin would have laughed, but she heard the ring of truth in the girl's voice.

"Why?" said Rilsin, bluntly.

"Because he cannot win," said Phara. Then she added, "And because I do not like war."

She twisted back slightly to look upward into Rilsin's eyes, willing her to understand. As she did, the branch she held gave another crack. A small shower of dirt, ice, and rock cascaded into the depths below. Phara gave a short cry and grasped for the trunk of the bush. She held on, but her feet lost their tenuous purchase on the side of the cliff, and she swung over the long drop.

"Why?" said Rilsin again. She understood why someone would not be enamored of war, but why did this girl think she could stop one?

Porit knew Phara was going to lose her grip any moment now. He couldn't stand to think of it, and he couldn't stand to think of Rilsin doing nothing. He had seen many things in his short life, had been in many fights, had killed. He knew Phara was Runchot, an enemy, and not just any Runchot at that. But he couldn't bear to see her die, especially not like this. He realized that he felt sorry for her.

Wrapped in these thoughts, he wandered away from the edge of the fissure, walking back toward the rocky hillside. He knew that Phara was going to die, and he knew that she must. He just did not want to see it.

Rilsin was leaning over the edge of the fissure. Beside her, Chilsa whined and tried to pull her back with one huge paw. "Chilsa, stop!" she said. "Go and sit!"

"I will not see my brother sacrificed." Phara sounded not only hoarse but breathless. "My father made a grave mistake when he sent my brother into your lands. He was taken in by Sithli sae Melisin and by his own greed. My father," Phara spat out the word, "is not usually taken in by women. His own desires are another matter. Tonar should not die for them!"

Rilsin was taken aback. All reports indicated that Raphat was ruthless, but she had not known there was any dissent within the prince's own family, let alone such obvious hatred on the part of one of his own children. And why did Phara think her father was sacrificing his son to his own desires? If not for sheer chance, Tonar's surprise invasion might have worked. Might still work, Rilsin reminded herself. She was about to ask Phara this question when there was a shout from behind her, and a snarl from Chilsa.

Porit had perched on a boulder at the bottom of the stony hill. He sat there feeling cold and miserable. He had thought it would be an adventure to go north with the army, to fight for his SaeKet. He had never imagined that it would turn out as it had. He was brought from his thoughts by Chilsa's sudden snarl. Three men had come out of the forest around the base of the hill, dressed in the drab russet colors of the Runchot winter army.

"SaeKet!" he shouted. "Look out!"

Rilsin jumped back from the edge of the fissure. It seemed to her that there were Runchot everywhere. She flung back her cloak and drew her sword in one fluid motion. All other thoughts fell away from her as she focused on her enemies.

From the corner of her eye she could see that Porit was engaged with one of the Runchot troopers. Although he still had the regulation short sword that was given to all Saeditin soldiers, he obviously preferred his own long dagger. He had drawn this and was warily edging back from his opponent. Chilsa was snarling at another of the three Runchot, but keeping his distance. The man stabbed his sword toward the big cat with an expertise that spoke of experience.

She had no time to see more. Her own opponent was skilled, and meant to keep her near the edge of the fissure, so that she would be unable to retreat, unsure of her footing. Rilsin had to work hard to avoid tumbling over the edge. Down below her, Phara had fallen silent.

Her attacker was a tall man with a long reach, who moved in rapidly. He was smiling, sure of his advantage. His smile broadened as Rilsin stepped back and slipped on ice near the edge of the fissure. She caught herself in time and felt the familiar flood of anger, followed by the equally familiar calm clarity which had aided her in so many battles.

She smiled back with a cold ferocity that unsettled her opponent. Everything around her seemed unnaturally bright. She could see the stones, and the ice crusted over them, and the snow at her feet, and she was now completely in control of all her movements. Her sideways steps along the fissure's edge were dancelike. At the same time, her sword flicked out and back with lightning speed, engaging her opponent's sword, deflecting it. While he watched the blade, waiting for an opening, she reached up with her left hand and undid the clasp of her cloak. She stepped back, balanced on the very lip of the drop, and saw the Runchot soldier's eyes widen, as he realized where she was. He moved forward quickly to try to force her back, over the edge. From within her crystal-clear space, Rilsin watched him come. Then she swirled the cloak forward.

The cloak entangled his sword, entangled him. He cried

out and tried to fight his way free, but Rilsin was too quick
for him. Having caught him in her cloak, she yanked him
toward her, aided by his own forward momentum. As he
fell, she dropped her cloak, ran him through with her
sword, and then pulled it free. The soldier was still falling
toward her, so she stepped to the side, still on the brink of
the chasm, and pitched him forward. He tumbled over the
edge with a cry.

From below, Phara cried out, too. Rilsin glanced over
the edge and saw the Runchot princess still clinging to the
bush. Then she stepped back again. The whole engagement
had gone by quickly, and now that it was over, Rilsin felt
only an icy satisfaction. There was one advantage to having
lost those she loved, and that was an insulation from caring
about smaller deaths, like those of the trooper or the Runchot princess. Why they were smaller she could not at that
moment have said, but she felt it and congratulated herself.
There was a freedom in not caring.

She looked up and saw Porit fighting hand-to-hand with
an opponent much bigger than he. The boy was fighting
desperately, but he was losing. The protective bubble
around her heart dented, as if pricked by an unseen weapon.
Porit needed help. Then she glanced across the rocky scree
to the third Runchot soldier. His uniform was ripped, blood
flowing from a great tear in his arm and from another in his
side. But he was rising from the ground. At his feet was
Chilsa, and the big silver cat was not moving.

The protective bubble around Rilsin's heart broke violently. She found she had closed the distance between herself and the third Runchot without realizing it. Someone
was screaming in what sounded like her voice. She saw the
trooper's mouth open in surprise, and then he was dead.
She had run him through.

She found herself next behind the soldier attacking
Porit. The boy was on the ground now, desperately trying to
hold off the larger man with his long knife. It was only a
matter of moments before the Runchot killed him. Rilsin
found that her sword, somehow, was still in the last man she

had killed. It did not matter. She yanked the Runchot off Porit with a strength she did not realize she had. As his eyes widened in surprise, she wrenched his own sword from his hand and cut his throat. She stepped back, neatly avoiding the blood that fountained from the lethal wound.

"Are you all right?" she asked the boy. Her voice sounded raw.

Porit stared at her, his eyes wide with shock. Finally, he nodded. Rilsin looked him over, not taking his word for it, and then walked over to Chilsa. She dropped to her knees beside the big cat.

Chilsa lay unmoving, and one silver ear was torn. Rilsin remembered him as a kitten, how he had saved her life when she gave birth to her daughter, how he had saved Reniat when Sithli had flung her from the balcony. She remembered how he had slept beside her every night, how he had tried to warn her, just minutes ago, and she had sent him away, thinking him a nuisance and a distraction while she questioned Phara. Something was blurring her vision. She leaned over the animal and then lay her cheek against his thick, soft fur.

There was a heartbeat. More than that, Chilsa's flank rose and fell slightly, shallowly. He was still breathing.

Rilsin sat up and reached out to touch the ripped ear. Behind the ear was flattened fur, and a lump.

"I think that soldier hit him with a rock," said Porit. He was standing at her shoulder, still shaky.

Rilsin took her waterskin and gently washed the blood and dirt from behind the big cat's ear. As she was cleaning this away, Chilsa's eyes opened, and he grunted slightly. She felt a flood of relief.

"Stay," she told the cat. She looked around for something in which to wrap him. She didn't want him moved just yet, and she wanted him warm. Her eyes lighted on the russet cloaks of the dead Runchot troops, and she grabbed one and tucked it around Chilsa. She was beginning to feel more like herself now that she knew both Porit and Chilsa were alive, and she was recovering from the battle trance.

Then she blinked suddenly and jumped to her feet. How could she have forgotten?

Rilsin leaned over the edge of the crevasse. Phara was still there, clinging to the small bush, which had pulled outward from its roots and now dangled her even more precariously above the drop. The young Runchot was obviously weakening. Phara heard her and looked up.

"I want you to know one thing, Rilsin SaeKet," she said. Her voice was little more than a whisper, but Rilsin heard her clearly.

"Sithli sae Melisin is with my father. He's helping her. She will come over the border with troops, but she does not have the support she thinks she has. My father is a fool, and he will get Tonar killed. Sithli sae Melisin—"

There was a loud crack. The trunk of the small tree snapped partway through and fell. The tangled little branches at its crown dragged downward, sweeping Phara from her hold. She screamed and reached up. Her fingers caught in the branches, and she swung there. The tree itself swung over the drop, the top half of the trunk attached to the bottom by only a few tough woody strands.

"Don't move, Phara! Just hold on!" Rilsin turned. Porit was beside her. "Look in the Runchot packs and see if they have any rope," she said. "Hurry!"

"I can't," said Phara from below her. "I'm so cold. My fingers are cold."

"Don't let go," said Rilsin. "We'll get you out."

Porit had returned with something in his arms.

"No rope, SaeKet," he said, "but there were these." He dropped a bundle of cloth at her feet: two of the Runchot cloaks.

"Good thinking." Rilsin snapped a cloak open and rolled it rapidly into a long, tight tube and then did the same with the second cloak. She tied them together, knotting them as tightly as she could.

"Hold on, Phara!" she repeated. "I'm coming to get you." She knotted one end of her makeshift rope around a small tree and went to drop the rope over the side of the cliff edge.

"SaeKet, wait! What are you doing?"

"Going after Phara," said Rilsin. "Stand back. When I tell you, pull hard and pull us up." She didn't want any objections from Porit, not now.

"No, SaeKet, please—"

"I am going to get her out, Porit; she has information I want." She glanced at him. "I'm not letting her die. At least not like that."

"That's not what I meant! SaeKet, I'm smaller than you. I don't weigh as much. On that rope—" He paused.

"Have you climbed before?"

Porit desperately wanted to say he had, but he couldn't lie, not looking into her eyes.

"I didn't think so."

There was another crack from below them. They both looked down. Phara and the tree were still there, but barely. Rilsin looked at the rolled cloak in her hand, but instead of tossing it over the side of the fissure, she knotted the loose end around her waist.

"I haven't, either." Then she leaned back and walked backward over the edge of the fissure.

It was strange to trust her weight and her life to the makeshift rope. Phara looked at once very close and incredibly far from her. Rilsin drew in a deep breath. She could feel the land below her, the drip of water, and the cracked stone, the bones of the ridge that ran beneath her and deeper under the soil. It seemed to her that she could even feel the little tree, feel its pain. *Hold on, little tree,* she thought, *just a little longer.*

Her feet touched the tangled branches, and she felt them give slightly. Phara was still holding to the tree with both hands. Her feet were in the tree's outer branches, but they had no support there.

"Can you reach me?" Rilsin asked.

The young Runchot looked up at her. This close to her, Rilsin could see the pallor of her skin, the tired lines around her eyes. Her gloves were torn, and through one of the rips Rilsin could see that her flesh was dead white in splotches. Frostbite.

"Can you reach me?" she asked again. "You will have to let go with one hand when I tell you. I will reach down and grab your hand and pull you up. Can you do it?"

"I don't know." Phara was obviously terrified, but she did not look ready to give up. "I will try." She suited the action to the word, letting go with her left hand and reaching up.

Rilsin was taken by surprise. She had meant to prepare herself and to tell Phara when to make the attempt. Now the younger woman was swinging by one hand. At the same time, the tree gave another great crack: its last. The trunk finished the split it had earlier begun, and the top portion ripped loose and fell.

Rilsin saw Phara begin to fall. She reached out with her right hand and saw that it would not be enough. She let go of her makeshift rope with both hands and plunged head downward, held only by the cloth knotted around her waist. She reached down and forward and caught Phara as she fell. The two of them hung there, Rilsin held by the cloth at her waist, Phara held only by Rilsin's hands, swinging. Rilsin felt the blood rushing to her head.

"Climb up me, Phara; climb up and grab onto the rope." Rilsin's voice was calm. "Do it, Phara!"

The princess clumsily grabbed her around the torso and began to heave herself up. Rilsin felt the knots at her waist pull and loosen.

"Grab the cloth as soon as you can," Rilsin said. "Try not to pull on me any longer than you must."

Phara's foot kicked her in the chest. Rilsin grabbed it and heaved her up. She felt the weight on her lessen. Phara must have grabbed the rope. Rilsin hoped so. She swung herself deliberately, and used the motion to swing up. She reached around Phara and grabbed the rope again with one hand. With the other, she pulled Phara to her. The two women swung like a pendulum above the drop, but at least they were upright now. For a moment, Rilsin wondered just how deep the drop was. Then she looked up.

She could see Porit above her. It occurred to her that she might have made a mistake: surely her weight and Phara's combined were too great for Porit, by himself, to pull up. Rilsin gritted her teeth. Still holding Phara, who was now rigid, she inched herself around until both hands were on the rope. Then she let go with one hand and reached higher, and pulled herself, and Phara, up. Phara grabbed onto their new position. The two of them swung there, breathless. Rilsin glanced up. Porit was gone.

Suddenly the makeshift rope jerked and began to pull them upward. Phara screamed: the rope had caught a finger. Rilsin choked, taken by surprise.

"Hold on!" shouted Porit. He was leaning over the edge. "I'll have you up soon! I wrapped the rope around another tree, like a pulley. It makes it easier!"

Rilsin held her breath. The rope jerked violently upward, jerked again. She could see the top of the fissure now, could almost reach it. The rope jerked again. The knots at her waist loosened, and there was a ripping sound. Rilsin shoved Phara upward, feeling her shoulders strain.

"Grab on!" she shouted, and pushed Phara hard.

Phara sprawled across the lip of the fissure. Rilsin felt the cloth rope tear and knew she was going to fall. Then a small hand clutched hers. Rilsin grabbed the hand, kicked hard against the side of the cliff, heaved herself, and was pulled up and onto solid ground. She lay with her legs over the edge, gasping for breath, while Porit threw his arms around her and sobbed. Rilsin pulled her legs up.

"Great freezing Runchot hells!" she gasped. "You are making a habit of this, Porit." She pulled the remnants of the ripped cloak away from herself and lay back on the cold ground. Nothing had ever felt so good, and she closed her eyes. Something was chuffing at her, licking her face. Chilsa had ignored her command to stay where he was.

21

PLEFFIN WAS GLAD THAT THE WEATHER HAD STAYED CLEAR
for the past days, since it had given him time to reorganize
the troops. He had made it to Hoptrin in record time, once
he and his Wilfrisin companion had managed to comman-
deer horses from some traveling tinkers, and they had
brought Meffa to the physicians. He had set up headquarters in the Sudit manor, the seat of Sudit saedhold, and had
immediately sent a message south to Essit sae Tillit, in Petipal. He had received his reply, but he was worried.

It had been over a week since he had returned. He was
concerned that the Runchot would invade from the south,
and he still had not managed to find Tonar's force. He had
sent out scouts, but they returned with no information. He
couldn't leave Hoptrin undefended, but he couldn't let
young Essit try to defend both Saeditin's capital and its
southern border with the troops he had.

And on top of all this, there was still no sign of the
SaeKet. Pleffin had scouts out looking for her, too, but she
had vanished as completely as the Runchot noblewoman

she trailed. He told himself repeatedly that Rilsin sae Becha was protected by the Great Mother, as the commoners believed. But if Rilsin disappeared, may the Mother help Saeditin. It was certain, at least, that Rilsin sae Becha had come through worse times than this and prevailed, so he tried to have faith.

When he looked out the window again, there were fat flakes of snow drifting down. He needed to get some of his troops out of Hoptrin and south to Petipal before the roads closed again. He would do it now, immediately, but for the uncertainty about the Runchot invaders.

Pleffin paced. He hated being cooped up with too little information. He stopped his pacing abruptly and turned on his heel. He would go out himself and inspect the troops. He might take a few soldiers with him and go out into the countryside, do a little scouting for himself before the storm got too bad. He was bothered by a feeling, a sort of visceral, gut expectation that something important was about to happen. He had never mentioned this feeling to anyone, but he knew from experience not to ignore it.

Within minutes, he was in the saddle. The shaggy Saeditin horse seemed glad of the opportunity for exercise, despite the cold and the occasional spits of snow. The troopers with Pleffin were not as pleased, but they knew better than to voice a complaint.

They rode out past the camp, into the rolling hills around the city. The fields had recovered remarkably from two autumns previous, when Kepit sae Lisim's troops had burned them during the siege of Hoptrin. Now they lay fallow under the snow. Southward there were villages like Mills Crossing, but to the north there were only isolated farms and more woods, approaching the border with the Confederacy lands. It was north that Pleffin rode, and east.

Toward midday the snow was swirling down in stinging flakes, more like sleet than snow. They rode through icy woods, where even the snow underfoot had a treacherous glaze. The sky was so dark that it seemed more like dusk than midday. Pleffin called a retreat, to the unspoken but heartfelt relief of his escort. He could not have explained just what it was that made him go out on this inclement day, or for what he had been searching. Nonetheless, he felt frustrated, bothered with a lingering sense that there was something out here that he should know. So it was with a sense of both relief and justification that he saw the rider coming toward him, pushing his horse as hard as he could over the treacherous forest floor.

It was one of the Saeditin army scouts, more surprised to find his commander out than the reverse. The news settled into Pleffin sae Grisna and left him with a sense of both satisfaction and concern. The Runchot troops had been found. They were some miles to the east, apparently hoping to skirt Hoptrin on the sly, to evade any Saeditin defenses, and to approach Petipal by surprise.

The other piece of news was instead a lack of news. There was no sign of Rilsin SaeKet Becha, and no sign of the commoner boy nor of the Runchot princess. There was not even any sign of the hunting cat. This last disturbed Pleffin more than he wanted to admit. He had expected Chilsa to protect his SaeKet and to bring her through. This brought him back to the matter of faith. He would have faith that Rilsin still lived, and he would do everything within his power to keep Saeditin safe for her return.

A∏XiOUS tHOUGH SHE was to move on, Rilsin had insisted that they camp for a time to give them all a chance to recover. Chilsa certainly needed it, as did Phara. Even Porit, youngest and most resilient, was exhausted, and although she would not have admitted it, Rilsin was, too.

The only traveling they did was to move a goodly distance from the fissure that had almost claimed their lives. Rilsin scouted thoroughly to be sure they were as safe as possible from Runchot troops. The Runchot seemed to have moved on, and the three who had attacked them must have been stragglers. They salvaged what they could from the bodies, and then Rilsin, with Porit's help, tumbled them into the fissure. Phara watched, and if she did not help, neither did she protest.

Phara's left thumb jutted out from her hand at an odd angle. It had been pulled partway from its socket when Porit had begun to drag them up from the fissure. Rilsin examined the hand and wondered aloud about wrapping it, but it was Porit who proved useful in this regard.

"It's pulled loose, but I can get it back where it should be. It will hurt, and it will be swollen afterward, but it will hurt less than it does now, afterward, and it will heal and be fine," he told Phara. "I've seen this before, from tavern fights. My uncle has done it many times, and he showed me how."

Rilsin wondered if Phara had heard what she did in Porit's explanation: that he had never done the procedure before himself. If Phara knew this, she was willing to let him try despite it. It was over more quickly than Rilsin would have imagined. Porit grabbed the young woman's hand, braced her arm against him, grabbed her thumb, and pushed it.

Phara screamed once, a high, shrill scream that echoed back from the frozen forests and set Rilsin's teeth on edge. Then Phara looked at Porit, and then at her thumb. She wiggled her thumb.

"It's better!" she said in amazement. "You were right! The pain is much less."

"It will be swollen for a time still, so be careful with it, Sae." Porit had taken to treating the Runchot princess like a saedin.

Two of the dead Runchot had bows and quivers full of arrows, which Rilsin immediately appropriated. She ordered Chilsa to stay with Porit, and Porit to stay with Phara, and then went hunting on her own. She did not return until almost nightfall, carrying a small deer across her shoulders. As she staggered into their small camp, she saw that Porit had laid a fire and was waiting only for her permission to light it.

"We might as well," said Rilsin. "I think the enemy

troops," she glanced sideways at Phara, who did not react, "are far enough off not to see the light. And I, for one, have no desire to eat raw venison."

Chilsa did, however, which Rilsin took as a sign that he was recovering. The big cat ate his share noisily, while Rilsin set to work with the butchering, an art she had learned in her childhood from the palace woodsman.

"Let me help."

Rilsin looked up, bloody to her elbows, to find Phara standing over her. A number of questions occurred to her, but all she said was, "You need to care for your hand."

"I will be careful. And yes," Phara smiled slightly, "I do know what to do." She had already dropped her cloak, and now she pushed up the sleeves of both overshirt and undershirt.

"My brother took me on hunting trips with him when I was a child," she said. "He taught me."

Rilsin did not reply. The two women worked in an almost companionable silence, while Chilsa ate whatever scraps they tossed him. Porit, a true son of the city, watched in horrified fascination.

Later, as the fire flickered and the night grew colder, they sat quietly, comfortably full. The only sounds were the popping of wood in the fire and Chilsa's occasional sigh. The big cat lay on his back, exposing the thick silver fur of his stomach to the heat. Porit was curled into a pile of cloaks and furs, sleeping soundly. They had no shelter this night but were camping under the ice-bright stars.

Rilsin knew she must break the silence. She needed whatever Phara could tell her, but she was afraid to go about it wrong. Despite Phara's surprising capabilities, there was something about her that seemed fragile to Rilsin. She was surprised at herself, too. She had been willing to let the girl die, but now she was reluctant to try to force Phara into sharing what she knew. Phara solved the problem by beginning to speak in a low voice.

"You saved my life today. I suppose I should be grateful.

After all, you are *his* friend. He would not trust you as he does without reason."

It took a moment for Rilsin to realize that *he* was Chif. She remembered how Chif had looked at Phara, and how Phara had looked at him. It was difficult to imagine a more incongruous pair, and she wondered if Phara even recognized the character of her own feelings. The Runchot princess seemed much younger than she was. Rilsin tried to remember how it was when she thought she was in love with her husband—no, she *had* been in love with Sifuat—and how she had known she loved Sola. It seemed that last was something she had always known.

A wave of loneliness hit her so hard that she struggled for air. If only she had been more aware of how she felt in the past, if only she had been more willing to take risks, if only she had told Sola just what he meant to her, then perhaps, somehow, he would have been safe. She pulled herself back abruptly from where her thoughts were leading. Sola was gone, murdered in a Petipal alley. All she could do for him, if she ever got back to her capital, would be to find his killer and avenge him. She would have to do the same for her daughter, but neither would be possible unless she could save her land, unless she could find out what this enemy princess knew, this sister of the enemy commander, this sad young girl. Suddenly Rilsin knew the question she needed to ask.

"Phara," she said gently, "why did you run away from home? You did, didn't you? That's part of why you are here."

The Saeditin ruler's face was softened by the firelight, and for a moment, Phara felt safe, reminded of times long ago, when politics and treachery and death were things she could not even imagine.

"Yes." Phara looked away from the other woman, into the fire. "I ran away. I had to get away from my lord father. He—he had my mother killed." Phara heard Rilsin draw in a breath and misinterpreted her shocked silence. "He did," she said. "I know it. I can't prove it, not that it would matter if I could. But I know it."

"I do believe you. Phara, I am sorry for you."

The sympathy in the other woman's voice unlocked something inside Phara. "He killed her; he wanted to be free of her! My grandfather, her own father, would not believe me! Or rather, he did believe me but would not act! Not even for his own child. And then my father took Sithli SaeKet for his mistress." Phara paused, remembering that the woman across the fire from her was the SaeKet in fact. "Sithli sae Melisin," she amended. "And then he, my father—he—he was going to marry me off, and he told me not to disobey him, that I should know the cost of that. I ran. Kirra took me in."

Phara looked across the fire again. It was difficult to read expressions in the firelight. Rilsin had not moved, and it seemed she barely breathed, so Phara continued. "Kirra hates Sae Sithli and will do anything to bring her down. Bringing her down would hurt my lord father. Not enough, perhaps, but it would be a start. I didn't find out until later that he had sent my brother north. That he had sent Tonar—" Phara bit off her words, near to tears. She didn't want the Saeditin woman to see her cry. Tonar would die if she could not find him and warn him.

"I am sorry," said Rilsin again. She would have said more, but Phara interrupted.

"You say you are sorry, but you don't know. You don't know Lord Raphat, my father. He poisoned my mother." She spoke coldly, without passion now, the tears gone. "She died in front of me. You don't know what that's like."

Rilsin got up and crossed the distance between them. She perched on the downed tree trunk they had pulled close to the fire as a bench. Phara said nothing to her but merely looked into the fire, her face drawn in, the muscles around her mouth clenched tight.

"No," said Rilsin, looking into the fire herself. "I have not seen anyone die of poison in front me. But I have lost those I love to treachery. I was not so old as you when it happened, but I did see my mother die, slain before my eyes." A log in the fire popped as sap boiled and exploded. Sparks flew up into the night. "I was very little then, only eight years. But it is not something you forget." She kept her eyes on the fire. "And I saw my husband executed from my prison window." She did not mention all those who had died to help her win back Saeditin from Sithli.

Phara looked up from the fire. Rilsin's face seemed to waver in front of her, half-blinded as she was from the flames. She had never before considered the Saeditin ruler as anything but an enemy, as she had been taught from childhood, or as a remote game piece on a political game board, one that even Kirra hoped to use. Now there was a living, breathing woman in front of her. The world was turning out to be much more complex than she had ever imagined. This was someone, it would seem, who understood pain.

"Tell me about Kirra," said Rilsin.

"She is, she is, she gave me—"

"I know. She gave you shelter. And I know—" Rilsin paused. She almost said that she knew that Kirra owned a brothel, and that she suspected it was a haven for spies. That the Runchot princess had found a haven there was more than strange, but then the Runchot were known for eccentricities.

"What I want to know," she amended, "is how Kirra fits into all this and why you are here in Saeditin, looking for your brother." *And why you believe that your brother cannot win victories here,* she thought.

"I cannot bear to lose him! He is all I have left. He would not have done this, would not have invaded your land if he knew . . . You have to promise me," Phara found she could not continue.

She did not know how to ask what she needed to. She realized how strange this must seem to Rilsin sae Becha, that the daughter of an enemy and the sister of one would try to stop this attack. She did not think Rilsin would believe her.

She wanted to offer what she knew for her brother's safety, but she could not imagine how to begin.

"This is not what you think," was all she could manage. "My brother—he . . . he doesn't know, but you can't . . ." She looked desperately at Rilsin, unable to continue.

"I can't promise you that I will not harm him, Phara." Rilsin heard what Phara did not say quite as clearly as if she had spoken. "Saeditin comes first. I will do whatever I must to keep my land safe. I will stop your brother if I can, any way I can. I have no desire to kill him, but he has come against me with force, and I will meet it."

She hoped she would, anyway. She hoped that Pleffin had made his way back to the army, and that she would be able to join him soon. The easiest thing would be to kill Phara now, but she had put that plan aside and would not go back to it now.

"I had always hoped for peace with Runchot," said Rilsin, almost meditatively. "I tried to convince Sithli to open up trade. But even now that she is no longer SaeKet, she manages to bring strife. If your father had given me Sithli sae Melisin, and also Kepit, and if he had not stolen and murdered my child—"

"He didn't steal your child. Sithli sae Melisin did, but she does not have her. Something went wrong. Your daughter never entered Runchot. Kirra would have known."

Phara stopped, suddenly frightened. Rilsin had turned toward her. She made no other move, but Phara felt pinned by the intensity of her gaze. Somewhere in the nearby forest, an owl hooted, but neither woman heard.

"You had better tell me everything," said Rilsin, "and you had better tell me now."

IT WAS MUCH later when Phara had finished explaining what she could. She was exhausted and had barely enough strength to roll herself into her cloak near the fire. She did not think she would sleep, but within seconds her eyes had closed, and she was breathing deeply.

Rilsin watched the Runchot princess for a few moments.

Then her gaze shifted to Chilsa, who was still sleeping beside the fire, but curled now into a large, silver ball. She believed that her daughter was dead, now more so than before, since Sithli's kidnap plan had gone awry. It was one more crime for which she would call Sithli to account. As for everything else that Phara had told her . . . She sighed. One of the sleeping lumps near the fire shifted, and she looked down into Porit's eyes. The boy was wide awake.

"Do you believe her, SaeKet?" he whispered.

"Yes," Rilsin said slowly, "I think I do. It's a strange story, but the Runchot are a strange people, and these are strange times." She looked down into Porit's eyes, which reflected the firelight back at her. "I cannot promise to spare her brother, as I told her, but neither do I wish to kill him. It would be a shame if he dies before I can meet him. If he is anything like his sister, he is an interesting man, perhaps more straightforward and honorable than Prince Raphat. So yes, I do believe her."

"So do I," said Porit, settling back to sleep.

22

THEY HAD BEEN WALKING FOR OVER A WEEK. CHILSA
seemed completely recovered, as did Phara. Rilsin rarely let
Phara out of her sight. Although she was inclined to believe
the story the girl had told her, she was not inclined to trust
her. They had been moving fast, catching up to the slower-
moving Runchot band.

It was easy to follow the trail of the Runchot invaders,
although Rilsin could see that Tonar was trying to keep
away from settled areas. She knew his strategy now: to approach Petipal as stealthily as possible. He wanted to avoid
confrontation until the last possible moment, if he could
sneak past the northern towns. He wanted to give his father's troops and Sithli's forces time to come over the border, so they could catch Petipal between them. Rilsin knew
Raphat's spies would have brought him the news that she
was missing. Although Tonar could not possibly know that
yet, it would give Raphat a sense of advantage, and Sithli,
too. She hoped to play on that and give them a nasty surprise.

The skies had clouded over again, and a wind from the lands beyond the mountains brought a threat of snow. Porit had wrapped his cloak as tightly as he could manage around himself, and was trying not to look forlorn. Rilsin watched him with more than a little concern. He had been right about coming with her; she had needed him. But he was young, and in her charge, and she wanted to see him safely home again. As she thought this, she suddenly realized that she knew where they were.

They were walking a rocky, forested hillside, which at first seemed no different than all the other hillsides they had so recently traversed. Some of the land had once been cleared but had then been abandoned and overgrown with snow-rose brambles, bare now of roses but still prickly.

There was something about the way the land rolled downward in gentle slopes. Rilsin could feel it under her feet in its winter sleep, and deeper below that, like a dream of the earth itself, a memory of raiders and burning. With a start, she realized that she was in the same countryside where three springtimes before, her husband Sifuat had been captured by the Wilfrisin. It seemed like a lifetime ago.

They were not far from Hoptrin. Rilsin, examining the ground, decided they were almost on top of the Runchot. Chilsa confirmed her deduction by drawing back from a patch of ground he had been sniffing, his lips drawn back in a grimace at the scent of strangers.

Now that she saw how close the Runchot were to Hoptrin, Rilsin abruptly made up her mind. Inclined though she was to believe Phara, she knew that Phara's brother wouldn't allow himself to be discouraged from or talked out of his attack. She would send Porit to warn Hoptrin, and thus get him, coincidentally, to safety. With any luck, Pleffin would be there already, but he might not know how close the Runchot were. She herself would scout the Runchot, since she was almost on top of them now. She could do this quickly and quietly, but her problem was the Runchot princess.

She covertly regarded Phara, who had taken advantage of their pause to sit down on an exposed bit of the hillside where the south-facing slope had allowed the sun to melt off some of the snow. She looked cold, tired, and hungry, and she obviously did not realize how close she was both to her brother's troops and to a Saeditin city. Rilsin motioned Porit aside.

"We are near Hoptrin," she told him in a low voice. "I want you to go there, find Sae Pleffin, and warn him that the Runchot are here. I will follow you soon."

"But SaeKet," Porit made a show of searching the briars for berries and kept his voice low, "I don't know how to get to Hoptrin. And what about Phara?"

"I will send Chilsa with you; he will get you there. It's not far, less than a day. I need to find out the Runchot numbers. And I will take care of Phara."

Porit blinked at her, opened his mouth. Rilsin knew that he wanted to know if she planned on letting Phara find her brother and talk to him. He was going to ask her, but his mouth froze in the open position, and his eyes widened.

She knew immediately, and drew her sword even as she turned. There were Runchot soldiers on the hillside behind her, three of them. There was a snarl from Chilsa, who crouched near her.

"Chilsa!" Rilsin spoke low and sharply. "Find Pleffin! Guard Porit! Go!" She looked into the cat's green eyes, filled with an intense animal intelligence. She tried to do what she had been taught when she had trained him as a kitten, tried to visualize Hoptrin, and Pleffin's face. She had no idea if this technique worked, but she trusted her cat, trusted him to remember and know Pleffin and how to find him.

"I can't leave you!" Porit had drawn his knife and now danced beside her, watching the oncoming troopers, who were fanning out to surround them. "SaeKet, I can't leave you here!"

Rilsin saw one of the Runchots' eyes widen. He had heard her title and knew who she was.

"Damn it!" said Rilsin. "Damn it to a freezing Runchot hell! Go, Porit! Sae Pleffin must know! Now! Tell him to scout now and attack immediately. If there is no word from me, he must assume I am dead. Run! Chilsa, find Pleffin, go!"

Porit obeyed her at last. The big cat was reluctant to leave her, too, but now Chilsa vanished from her side, and she heard Porit crash through the brambles behind her, the most direct if painful way to safety. She wanted to look to see what had happened to Phara. She was afraid the girl had already been killed, but she couldn't turn to search. The three enemy soldiers had her surrounded. She stepped back and felt the brambles catch her cloak.

"Stop!" she called in Runchot. "I need to talk to your commander, to Prince Tonar!"

The soldier who had recognized her hesitated and glanced at his companions. One of these was no longer in sight, and the other had slowed. Rilsin ripped her cloak free of the brambles behind her, and under cover of this, pulled her knife from its sheath and flipped it. It caught the first soldier in the left eye. His mouth made a little circle of surprise, and he went down without a sound.

The other Runchot shouted and charged her. He was very young, not much older than Porit, and more enthusiastic than skillful. It did not take her long to finish the fight. She stepped to the side, feinted high, and then came in low, killing him almost regretfully. Then she looked around for the missing Runchot trooper and for Phara.

They stood close together. It looked as though Phara and the remaining soldier had been in brief but close conversation. Rilsin frowned. After she dealt with this soldier she would find out just what it was that Phara had told him.

He was unprepossessing as warriors went. He was short, somewhat round and barrel-shaped, and his hair, which was rolled back in the tight bun of a Runchot noble, was strawberry blond and beginning to recede from his brow. His eyelashes were so pale they seemed almost invisible. As Rilsin moved to face him, he raised his sword. He did not look much like a fighting man, and Rilsin did not expect much trouble from him, but she immediately revised her opinion when she saw him move. This man knew combat. He saw the realization in her eyes and smiled as he moved forward, almost dancing.

Rilsin leaped forward, hoping to take him by surprise. Her sword flicked up, slicing through his woolen uniform shirt and drawing a thin line of blood along his collarbone, and then upward still, cutting a gash just below his receding hairline as he jerked away.

Phara screamed. The sound split the cold afternoon air like a fall of ice, searing a sudden bright flash of knowledge through Rilsin's mind. Surprise slowed her, and she barely moved back in time from the small man's assault.

"Phara," said the man, in Runchot, "do not do that again! You distract me!"

His onslaught was furious now, and Rilsin was being forced back. But she had recovered from her surprise.

"Prince Tonar," she said in Runchot, parrying rapidly, "you are not what I expected."

"Nor are you what I expected, SaeKet," he answered, in Saeditin. "I thought you would be more like your cousin."

Rilsin did not respond. She knew what he was trying to do, but he could not provoke her into acting rashly. Instead, she shifted to the attack and pushed harder.

For a moment she made no headway, but the lucky cut she had made on his scalp was bleeding copiously. The blood dripped into his eyes and obscured his vision. He tossed his head in annoyance, trying to shake the blood from his eyes, and moved sideways across the hillside. His left hand disappeared beneath his overshirt and reappeared with a knife in it. Now Rilsin had two weapons to watch. Her own knife was gone. She needed to resolve this soon, but she seemed unable to break his guard, no matter how hard she tried. It seemed that the only way she might win this would be to kill him, if she were lucky. She would if she must, but she had hoped to disarm him. If she could bring him alive to Hoptrin, it might go some distance to resolving one of her problems. For that reason, she was reluctant to attack too hard.

Her hesitation cost her. Their duel had taken them across the lower part of the hillside, into the edge of a small stand of bushes, covered with the ubiquitous snow-rose briars. Rilsin could neither retreat nor even see clearly past these. Tonar came in under her guard. He slammed his arm against her sword arm, temporarily numbing it, and thrust the dagger in his left hand against her throat.

"Don't move," he snarled.

Rilsin dropped her now-useless sword. She pulled back very slightly from the knife and then rammed the heel of her left hand into her opponent's solar plexus. Tonar grunted and hunched reflexively. If Rilsin had not pulled back slightly, his dagger would have sliced along her throat. As it was, the point nicked her under the chin in a painful cut. She grabbed the weapon as it slid from Tonar's hand. Moving lightning fast, she spun him around, yanked his arm back before he could recover his breath, kicked the back of his legs, and dropped him to the ground on his knees. She dropped right behind him, pulling him tight against her. Then she whipped the dagger around so she was now holding it to his throat.

"Damn it," she said in Runchot. She was out of breath. "I just wanted to talk to you."

"Lucky for you," gasped Tonar, in the same language.

Looking up, she saw why. She also saw why Phara had neither cried out again nor tried to interfere with the fight. Surrounding them, with bows drawn and arrows nocked at the ready, were several Runchot archers. Phara stood well back among them, her knuckles pressed to her mouth. If Rilsin had not dropped behind Tonar and pulled him against her, effectively shielding herself, she would have been shot.

Rilsin frowned. She kept the knife pushed tight against Tonar's throat but shifted slightly, rising, attempting to pull him to his feet. He resisted, and small though he was, he was strong, and she could not force him.

"Get up," she said, still speaking in Runchot. Then she

raised her voice slightly. "If you shoot me, he dies," she said. "I swear it."

Tonar climbed to his feet, clumsily because she still held his arm wrenched behind his back, and she held his own dagger to his throat. The blood continued to drip down into his eyes from his scalp.

"Truce," he said to her.

Rilsin couldn't see his face, but she thought she heard the bare hint of a smile in his voice. She kept the knife in place.

"I would like to take you at your word," she said.

"You can trust me." Toner raised his voice slightly. "Stand down," he told his archers. "She has my word of safety."

The archers took the arrows from their bows. Rilsin took the knife from Tonar's throat. Tonar sighed and straightened, rubbing his wrenched arm and then his bruised stomach without embarrassment. He tried to tear a strip of cloth from his overshirt, but it would not rip properly, so he looked up at Rilsin.

"May I borrow the knife?" he asked politely.

Without hesitation, she gave it to him, hilt first. She knew there was no way for her to maintain her advantage, outnumbered as she was, and killing him now would not serve any good purpose. From the corner of her eye she could see the archers truly relax now, and she braced herself, expecting them to try to take her. They did not, nor did Tonar give the order. Instead, he used his knife to finish cutting the strip from his overshirt, which he used to wipe the blood from his eyes. He then rolled the strip into a makeshift bandage, which he tied around his head. It gave him a raffish look, rather like a bandit. He then cut another, smaller strip, and proffered the woolen cloth to her.

"You're bleeding," he told her. "Under your chin." He started to point to her and then paused, and pointed to the same spot, but on himself. "There," he said.

"Ah," said Rilsin. She took the strip of wool. "Thank

you." She wiped at the blood under her chin, dabbing at the sore spot, and then pressed the cloth against it.

Tonar sheathed the knife, found his sword, and sheathed that. One of the archers had already retrieved Rilsin's sword and obviously had no intention of returning it to her. Rilsin did not ask for it. She glanced at the brush and the brambles, seeing the bent and smashed vegetation where Porit and Chilsa had made their escape. She hoped they were well on their way to Hoptrin by now.

"SaeKet, come with me." Tonar bowed slightly, courteously, but the authority of his tone made the command obvious, and Rilsin knew she had no choice.

She picked up her torn and much abused cloak, under the watchful eyes of the Runchot. She was careful to make no sudden moves. Two of the Runchot troopers came to stand by her, hands on their swords. Rilsin stood quietly between them, ignoring them as best she could.

Raphat was standing beside Phara again, saying something to her in a low voice. Seen together now, their relationship was obvious. Tonar's strawberry blond hair was the exact shade of Phara's roots, where the blonde was growing out through the brown. Phara's face was heart-shaped and slender where Tonar's was round, but the fullness of their lips was the same, and the arch of the nose, and there was something about the expressiveness of their faces that was similar. Right now, Phara's face was expressing annoyance and insistence both.

"I have already said so." Tonar raised his voice slightly, silencing his sister. She looked mutinous, and it was obvious that the discussion was far from over.

Rilsin studied the Runchot prince carefully. From the way Phara had spoken of him, she had envisioned a young, vital, and handsome man, tall, and not much older than Phara. Tonar was vital, certainly, but obviously a number of years senior to his sister. Nor was he beautiful in the way that Phara was. His features were pleasant enough, but his face was interesting rather than traditionally handsome, a fact accentuated by his receding hairline. The thing that

struck Rilsin most forcefully, however, was his obvious intelligence and his lack of ostentation, a trait she admired,
since she shared it. His uniform was that of an ordinary
Runchot soldier, with no sign of his rank. Tonar looked up
from his conversation to find Rilsin watching him.

"Please accompany us back to our camp, SaeKet," he
said. "My sister informs me that you have been traveling
for some many days through this wilderness, so perhaps
whatever poor amenities we can offer you might be welcome."

As he spoke, several more of the Runchot soldiers
closed around Rilsin, hands on their swords. One of them
reached out to take her by the arm, making it clear that this
was not an invitation she could refuse.

"That is not necessary," said Tonar, coming to her side.
"The SaeKet is our guest, if an unwilling one. We offer her
our hospitality."

"Thank you," said Rilsin. Despite her predicament, she
found herself liking the Runchot prince. "It is a most generous offer, which I hope to repay soon enough." She was
rewarded by an appreciative flash of humor in Tonar's eyes.
He seemed to have a genuine admiration for her, which
puzzled her.

"I am afraid I must decline your offer," he said. "And I
am sorry that your young friend is not here to join us. It
would be a shame to have him lost and unprotected in such
rough country. I fully expect my scouts will be able to find
him and bring him safely back."

Despite Tonar's ostensible courtesy, Rilsin noticed that
his troopers stayed close to her as they made their way back
to his camp.

The camp was well hidden in a tiny valley, more a cleft
in the hills than a true valley. The tents were gray, blending
into the snow and bare land, and camouflaged with brush.
What surprised Rilsin was the size of the force that Tonar
had brought with him. As best she could tell, making a
hasty, surreptitious estimate, Tonar had brought a little
under two hundred troops. It was a small contingent in the

general scope of things, but quite large enough that to move without being detected was a real feat.

"We intended to distract you," said Tonar, who had been watching her, seeing where she looked, watching her calculate. Rilsin frowned. She had not meant her thoughts to be quite so obvious.

"We did not really think to be able to take your capital by ourselves or even to get to it unhindered and in secret. But we planned to distract you, to make it easier for my lord father to cross the border and come up from the south. Now, instead of distracting you, I suppose we shall be distracting your first minister. That is young Essit sae Tillit, is it not?"

"It is," said Rilsin. It was apparent that Tonar did not realize how close he was to Hoptrin. She hoped, fervently, that Pleffin was there now, and that much of the army was still there. If Porit got through, and if Pleffin followed her instructions, Tonar would have a surprise.

"A very nice young man, and able, so I am given to understand. My sister," Tonar glanced at Phara, who had kept pace with them, "tells me that you have been missing from your people for some time."

"What else did your sister tell you?" Rilsin asked. She tried to keep her tone light, but she did not succeed, not to judge by the way Tonar glanced at her sharply.

"We can talk at dinner," said Tonar, "where you will be my guest, SaeKet. I am very much looking forward to it."

Dinner was in Tonar's tent. It was a surprisingly comfortable accommodation for someone who had been on the march, secretly, through difficult terrain in even more difficult weather. There was no cot, but there were piles of comfortable skins and furs. A fire had been lit outside the tent; in fact, there were a number of cook fires throughout the camp, confirming Rilsin's opinion that they did not realize how close they were to inhabited Saeditin lands. Dinner was stew and roast venison and Runchot wine.

"The Clinsi helped to resupply us," Tonar told her frankly. "It is difficult to hunt when you are on the march,

as I'm sure you know. The wine, well. I could not bear to
go without some, for relaxation now and again."

Tonar seemed to have no reservations about discussing
what Phara had told him, and it appeared that she had told
him everything.

"Of course I believe my sister." Tonar leaned over to
offer Rilsin another slice of venison. Although he had removed the bandage from his head, the cut was still quite
visible and made him look rather disreputable. "It is a concern to me, of course, that all of my father's troops, or
rather, Sae Sithli's, may not be loyal. That little problem
may possibly be offset, though, by the fact that I have you."

"Possibly," said Rilsin, "and quite possibly not." She did
not mention the other problem that she knew was on his
mind: the problem of keeping her. He would have to guard
her very carefully so that his valuable prize did not escape.
She knew that Tonar's scouts had not found Porit. If they
had, Tonar would have told her. She only hoped that the
scouts did not track Porit to Hoptrin, realize how close they
were to the city, and cause the Runchot to retreat before
Pleffin could find them. If that happened, escape would be
even more imperative.

"You will not escape me, SaeKet, believe me. But there
are far more interesting matters that I would like to discuss
with you." Tonar looked at her with such earnest intensity
that Rilsin was taken aback. What could this strange, ruthless, yet courteous enemy have to discuss with her?

"I have hoped for so long to meet you, someone who is
interested in the new natural science. Especially in the new
art of astronomy. I hear that you have ordered a new tele-
scope, specially made, and that you wish to provide for a
school for this study. And I have read your essay on 'The
Planets.' Truly a remarkable piece, remarkable! It is so
wonderful to find an aristocrat who cares for such things.
Unfortunately, my lord father—our lord father—" he
glanced at Phara, who sat quietly sipping her wine, "is of
the opinion that the planets, and the sun itself, orbit the

earth. I requested that he read your essay, but I am sure he has not had the time yet."

"He will never find the time," said Phara acidly. "He believes such pursuits are foolish fantasy."

"Yes. I'm afraid he does," Tonar agreed. "But I do not."

Rilsin looked at Tonar with astonishment and increased respect. The admiration for her that she had sensed in him now made sense. He was another who shared an interest in the new sciences. That he had read her essay surprised her, but what surprised her more was the mixture of enthusiasm and deference with which he engaged her in discussion. Rilsin found herself briefly forgetting that she was not this man's guest but his captive. Phara sat listening to them but did not join the conversation, and it was her yawns that finally brought both Rilsin and Tonar back to the present.

"It's late," said Tonar regretfully, "and we must be on the move shortly after dawn. SaeKet, I placed you in a tent with my sister. I hope you do not mind this, but we have few guest accommodations."

"I am sure our tent will be well-guarded, to keep us safe," said Phara. Another yawn detracted from the acerbity of her comment, and Tonar tried unsuccessfully to hide a smile.

"Yes, indeed," he said, "although you, sister, may leave the tent any time you please." He smiled at Phara and walked with her out of the tent, saying something to her in a low voice.

Rilsin was escorted to the tent by six Runchot troopers, who saw her safely inside and then took up positions outside. Rilsin considered the size of her guard and wondered how she could possibly elude all of them, while Phara combed out her hair by the flickering light of their torch.

"My brother likes you," Phara remarked.

"I like him, too," Rilsin admitted, before she realized just what Phara meant.

"I have never seen him so taken with any woman. He told me that he thinks you are beautiful as well as educated.

He said that when you lose this war, he will protect your life and take you back to Runchot with him."

Rilsin knew her mouth was open slightly, but it took her a moment to regain control of herself.

"A sense of humor runs in your family, I see," she said.

"Perhaps it does," said Phara, "but I did not inherit it, and I was not joking. My brother is infatuated with you." It was impossible to tell from her tone whether or not she approved of her brother's feelings, but Rilsin was inclined to believe she did not. Phara extinguished the torch and settled into her pile of furs. Within moments, her breathing evened.

Rilsin sat in the darkness, listening to the princess sleep. She was exhausted, but she knew she would not sleep, herself. She pondered Tonar and his behavior, and what advantage she might have if Phara spoke true. She believed Phara; Tonar was attracted by her intellect, but by more than that. He found her beautiful. It had been so long since she had seen herself in a mirror. Her appearance had never much concerned her, but she could not imagine that weeks in the wilderness had done it any good.

Thinking about Tonar and his infatuation, as Phara had called it, made her think of Sola. She had been avoiding thinking of him because she could not afford to fully grieve yet, and because, she realized, it was easier to cloak her grief with anger. Her time with Sola had been too short. She had loved him for years, and been afraid to love him, with good reason. When that reason was gone, along with Sithli sae Melisin, its author, Rilsin had still been afraid. The habit of fear had kept her from happiness. As she realized this, the anger surfaced again. Sola was gone, and Reniat was gone. Tears would not serve her, but anger would. Saeditin remained to her, and she would save it. Somehow, she must.

Her eyes had become accustomed to the dark. She could see the dim shape of Phara, curled into her furs. She could see her torn cloak, where she had tossed it. She had no weapons, nor did Phara, but that did not matter. She could not get out by fighting.

She walked softly to the tent flap and pulled it back slightly. She came face-to-face with a Runchot soldier, who put his hand on his sword. Rilsin stepped back into the tent, letting the flap fall. She could see the shadows of the other troopers against the outside wall of the tent. Frowning again, she sat down on the pile of furs heaped for her bedding. She placed her palms against the earth, trying to feel the song of the land. She could feel the cold earth and the forests around her, dreaming of the spring that was almost here. She tried to sense outward toward Hoptrin, to feel the life of the city. She remembered the feel of those lives that were Saeditin's, linked to it. She wanted to feel the massing of her armies, to feel Pleffin and Porit and Chilsa.

She did not. All she felt was the earth and the trees and the stone, and above it all, the dark fire of her own anger. Frustration almost overwhelmed her, and then she remembered what she had felt in the caves and on the Demon Bridge: the sense of two lives, Reniat's and Sola's. It had been delusion, self-delusion and fantasy. If the song of the land could trick her in this way, or rather, if she could trick herself with the song, then she could trust neither the song nor herself. Confused and frustrated, she eventually drifted into sleep.

23

RILSIN WASN'T SURE WHAT WOKE HER. THE SKY WAS BE-
ginning to lighten; she could tell even through the walls of
the tent. She was filled with a sense of urgency and knowledge. Phara was still sleeping peacefully. Rilsin ran her
hand quickly through her hair, tugged her overshirt straight,
walked to the tent flap, and pulled it back. A Runchot guard
faced her, hand going to sword. Rilsin nodded to him, saying nothing, and took one step out of the tent. His sword
hissed free of its scabbard. She ignored him, concentrating
instead on the earth beneath her feet and on the very air
around her.

It was cold predawn, and the gray light seemed almost
brittle. Rilsin drew in a deep breath. Now she was sure.

"Take me to Prince Tonar," she told the trooper in Runchot. When he frowned at her, sword still drawn, she lost
patience. The back of her neck itched with impending ca-
tastrophe.

"Now!" she said. "It's urgent."

"You will see the prince when he wants to see you," said the guard, "and not before."

"I said it's urgent!" Rilsin took another step forward, but the other guards had come at the disturbance, and she now faced a wall of six armed enemy troopers.

"What is going on out here?" Phara stood in the open tent flap, looking out. She was wrapped in a soldier's russet uniform cloak, but her hair was in disarray, her face still slack from sleep.

"I need to see your brother," Rilsin told her. "Immediately."

Phara stared at her. "Surely it can wait a little," she began.

"No," Rilsin interrupted her, "it cannot. It's a matter of his life. And yours. And," she added, glancing at the troopers who still surrounded her, "their lives, too."

That no one believed her did not matter. Phara made the decision to go to her brother, so they went.

Tonar was up and had been alerted. He came out of his tent, looking more rested than he had a right to, Rilsin thought.

"Good morning, sister, SaeKet," he said courteously, "what is it that brings you out so early?"

"She insisted on seeing you, and right away," Phara said. "She—"

"Excuse me for interrupting," Rilsin said. Her shoulder blades prickled, her whole skin crawled uncomfortably as she looked around the camp, nestled in its tiny cleft in the hills. She remembered that her husband Sifuat had lost his first and final battle because he made the mistake of camping in a valley. Her unease intensified, almost choking her.

"Lord Prince," she said, "I have some bad news for you. You are—"

A trooper ran up to them, breathless. "Surrounded!" he gasped. "By Saeditin troops! The camp is surrounded!"

Tonar reacted immediately. He nodded at two of his men. They grasped Rilsin by the arms and pulled her hands behind her back, tying them. Rilsin made no resistance, but she looked to Tonar, who was barking orders.

"Lord Prince!" she said. "Tonar!" Her voice cracked through the confusion. Tonar looked at her, obviously struggling to retain some of his former courtesy in the face of potential disaster.

"I am sorry, SaeKet, but you are my hostage."

"And I will die your hostage, right along with you, and your sister, and all your men, if that's your choice." Rilsin willed him to look at her, to really hear her. "We can have this battle, and you will lose. No," she shrugged, forestalling what he would say, unable to gesture with her hands bound behind her, "you *will* lose. You are gravely outnumbered, and from all sides." She looked at the trooper who had brought the news. "Tell him," she ordered.

"She is right." The man's eyes were wide, and he was pale. "There are hundreds of Saeditin troops all around us!"

"And we haven't much time," continued Rilsin. "They will attack soon, unless I stop them. So we can have this battle, or we can have a truce, if you will hear what I have to offer."

"You have nothing to offer. I do. You are my captive, and I am going to offer them your life," said Tonar grimly. "If Sae Pleffin does not accept, we will fight our way out. I am sorry; I would hate to kill you."

"It will be necessary." It was her calm and her apparent complete lack of fear that finally made Tonar stop and look at her.

"Pleffin sae Grisna commands those troops, and he will not bargain for me. If I die in this attack, then I die." Rilsin shrugged. "You and all your troops die, and Sithli sae Melisin and all her troops will be massacred as soon as they cross the border. And anyone with them, even Prince Raphat, if he comes. Saeditin will be free, whether I live or die."

She felt it was true, and she willed Tonar to believe it. Pleffin thought she was dead or would act as if she were. If Tonar offered Pleffin her life, Pleffin would assume it was a ruse. What would happen to Saeditin if she died? With Reniat gone, she had no heir. Rilsin put the thought from her mind. She looked down at Tonar.

"What happens now, Prince, is your choice."

"What is your proposal?" Tonar was grim and unhappy, but he was no fool.

"A truce, and peace between us. You come with me, and I will signal my commander. You and all your men will give up your weapons—"

"No! We will not surrender to you!"

"Listen to me. You give up your weapons, and we will give you your lives, and more, we will give you safe conduct through Saeditin to the border. Surely you don't think I will let your force, however outnumbered, march through my land armed! But you, Prince, and your troops can be my guests. I told you I would return your courtesy and your hospitality, at least until this business with Sithli is over. Then you can go home. I want no conflict with you."

Tonar turned on his heel, away from her, and spoke quietly but fiercely with some of his men. Try as she would, Rilsin could not overhear what was said. Phara remained, looking at Rilsin.

"You would have my brother go home in disgrace," she said bitterly.

"What did you expect?" Rilsin felt surprise and a little pity. Phara seemed so tortured by her own thoughts and her own past. *As am I,* Rilsin thought fleetingly. She pushed the thought aside. "You are the one who came to save your brother at all costs, so he will not go to worse defeat and certain death when Sithli's troops turn on her, and Prince Raphat's plan fails. I do not know what you expected here, but this is how to save your brother. What will your father think, if both of you die here? What will that do to the land of Runchot?"

Phara lifted her head. "I know you're right." She was far from happy about it. "I do not care in the least what my lord father thinks, but I do care for my own land. I know this is what we must do."

"I know it, too, I am sorry to say. SaeKet, I would talk with you more on this." Tonar looked as unhappy as his sister.

"We have no time. We need to act now, Prince, or it will soon be too late." The sense of something impending, of a wave cresting, was huge and almost unbearable.

"Where is your commander, SaeKet? How do you know where he is?"

Tonar took her by the elbow, as her hands were still bound, and was leading her away from the center of the little camp. Several of his captains followed him, with Phara trailing them all. Rilsin stopped, resisting Tonar's grip. She frowned, concentrating. The feeling of the storm about to break was not weather sense, such as the priests had. The storm she felt was human, and she sensed its apex, and its point of power. She turned toward one low hill and pointed with her chin.

"Up there!" she said. "Sae Pleffin is up there. Untie me! Now, before it's too late!"

Tonar unsheathed his knife in one quick movement. He stepped behind her and cut the ropes around her wrists. Rilsin rubbed at her wrists briefly, then grabbed his arm.

"Come on!"

Half striding, half running, they left the outskirts of the tiny camp. Rilsin looked up. The hills were dark with Saeditin troops. Her troops. She knew where Pleffin was, she could feel him now, but she knew what he saw when he looked down from his position. He saw a small group of the enemy leave their camp, walk out, and stare upward toward him. She stopped. She had not thought this through. It could still end in disaster.

"Stay back." Rilsin glanced around to be sure Tonar and his captains obeyed. All of them were staring up uneasily at the Saeditin troops around them. Rilsin stepped forward.

She was conscious of the gaze of the soldiers on the hillsides. She could actually see archers at the front, training her in their sights. Her gaze swept the hillside: yes, there was a small company with fire-tubes.

"Sae Pleffin!" Rilsin raised her voice and pitched it to carry. "Commander! Can you hear me?"

"He should hear you, but I don't know if he can make out the words." Rilsin turned to find that Tonar had come up behind her.

"Great freezing—damn it! I told you to stay back, Prince!" As she watched, the fire-tube company lifted their tubes. Were they in range? The sleet began to fall harder, and the wind tore at her clothing.

"Pleffin sae Grisna!" She put all the force she could into her voice, and she heard her words echo back from the hills. Surely Pleffin had heard that.

There was movement from where she knew Pleffin stood, a shifting and roiling, and then suddenly a sleek, silver form shot out of the assembled troops and raced down the hillside: Chilsa. The hunting cat covered the distance in what seemed the blink of an eye. He flung himself against Rilsin's legs, chuffing and purring simultaneously. Rilsin grinned. She reached down and hugged the cat and began to scratch behind his ears. Then Chilsa turned his green eyes on Tonar, his body tensing.

"Father of Battles," whispered the prince, retreating a step.

"He's a friend, Chilsa," said Rilsin, anxious to forestall at least that attack.

On the hillside, someone shouted a command. The fire-tube company lowered their tubes; the archers slipped the arrows back into their quivers. The troops were parting. A figure mounted on a horse rode out, alone, partway down the hill.

"SaeKet! Rilsin SaeKet!"

Rilsin glanced back at Tonar, who was flanked now by his captains and by Phara.

"This time, Prince," she said, "stay here. Do not follow me. If you hold your troops back, I give you my word we will not attack you."

She did not wait for his reply but walked forward, between the two forces, with Chilsa at her side. For a moment

she stood alone between the two armies. Then Pleffin rode
forward and reined up beside her, dismounting in a practiced glide.

"SaeKet," he said again, this time in almost a whisper.
He looked as though he fought back tears.

Rilsin looked at him for a moment, and then walked forward and embraced him. Pleffin sae Grisna, tough old soldier though he was, sobbed. The troops on the hillsides
began to cheer.

THANK THE MOTHER they were at last ready to leave, Sola
thought. It had taken less time than he had feared to reach
First Man Bilt of the Wilfrisin in his winter village, but it
had taken far more time than he liked for him to explain
things to Bilt. No, that wasn't strictly true. It had taken Bilt
virtually no time to understand the situation. What had
taken time was Sola's advocacy of the Clinsi. He had become the Clinsi advocate and simultaneously an aid to First
Man Bilt in the saving of the Confederacy. The first seemed
expected of him as Solstice Warrior, the second seemed expected of him as unofficial representative of Saeditin.

On his way down the river with Chif, they had come
across still more Clinsi who had no wish to leave their new
nation. Sola found himself, as the Solstice Warrior, already
well-known and credited with powers of persuasion. The
news had spread fast. Finding himself cast in the role of
peacemaker and arbitrator of the northern tribes was something he would never have dreamed, but he was good at it.
The Clinsi listened to him. The Wilfrisin listened to him.
He consulted Bilt on every matter. He trusted Bilt since
Rilsin did, but with typical Saeditin arrogance, he would
never have imagined that a northerner, barbarian or not,
could have anything to teach him. Sola, watching and listening to First Man Bilt, began to learn something of northern politics and also of the art of persuasion. He spoke
Wilfrisin well now, and he spoke Clinsi better than he had.

Throughout all of this, Sola wanted to go home. He
missed Rilsin desperately. She could not know what had

happened to him, why he had vanished. Did she believe him dead? He wanted to get Reniat back home safely. Bilt agreed with him that Rilsin needed to know that her daughter was safe, and he had sent a messenger south to Saeditin to inform her. It was only much later that they heard that the messenger had not arrived and that the SaeKet herself was missing. He did not even know if Rilsin had found her way back from the Demon Bridge. So close, thought Sola. He had been so close to her and had never known.

Every minute spent in the Confederacy was too long. The thought that he was doing nothing to find her, to help his own land, was almost more than he could bear.

"Sola dira, I agree, you must get back. But going unprepared is as dangerous as not going. Now I have your escort ready. We can go in two days' time, if the weather holds." Bilt watched Sola pacing the hard-packed earthen floor. "I am taking my warriors to your SaeKet's aid, as promised by our treaty. The treaty would not be worth much if my Confederacy had failed," Bilt reminded him. "It will not now, in part because of your efforts. So we will go. And you will bring the Suncat SaeKetti Reniat." Bilt smiled.

Most people smiled when they spoke of Reniat, Sola had noticed. The little girl seemed to have a knack for winning hearts. She had even won the heart of Lendis, Bilt's young son, who treated her like another little sister. The two were playing now in a corner of the cabin, and from the sounds of it, Lendis was gently tickling the little girl.

Sola and Bilt sat near the fire in the warm, earth-covered cabin in Bilt's winter village. It was a village deep under the shelter of the northern forest, hidden on a small flat-topped hill. The two dozen or so small cabins were all earth-covered for added insulation, and all set back under the trees, which gave additional cover. The smoke rising from their smoke holes and chimneys seemed to arise from the earth itself, and mingled with the icy mists.

"Sit down, Sola, my friend. Walking the floor will not help you leave any the sooner."

Sola forced himself to sit. Ticha, Bilt's wife, came in

with some of the deep-fried cakes the Wilfrisin loved. Bilt helped himself to several, and he and Ticha exchanged a fond glance before she carried Reniat away, trailed by her son.

Sola watched the quiet affection between Bilt and Ticha, which ran so deep it seemed to need no words. He took a fried cake himself, but he could only nibble at it and fidget, lost in thoughts he could not formulate clearly, even to himself.

"You miss her badly."

Sola jumped. He had been so distracted he had not noticed when Bilt's attention returned to him.

"Without her, Saeditin falls apart. She hasn't had the time yet to restore Saeditin from the wreck Sithli sae Melisin made. And she has no heir but Reniat. Even if I bring Reniat home safely—"

"Tch." Bilt made a disgusted noise. "I am not speaking of Saeditin politics, friend Sola; I am speaking of your heart. You miss Rilsin sae Becha because you love her. And you hope she loves you, but you are unsure."

Sola stared at the big northerner and then looked away, tugging nervously on his short brown hair. It was growing out again, but not much, and he was unused to its cropped length. Bilt did not appear to be a perceptive man, but then, he would not be first man and the founder of his new nation if he were not.

"I did not know you were as expert as a grandmother in love matters." He tried to make a joke of it.

"I don't know how expert I am, my friend, but I know how it is between Ticha and me, and I see how it is with you. And I have seen how it is with Rilsin, who is also my friend. I hope you do not mind if I tell you what I think."

"I don't mind," Sola muttered. He did mind because he was embarrassed, but he tried not to let Bilt see. He was also horrified that his private concerns should have been so obvious.

"Well then, here is what I have seen." Bilt settled himself back comfortably in the heavy wooden chair.

"I believe Rilsin has loved you for a long time. Not just because of what my spies have told me of your history and childhood together," Bilt grinned when he saw Sola start, "but from the way she would look at you and speak to you. Yes, she loved her husband, but he is gone now and no longer in your way. He was never the right man for her. She knows this." Bilt dismissed Sifuat with a brief wave. "That is not the problem. If Rilsin SaeKet has loved you always, and if her husband no longer stands between you, then what is the problem, my friend?"

"I don't know," muttered Sola.

"You are. And she is."

Sola sat up straight. Bilt smiled slightly when he saw that he had his guest's attention. "Rilsin has put Sifuat aside, but you cannot. You could not get past the fact that the child of your beloved was the child of your rival." Bilt held up his hand when he saw Sola open his mouth. "That is no longer the case."

Bilt glanced in the direction in which Ticha had gone, taking the children with her. "I have seen how you love that child, Rilsin's child, and you have risked your life for her, for love and not for duty. I think the problem you face now is with Sae Rilsin. She loves you, but she is afraid."

"Afraid?" Sola knew he sounded as astonished and stupid as he felt. "What has she to be afraid of?"

"Think, my friend. She was never able to love without fear, never in all her life. Sithli did that to her. She is still afraid to love. She is afraid of what that will do to you, since it is you that she loves. She is afraid that it will put you in danger. Look what has already happened to you. You vanished from her side. She could love only her child without reserve, and look what happened then, even to her child."

Sola realized that his mouth was hanging open, and he shut it with an audible snap. He forced himself to draw a breath. Beneath his bluff exterior, the Wilfrisin first man had not only a mind that missed nothing but also a heart that missed nothing.

"You are right," Sola said at last.

"I know that. I am glad that you know it, too. The question, my friend Sola, is whether or not you can help Sae Rilsin overcome her fear."

"I am going to try."

"Good. Because if you don't, someone else will. I would hate for that to happen, my friend."

Bilt leaned over and gave Sola a friendly thump on the shoulder. Sola tried not to wince.

24

Hoptrin and the Sudit manor house were both just as she remembered them from weeks before, and yet they seemed strange to Rilsin. She had been too long in the northern forests and in the caves, but the initial sense of being out of place soon passed. What did not pass were the reminders of the past. The house spoke to her of Sifuat, and even more of his powerful mother Norimin, and Rilsin supposed it always would.

There was no time to brood. Accommodations had to be found for the Runchot troops, and arrangements made. Finding space was not difficult, as Tonar had with him less than two hundred men, and Hoptrin had long been a garrison for thousands. Rilsin ordered that the Runchot be split apart, spread out among the Saeditin troops, and disarmed.

"They are to be treated as much like guests and as little like prisoners as possible," Rilsin told Pleffin, "but take no chances with them."

Prince Tonar, Phara, and the Runchot captains were lodged in the manor house, as were she and Pleffin. All of them had guards at their doors, so in this the Runchot were no different than their Saeditin hosts, at least ostensibly. Tonar knew the difference, but he said nothing of it, and if he missed his weapons, he said nothing of that, either. He accepted the turning of fortune with such apparent good grace that Rilsin was surprised and also a little concerned. She had the distinct impression that there was something she should know but did not.

They ate in the Sudit banquet room, a large room for what was a small group: Rilsin, with Chilsa at her feet, and her officers, Tonar and his officers, and Phara. The lavender and silver Sudit colors were everywhere: in the curtains, the hangings on the walls, even in the carpets. Their carved wooden chairs had been touched and ornamented with silver paint. It was meant to overwhelm the diner with sophistication and luxury, and although it was not to Rilsin's taste, the Runchot were suitably impressed.

"I want to get word to my lord father," Tonar leaned forward to speak to Rilsin, who was opposite him at the table, but his words carried in a sudden lull.

Pleffin leaned back in his carved chair, regarding the Runchot prince. He was disinclined to like any Runchot, however courteous, and he wished they were all under lock and key. His SaeKet made him nervous by treating them this well.

"Send word to Raphat?" Pleffin's raised eyebrows spoke volumes, as did his lack of a title for his guest's father.

Rilsin frowned at her commander. She understood how he felt, but his rudeness was out of place. It was possible that Tonar might someday rule in his father's stead, and she wanted a better relationship with their southern neighbor.

"What message, Prince Tonar?" she asked.

"I wish to tell my father what most of us here at this table already know. If he persists in what was a good plan, a very good plan," Tonar looked completely unabashed, "Runchot will lose. My father may put himself in danger. You have said you do not wish a war with us. Let me warn my father the prince of what Sithli sae Melisin is leading him into."

Pleffin laughed. Some of the Saeditin officers followed suit, but Rilsin did not. She stared down at her plate, thinking. After a moment, the laughter ceased.

"Why not?" said Rilsin slowly. She looked up to find Pleffin staring at her, his mouth slightly open. "Really, Commander, why not?" she said again. "We do not wish to fight the Runchot. If we can discourage them from attacking us, it would suit all of us. I have no desire to lose even one of my troops," she looked around, "if it can be avoided. If Prince Raphat insists on fighting us, he will lose, as we will be ready. If he knows he cannot win, perhaps he will give us Sithli sae Melisin and Kepit sae Lisim. If he will not," she gazed briefly into the distance, and then turned her icy gaze on Tonar, "then we have no choice." Complete silence followed her words.

Then they all began to talk at once. Rilsin sat back and listened for a while. She valued what her officers had to say, but she knew they would all end up in agreement with her, and she had other matters she wished to deal with. She wanted this dinner finished.

"Prince Tonar will send no word. The message will come from me, but not until we are back in Petipal. Then we will see how Prince Raphat of Runchot responds." Rilsin rose, ending the dinner.

"Thank you, SaeKet. Your reputation for fair thought is well-deserved." Tonar leaned toward her for a moment. "I want nothing more than good relations between us." The smile he gave her was more than cordial.

Rilsin frowned, but Tonar was already being escorted down the corridor. She found the Runchot prince disturbing in a number of ways. The balance of power had shifted in Saeditin's favor, but he seemed unperturbed. Once again she had the feeling that there was something she should know, but there was another matter that demanded her attention first. She turned to Pleffin.

"Where is she, Sae Pleffin? Where is Meffa?" Pleffin

seemed not to hear her. His eyes were following Tonar
down the corridor. "Commander!"

Pleffin turned from glowering after the Runchot prince.

"I said, where is she? You told me she was still in the
care of a physician, but you did not say where the infirmary
was."

It turned out that Meffa was not in the infirmary. She had
been given a small room of her own. Rilsin went alone, refusing Pleffin's offer of a guard. Now that she had finally
returned, events were moving quickly, and she desperately
wanted a little time to herself.

There was no guard at the door of Meffa's room, but
there was someone in the room, sitting in a chair near the
bed. It was Porit, looking at a book, turning the pages
slowly, frowning. He looked up as Rilsin entered and then
jumped to his feet, hand to heart, stuffing the book behind
him on the chair. Rilsin smiled at his sudden formality. She
crossed the room and grasped his hands.

"I am so glad you are safe," she whispered. Meffa was
asleep, and Rilsin did not want to wake her, but she realized
just how worried she had been about the boy.

Porit burst into tears. "I should have known they
couldn't kill you," he sobbed.

Rilsin stared at him, touched, and gathered him into her
arms. She realized suddenly the place she had taken in the
life of this boy who had lost his mother so young, and she
wondered why it had taken her this long to see it. Porit
snuffled noisily, trying to control himself. The sound woke
Meffa.

"SaeKet," Meffa whispered. Her voice was thin and
raspy, and she coughed, but she tried to sit up. In a flash,
Porit was beside her, helping to prop her up. Rilsin took the
pillows from him and finished the task herself.

"I am so sorry," she said, smoothing back her friend's
hair. She could see the bandage now on Meffa's left arm, or
what remained of her arm.

"They say I will recover, SaeKet, and that I will learn to
manage with one hand almost as well as two." Meffa

smiled bravely. "At least it was my left hand, and I have always favored my right. The doctor says I am fortunate."

"I am the one who is fortunate. I don't know what I would do without you." Rilsin leaned over her friend, wanting to say more, but she saw Meffa's eyelids flutter.

"The doctor gave her something to make her sleep," said Porit.

Meffa yawned.

"Sleep, then," said Rilsin, settling her back against the pillows. She fought the sudden lump in her throat and turned to leave.

"SaeKet." The whisper was faint but urgent, and Rilsin turned back.

"Don't leave me, SaeKet. I know you are going back to Petipal. I want to go with you."

"If the doctor says you are strong enough to travel, then you may. I will ask him—"

"I must go with you!"

"All right, Meffa, I will see to it."

"Please, SaeKet, I have to tell you, you must know—" Meffa began to cough.

Alarmed, Rilsin went back to her and held her. When Meffa had finished coughing, she dropped back against the pillows and was asleep almost instantly. Rilsin walked quietly from the room, motioning Porit to follow her.

"What did she want to tell me?" Rilsin asked.

"I don't know, SaeKet. She has been having waking dreams, the sort that go with fever, the doctor said. She says she has seen things, people—men, coming to kidnap the SaeKetti. The doctor says the dreams will go once she is well again." Porit stopped. His eyes filled with tears, try though he did to fight them back. "This is my fault, SaeKet! I know you said it isn't, but Meffa would not have come if it were not for me! If she had stayed in Petipal, she would not have been hurt!"

"Meffa is a grown woman. She did what she did not just for you but for me, Porit." Rilsin put her hand on his shoulder and turned him to look at her. "Porit, it's not your fault."

He looked up at her and tried to smile bravely. Rilsin asked to see the book he had been looking at. It was a small book, made for children of saedin, to teach them. During her more lucid moments, Meffa had already started teaching Porit to read. By the time Rilsin had walked the boy to the room he shared with two junior officers, he seemed to be feeling better. Rilsin was not. She did not blame Porit for what happened, but she did blame herself. It seemed that no matter whom she loved, she could not keep them safe.

She reached the room that had been set aside for her and watched the guard snap to attention, hand to heart. Inside, Chilsa was sprawled on the bed, shedding silver fur on the lavender velvet of the coverlet. The room had been Norimin's once. Rilsin was not entirely happy at being in her mother-in-law's old room, but it was better than being in the room that had been Sifuat's. She sat on the bed, scratching Chilsa behind the ears. The big cat sighed. Rilsin pulled off her boots and stretched out on the bed beside the cat.

She wondered what Meffa had wanted to tell her. And she wondered why Tonar had seemed so calm at finding himself in Saeditin custody. Perhaps the clue was that he only *seemed* complacent. Rilsin frowned, wanting to pursue the thought, but there were too many mysteries, and she was too tired to stay awake to think about them.

ESSiT HAð BEEΠ monitoring the border for the past two weeks, but his spies told him nothing new. He had no spies as good as the missing Gigrat, but he would have known if Raphat were moving his troops. His intelligence was certainly good enough for that. Raphat had massed his troops across the border, but he seemed to be waiting for something. It made Essit jittery. He wanted to do something now, but he couldn't go over the border and start a war without his SaeKet's authorization, and he couldn't leave the capital undefended.

He wished he knew that Rilsin was in fact safe, but no messenger had come from the north, not surprising since the weather was bad, which also meant that communication by sun-flash was not possible. So Essit waited and worried and kept the roads open. At last the messenger came. Rilsin SaeKet Becha was in Hoptrin and had captured the surprise Runchot invaders from the north. Essit felt a huge joy that was overshadowed only by an equally huge and overwhelming relief. He found he could not stop smiling. The SaeKet had returned, and the city was safe. He called in Dremfir and the SaeKet's council to give them all the good news, and he had the bells rung in all the temples.

When the word came up from the south by signal fire that the Runchot were sending raids over the border, Essit hesitated no more. It was more like the northern barbarians than the Runchot, and the thought made him smile, as even the northern barbarians no longer acted this way. He had no doubt that this was the prelude to the Runchot invasion, and he thought it was careless of them to tip their hand this way. He would go south and stop the raids before they became an invasion in force. He would get this under control before Rilsin returned to Petipal.

Essit left Petipal and took most of the city forces with him to reinforce the troops at the border, now that there was no danger to the capital. The SaeKet and Commander Pleffin would bring the rest of the army down from the north as soon as the weather permitted.

Unfortunately, the weather was terrible. They were not far past the midpoint day between winter solstice and spring equinox, the coldest time of the year. The temperature had warmed briefly, melting some of the snow, and then suddenly plunged, turning the melt to an icy crust above the deeper snow. Roads were treacherous. Essit took the troops south and camped with them near the southern town of Aphala Tree, just across the border from Runchot. He was convinced that even the raids would stop now, because of the weather, and certainly any invasion must wait. He was very unhappily surprised to be awakened just before one icy dawn with the news that the Runchot were already across the border.

It did not take long to get the troops alerted and ready to march. The weather was gray, and it was sleeting, once again useless for sun-flash. Essit would have to send a messenger north to Petipal and then onward to Hoptrin and the SaeKet. It would take days, even with the fastest horses. The traditional signal fire alerting of Runchot invasion would have to be lit, but Essit felt it was a crude message, one as likely to cause panic as to warn and alert. He delayed very briefly, only the day, before ordering the signal fires lit. It gave him time to move his troops to meet the Runchot force. It also almost cost him the war.

"SAEKEȚ, WAKE UP!"

Someone was pounding on the door, and then, when she groggily gave permission to enter, came in still shouting. It was Pleffin sae Grisna.

"Signal fires, SaeKet! From Petipal and the south. A Runchot force has come over the border!"

Rilsin sat up. It was still dark, but it had the feeling of just before dawn. She remembered the first Runchot invasion, when Essit had awakened her with the news in Petipal, when Sithli was SaeKet, and she had had to leave her husband and go, pregnant, to repel the enemy. Before Reniat was born. The stab of loss was sharp and sudden. She doubled over briefly with a grief so intense it was physical, but she rubbed her eyes and straightened. Her husband was dead. Her daughter was dead. Sola was dead. She was not in Petipal but Hoptrin, and she was SaeKet, not Sithli.

"Is there a messenger, Sae Pleffin?" She waved the guards out and swung her feet over the side of the bed.

"Not yet. SaeKet. The weather."

Pleffin was not in the least embarrassed to see his SaeKet barefoot and in the thick nightshirt that reached to her ankles. He handed her the clothes she had tossed on the corner love seat the previous evening and turned his back while she dressed.

"Sae Essit should be able to hold them while we come south." Rilsin dressed quickly and reached for her sword.

"We will need to go back to Petipal immediately. What is the weather today? I wish we had Mage Dremfir with us, but perhaps he will be of more help to Essit."

She paused in the act of buckling on her sword. Pleffin, about to give her the bad news about the weather, stopped. He recognized the abstracted look on his SaeKet's face with a prickle of awe. He had seen her listen to the song of the land before, but it was not something he would ever become accustomed to.

"It's not right," said Rilsin slowly. "There's something not right." She looked up, right at Pleffin, but she did not see him. He took a step backward. "In the south, yes, the Runchot. Over the border. A lot of them coming, I think. And just to the north, something else, the land is friendly to them now, not in the past, but now, they are friendly. Friendly, and, and—" She blinked, actually seeing Pleffin now, and distracted by him. What had she felt there?

"I think First Man Bilt is bringing troops south. I imagine we will receive his messenger soon, Sae Pleffin."

First Man Bilt, who else could it be? But what else had she felt? For a moment she had thought of Sola and her child. She could not let herself be so distracted. But farther south, in Saeditin itself, farther south than Hoptrin, something was wrong.

She looked at Pleffin with frustration. He shook his head, helpless, and shrugged and spread his hands.

"It feels wrong," said Rilsin again. She shook her head, irritated. "It is like a sickness, a moving sickness." She put her hand over her stomach, as if she felt ill, and then suddenly her gaze sharpened. One of the mysteries began to resolve itself.

"Where is Prince Tonar?" Her voice was like icy steel, and Pleffin actually jumped.

"Asleep, SaeKet, under guard."

"Get him up." Rilsin forced the words out between her teeth. "Get him up now, and bring him to me."

She waited in what had been her mother-in-law's audience hall for them to bring in Tonar. Rilsin had chosen this

room, with its huge, ornate carved chair on the dais because
of its formality. She had a point to make to her unwilling
guest.

It was clear that the Runchot prince took her point immediately. He glanced around the room, seeing the typical
Sudit ostentation but also the Saeditin troopers lining his
path. They brought him to the foot of the dais. He looked
up at her calmly but warily.

"How many troops did you bring with you on this expedition?" she asked him.

Something flickered behind Tonar's eyes. He would
have looked away, but he seemed incapable of breaking
Rilsin's glance. There was absolute silence in the hall.

"How many?" said Rilsin again.

"You have surely counted us, SaeKet; I know you have."
Tonar had regained his smooth and courteous manner.

"That is not what I asked you, Prince."

Pleffin, standing beside Rilsin, did not flinch. He would
have, had that icy cold voice been directed at him. He felt a
certain grudging respect for the Runchot commander, who
still seemed completely at ease in the midst of enemies who
were far from well-disposed to him.

"I have one hundred thirty-one men with me, SaeKet.
There were one hundred fifty with me, but some died crossing the mountains and the forests."

"With you," said Rilsin. "And how many did you detach
and send a different route?"

The silence in the hall lengthened. Pleffin put his hand
on his sword. He looked at Rilsin. If she so much as
breathed the word, he would kill this Runchot where he
stood.

"Two hundred and fifty more." Tonar sighed and
shrugged. "I don't know how you found out, SaeKet, since
obviously you have not found them. With the help of the
Father of Battles, you will not find them in time."

"I don't have to," said Rilsin, "since we are warned. It is
not a huge force, Prince."

"It does not have to be." Tonar met her eyes. "It merely

has to move quickly and come upon your capital unaware. Your army has enough to deal with at our border. And you have been delayed here with us. My lord father will have the advantage after all."

Rilsin stood up. "I underestimated you, Prince, but that has been remedied." She surprised herself by smiling. "It was not much of an advantage, and it will be neutralized." She glanced at her commander, who was rigid at her side. "No, Sae Pleffin, you may not kill him, although I understand the urge." Her glance flicked back to Tonar. "He may still have some value for us."

"I am glad," responded Tonar, with a slight bow, "to be considered of value to such a talented and beautiful enemy. I do hope that we will not always be enemies."

Rilsin barely stopped herself from gaping at him. She looked for a sardonic glint in his eye or a trace of sarcasm behind his words. There was none. He met her astonished glance warmly. Rilsin drew back.

"Get him out of here," she said, "before I kill him myself."

25

THEY WERE MARCHING SOUTH AS FAST AS THE WEATHER
would permit them. It was not nearly fast enough for Rilsin.
The weather had been unremittingly bad, as if somehow it,
too, had turned against them. Rilsin knew Tonar's second
force was ahead of them, closer to Petipal, but she did not
know where. Either the song of the land could not give her
information that exact, or she was not capable of hearing
what was required in the song, she did not know. All she
knew was the sense of desperation she felt, as the icy roads
impeded the progress of her troops and made every mile excruciating.

She knew that Tonar's small secondary force intended to
get as close to Petipal as they could before their presence
became known. Then they would burn and lay waste what
they could, as fast as they could, right to the gates of the
city. They did not hope to overwhelm a large Saeditin force;
their advantage was all in surprise and confusion.

The timing was to coincide with Raphat's attack over the
border. One problem for Tonar was that communication

had failed. Whatever message was to be sent between Tonar's band and his father had gone astray; no doubt a messenger waylaid or dead, so that Raphat, tired of waiting, had attacked first. This might not prove to the disadvantage of the Runchot, if Essit had taken most of the troops in Petipal to the border, as Rilsin was very much afraid he had.

She had sent three messengers, separately, to find Essit and give him warning. Toward the end of a week on the road, painfully inching south, a return messenger had arrived. Essit had most of the troops at the border, as she had feared. And he was the first messenger Essit had sent; he had not come in response to her messages.

"What troops are left in the city?" she asked him.

"The Petipal Guard, SaeKet."

"Send another messenger to Sae Essit." She frowned upward at the leaden skies. "Make that two messengers. We need more troops in Petipal."

Tonar and Phara were still with her, although the other captured Runchot remained in Hoptrin under guard. She had the prince and princess kept away from her. She believed they might prove useful eventually, but she was reluctant to see them now. Tonar disturbed her in ways she did not wish to analyze, although she found her thoughts drifting to him frequently.

As they were making camp in a field crusted with icy snow, a trooper approached her, putting hand to heart.

"I am sorry, SaeKet, but the Runchot saedin is demanding to see you. He claims it is very important. He will not be silent."

"I'll see him," she said, "and find out what is so urgent. Bring him here."

When they brought him, it was hard to imagine him giving his guards no peace. He was polite as ever, and despite the hard travel, the difficult conditions, and the uncertainty he must feel, Tonar looked well, as if hardship agreed with him. His own russet uniform cloak had been taken from him, and he had been supplied with one of gray wool, nondescript but thick and warm. He had this wrapped around

him against the bitter evening cold, with the gray hood
drawn up over his head. Wisps of pale red-blond hair escaped from the sides of the hood, making him look almost
comical and certainly harmless. Rilsin reminded herself
that he was not.

"What is it, Prince?" Her tone was more clipped and
abrupt than she had intended.

"My sister, the Princess Phara. I am concerned about
her."

"In what way?" Rilsin was genuinely puzzled. She had
ordered that both Tonar and Phara be treated well, that they
be as fed and warm as any of her troops.

Tonar's hood fell back. His round face was flushed from
the cold, and it seemed to Rilsin that even in the flickering
firelight, his eyes were intensely blue.

"I am concerned about what will happen to her if you
bargain with my lord father. You must understand," he
paused, and Rilsin felt the weight of his regard again, "that
she would not fare well if she is returned to him. He will
consider her actions treasonous."

"And you do not." It was not a question.

"No, I do not. She came to save my life, she believed,
and also to save Runchot from defeat. And I do not consider
her refusal to wed at my lord father's orders treason, and
worthy of death."

"Ah," said Rilsin. "Well, I do not either, Prince. I will do
what I can to safeguard your sister." She was careful not to
promise. She hoped that if it came to bargaining with
Raphat, he would not insist on the return of his daughter.
The Mother willing, he would not be in a position to do so,
but luck did not seem to be with her recently, and she would
use Phara if she had to.

"There is one more thing, Rilsin SaeKet. I am sorry that
we met under the circumstances we did, and I am sorry that
we must, at least for now, continue in this way. I have long
admired you, as you know."

Tonar knew how to focus his intensity, to turn it on her
like torchlight. She drew back slightly from this heat.

"I want to assure you," Tonar continued, "that you need have no fear, when this, ah, matter is concluded, for your personal safety. You know now that my lord father will almost certainly win. I doubt you can even reach Petipal before my troops do and before my father comes up from the south. If you stay with me, I will see to it that you come to no harm. Whatever my lord father's intentions, I will not let him give you again to Sithli sae Melisin, once she is back in Petipal. I am sorry that you cannot remain Saeditin's ruler, but my father will not allow that. You will be a captive in Runchot, but it will not be so bad. In time, I think, you will come to appreciate Runchot, if not enjoy it, especially in my company." He smiled at her again, even more warmly.

Tonar's escort of Saeditin troopers had heard this speech. Without exception, they bristled, hands going to their swords.

"I will kill you now, which is better than you deserve," snarled their captain.

"Stop," said Rilsin. "Do not harm him." Her voice sounded strangled, and she seemed to be struggling for speech.

The captain slid his sword back into its sheath reluctantly, peering in the dusk at his SaeKet.

"Thank you for your concern," Rilsin gasped, "Prince Tonar." She paused, and made an odd croaking noise, which turned into a cough.

She turned away from Tonar for a moment and glanced at her guard captain. He stared back at her, concerned. Then his lips began to twitch. Rilsin dropped her gaze, shoulders shaking slightly, but when, a moment later, she turned back to Tonar, her voice was under control.

"I will remember your concern, Prince, and I will do what I can for your sister Phara and for you."

"I know you do not take this seriously, Rilsin SaeKet, although at least your soldiers do. But you should take me seriously. I am your prisoner now, despite your talk of hospitality, but you, and Saeditin, will fall. When that time comes, and it will not be long, I will remember my promise to you. Don't you forget it."

There was something about him that was convincing, and Rilsin felt the urge to laugh fade abruptly. Tonar, at least, believed completely in what he said.

"Never fear, Prince," she said, grimly, "I will not forget." She looked at her captain. "Take him back," she said. "No one can ever claim that you lack self-confidence, Prince," she added.

Later, during the night, she woke. Chilsa was sprawled beside her on the small camp bed, and through the walls of the tent she could see the silhouette of the sentry against the fire. The night was bitter cold, and she curled down under the thick furs and drifted back into sleep. She dreamed of Sola. He was trying to tell her something, but she couldn't hear it. She tried to ask him to repeat it, but he turned away from her. Then he reached down and picked up something, no, someone. It was Reniat, and she smiled at him, and laughed, and threw her little arms around his neck. Rilsin called out again, but neither of them heard her.

She woke in the gray light of predawn, whispering the names of her lost lover and her lost child. She felt completely abandoned. Even Chilsa was no longer on the bed to keep her company but was sitting in front of the tent flap, waiting to go out.

SiTHLi HAƏ ΠEVER imagined it would be this uncomfortable. The most discomfort she had ever had to experience before this was in her flight from Saeditin, after Rilsin's successful rebellion. But even then it had not been all that uncomfortable, however infuriating and humiliating it had been. Kepit had contacts in Saeditin, members of her own Lisim clan, who had spirited them quickly out of the country. They had taken care of her, and it had not taken long to get into Runchot, claim the status of exiled SaeKet, and live in at least a certain degree of luxury.

This was different. It was winter, and bitterly cold. Her tent did not keep out the cold, and building a fire outside the

tent was barbaric and ridiculous, and bringing in fire pots
did not help much. Raphat had refused to let her build a fire
under the smoke hole of the tent, since she had come close
to burning it down, so now the smoke hole was kept closed.
Sithli complained almost constantly, and she was always
bundled in furs.

Then there was the fact that she actually had to move
with the troops, which meant being on horseback more
hours of the day than she liked to contemplate. Getting
heated water for bathing was a problem. Keeping her
makeup in good repair was a problem. Keeping her hair
properly braided and jeweled was a problem. Sithli didn't
understand how anyone of true quality could be expected to
endure this.

It was all very well for Raphat. He was a man bred to be
a soldier. It was all very well for Kepit, too, who had commanded a number of campaigns, although Kepit was now
getting old, and Sithli knew she would rather not be doing
this. Despite herself, she felt a certain grudging respect for
the soldiers and captains, and this made her think of Rilsin.
Rilsin had been the best commander she had ever known,
at least until she met Raphat, but more than that, Rilsin had
been her friend. Sithli had been able to rely on her cousin
for everything, which made the final betrayal so very much
worse. Even more horrible: Sithli missed her now. This was
not acceptable, and she reminded herself of all the wrongs
Rilsin had inflicted on her.

Sithli pulled her cloak more tightly around her. It was of
fox and ermine fur, wonderfully rich and expensive, and a
gift from Raphat. It was not as rich or as expensive as her
old cloak of valley slipe fur, which had been blindingly
white. She had been forced to leave the cloak behind, along
with so much else, when she had fled Petipal. Rilsin owed
her for that, too. Sithli blinked back tears, feeling very sorry
for herself.

She frowned out into the sleet. It seemed spring would
never come. Then she stopped frowning; it was bad for her
face. She sniffed back the tears. It was no use missing

Rilsin, and it was less use crying about it, which was not good for her complexion, either. Besides, someone was approaching her tent. The sleet came down harder, stinging, and Sithli pulled back into her shelter. After a moment, she was able to make out her visitor's identity. Her guard, hunched over in the sleet and his cloak over his head for protection, gave only a cursory challenge, and then Kirra stood before her.

Sithli knew more about the Runchot merchant now. She felt no disdain for Kirra due to the nature of her business. Kepit had owned numerous similar establishments back in Petipal, and some of the profits had made their way to Sithli. Kirra intrigued her. There were a number of mysteries surrounding her, and Sithli was surprised not to have learned more. Meeting her had not clarified much, certainly not as much as she had wanted, and being in her company on this campaign had only deepened some of the mysteries.

"Come in." Sithli held aside the entrance flap for her visitor. Servants were unavailable on this expedition, another barbarism. "You will freeze in this weather," she said.

"Thank you, SaeKet." Kirra spoke Saeditin perfectly. She had always spoken it to Sithli in the few times they had met, a courtesy Sithli appreciated since her own Runchot was less than perfect, but Kirra did not put hand to heart as a Saeditin would have when facing her SaeKet, or in any other way behave as a Saeditin. Sithli was not certain that she believed the assertion that Kirra had left Saeditin as a child, or even that she was Saeditin at all.

"I came to bring you word that my troops have come through the recent skirmish with the Saeditin scouting party with no casualties. Despite this weather, they are strong and prepared, SaeKet."

"I do not understand why you came on this campaign, Sae Kirra, when you could have remained in much more comfortable surroundings." Without thinking, Sithli gave Kirra the honorific of a noble, addressing her as a saedin.

An odd, ironic look flickered briefly across Kirra's face. Sithli squinted in the dim light of the tent. She wondered if she had seen Kirra before, if perhaps she knew her from Saeditin after all. She seemed familiar in an odd way. Sithli was sure she had never met Kirra before Kepit made the introduction. Nonetheless, something prickled along the back of her neck. Sithli had been trained, growing up, to remember faces and names.

"I could not be anywhere else." Kirra's voice was low, intense, and full of passion. She spoke the truth, and Sithli heard it in her voice.

"There is a certain Saeditin whom I hate and detest above all others. I have told you this before, SaeKet. That saedin is about to be brought down. I want to see her destruction with my own eyes. I do not want to hear of it only later and after the fact. If it is possible, I want her to know that I have had a hand in ruining her."

The intensity of Kirra's hatred caused the prickling at the back of Sithli's neck to grow stronger. "Why do you hate her so much?" she asked.

"You know I was once Saeditin, but now I am Runchot. This saedin, she destroyed my family in Saeditin. I lost everything because of her. I have no family left to me. I searched, but there is no one." Kirra looked out at the falling sleet, her face as bleak as the gray sky. "All I have left to live for is my vengeance."

Sithli drew in her breath. It was a motive she could understand, for it was what she herself wanted: vengeance against Rilsin for taking from her what was hers.

"We have the same goal," Sithli said. For a brief instant the ironic look flickered again on Kirra's face. Sithli saw it. She considered asking Kepit about it later, but she decided she had been mistaken.

"Stay by me, Sae Kirra, and you will see what I see. We will both be satisfied." Sithli had made up her mind that Kirra was, in fact, the child of a saedin family, fled from Saeditin perhaps in the reign of Rilsin's mother. She would have Kepit dig more deeply. Perhaps, after she had her land back and had retaken the SaeKet's chair, she could reward Kirra more substantially.

*   *   *

"SUN-FLASH, FIRST Minister! Sae Essit! The SaeKet's message!"

It was just past dawn, and Essit had been dozing fitfully. They had been skirmishing off and on with Runchot contingents that sneaked across the border and then just as hastily beat a retreat back again. Essit did not feel free to pursue them without the authorization of his SaeKet. Messengers from Rilsin had not come, and the skies had been uniformly leaden for weeks. Essit could not understand why the Runchot were playing this game, which must be as wearing on them as it was on the Saeditin.

At first all he felt was resentment at being awakened, but then the import of the words jolted him. He stumbled from his tent, rubbing at the blond stubble on his chin. Sure enough, the sun had risen and had broken through the clouds. It looked to be a fine, clear day in the making. The winking of light from the north continued for a moment. Although the signalers were there, noting down the message, Essit didn't need them. He had learned sun-flash as a boy, and he read the long and short flashes easily. All color drained from his face as he did. He knew now what the Runchot had been waiting for.

Sithli peered at the flashes from the north, barely visible through the long-glass hastily handed her by the Runchot trooper. Beside her, Kepit and Raphat watched through their own long-glasses. Kirra stood in the group with no glass, looking concerned.

"As we hoped," said Kepit. Satisfaction was evident in her voice.

Sithli squinted, then looked down. She had neglected learning sun-flash among her studies. As SaeKet, she had not needed to know it; there had always been someone to read it for her. As, in fact, there was now.

"Prince Tonar has succeeded." Pride in his son was clear in Raphat's posture as well as his voice.

"Succeeded?" Sithli couldn't contain herself.

"My son has struck Saeditin from the north. He took a

force over the mountains and through the barbarians' land—the new Confederacy—and moved it through Saeditin in secret. He is near to Petipal and has put it under threat. First Minister Essit sae Tillit has just received his word of this."

Raphat smiled, looking as happy as Sithli had ever seen him. Kepit was smiling, too, and slowly, Sithli began to smile. Kirra looked shocked. It was obvious that the Runchot merchant had not known of Raphat's strategy. *Her spies failed her,* thought Sithli, *and she is not accustomed to that.* There was more to it than that, but Sithli could not determine just what that might be. Before she could pursue the wayward thought, Raphat spoke up.

"Now we teach Sae Essit the lesson he so desperately needs to learn. We attack him now and tie up his forces here, while Petipal, with any luck, will burn." Raphat laughed. "There is nothing Sae Essit can do about it. We are lucky that Rilsin SaeKet," he glanced sideways at Sithli and then amended this, "Rilsin sae Becha is still missing, and her commander, Sae Pleffin. Without them, Saeditin will fall. The gods have favored us."

Sithli realized several things simultaneously. Kepit had known of this plan for a long time. Kirra, however, was shocked, and for reasons that were not obvious. It was not simply because her vaunted intelligence system had failed her; there were other forces at work. But what struck Sithli most of all was that Raphat knew that Tonar almost certainly would be sacrificed to bring about the opportunity for a Runchot victory. And Raphat did not seem to care. No, that was not right. Raphat cared about victory, not about his son. His heir. Sithli looked at Raphat with open admiration.

26

THE WEATHER HAD FINALLY BROKEN. THE CLOSER THEY
got to Petipal, the clearer the roads were. There had been no
sign of Tonar's raiders, and she began to hope that they had
been lost in the forests or had met with some accident. As
the days went by and they drew nearer to Petipal, she became more cheerful even as Tonar became more glum. And
then, still five days or so out of Petipal, they saw the sun-
flash.

Tonar's raiders had sneaked through the countryside,
traveling at night. They might have made it all the way to
Petipal, but their luck failed as they approached the larger
villages. They had stumbled across a group of shepherds
making their way to the outer pastures to repair their huts in
preparation for spring. Four of the shepherds had been
killed, but the fifth, a young girl, had escaped and raised the
alarm. But this was not all. Hard on the fading of the first
message had come the second. The Runchot were no longer
skirmishing along the border but were attacking in force.
The little town of Aphala Tree was burning. Essit was

pinned down in the south and could not send any help back to the capital.

"We have to get to Petipal, and we have to get to the border," Rilsin told her captains. It was a hastily called meeting even as their camp was being struck. "The Petipal Guard will do their best, but they are needed for order within the city. They are not strictly trained for this and may not be able to stop this Runchot force."

"We can't get all the troops to Petipal fast enough." Pleffin looked around at the supply wagons loading up and the horses stamping in the snow.

"We don't have to," said Rilsin. "The raiders are a band of only two hundred fifty. We need a fast-moving force, so the wagons and most of the body of troops must follow later. You and I will take a smaller force, Sae Pleffin, and we will get to Petipal and stop the raiders. The rest of the army can catch up to us, and we will take it south, to the aid of the first minister." She stopped, frowning. She could feel the anger building. She remembered the little town of Aphala Tree.

"What about the Runchot saedin?" asked one of her captains.

"The prince and princess will remain with the main army, under guard. I will want them when we reach the border; they are our hostages." She saw Tonar and knew that if he could have spoken with her, he would have. She did not give him the opportunity.

She took four hundred of her best troops. Pleffin suggested more, but Rilsin wanted speed. She took both archers and the finest marksmen of her fire-tube company, all of them mounted, and they rode hard, stopping only when they must, so as not to kill the horses. The weather remained good, crisp and cold, but with no snow, and better still, no sleet. By the morning of the third day they were on the Petipal Road, approaching the city. They had been forced to stop for the night for rest, but Rilsin had them up before dawn.

There had been no further messages, by sun-flash or

messenger. There was no need; the message was clear. Farms along the road were abandoned, and some were burned. There was no traffic. *How could this have happened?* Rilsin asked herself repeatedly. It would never have occurred to her that such a small force could have come so far, and worse, so secretly, and do such damage. She would see to it that this never happened again.

Luck was with them. Ahead of them they saw a small, moving fog of ice and dust. And then from the top of one of the hills outside the city, they saw the source of the fog: Tonar's raiders. They had not yet attempted to enter the city. The city gates were closed, but Rilsin could not see any of the Petipal Guard.

There was no time to lose. They thundered down from the hill, fanning out in a crescent to attempt to surround the Runchot and to keep any from doubling back. The Runchot turned and drew themselves into a tight group partway to the main gates of the city. Rilsin drew her sword, leading the charge.

She wasn't sure just what made her draw back, and what caused her to signal her troops to pull back. She could see the Runchot archers, of course. They were mounted, and she could see them draw their bows, aiming at the oncoming Saeditin. But it was the Runchot troopers in front of the mounted archers that drew her attention. There was something unusual about them. They knelt down on the packed snow of the road and looked toward the charging Saeditin. Each one held something, some device. Abruptly, Rilsin realized just what those devices were.

"Fire-tubes!" she shouted. "They have fire-tubes!"

Her cry was drowned out by the sound of small explosions: the tubes were being fired by the Runchot marksmen.

They were just within range. Around Rilsin were shouts and cries. She looked around her. No one seemed hurt, but one horse was streaming blood where a shot had grazed its shoulder. She felt shock but pushed it aside. The Runchot had moved fast to make their own fire-tubes. And if these troops had fire-tubes, what about those Essit faced? She must answer these questions later.

"Fall back!" she shouted, giving the hand signal to be sure she was understood.

Her troops drew back, just out of range, the captains gathering around her. Pleffin was pale, his eyes wide.

"How did they get them so fast, SaeKet?" he asked. "How did they get the plans?"

"The plans aren't much, Commander," Rilsin reminded him, "nor are the tubes difficult to make. Look what Dira Sola accomplished in only a few months."

Saying his name gave her a sudden pang of loss. Sola had been right, she thought. This invention of his was going to change not just warfare, but everything, and in ways they could not now understand.

"Let's show them how it's done," she said.

Her own fire-tube company prepared their weapons, Rilsin with them. When Pleffin started to argue that she stay back, he took one look at her face and swallowed his objections.

The Runchot had not been patiently waiting for the Saeditin to regroup. They knew they were outnumbered and had to act quickly to secure whatever advantage they had. The ranks of their fire-tube company parted, and their archers rode forward, firing as they came.

This was a mistake. Rilsin's troops were ready. Her fire-tube company knew how to use their weapons from horseback, and they charged into the archers, firing their tubes and then drawing their swords for closer combat once their shot was expended. The Saeditin archers swung to one side, blocking any escape for the enemy. The Runchot marksmen, on foot, found themselves caught between their own mounted archers and the Saeditin. This was when the gates of Petipal opened. A company of the Petipal Guard rode out, having been alerted by their lookouts and sentries.

The Runchot were surrounded, but to their credit they did not give up easily. In fact, Rilsin realized, when at last the battle was over, they had not given up at all. They had

fought to the last man. Those who were wounded asked for
no mercy but attempted to fight as long as they had breath.
Not that she would have been inclined to grant mercy in
any case, Rilsin thought, as she stepped across the body of
an enemy she had just dispatched. Tonar's plan to destroy
her city had come very close to succeeding.

The air was thick with smoke from the fire-tubes, and
the ground was littered with bodies. Her troops had not escaped the carnage, and she knelt by one of her own
wounded, trying desperately to bind up an arm shattered by
fire-tube shot. Eventually, carts came from the city to take
the wounded to physicians, and Rilsin was escorted by her
troops and the Petipal Guard through the streets. The people cheered her, relieved to see their SaeKet safely home,
certain now that the Runchot invasion would soon be a
thing of the past, and all would be right with the world.

"No, they don't understand, SaeKet," said Dremfir, later,
listening to her fret about this. "They know the war is not
over yet, but they also believe the worst danger has passed,
now that you are here. They are glad to have you back."

Rilsin was back in her old rooms. She had not wanted to
even enter the city, but she knew it would be foolish to continue south immediately. They needed to wait for the rest of
the army to catch up with them, and one night's rest, at the
least. Chilsa was stretched out in his accustomed place on
the rug, but all else was strange. Meffa was not there, having been left with the main body of the army, still under a
physician's care. Rilsin had not had either the courage or
the mental strength to look in Reniat's room, and there were
reminders of her everywhere.

"SaeKet," said Dremfir. He had seen her eyes flick in the
direction of the room with the door still closed, and he saw
the tight lines around her mouth. "Rilsin," he said, gently,
"perhaps she is not dead."

Rilsin looked at him, Dremfir sae Cortin, mage to the
SaeKet, but more importantly, a friend who had been
through so much with her, and she felt the sadness rise
higher, like a tide. "She is. She cannot be other than dead.

Sola, too." She spoke before the waters rose too high for her to breathe.

"I am sorry, Rilsin, so very sorry." Dremfir reached out and put his hand consolingly on hers.

The waters rose and choked her. For a moment she fought furiously against the tears, but then she simply let them roll down her cheeks. She said nothing, did not sob, made no sound at all. She sat like a statue. Dremfir sat with her, making no further move to comfort her, until the tears stopped. Eventually, they did, and Rilsin sighed, wiping her eyes with the back of her hand.

"I once thought I felt them," she said, in a tone that was almost normal, "both Reniat and Sola." Her eyes flicked up to his now, and they were sharp and penetrating, with no sign of the recent tears. Dremfir sat up straighter, alert to the change in her as much as to what she said.

"I thought I felt them when I was listening to the song. I need to ask you, Dremfir, about the song of the land."

"What is it you wish to know, SaeKet?" Dremfir was cautious. The priests had been studying the song as best they could, for as long as there had been priests. Although they had learned some, there was far more they did not know.

"You know that I have not heard it myself, SaeKet," Dremfir continued. "And I will not until I die. You know far more than I about the song, SaeKet."

"I doubt that, and certainly not about its history," Rilsin said dryly. She felt better now, more like her normal self. "The priests know more of this than anyone, and I was not taught about it as a child." It was her birthright, and therefore the knowledge had been kept from her. "Is it possible, has any SaeKet ever—" Rilsin paused, then seemed to gather her thoughts. "I have felt people moving on the land, groups, forces. Sometimes I can tell if they are friendly or hostile." Rilsin glanced over and met Dremfir's eyes.

"Indeed!" said Dremfir. "I suspected so." He was extremely interested. "A few SaeKets in history have been reported as having this ability, but only a few. Your great grandmother was one. But you wished to ask something."

"Has any SaeKet, has *anyone,* ever been able to sense individual people upon the land?"

Dremfir looked at her for a long moment before replying. "Yes," he finally said. "It has been reported twice in all of Saeditin's history. Can you do this, Rilsin?"

"No." she said abruptly, too abruptly. She could feel Dremfir's skepticism and excitement both, and she wanted to defuse them. "I was merely curious."

It would be only natural if you could do this," said Dremfir thoughtfully, refusing to be distracted. "Some have speculated that hardship, and the pressure of great events, and the land's need can bring forth a stronger sense in the SaeKet. You most definitely had the pressure and the need, so yes, it would be natural." Dremfir seemed to be speaking as much to himself as to Rilsin.

"Natural?" Rilsin raised her eyebrows at him. "Natural and not the Mother's magic?"

"Yes," said Dremfir, "natural. I believe in the Mother and Her works but not in magic, as you well know, Rilsin. The ability in you to hear the song is the Mother's work, but it is just as natural as the rain." He grew more animated, caught up now in a matter of great interest to him. "As natural as the rain, only less explicable. I believe it is more like the reason some have blue eyes and others green or brown. Someday, perhaps, we shall know why it is the Mother arranges things in this manner. Perhaps we may even learn some of the rules by which she does this. When I have time, SaeKet, I would like to grow rock roses, to learn why some are white and some are pink and a few are even lavender. I started to work upon this puzzle when I was in the employ of Sae Norimin, and she let me grow the roses in a portion of her gardens. I know I differ from many fellow priests in this belief that the Mother works by laws we can hope to comprehend."

"I hope more priests will begin to share your opinion, my friend." Rilsin was quite aware that she had not truly lured him away from the question of her ability, but she was grateful that he did not choose to pursue it and that she did not have to put an unpleasant end to the discussion.

MEFFA WAS NOT happy to be riding in the surgical wagon, with its heavy canvas roof that kept out snow and sleet but not the chill. But she was grateful that at least the SaeKet had not left her behind in Hoptrin. Porit stayed with her as much as was possible, seeing to it that she ate and took her medicines, and that the bandages on her arm were always clean.

At first Meffa had not wanted to look at the stump that had been her left hand. Despite her brave words to Rilsin, she felt a profound sense of loss and a deep depression. In some ways it seemed that her life was gone. Nothing would ever be the same. She had never married but had dedicated herself to the service of Rilsin sae Becha when she was first minister and then as SaeKet. She had never had children, but in many ways she had thought of little Reniat, the SaeKetti, as her own, the Mother forgive her. Now she had failed her SaeKet, and she had failed little Reni, and she had failed herself.

In her fever and delirium in Hoptrin she had thought she had seen the man who had come into the SaeKet's rooms, the man who had almost killed her and who had stolen her Reni on that night of terror. The physician had convinced her that it was merely a fever dream. Meffa believed him, but in a strange way, she was disappointed.

"Are you tired, Meffa?" Porit had been going over his lesson under Meffa's guidance. She had been teaching him to read, and he was a good student.

"Yes, Porit, I am. I am sorry." She was no more tired than usual, but she had no more heart to help the boy learn, not when she had been thinking of her Reniat again.

"We are stopping soon; I heard the order from the soldiers up the column. We are almost to Petipal, to rejoin the SaeKet." As he spoke, they felt the wagon come to a halt. "Here, do you want something to drink?" Porit poured a little wine mixed with water into a metal cup and offered it to her, but Meffa shook her head, and he put it on the wagon's floor. "I will get you something good to eat, Meffa. You are getting too thin. I'll be right back!"

When he did not return, Meffa pushed herself up with her good arm. The physician had been telling her recently that she needed to try to be active. She couldn't seem to care, particularly, but she found now that she was worried about Porit. There were any number of things that could have delayed him, but Meffa decided to try to at least look out to see if she could see Porit coming back. She was also bored. For far too many days she had seen no one but Porit, the physician, and the physician's apprentice, and always in the wagon. It was time to move.

It was far harder than she thought. She felt dizzy, but she swung her feet down and managed to stuff them, somehow, into her boots. She couldn't get her cloak around her, not one-handed without practice; it was too hard. So, shivering and cloakless, she made her way to the entrance flap on the wagon and twitched it slightly aside.

It was a gray day, following the string of a few clear days they had recently had, according to Porit. The trooper who drove the wagon was gone, off to eat his own lunch, undoubtedly, with friends. Soldiers moved here and there purposefully, but no one glanced at her wagon. And it was cold. There was a metallic taste in her mouth, and she was dizzy, and Meffa started to let go of the flap. She would go back to the pallet that was her bed. Porit would come eventually, or someone would.

"Around the corner here, by this wagon. No one will pay us any attention. Just act natural, Nacrit, you fool! If you look as though you belong, no one will question it. If you look around all shifty-eyed, you will have them down on us. Here, take this bread; let's try to look as if we are eating our meal."

Meffa let the canvas fall, but she left a small gap out of which she could see. The words by themselves were enough to set her on guard, but there was something about the speaker's voice that was familiar. She couldn't place it, and the name Nacrit meant nothing to her. She could see only the back of one man, Nacrit, presumably, since he held a hunk of bread and tried to lounge against the side of the surgical wagon.

"Relax," said the man she couldn't see. "No one expects me to be here, and I've grown a beard, and I'm with the commoners. They haven't recognized me."

"The SaeKet would know you." Nacrit had a nasty note in his voice. "So don't pretend to be the hero. You wouldn't be here at all if your aunt hadn't sent you to keep track of the Becha. Which you failed to do when she disappeared."

"Well, I found her again."

Meffa drew in a quiet breath. She recognized the voice now. It was Philla sae Lisim. Whoever this Nacrit was, he was right. Philla was no hero. He was here only because he feared his family chief, Kepit sae Lisim. Meffa's right hand clenched on the wagon support.

"There's no one here who knows you," Philla continued, "so you have nothing to be so twitchy about."

"There is one here who knows. Two, really. There's that boy from the tavern. But he doesn't know what I do, so he's no concern. For all he knows, I joined the army to fight for my SaeKet, like he did." Nacrit laughed, and Philla joined in. "But that woman who works for the Becha SaeKet, she's here."

"She's wounded, sick, and not likely to live. She won't be a concern for long."

"If she lives, she would know me. And she did see me in Hoptrin. If she remembers—"

"Well, you'd best make sure she doesn't. Why'd you let her live back in Petipal? She's right here; this is the surgical wagon. What, you didn't know that? You *are* a fool."

"Not such a fool that I can't take care of a threat." Nacrit spat out the words and turned, his hand going to his knife.

When he turned, Meffa saw his face. It was the man who had broken into her apartment, Rilsin's apartment, who had forced the drug on her, who had stolen Reniat. During that awful night he had never spoken but only acted, quickly and brutally, grabbing her by the throat, forcing some liquid from a vial into her mouth, crushing her against him until she swallowed, forcing more down her throat as her muscles slackened, and then holding her until she went completely limp. Then he had gone for Reniat. In the aftermath of that terror and guilt, she could not remember clearly what he looked like. Now she saw his face, and the memory came back as fresh as if she lived it again. Meffa gasped.

Both men's heads snapped up. Nacrit's eyes met Meffa's through the slit in the canvas. He drew his knife and leaped up into the wagon. Philla grunted with surprise and then followed him.

Meffa staggered back, away from the opening. She drew breath to scream, but before she could, Nacrit reached out and grabbed her by the throat. It was a repeat of that terrible night. Meffa flailed, struggling to escape. She could not fight, not unbalanced, weak, and with only one arm. But her unsteadiness proved to be to her advantage. The stump of her left arm popped up as she flailed and hit Nacrit's nose.

Nacrit swore and lost his grip. Meffa fell backward, hitting the floor of the wagon with a painful thump, the stump of her arm throbbing. Her throat hurt and she couldn't breathe, let alone cry out, and she had hit her head in the fall, making her even more dizzy, but her hand found the cup of wine Porit had left.

"What in the Mother's name are you doing, Nacrit? Making love to her? Finish her!" Philla crowded up to Nacrit, causing the big man to lose his balance and stagger slightly.

"Damn you, Philla, you are next, I swear it!" Nacrit fumbled for the knife he had dropped, going to one knee on the floor beside Meffa. He put one large hand on her chest, pushing her down, holding her.

"I don't know how you managed with the SaeKetti," said Philla. "You are completely inept. Why didn't you kill this one then? Here, let me do it." Philla had drawn his own knife, and he came up behind Nacrit again.

"Stay back," snarled Nacrit. He had found his knife at last, and he flipped it over in his hand, shifted his grip on Meffa, and leaned down for the strike. Meffa threw the wine in his face.

Nacrit roared and reared back, blinded. At that moment, the canvas door flap was yanked aside, and Porit jumped up into the wagon. The boy took one look at the scene before him and recognized Nacrit. He grabbed one-handed for the stool on which he had been sitting not that long ago, and with the other hand drew his own long knife. He flung the stool into Philla's legs, tangling the older man, who went down with a cry. Nacrit tried to pull out of the way to face this new threat, but now Meffa grabbed him and yanked him down. She rolled to one side and attempted to smash his face into the floor. She had difficulty doing this one-handed, so she pulled herself up and onto his back and sat on him.

Porit wanted to help her, but he found himself facing Philla again. He gauged Philla in one practiced glance, flipped his knife over in his hand, and prepared to throw it.

"Don't kill him, Porit!" cried Meffa.

Porit hesitated, and Philla rushed him. Porit stepped aside, hard to do in the confined space, tripped him, and then grabbed up the stool again and smashed Philla over the head with it. Philla slumped to the wagon floor, out cold. *Just like a tavern fight,* Porit thought. He glanced at Meffa. She was desperately trying to keep Nacrit from bucking her off, and to keep his head pushed down into something. She was having a hard time doing this with only one hand. Porit peered over her to see that she had Nacrit's head in the wide-mouthed chamber pot, more a slop bucket, which from the smell of it was almost full.

"Help me!" said Meffa. When Porit hesitated, wrinkling his nose, she glanced up at him. "I need answers! This is the man who stole Reniat!"

It looked as though Nacrit would have her off him soon.

Porit squatted beside her, pulled Nacrit's left arm behind him, and broke it. When Nacrit screamed, Porit lent his strength to Meffa's and pushed his head into the slop bucket again, letting him up only briefly for air. It turned out that Nacrit did not much like drowning in the chamber pot.

"Stop!" he pleaded when he caught a breath. "You're killing me! And my arm!"

Porit shoved his head into the gloppy mess again, then let him up. Nacrit's face was streaming with filth.

"What did you do with the SaeKetti!" demanded Meffa.

"Gave her to the Runchot," gasped Nacrit. "Well, Sae Philla gave her to the Clinsi, who were supposed to give her to the Runchot. Please, no more, please!" He glanced sideways, moaning with pain, trying to see their faces. "I don't know where she is now, I swear it!"

"Why didn't you kill me back in Petipal?" Meffa was curious.

"I thought you *would* die. Eventually. And I wanted to have a little fun with you before I left. After you were asleep, when you were dying. But there wasn't time. You looked pretty good then. Before you lost that arm."

Meffa shoved his head into the pot again and held him there. Nacrit thrashed and struggled and tried to get away, but he could not use his broken arm, and he could not break free.

"Meffa, stop it! You are really going to drown him!"

"Good." Meffa continued to hold Nacrit under.

The canvas flap was pulled suddenly open, and several troopers, swords drawn, entered, followed by the physician. It took a few moments to sort things out. Nacrit was pulled out of the slop bucket, amid general expressions of disgust. Philla, who was regaining consciousness, was taken away.

"Why didn't you want me to kill him?" asked Porit, watching Philla taken out. "You had no second thoughts about killing Nacrit."

"That's Philla sae Lisim. He's a saedin."

Porit frowned. "You didn't want me to kill him because he's saedin?"

"No, I didn't want you to kill him because he's a traitor, and Rilsin SaeKet will want him."

Porit blinked and drew in a breath. Of course she would. Philla would be executed in the Mother's Square.

"You must get back to bed after I examine you," the doctor was telling Meffa. He was a beefy middle-aged man, a saedin. His hair was graying and pulled back in a tight, utilitarian braid with no ornamentation. "I do not want you reinjuring your arm before it is fully healed. And I do not want you exerting yourself too much."

"You told me, Sae Rollo, that activity would make me feel better."

"I meant mild activity, not life-or-death battles!"

"Well, you were right, sae." Meffa allowed herself to be guided back to the pallet. "I am feeling very much better now."

The doctor muttered something under his breath, and Meffa smiled.

27

"SaeKet, I apologize with all my heart. I had no idea the Runchot could attack Petipal. I truly believed all the threat was from across the border, after we heard from Commander Pleffin." Essit stopped. His distress was real and just as strong as his relief at seeing Rilsin again. His unhappiness and embarrassment were excruciating and counterbalanced his joy at the arrival of the SaeKet.

After the first greetings, she was meeting with him, Pleffin, and some of the captains. The main body of the army had caught up with Rilsin's advance party, and they had moved south toward Aphala Tree and the border.

"No one could have guessed what the Runchot had planned, Sae Essit. It was," Rilsin admitted, "a very daring move on the part of the Princes Raphat and Tonar."

"Our intelligence failed," said Essit.

"It did, indeed." Pleffin was irritated.

"It should not have. My best spy disappeared, and I fear the worst." Essit frowned. Gigrat was undoubtedly dead.

"That is of no help now, Sae Essit," said Pleffin, "and it

is of no use to replow the same worn-out field. You said you thought there was no danger to Petipal from my message, but in truth, First Minister, I knew no more than you." Pleffin was stung by the implication that he should have somehow alerted the first minister.

"Enough, Commander! And Sae Essit, you, too. We cannot argue this, especially now. If there is dissent among us, the Runchot are nearer to winning. This is no one's fault." *It is, though,* thought Rilsin. *The blame falls on me.* "Tonar's mission was utterly secret. Very few knew of it; even his sister found out by accident only."

"Where are these Runchot?" asked Essit. No one needed to ask; they knew exactly which Runchot he meant.

"They are here," said Pleffin. "Under heavy guard."

"They can be useful to us," said Rilsin, "as hostages, at the very least." Personally, she wondered if Raphat valued either of his children, even his heir, enough to bargain for them. She was beginning to believe he might not, hard though that was to understand.

"The information Phara gave you was designed to mislead," said Essit. "There is no indication that any of Raphat's troops are disloyal. Raphat keeps shifting their positions, and they have undertaken some forays and some much more serious attacks. We have been holding them back, but I do not understand why. From all I know, they outnumber us, yet they retreat when we chase them. I do not understand why they have not attempted to advance again."

"Because they are in a position of strength," said Pleffin. "The rocky terrain to the south suits them, and they want to draw us into ambush. We need to draw them out instead. There is something more here than an attempt to simply lay waste to our lands."

"That," said Rilsin, "is because they were waiting for me. They know by now that their attempt to terrorize Petipal and throw the city into confusion has failed. They know that we stopped it, and that we rode hard and fast, that we pushed the army, to come here to stop them. They want us

tired, they want us outnumbered, and they want my life.
They are hoping to draw us into ambush, and they are hoping that I will be unwary."

A murmur of distress and defiance, almost a growl, met
her words.

"I think they mean to offer some bait to draw me in,
probably the chance to capture Sithli sae Melisin. I recognize Sae Kepit in this. Together with Raphat, she is even
more dangerous."

"We need more troops for when the Runchot do make
their push." The speaker was a young lieutenant, Effell sae
Tillit, one of Essit's many relatives. She was only eighteen,
but brilliant and dedicated, a true member of her family.

"We are getting them, Sae Effell," Rilsin assured her.
"We had a partial communication from the north, by sun-
flash, before the skies closed up again. First Man Bilt is
coming south." She saw the way some of her captains exchanged glances. "They may not be trained quite as we are,
but they do know fighting in rough territory." Rilsin
glanced aside, out over the encampment. Bilt's message
had been cut short by the damnable late winter weather. He
had said he was bringing something or someone. Rilsin
shook her head. Whatever it was that Bilt was bringing, she
would have to wait until he arrived to find out.

"SHE WOΠ'T BE easy to trap, Prince; believe me, I know
Rilsin sae Becha all too well." Kepit hunched forward on
the camp stool to be slightly closer to the fire. It was growing colder as the dusk slid into night, and Kepit wished for
far more warmth than she was likely to get. She was too
old to have to put up with another campaign, especially in
winter. She did not know how Raphat could bear it at his
age, but war seemed to suit him. Well, with any luck and
the Mother willing, this would be Kepit's last such adventure. If any military expeditions were needed in the future,
she would be the one to order them from the safety of the
palace in Petipal.

"I am well aware of her cleverness, but it is possible, Sae

Kepit, to trap any animal if you have the right bait and the right strategy and enough patience."

"And what bait do we have, Lord Prince?"

"You know perfectly well what bait." Raphat moved closer to the fire himself. It looked as though it were going to sleet again. This had been a miserable winter, but he had been blessed with a robust constitution. The cold invigorated him, and he took bad weather as a challenge to be met. He was well aware of how Kepit felt, however, and he was quite willing to use this to his advantage. He watched his Saeditin ally critically.

"The bait, Sae Kepit, is Sithli sae Melisin, your SaeKet. If we dangle her enticingly, Rilsin cannot resist. We will have Sithli in the front of a foray; leave it to me to arrange this. We will render her apparently helpless, and make it seem as safe as possible for Sae Rilsin to swoop in and take her, but then we shall spring the trap."

"It sounds wonderful, my lord, but pardon me for pointing out just a few weaknesses." Kepit was well aware of Raphat's scrutiny. It did not disturb her, and she gave as good as she got. "How can you insure that Rilsin herself comes to your bait? However well you set it up, she could simply send troops to take Sithli."

"Oh she will go." Raphat smiled slightly. "I can arrange for word to be sent that Sithli wishes to speak with her in private. Perhaps about her missing daughter." Raphat did not let a flicker cross his face, even though his thoughts went to his own missing and traitorous daughter. "I will arrange it so that Rilsin herself will go, have no doubt."

Kepit looked at him. Perhaps he could, she thought. Of course Sithli herself would not agree to meet with Rilsin, so Raphat would have to set her out as bait without her knowledge. That would be tricky. "How will you keep Sithli safe, if you arrange matters well enough to tempt Rilsin sae Becha?"

Raphat leaned back for a moment. He had an actual chair, a small, lightweight one. He knew it made Kepit envious and even more uncomfortable to see him in it. He had another chair, but he did not intend to offer it to her. Anything that kept her uncomfortable was to his advantage.

"Do you really want her safety assured, Sae Kepit?" Raphat smiled, but his eyes did not, and they were intent on Kepit. When he saw her shift uncomfortably on her stool, he rose. He walked over to her and looked down, directly into her eyes. The fire was at his back now, and it haloed him with shifting light. Kepit sat completely still, not moving a muscle. Her eyes betrayed no more than her face, and Raphat was impressed.

"I know you do not," he continued. "And you know quite well that I do not care much for her safety, either. She has been useful to me, Sae Kepit, but she is quite expendable. I have enjoyed her company in many ways," he smiled slightly, "but as you are very aware, she can be quite difficult, also. I find you, Sae Kepit, to be more straightforward. I know I can count on you to be my ally both here, in the field, and later in Petipal. I believe we see eye to eye on this, do we not?"

Kepit looked up at him. She didn't trust him, but she knew he meant what he said. He would sacrifice Sithli without hesitation if it would further his goals, and it would. She would see to that. She knew his ambition was to eventually have all of Saeditin under his direct rule. He would never have that with Sithli. He would never have it with her, either, and she suspected he knew it. But for now, they both needed Sithli out of the way.

"We do indeed see eye to eye on this, my lord prince," she said. She smiled and stood so that they did, in fact, see close to eye to eye. "I would like to see you persuade Sithli to put herself as bait for Rilsin. That will be a feat I would love to see."

"Well, then," said Raphat jovially, "see it you shall. I will convince her now. Come and watch." He took her gloved hand and bowed slightly, and then took her arm.

Kepit tried not to smile. Raphat's charms were considerable, but he was sorely mistaken if he thought he could use them on her. She would not tell him so, however. Raphat's guard moved in around them as they walked toward Sithli's tent. This close to the enemy, Raphat took no chances. But then, Raphat never took any chances.

Sithli's tent was in the center of the Runchot camp, but it, too, was surrounded with Raphat's guards. It was large enough for Sithli and two servants, who slept in a curtained-off portion of the tent. The servants had been, only some days ago, camp followers who did some of the sewing and cleaning for the troops. As Sithli seemed unable to manage without servants, however, they had been taken into her service with a quick course of instruction. As Raphat and Kepit approached the tent, the sleet, which had been threatening all day, began to fall, making the night seem colder.

"SaeKet!" called Raphat. "Are you within?"

It was Sithli herself who pulled back the entrance flap.

"I dismissed the servants, Raphat; they can find somewhere else to sleep tonight. Come in before you freeze in that sleet—Kepit?" Sithli had obviously been waiting for Raphat, and she was just as obviously surprised and not especially pleased to see Kepit. "What are you doing here, Sae Kepit?"

"I asked her to come," said Raphat. "I would not, believe me," he forestalled her objections, "but this is very important. Please, Sithli, hear me out." Sithli had opened her mouth, but Raphat did not intend to give her time to complain. "It concerns Saeditin, and Rilsin sae Becha."

Whatever Sithli had been about to say, she swallowed it. "Come in," was all she said.

The inside of Sithli's tent never failed to amaze Kepit. Every time she saw it, Sithli had added to it. Since they had been camped in this one place for some days now, Sithli's tent was becoming almost luxurious. More and more furs had arrived from somewhere, to be heaped in great piles around the edges of the tent, right up to the curtained portion for Sithli's new servants. Several oil lamps were burning now, placed on overturned crates that had been covered with furs. The oil lamps lent not only light, but a small amount of heat to the space. Sithli had come up with one of the small camp chairs, too, and she immediately sat in this, leaving her visitors to seat themselves on crates and furs. Kepit glanced at Raphat and saw a quick gleam in the prince's eye. It had not escaped him that Sithli felt herself in command of all the resources of Raphat's army.

"I have thought of a way to bring this war to a quick close." Raphat came immediately to the point. "Rilsin sae Becha has rescued Petipal from my attack, as you know, and she has now come south. She is with her troops, facing us. I have thought of a way to bring Saeditin back to you and to destroy Rilsin, to give her to you. I need your help to do it."

That was straightforward, Kepit thought. She watched as Sithli sat up straighter and stared at Raphat. She was nosing the bait, but she was not hooked.

"I am no soldier," Sithli reminded Raphat.

"You do not need to be. Not for this. It does require that you go into apparent danger—but apparent only. I am sure you will be willing to undergo peril that seems to be real to recover the SaeKet's chair and to rid yourself of your cousin. The appearance of danger will make you all the more beloved when you return safe and in triumph to Petipal."

"Yes," said Sithli slowly. "I will do what must be done, and I will trust you to make sure that I am kept safe, Raphat."

Kepit deliberately avoided looking at Raphat, afraid that Sithli might read her glance. *He was right,* she thought, *it really was very easy.*

Shortly thereafter, Kepit rose to leave. It had been made plain that Raphat was staying, and Kepit had no wish to remain any longer than necessary. To her surprise, Sithli herself walked her to the tent flap and even stepped out briefly into the sleet with her. Raphat's guards were there, but at a slight distance, and both Kepit and Sithli knew they would not be overheard.

"I want you, Kepit, to be sure that I am guarded at all times," Sithli told her in a low voice. "Whatever arrange-

ments the prince makes, I want you to take extra care. Do
not rely on Raphat. I think you understand me. And I do not
wish the prince to be aware of what precautions you take."

Kepit put hand to heart. "Do not fear, SaeKet, I will take
care of you." She watched as Sithli went back into the tent.
She had thought it was easy before, but now it had just become even easier still. Kepit grinned into the sleet.

"I HAVE HAD word directly from Raphat, just a little while
ago, under flag of truce." Rilsin looked out across the
Saeditin camp, which blazed with the light of the rising sun
reflecting off the previous night's ice and sleet. She
squinted and turned away, back into the more comfortable
dimness of the tent. At her feet, Chilsa stretched and
yawned, showing his impressive dentition. "He says he is
willing to give me both Sithli sae Melisin and Kepit sae
Lisim, if I will make peace with him and agree to trade."
She smiled and looked over her captains, who were eating
a breakfast of bread and cider. "I would dearly love to accept his offer. How unfortunate that it is not genuine."

"Can we be sure it is not?" asked one of her captains.

Pleffin snorted in disgust, but Rilsin answered him courteously.

"We can be certain," she said. "This is Prince Raphat we
speak of here, and I have come to understand his character
a little. Why would he agree to this now, and not months
ago? He has been planning this attack for a very long time,
and he has built up a considerable force. I do believe that
all of his troops are loyal to him, no matter what the princess Phara told us. He wants to pull us into a trap. But let's
see what Raphat's children have to tell us." She turned to
one of the troopers near the entrance. "Bring me our Runchot
nobles," she said.

Tonar's guards had been waiting for her command. It
was a matter of only a few moments before Tonar and
Phara were brought in. Phara attempted to hide her nervousness beneath a haughty veneer but did not entirely
succeed. Tonar, on the other hand, appeared completely at

ease. He smiled at Rilsin and gave her a slight bow, cheerfully ignoring the almost tangible hostility of the Saeditin
around him. Chilsa, who had retreated to a corner of the
tent where he had been washing himself, lifted his head and
growled softly.

"Good morning, Prince and Princess," said Rilsin. "I
would not have required your presence so early, but I would
like your opinions on an offer your father made to me."

"An offer?" Tonar was composed and calm. "What offer
would that be, SaeKet?"

"He has offered me Sithli sae Melisin and Kepit sae
Lisim, as well as a trade agreement, in return for peace."

"That is wonderful!" Phara spoke for the first time,
looking so relieved that for a moment Rilsin felt sorry for
her. She obviously wanted very badly to believe that peace
was almost accomplished.

Tonar, however, looked slightly surprised. "That is a
very good offer; I would accept it, were I you."

"Indeed." Rilsin looked at him sharply. "It is a very good
offer, too good, perhaps, don't you think?" She saw Tonar
shift slightly and try to look away from her, but he could not
seem to do it. "I very much doubt that you would accept it,
after all, Lord Prince." She took one step closer to him, still
holding him with her eyes. "Would you?" Her voice
cracked like a whip. Phara flinched openly, and some of the
Saeditin officers jumped slightly. Tonar did neither, but he
did smile slightly and turn palms up in capitulation.

"No," he agreed, still smiling, "I would not accept it."

"Do you believe your father is acting here in good faith,
Prince Tonar?"

"No more than you," said Tonar with a chuckle. "I can
see there is no point in attempting to deceive you on this
matter."

"Good," said Rilsin, dryly. "Then perhaps you can help
me on another point." He said nothing, so she continued.
"How many of your father's troops are supplied with fire-
tubes?"

"Fire-tubes, SaeKet?"

"Don't play innocent with me, Tonar. The force you sent against Petipal was armed with them. None of that force survived, but their fire-tubes did. We have been examining them. They appear hastily and poorly made but nonetheless deadly enough. How many of your father's troops have them, Lord Prince?"

"I don't know." Tonar spread his hands. "Truly, SaeKet, I do not, nor, of course, would I tell you if I did."

Rilsin could feel the shifting intensity of her officers. She knew they would welcome the chance to attempt to find out just what the Runchot prince did know, in whatever manner they could obtain it. She briefly considered her hostages in this light but dismissed the idea. She was certain that Phara did not have this information, and for all of his charm, Tonar was as stubborn as he was intelligent. He had not made the hazardous journey into Saeditin unprepared for possible capture and questioning. If she attempted to use force, she had no doubt he could resist successfully for a considerable time. Every SaeKet in the past had resorted to torture when necessary, but for reasons she did not fully understand or have time to explore, Rilsin found the thought distasteful. Also, and despite herself, she believed Tonar when he said he did not know. Also, and despite herself, she liked him.

"Take them back," she told her troopers.

When they had gone, she turned again to face her officers.

"We will take a page from Prince Raphat's book," she told them, "and stall. We are still under truce now, and we shall attempt to remain so for as long as it suits our purpose. Raphat promised us peace, as well as giving us Sithli and Kepit late last autumn. He prepared his attack under cover of truce. We will do the same. Sae Pleffin, send a messenger to the prince telling him I am inclined to accept his offer, but I need a little time."

"Time will help a little, SaeKet, but we are still outnumbered. In any event, we cannot attack them in any numbers through the hills; it is too rocky. We must draw them out to

us. What will this time buy us?" Pleffin laid out the problem almost didactically, as if it were an exercise put forth
by a child's tutor. Rilsin appreciated his calm.

"It buys several things, Commander. First Man Bilt is
bringing us his Confederates as reinforcements. We need
them. And time gives us the chance to take another page
from Prince Raphat's book of despicable tactics." She
grinned at her officers and was rewarded with a few smiles
in return.

"Raphat used stealth to sneak a force through our own
lands. He outflanked us, or tried. We shall do the same to
him. I have a plan." Rilsin walked to the table set up in the
middle of the tent and motioned her officers around her.

The messenger went back to Raphat under flag of truce.
The calm lasted through the morning, and the strengthening
sun of the waxing year began to melt the ice of the previous night. Ice dripped off tents and puddled on the snow. It
was not only cold now, it was also wet.

Under such miserable conditions, Rilsin expected the
truce to last past nightfall and into the next day. She intended to carry out the largest part of her plan under cover
of darkness. The Runchot would not expect her to move
any troops through the treacherous terrain in the dark.

Early in the afternoon, the lookout called an alarm, and
the sentries parted to let in a gasping scout. The woman was
badly wounded, and her horse, one of the small, shaggy
Saeditin horses, had an arrow still stuck in his rump. Another was in the scout's saddle, and a third was below her
left shoulder.

"They are coming!" she panted. "Raphat's troops are
moving! They sent out advance riders to kill our scouts, but
I made it through. The truce is broken, SaeKet!"

"Damn Raphat to a freezing Runchot hell!" Rilsin realized she was not surprised, but she was furious. "We have
no choice but to fight now. Get Commander Pleffin, get the
captains!"

28

THE RUNCHOT ATTACK did not push through to the
Saeditin camp. In fact, the Runchot never got out of the
rocky terrain. Since Rilsin had warning and had fielded her
troops with what seemed a split-second response, Raphat
reverted to his earlier plan, attempting to draw the Saeditin
in, deep into the treacherous terrain, hoping the land itself
would work against his enemy.

At first Rilsin stayed back from the fight herself, coor-
dinating and directing her troops. It was difficult, between
the weather, the rough terrain, the lack of intelligence, and
the general confusion of battle. But Raphat and Kepit had
made at least one serious mistake. They had assumed the
topography would work against Rilsin and the Saeditin,
that they could entice the Saeditin troops into the rocky hillsides and tiny steep valleys, where they could be picked off
by Runchot archers and fire-tube companies.

They had overlooked that they were facing the armies of
the SaeKet, in whose blood ran the song of the land. Rilsin
directed her troops not only with her mind but with her

deeply felt communion with the very rocks and trees around her. She had not meant to follow Dremfir's advice, to draw on her link with the earth. Although she knew it was real, it seemed to her unreliable and incomplete, but now that Saeditin was in peril, she did follow his advice after all. Rilsin could sometimes sense where the enemy archers were and where the little pockets of Runchot troops lay hidden, waiting for the Saeditin to venture too close. It was an incomplete and unreliable knowledge, more a feeling, but Rilsin used it. It also exhausted her. By the time darkness began to fall she felt drained, barely able to keep her feet.

"You need to rest, SaeKet." Essit hovered anxiously at her elbow. He was dirty and exhausted himself, having personally just led a foray toward the Runchot, and his soaked boots squelched with icy water with every step.

"I need rest no more than you, Essit. Change your boots before your feet are frostbitten, or worse, freeze solid. Sae Pleffin, we know now where Raphat and the Runchot command are likely to be. Can we get one of the larger firetubes on the slopes above them, within range?"

"Not in the dark, SaeKet, and the range is not good enough, even on the big tubes."

"Or accurate enough, which is worse," agreed Essit, who was in the process of changing his boots.

"It appears their attack is pulling back," said Rilsin, rubbing her hand across her face wearily. "Raphat and Sae Kepit think they are safe enough on higher ground during the dark hours, that it is too dangerous for us to attack them further or even get close to them. The slopes above them are so steep, they think they cannot be climbed, especially in the dark. But as for rest, we cannot allow *them* to rest, Sae Essit. We must continue to harry them throughout the night, however hard it is for us, so that we may continue with our plan. And yes, Essit, I will at least eat something now." She smiled and shook her head at him. "You will make a wonderful father some day," she told him, "with all your care and fussing." Essit laughed, and dour Pleffin actually grinned, but Rilsin's smile faded. She was reminded of Sola, but also of Sifuat. Sifuat had been a terrible father, and now she would never know what kind of father Sola could have been.

It was a very difficult night. Rilsin found that food did revive her, but she could not afford to rest. She saw her plan begin to go into action, as those of her troops who were mountain born and bred formed into small companies and set out, a few at a time, to meet up in the scrub forests at the foot of the steep slopes. The rest of the troops stayed with Rilsin, creeping closer to the Runchot.

"We need the barbarians, SaeKet," Pleffin fretted. He was unhappy that they needed the support of their northern, non-Saeditin allies, but he was not foolish enough to hope it would not arrive. "Where are they? And why have we had no messenger from them?"

Rilsin knew no more than he. As the first light of dawn began to seep through the mountains, their skirmishing with the Runchot took on a new character. Raphat sent troops out in force now, countering the harrying, niggling attacks of the Saeditin.

"We have to commit now," said Rilsin, "whether the Wilfrisin are here or not." She frowned. "Have we had word yet, are the mountain squads in place?" She knew there had been no word, she would have been notified immediately. There was nothing for it but to fight now, as best they could.

"Keep our Runchot prisoners guarded," she said. "We do not want them escaping when we may need them." She had set Chilsa to guard them as well, knowing that if all else failed, the hunting cat would not let them go alive. She looked around her at Pleffin, as tired as she but not showing it, at Essit, gray with exhaustion, and at her tired captains.

"The Runchot and Sae Sithli are no better off than we," she told them, "and by the time this day is over, they will be considerably worse." She grinned at them and saw tired smiles in reply. "Let's go, my friends."

It was almost impossible to hold ranks on the rocky and uneven slopes. It was also impossible for Rilsin to stay back from the fight. She led their progress, with Pleffin and Essit close by. Their troops shielded them as best they could, but Rilsin knew the value in letting her soldiers see her leading them. Exhausted as they were, she gave them heart. The ground was slippery with ice and melting snow, snow turning to mud under the friction of battle.

A soldier in the russet uniform of the Runchot managed to fight his way through Rilsin's screen of guards, and she engaged him. Suddenly Essit was beside her, and together they killed him, and then Essit was drawn away again. Rilsin found herself fighting more and more to the front, and she had to remind herself to stay back, remembering the fight in the northern forest, seemingly so long ago, when she had helped Bilt form his new Confederate nation. She had almost lost her life then by fighting to the front and becoming separated from her troops. She had no desire to let that happen now. Slowly but surely, they fought upward into the mountains, pushing the Runchot back. If the Confederates did not arrive, but even more, if her secret squads were not in position, she and her troops would indeed be surrounded by the more numerous Runchot, and Raphat would have them in his trap. But there was no stopping now. If there had been time for even a spare breath, let alone a thought, Rilsin might have prayed. There was no time and no breath.

"THEY FiGHt WELL," said Raphat. He was standing on the slope outside the Runchot camp, long-glass in hand, watching the battle down the hillside.

"They should," responded Kepit. Despite her circumstances, she felt a sense of pride in her countrymen. Besides, they would be hers again soon enough. Raphat glanced at her and raised his brows slightly, but he smiled.

"And Rilsin sae Becha seems to lead a charmed life. I can see her there in the front. I assume that is the young

Essit sae Tillit with her, and also her commander, Sae Plef-fin." He passed the long-glass to Kepit.

"That is the Sae Tillit, indeed," she said, "right beside the Becha. Perhaps I will get my hands on him after all." She had never forgiven Essit for successfully resisting her siege of Hoptrin.

"We are safe where we are, aren't we?" Sithli couldn't refrain from asking. She knew how it sounded, but she had never been so close to an actual battle. Although she had wanted to be here, now she wished she had stayed behind in safety. Her hand trembled slightly as she looked through the long-glass.

"You are quite safe," Raphat told her, "as long as you are here with me."

"There is nothing to fear, SaeKet." Kepit was careful to infuse the right amount of sincerity into her voice.

"It's time to use Kirra's troops," said Raphat abruptly. "We can overwhelm the Becha now and put an end to this. Bring the Lady Kirra here," he said to the soldier nearest him. "She should see her troops go into battle. She re-quested it of me."

"My Lord Prince," said Kirra. It was clear she had been waiting for the summons, from the alacrity with which the soldier returned with her. She glanced at Sithli and Kepit. "SaeKet," she said. She looked back at Raphat. "Is it time, Lord Prince?"

"It is, indeed. I know you wish to give the order for the troops you have supplied. Do so now."

"Thank you, my lord." Kirra turned to the messenger. "My troops are to form a screen between us and the Saeditin. They are to swing down and overwhelm the enemy."

"See to it," said Raphat.

The messenger saluted and left. Raphat watched as Kirra's forces began to move. They could all see it clearly from their position on the hillside. Kirra's troops now gave them overwhelming force, numbers too great to be ignored. He glanced aside at Kirra herself, expecting to see her

watching her troops with pleased anticipation. There was
pleased anticipation on her face, certainly, but there was a
predatory aspect to it. And she was not watching the
progress of her troops. She was watching both Sithli and
Kepit.

Raphat felt something prickle up the back of his neck, a
sense that something was not right, that something was, in
fact, terribly wrong. He saw Kepit turn and glance at Kirra,
saw her recognize the expression on the other woman's face
and frown in puzzlement and growing alarm. Even as
Raphat frowned, beginning to wonder what was wrong,
Kepit stepped forward toward Kirra.

"Who are you?" Kepit's voice was harsh. "Who are you,
Kirra?"

"You know me, Sae Kepit. As does Sithli sae Melisin.
You know me well, but it is plain you do not remember me.
You should."

Whatever she would have said next was drowned out by
sudden shouts from the Runchot troops. Raphat felt the
blood leave his face. On the hillside right below them,
cheering began. The Saeditin army, so outnumbered, was
cheering.

"Look!" Sithli almost screamed. Raphat looked.

Something was coming up the hillside behind the
Saeditin. Men and women in leather and furs, some of them
with blue hair, shouting and screaming something unintelligible. The northern barbarians, arrived in time to aid their
Saeditin allies. Raphat snarled.

"I will see them all in hell!" he shouted. "Saeditin and
barbarian alike, it makes no difference to me! We still outnumber them, and we will prevail."

Raphat glanced at his companions. The Melisin looked
terrified. Sithli, he thought, never had any courage. *Some
SaeKet,* he thought, with contempt. Kepit sae Lisim, however, was not terrified, but she was concerned, and she was
still looking at Kirra. Kirra smiled at Kepit and at Sithli, a
smile that was feral, more a baring of teeth. Then she
stepped forward, drew a large, brilliant orange scarf from

within her sleeve, and waved it. Raphat gaped at this odd behavior, and then suddenly a possible reason for it flashed through his mind. He looked down at Kirra's troops. They had been waiting for this signal. Kirra's troops raised a banner: the blue and gold banner of Rilsin SaeKet Becha. Raphat could not help himself; he gasped, and he heard Sithli and Kepit gasp in concert with him. He took a step toward Kirra, his face like thunder.

"Why?" he snarled.

"Not because of you, Prince," said Kirra calmly. "You are merely the sugar on the muffin." She turned her attention back to Sithli and Kepit, her expression avid. It was hatred for them, Raphat realized, a desire for revenge so strong that it was a lust. Raphat shuddered despite himself. He knew just how overpowering lust could be.

"Don't you recognize me yet?" said Kirra. She was speaking in Saeditin now, and she did not appear to notice that she had changed languages. "Either of you? Of course, why should you? I was merely another commoner, someone of no account. Someone whose life you could destroy without a second thought, someone whose *child* you could destroy for your own gain."

The acid calm with which she spoke awoke alarm in Raphat far more than any screams or shouts could have done. The back of his neck felt cold. He realized that he was witnessing the culmination of a very carefully crafted plan, one that had been made to bring down the Melisin and the Lisim, but that might also bring him down.

"I am Cilla, Cilla of Blue Street, the washerwoman. I see you still do not remember. Again, how could you? You ruined the lives of more commoners, and even of honoreds, of dira, than you could possibly hope to remember. Well, they shall now have vengeance through me. You killed my husband, Kepit sae Lisim. You stole my daughter, my Gisi, my only child, and sold her into Runchot to a brothel. Why do you think I have the business I do now? I was looking for my lost child. You kidnapped and stole her, and when I went to you, Sithli sae Melisin, then Sithli SaeKet, when I went to you for justice, you had me taken and whipped and branded."

Oblivious to the cold, warmed by her hatred, Kirra pulled aside her cloak and ripped down the neck of her overshirt, exposing her left shoulder. The raised mark of a brand was there, the X of a prisoner. Raphat swallowed and backed up a step. He had never before felt that he was in the grip of a force stronger than he, but he felt it now.

"You would have sold me then, too," said Kirra calmly, "but Rilsin sae Becha, Rilsin *SaeKet* Becha saved me, until you took me by force again. Now do you remember me, Sithli sae Melisin? And you, Kepit sae Lisim?"

Raphat could see that Sithli did. Whether Kepit did or not, he couldn't tell. But Kepit took a step forward, her hand on her sword.

"You will die for this!" Kepit snarled.

Raphat snapped out of his trance. "Yes," he said, "she will, but not now." He stepped between Kepit and Kirra—Cilla—and put his hand on Kepit's sword hand, preventing her from drawing. "It is possible we can use her yet," he said. "We need to act quickly. We have not lost, but we will, unless we act now." He looked at his stricken and horrified troopers. "Raise a flag of truce and parlay!" he commanded.

It was done immediately, and in immediate response, he saw the corresponding parlay flag from the Saeditin down the hill. Raphat smiled. "She thinks we mean to surrender," he said, "and we want terms." His smile broadened, but it was not pleasant. "The message for Rilsin SaeKet," he said to the waiting trooper, "is that we have her daughter, the SaeKetti Reniat. We wish to negotiate."

He looked back at the little group, who seemed frozen behind him. "Now we wait," he said. "For the moment that is all we can do. Sae Kepit, you will not cut Kirra's throat. You will have your revenge, but when and in the manner I say." He fixed Kirra with an icy stare. "You have not ruined me," he told her, "although you have cost me dearly."

"I cannot say I am sorry." Kirra was speaking Runchot

again. "And I may yet ruin you, Prince, but it is certain that I have ruined these saedin."

"I claim a right to her, too." Sithli's voice was low and venomous. "Whatever is done to her, it must be slow. I will have you suffer for my amusement, Cilla, and I may take a hand in it myself."

"Enough." Raphat was perfectly willing to allow the Saeditin women to have their fun, but he had other matters to attend to first. "Guard Kirra," he ordered one of the troopers. "I do not want her harmed yet."

The man drew his knife and stepped up to Kirra, putting his hand on her arm. Kirra stepped back when he pulled her, offering no resistance. She dropped her eyes. "Please," she said, "don't bind me. I cannot escape you, and I do not wish to." Having accomplished her plan, she now seemed unable to fight any longer.

"Fine." Raphat waved his hand in acquiescence, and turned back to considering what Rilsin's response must be.

"Rilsin will want to see her child." Sithli had realized the importance of focusing on more than the thought of revenge against Kirra. "What will you do when she asks to see Reniat?"

"If we can get her up here, the question becomes unimportant, Sithli." Raphat was impatient and scarcely paying any attention to her. He noticed but did not care when she frowned at his abruptness and at his lack of title for her. He looked over at Kepit. "Can we get her up here, Sae Kepit? What do you think?"

"I think she cannot afford to pass up the chance that we might have her child." Kepit took the long-glass from the trooper beside her and looked down at the Saeditin army. Raphat's messenger had been received, she could see that much. There was a flurry of activity in the lines below, but she could not tell what was happening.

"We will see what can be done when we get her up here." Raphat kept himself from pacing by an effort.

"I hope she brings that Tillit boy with her," said Kepit.

*   *   *

RILSIΠ WATCHEÐ THE messenger head back up to the Run-chot lines. She did not know if what she was doing was the right thing. She had met only briefly with the chiefs of the Wilfrisin, sending them around to reinforce her flanks. One of the chiefs had informed her that First Man Bilt himself would be there soon. Rilsin hoped so on this account, too.

"SaeKet, do you really think he has the SaeKetti?" Essit was looking at her nervously, asking the question everyone had been thinking.

"I don't know." Rilsin turned abruptly and walked away from them all. She knew Reniat was dead. Reniat had to be dead, didn't she? She had been so certain. But what if she were not dead, what if Raphat and Sithli had had her child all this time? Would they have brought her on this invasion, a little child? Could she take the chance that they had not?

Rilsin stood still, trying to distance herself from the army, the interrupted battle, the confusion of war, from everything around her. She remembered how she had sensed her daughter the night she had been stolen, had felt her like a star, fading into the snowy night. She had never been able to feel that tenuous starlight again, though she had tried. The song of the land had failed her in this, or she had failed herself, and Reniat was dead. She remembered thinking she had felt her child once since then, on the Demon Bridge. Wishful thinking, a desperate attempt of her mind, or her soul, as the priests would say, to comfort herself, as it was so obviously ridiculous. Nonetheless, she tried now, tried again to feel that little bright star that was—had been—her daughter's life.

She could feel the song of the land; she knew it and could hear it now without much difficulty. The stony chords of the mountains around them, the rise of the hills, the trees and brushy forests beginning to stir toward spring. And the upset of battle on the land, and the knowledge of enemies who did not belong, who wished ill to the harmony that was Saeditin.

And then there were those that belonged, her troops, her officers, the shaggy little horses, Chilsa, her hunting cat. Those that were friends, the Confederate warriors. And mixed with the northerners were some of those who were native, those who loved Saeditin. Some Saeditin were with the Wilfrisin contingents, Rilsin thought.

And then she felt it. The starlight, the shining, bright daughter-star. It was with those northerners still behind her, approaching her, First Man Bilt and his warriors, and some Saeditin with him. Rilsin drew a breath. This was not to be believed. Was it wishful thinking again? Of course it was; she was deluding herself again. And one of those other Saeditin was familiar, too—no. Rilsin shook her head. Why did she torture herself this way? None of this was possible. Angry with herself for falling into the same trap, she walked back to Essit and Pleffin.

"The SaeKetti must be dead." Her voice was flat and emotionless. "Nonetheless. I will not take any chances, and beyond that, we have our own surprises for Prince Raphat, our own bargaining chips. Don't fret so, Sae Essit, I said I won't take any chances."

But she would, thought Essit. He knew her. She believed her daughter dead but hoped she was not, and she would put herself in harm's way to be sure. He looked at Pleffin with something like despair. Pleffin looked back at him in complete understanding and then turned abruptly to Rilsin.

"SaeKet," Pleffin said, "you are not going all the way up to Raphat's camp. I must say this, I am sorry. You are not going without escort—"

"Commander Pleffin, our forces are here, and some of Raphat's forces, for reasons we don't yet know, have raised our banner. What is there to lose?"

"You," said Pleffin. "If you are correct that the SaeKetti is dead, you are all Saeditin has now. We will not risk you." Pleffin stood his ground.

Rilsin stared back at him, astonished.

"Well, not more than we must," Pleffin amended, squirming only slightly under her scrutiny.

"I understand you, Commander." Rilsin was tempted to smile, but she did not. Pleffin would not take it in the right spirit. "And thank you."

29

CHILSA WAS BESIDE HER AS SHE RODE UP THE STEEP, ROCKY hillside. The hunting cat had whined to come, as intent on guarding her as her commander and her troops were. The truth was that she felt safer with the big cat along. But Rilsin also had troops around her, and they were alert, scanning everything around them.

With her rode her Runchot hostages. Tonar's hands had been bound before him, as had Phara's. Both had been gagged, which Tonar took with good grace, but Phara did not. They were between troopers ordered to guard and restrain them. Rilsin trusted neither Runchot noble, but she had to admit that Phara had spoken the truth. A messenger had come from Raphat's turncoat troops. They were indeed the troops supplied by Kirra of Runchot.

"Please, SaeKet," Phara had said earnestly, "please make peace with my lord father. That is the only good ending there can be to this long history of distrust and war. Now you see that he cannot harm Saeditin and has no power to attack you, so let there be an end."

"I want nothing more than to end this, Princess," said Rilsin more gently than she intended. And then she thought, *but I do want more than that, much more.* Phara was right, though. No good could come of the continued hostility between Saeditin and Runchot, but she doubted that Raphat would see this as clearly as his daughter did. And she doubted that Raphat had no more power to harm Saeditin.

The horses' hooves crunched on the snow and ice. Her troops had swords and fire-tubes at the ready, but Rilsin herself kept her sword sheathed, her fire-tube in her belt.

They came to the lines of Kirra's troops, and the troops parted to let them through. The soldiers saluted her, not hand to heart as Saeditin would, but hand to brow, in the Runchot manner. Rilsin and her escort rode through unharmed, and the troops closed ranks behind her. Then they were just downhill from the main body of the Runchot army.

They pulled up short, partway between Kirra's troops and the Runchot forces. Pleffin noticed something in the nearer rocks and nodded to Rilsin. She looked. It was Runchot marksmen. A cold wind had sprung up, and the banners over their heads, the flag of parlay and the Sae Becha banner, snapped briskly. Chilsa's silver gray fur ruffled slightly.

"This is as close as we get," said Rilsin. "We wait."

She could see the group coming down on foot through the Runchot lines: a rather sizable body of guards surrounding several individuals. After another moment she could see their features. She slid down from her horse, and Essit and Pleffin did the same. They handed their reins to a trooper and walked forward a few paces, surrounded by their own soldiers. Behind them came a tight knot of Saeditin troopers, screening and hiding Tonar and Phara, who had also dismounted.

Several yards away, the Runchot party stopped. In front of the little group, with armed guards on either side of him, was a handsome man of about forty or so years, with wavy hair, still mostly chestnut brown, caught back in the bun of

a Runchot noble. His full lips and bright blue eyes were like
those of Tonar and Phara, but even without this resem-
blance, Rilsin would have known him from his air of command. But her eyes went past him to the three women
behind him; two of them she knew. The one she did not
know seemed to be a prisoner, and Rilsin wondered briefly
why she was there, but her attention was drawn and held by
the two she knew. Chilsa's attention was on them, also, and
he growled once, low in his throat, but stopped when Rilsin
touched his head.

Kepit sae Lisim had aged a bit, her gray hair in a long
braid, her face lined and sharp. Sithli was still beautiful,
with her long blonde hair tightly braided in one long plait
down her back, but there were no emeralds twined into it
now. Her powder was flaking from the scar on her face, the
reminder of the attempted assassination from which Rilsin
had saved her. Rilsin saw that she still wore her emerald
cuff bracelet. What shocked her most was how tired and ill
her cousin seemed. Sithli met her glance, staring back at
Rilsin with a burning and incandescent hatred.

"Rilsin SaeKet Becha. I knew you would come."

Rilsin snapped her attention back from her cousin to the
man in front of her, the ruling lord of Runchot. She took
several steps toward him, keeping her eyes on his face. She
was aware of her troopers behind her, hands on their swords
and fire-tubes, of Chilsa still crouched and ready. She did
not look away from Raphat's face.

"Where is she, if you indeed have her?" she said.
"Where is Reniat SaeKetti Becha?"

"She is behind the lines, back at my camp," said Raphat.
"Surely you did not think I would bring a baby down into
danger, between the armies."

Rilsin, watching his face carefully, listening to more
than his words, heard the lie. There was no doubt that
Raphat was a very accomplished liar, and she was not sure
just how she knew, but she had no doubt now, none at all.

"Come with me," said Raphat, "and I will take you to
her."

Pleffin put his hand on Rilsin's arm, but she glanced at him sharply and he removed it quickly. Rilsin looked for a long moment at Raphat. He looked back at her, but he broke the glance first, shaking his head slightly. Rilsin realized that she was not the only one to understand more than what was spoken.

"You are right," said Raphat. "I can see you have guessed the truth." He smiled faintly, but the smile faded immediately. "She is dead, SaeKet, but we have her. We have her body."

Rilsin said nothing, but she felt as if a vast chasm had opened up at her feet. She felt as if she stood above a drop far higher than the Demon Bridge. She could not tell any longer whether or not Raphat spoke the truth; his words had robbed her of breath and thought. Her sight grayed.

"She was kidnapped," said Raphat, "by Kepit sae Lisim, acting for Sithli sae Melisin." He did not look at the two women behind him and did not see Sithli start with surprise, while Kepit remained impassive. "She was brought to us, but something went wrong. I don't know what it was, but the child was dead by the time she came to my attention. I had her little body wrapped in snow and ice, to preserve it for you. Come with me, Rilsin SaeKet, and I will return it to you. Just you and your escort, as many as you like. You will be safe, I give you my word."

Rilsin looked at Raphat. He looked into her eyes and drew back, for the gaze that was fixed on him was as sharp as a sword. Despite himself, he drew in a quick breath.

"If I could have saved her, SaeKet, I would have, believe me."

Rilsin continued to watch him, saying nothing. She knew her silence made him uneasy, and worse, and that was fine. He had begun well, and the shock of his announcement had almost undone her, but he had betrayed himself. It was the word "little." Raphat had said, "her little body," hoping to increase her agony, to blind her further with grief. It had backfired; the ploy had failed. As for his word on her safety, it was as flimsy as the thin film of frost that was

forming even now on the rocks around them. She had taken
Tonar at his word, but she would not do so with Tonar's father.

"I don't know, Lord Prince, whether or not you would
have saved her, had you been given the chance. Perhaps
you would have. But, my Lord Prince, I would like to know
just what makes you so certain my child is dead. I am certain you do not have her body." Her tone clearly called him
a liar.

Some of the Runchot troopers put hands to their swords,
and behind her Rilsin heard her own escort draw in their
breath. They had believed Raphat. Raphat himself did not
take offense, however.

"You are a hard one to deceive, Rilsin SaeKet. I do not
have her body. I believe she is dead because what else could
she be?" He shrugged, a brief lift of the shoulders, a quick
sneer with it. "Where else could she be but in the ground
somewhere, or left out for beasts? Your cousin had her
stolen, I do know that, and something went wrong, and now
the child is dead."

"How fortunate for you that you had no hand in it."
Rilsin's voice was cold, and as she spoke, the wind lifted
their cloaks, as if to underline her words. Despite herself,
Kepit shivered, and when Raphat looked into Rilsin's eyes,
they were like ice. He smiled.

"Why, would you kill me now, SaeKet, if you thought I
had killed your child? Will you try to kill me nonetheless?
Am I no longer quite so fortunate?" Raphat appeared perfectly at ease, and Rilsin could see where Tonar had come
by his own grace under pressure. "If you do, or if you try,
the battle will begin again. You have us outnumbered now,
SaeKet, and you may think we have lost—"

"You *have* lost," Pleffin interrupted. He was furious with
the way this Runchot had tried to manipulate his SaeKet. At
least Rilsin had seen through him. And he was furious over
the death of the SaeKetti. "You *have* lost," he repeated.
"Anyone can see that."

"But the battle will cost you dearly," said Raphat, ignoring Pleffin, "and I doubt you can kill me."

"Oh, I think I can kill you," said Rilsin. "You can die, as can we all, but that is not what I meant. I meant simply that you are fortunate to have both your children still." She motioned behind her, and the screen of troopers around the Runchot brother and sister parted. Tonar and Phara, still bound and gagged, were led forward.

"Remove their gags," said Rilsin. "And cut their bonds." When the troopers hesitated, she repeated it. "Cut their bonds, but do not release them yet."

"Ah," said Raphat. "My children. I do not have my children, Rilsin, you have them."

"That is Rilsin *SaeKet*," said Essit, stepping forward.

Raphat looked at him. "Young Sae Tillit, is it?" He smiled charmingly. "Speaking of children, you are still quite the child yourself. Your SaeKet should send you back to your tutor."

Essit flushed bright pink and would have spoken again, but Rilsin shook her head at him.

"Here are your children, Raphat. You may have them back again, with conditions."

"Let me see if I can name some of those conditions. You wish me to leave Saeditin. You wish an end to this war, and you want your cousin the Melisin and also the Lisim given to you."

"Raphat," said Sithli, speaking for the first time, "how dare you speak so of me! I will not permit this!"

"Silence, Sithli!" When she continued to sputter, Raphat looked at her. "Or I will have you silenced."

Sithli turned pale and stopped. She opened her mouth to say something again, and then glanced briefly at Kepit. Kepit was looking at Raphat with concern and with something else. Raphat glanced at Kepit and gave a very slight inclination of his head. It was that, and something in his glance that spoke to Kepit but also to Sithli. Sithli suddenly saw what had been hidden from her before, what she had not permitted herself to see. She realized that she had put her future and her life in the hands of two people who cared nothing for her.

Rilsin saw everything, too, in the same sudden flash that illuminated Sithli. Kepit had sold out her cousin. It was exactly like Kepit. Rilsin was surprised by a wave of sympathy for Sithli, who had once again brought about her own destruction.

"Perhaps I will let you have Sithli sae Melisin," said Raphat.

"No!" It was a scream more than a shout. Sithli was both shocked and furious. "Raphat!"

"And perhaps I will not." The wind had picked up, and Raphat raised his voice slightly over it.

Sithli, who had taken several steps away from the little group, stopped. She was hemmed around by Raphat's men, but now she looked at Raphat and smiled tentatively, as if she thought he made a joke in poor taste. Rilsin swallowed. She had never seen her cousin, Sithli the imperious, look so unsure.

"Why not make peace, my lord father? Why will you not consider it?" Phara could no longer keep silent, and she attempted to step forward, but the Saeditin soldier beside her grasped her arm, preventing her. Tonar said nothing, but he watched his sister intently.

Raphat looked at her. "Phara," he said, "my daughter. My worthless daughter. Still going on with that foolish nonsense about peace. Is this what you would trade to me, Rilsin, for the Melisin and the Lisim? She has no value to me. If you give her to me, I will put her to death or perhaps imprison her or sell her. She ran from me and from her duty. She has proved herself a traitor like her mother."

"Father." Despite her best resolve, Phara was struggling to speak, fighting against tears. "Why? Why did you kill Mama?" The raw agony, the anger, and the fury were mixed with something. Rilsin, listening, realized it was love, and not just love for Phara's mother but for Raphat, too. Couldn't Raphat see this?

Raphat began to flush with anger. The watching Saeditin expected him to explode, to rave and shout, but he did not.

"She was useless to me," he said coldly. "She gave me no more pleasure. And you have no right—*no right*—to question me. You are no longer my child."

"Father." It was a little girl's voice. "Please. Don't you still love me?"

Rilsin felt her heart tear at the tone. For all of Phara's courage, for all of her anger, for all of her daring, this was what she wanted: her father's love. Rilsin realized that Phara herself had not understood this until now.

"You are nothing to me," said Raphat. "You failed me. You were mine to use, but no longer. If you give her to me, SaeKet," Raphat looked at Rilsin, "her life is forfeit."

Rilsin wanted to put her arms around Phara, to comfort her, to tell her it did not matter. But it did. "I will not give her to you," she said. "She has a home in Saeditin, if she wants it, as long as she wants it."

Phara, struggling to control her sobs, gave Rilsin a glance of pure resentment. Rilsin repressed a sigh. She had not expected her to be grateful.

Tonar attempted to come forward to comfort his sister. His guard would not permit him to do so, but the movement drew Raphat's attention.

"Have you turned traitor, too?" Raphat asked his son.

"You know better than that, sir." Tonar seemed to take no offense. It appeared to those watching that he was accustomed to this sort of response from his father. "I am sorry to hear you speak as you do of my sister."

"You were intended to succeed or die. It does not look to me as if you have done either."

Succeed or die, thought Rilsin. She did not understand. Tonar was Raphat's son, and the Runchot put more stock in sons than in daughters. If Raphat cared nothing for Phara, he should have more care for Tonar. Tonar was his child, but more than that, Tonar was also his heir. It would seem that Raphat had no regard at all for his children. How could this be?

"Why should I care, SaeKet?" Raphat had been watching, her, too, and had seen her puzzlement. "I can always get more children, as you, so I understand, cannot. So why should I care what happens to these children of mine?"

"I understand you," said Rilsin. The last piece of the puzzle that was Raphat fell into place. He was completely ruthless because he believed himself immune from misfortune and disaster. His family, even his children, were merely game pieces to be played as he thought best. It was the ultimate version of the game all rulers played. "I understand you," said Rilsin, "and I pity you." A movement on the rocky heights above them caught her attention. "Not everything is a game to be played, Lord Prince. But if this war is a game, you should know that you do not control the board. We have you now. Look up."

Shouts rose from the Runchot troops behind Raphat. They were pointing up. Around them, too, the soldiers of both escorts were pointing up at the steep slopes, the impassable rocky terrain, the high, jagged cliffs around them. Raphat looked up. On those very cliffs, where surely only mountain goats and hunting cats could climb, were Saeditin soldiers. Saeditin archers with arrows trained on them and also squads with fire-tubes aimed down at them. Here and there a winking flash showed where a long-glass caught and reflected the shaft of weak sun that briefly broke through the clouds.

"Are we in range?" asked Raphat. He did not need the answer. Looking up, he knew they were. Above them on the ridges, the Saeditin marksmen held their fire. "No," said Raphat, "you do not have us. Not yet!" He signaled his own marksmen in the lower rocks. "Kill them!" he shouted. "As for you—" he turned on Tonar and Phara, still in the custody of their Saeditin guards, "I will kill you myself! No one betrays me!"

A number of things happened almost at once. Raphat had a fire-tube beneath his cloak and drew this forth. He struggled to prepare it for firing. Phara screamed. The trooper guarding her, distracted by events around him, did not have a strong grip on her. She pulled away from him and leaped forward.

"Not Tonar!" she cried. "You will not kill him, too!"

She reached her father just as he had finished preparing his fire-tube, and had lit its short wick. Phara grabbed it from him. Raphat backhanded her across the face, struggling to retain control of his weapon, but Phara would not relinquish it. There was a muffled report. Raphat looked surprised and staggered back, looking down at himself. A red stain began to spread across the front of his overshirt. Raphat sat down abruptly on the ice-crusted snow. He opened his mouth to say something, but whatever it was, it was drowned out by the screams and commotion. He blinked and then slumped over.

"No, oh no oh no!" Phara was still screaming. "No, oh please, Father, Dada, no!"

"Get down, SaeKet, get down!" Pleffin had Rilsin by the shoulders and threw her to the ground, throwing himself on top of her. Runchot arrows were clattering around them, and a hot puff of air passed close to Rilsin's cheek. She realized the shot from a fire-tube had just barely missed her.

There were more shots and cries. The Saeditin marksmen on the heights were targeting the Runchot snipers below them. There were shouts from down the hill, as the Saeditin companies prepared to charge upward. Rilsin turned her head and spat out gritty snow.

"Get off me, Sae Pleffin! Commander, get off!" With a mighty heave she dislodged him and staggered to her feet.

It would seem that there were no more hidden Runchot snipers, at least none who could still shoot. But the main body of the Runchot troops remained intact. Rilsin looked around and saw Tonar, still somehow in the grip of his guards.

"Let him go!" she commanded. "Prince Tonar," she said, "your father's troops will attack unless someone they trust orders them to desist. If they attack now, we will kill them all. Do not doubt it."

Tonar stared at her. He was struggling for control, strug-

gling even for breath, it seemed. He tore his eyes away
from the sight of his moaning sister cradling the body of his
father and looked to the Runchot captains and lieutenants
around him.

"There is a truce," he said. He cleared his throat and
spoke more forcefully, his voice carrying. "A truce!" he
said. "Call off the attack!"

After a second's hesitation, they obeyed him, turning to
relay the order. Rilsin raised her hands and, looking up at
her troops on the ridges, made the sign for "stand down."
Pleffin was already giving the order to the troops behind
them. It was then that Rilsin looked around for Kepit and
Sithli.

Sithli had her back to a rock wall. She seemed unharmed, but she could not move, for in front of her, fur
raised and teeth bared, a silver hunting cat snarled every
time she shifted position even slightly. Her golden complexion was slightly gray, and her eyes were wide, but otherwise she was calm.

"Easy, Chilsa." The big cat stopped snarling at Rilsin's
command but kept his eyes on Sithli, staying alert. "Prince
Tonar," Rilsin said, "this woman is mine."

"She is yours," agreed Tonar, "as is the other, the Sae
Lisim." He looked at the officers around him. "Find Kepit
sae Lisim," he said. "She and this woman, Sithli sae
Melisin, were responsible for this war. They are responsible
for the death of my father, Prince Raphat." He raised his
voice. "There is a truce and peace with Saeditin and with
Rilsin SaeKet Becha!" Tonar had a strong voice, and it was
pitched to carry. "The war is over! We will have peace, and
we will go home to mourn." He looked at Rilsin and nodded slightly at her.

"It will be as he says." Rilsin pitched her own voice to
carry, speaking in Saeditin now, so her own troops would
understand. "The war is ended!" She was impressed. Tonar
was moving rapidly to solidify his position as the new lord
of Runchot. It was inspired of him to blame all of the mis-

fortune on Sithli and Kepit, although in a way, Rilsin reflected, it was not far from the truth.

"I am not going back with you, Rilsin. I am not going to Petipal, to let you cut my throat in the Mother's Square. I will not!" Sithli was still against the rock wall, looking askance at Chilsa but also at the troops who stood ready to take her, as soon as their SaeKet called off her cat.

"Sithli." Rilsin looked at her cousin. She walked closer to her, examining her.

On closer inspection Sithli looked even worse than Rilsin had initially thought. Her face was puffy, and there were lines of tension and distress around her eyes. She looked drained and ill. Rilsin remembered the young girl she had grown up with, whose beauty had been the talk of the land. She was swept by a sudden compassion for her cousin. She was about to speak when she felt someone close behind her. Turning, she saw the third woman from Raphat's group, the prisoner she had not recognized. There was something vaguely familiar about her. Rilsin turned back to her cousin.

"Sithli," she said again. She sighed. "I don't know what I am going to do with you. Yes, I should take you to the Mother's Square." She shook her head, disturbed despite herself by the thought of Sithli facing the knife. "Whatever I do, you will never be able to cause trouble like this again. That day is over, Sithli."

"You can't kill me, Rils, you can't!" Despite Chilsa's growl, she shifted helplessly against the rock, tears forming in her eyes. "You can't! Please, Rilsin!"

Rilsin had never seen Sithli desperate before, not like this, not pleading for her life, before all the troops. The scar stood out on Sithli's face, and her hair had come out of its braid. Rilsin was unaccountably embarrassed for her.

"I don't know, Sith," she said gently in a low voice. She had no desire for anyone else to hear any more of this. "I don't know. But you will not have your freedom." She would have said more, but the woman behind her stepped forward.

"She must die!" The voice was low, strong, and some-how familiar. "After all she has done, SaeKet, after she killed my child and yours, and all those others. She does not deserve your compassion! She must not live!"

Rilsin turned. The familiar voice, the face of the woman before her—suddenly she saw the audience hall, with Sithli as SaeKet presiding over the Common Audience, when commoners came to present their grievances. She saw the washerwoman from Blue Street, who had cried out for jus-tice for her husband, murdered by the agents of Kepit sae Lisim, for her stolen daughter—

"Cilla?" Rilsin stared. "Cilla?" she said again.

Sithli chose that moment to run. She pushed away from the rock wall and tried to force herself past Rilsin. She would not have succeeded: Chilsa snarled again and stood up, showing his teeth. But the cat had no time to stop her. Cilla pushed past Rilsin, leaning around the big cat. Too late, Rilsin saw the knife in her hand.

"You deserve this," said Cilla calmly. "I have owed this to you for a very long time. You will cause the deaths of no more children!"

As she spoke, she grabbed Sithli by the front of her over-shirt. She did not attempt to stab her in the heart but pushed her back against the rock and went directly for her throat. The knife went in once, before anyone could react, and then again, even as Rilsin reached forward to pull Cilla away, even as Chilsa reared up and dragged her back.

"Chilsa, down!" Rilsin could see that Cilla had no desire to escape. Her vengeance taken, she had let the knife fall.

Sithli had fallen back against the rock wall. Blood poured down from her throat, and she put her hand up, weakly, as if to stem the flow. Then she collapsed in a heap. Her lips moved. Rilsin leaned forward.

"I hear it, Rils." It was a mere whisper, a thread of sound, all Sithli could manage. "I hear it at last. I hear the song of the land." Her eyes closed.

Rilsin stood up. She found that she was shaking. Some-thing was thick in her throat, almost preventing her from speaking. "Sithli," she whispered. "Oh, Sithli." She felt the telltale prickling behind her eyes and fought it back. She would not weep for her cousin, not now and not here. She looked up to find that Pleffin and Essit had both come up beside her. For a moment, neither spoke. Then Essit cleared his throat.

"SaeKet," he said. He tried again. "SaeKet," he repeated. "It's the dark moon."

Rilsin looked at him. The dark of the moon, sacred to the third aspect of the Mother, the traditional time of execution, when condemned saedin had their throats cut.

"It's the will of the Mother, SaeKet," said Pleffin.

There was shouting from down the hill. It took a moment for this to register with Rilsin. She straightened, looking from Essit to Pleffin, and then strode forward to see what was happening. It was more northerners arriving. The Confederate warriors already with her troops were cheering, shouting and screaming victory cries.

"It's First Man Bilt," said Essit.

Rilsin looked at some of the troopers beside her. "Cover her," she said of Sithli's body, "and take her back to camp." She would deal with it later. She looked for Cilla, but she was already gone. That, too, must wait.

"Let's go meet Bilt," she said.

It was Bilt, indeed, still on horseback, coming up the mountainside, through the cheering troops, both Saeditin and Confederate, and also Kirra's—Cilla's—mercenaries. It was almost as if Bilt had either won a battle or prevented one, Rilsin thought. Then she saw why the troops were cheering. There was someone with him. Rilsin felt the land throb beneath her feet. Not one person with him, but two, both on horseback themselves. An adult and a child. Bilt was near her now, and he dismounted with a flourish and a grin.

"Sae Becha, my friend!" he cried. "I see I am not too late for this latest of battles, since there was no battle." He was grinning so broadly Rilsin was afraid his face might split.

"Sun-flash failed, and my messenger failed, also. So I bring you good news myself!"

Rilsin opened her mouth to answer him, but she never did. She could feel it through the land again, much stronger than before. It was the glow, the shining of the daughter-star. And also someone else, someone she knew. Rilsin took several steps to the side and around Bilt. The second rider had reined up his horse. A small figure squirmed in his arms.

"Mama!" the little figure cried. "Mama!"

The rider dismounted and placed the child on the ground. The girl took a step toward Rilsin with her short little legs, and then Rilsin ran forward and caught her up. She knew tears were streaming down her face. She knew the troops could see, that Tonar, returning from organizing his officers, could see. She did not care.

"Reniat," she said. "Reni, my sweetheart."

"Don't cry, Mama," said Reniat, hugging her back. "Dada Sola brought me home."

Rilsin looked up. Sola was standing there, waiting. His hair was short now, and he looked thin and somehow harder, but he was there. Still holding Reniat, she took a step forward, and then another. She tried to think what to say, what words were best to welcome him home. She could think of none. She walked forward and embraced him, at first awkwardly, because of the child still in her arms. But then Sola put his own arms around them both. Rilsin heard Bilt laugh, and then the Saeditin troops began to cheer.

30

THE WINDS OF THE PREVIOUS DAY HAD PUSHED THE CLOUDS through, and morning dawned bright and clear. Rilsin was up before dawn, having had very little sleep. She accepted another mug of warm cider from the young trooper and tried to make herself comfortable in the camp chair set up for her. She was exhausted but still extremely alert, a combination that made it difficult for her to relax. The tent flaps were open despite the cold of the morning, as so many people kept coming and going.

"He's coming," said Essit, the latest person to enter the tent. "The sentries at the perimeter just let him through. He should be here in a few minutes."

"Good." Rilsin sat up straighter, tugging down her uniform shirt, running her hand over her face, smoothing her hair. She felt at ease back in uniform, her old plain black, as if she were still commander of the army herself.

She looked around the tent. Bilt and some of his officers, including Chif, stood near the entrance. Around the sides of the tent were crammed as many high-ranking Saeditin,

Confederate, and even mercenary troopers as were invited
or could fit. Chilsa was there, too, stretched at her feet like
a silver rug with a twitching tail. Despite the chill of the
morning, the tent was almost overly warm with the heat of
so many in a confined space. Sola was missing, at his request. She had had no time as yet to talk to him.

Essit took his position at one side of her camp chair,
Pleffin at the other, as if this were the audience hall in Petipal. That was how Tonar found her when he was ushered in,
blinking at the change from the bright light of the dawn to
the dimness of the tent. Behind him came other Runchot officers, and Phara.

"SaeKet," said Tonar, inclining his head slightly.

"Prince Tonar," said Rilsin. She did not rise.

Tonar was in the russet uniform of the Runchot winter
army, and his cloak and the sleeves of his overshirt were
sewn with the gold eagle feather pattern of House Merri.
His hair had been rolled back neatly into a tight bun. He
seemed to Rilsin to be taller, which surprised her for a moment until she realized it was an illusion born of Tonar's
ease with his new authority.

"I am sorry I cannot stay for anything more official,"
said Tonar, "but I must return as soon as possible to Runchot, as I am sure you understand."

"I do," said Rilsin. Tonar needed to go home to consoli-
date his new position. She knew he had enemies almost as
dangerous, in their own way, as any of her troops on the
battlefield. "This is official enough for now, Lord Prince.
We will await your emissary in Petipal when the details are
agreed upon and the copies are ready." She nodded to Essit,
who brought out the carefully written treaty she and Tonar
had agreed upon. It was preliminary, but the intent was
there, and it was binding as long as it was backed by the
goodwill of the signatories, she thought cynically.

"Perhaps I will be able to come to Petipal myself,
SaeKet, when the copies are prepared." Tonar straightened
after signing the paper. He bowed slightly to her again. "Or
perhaps you could come to Tressig; you would be most

welcome. I would be pleased to show you my capital."
Rilsin noticed again how blue his eyes were, and how intense.

"Thank you, Prince," she said noncommittally. She was
remembering what Phara had said about her brother's feelings. She looked around the tent, but Phara was no longer
in evidence.

"Prince Tonar," Rilsin said quietly, "your sister, I saw
her come in. How is she?"

"The Princess Phara may not return to Runchot. If she
sets foot in the land of our fathers, she will be condemned
to death for the murder of Prince Raphat of Merri." Tonar's
voice carried through the tent, hushing the buzz of individual conversation that had sprung up. Tonar wanted this information to be well-known, but Rilsin was in a position to
see his eyes, and she saw the sorrow there.

"I regret that, Prince, more than I can express." Rilsin's
voice carried, too. But then she lowered her voice. "I am so
sorry, Tonar."

"So am I," said Tonar quietly. "I hope in time, perhaps
only a few years, I will be in a position secure enough to
pardon her. I hope when that time comes, she will wish to
return."

Rilsin nodded. "The Princess Phara," Rilsin spoke again
for everyone, "has a home in Saeditin as long as she desires
it."

"Thank you, SaeKet, but I will not accept your offer."
The knot of Wilfrisin near the entrance parted, and Phara
came forward with Chif at her side. She looked haggard,
and she glanced once at her brother, a glance filled with
pain, and then looked away. She obviously had not slept at
all, and her face was blotched from tears. But she seemed
calm.

"She has a place in the north, SaeKet," said Chif. He put
his arm around Phara and smiled, turning to look at her.
Phara smiled back at him. It was a tired smile, but it had a
brilliance that lit up the tent.

"I can see that she does." Rilsin couldn't help smiling in

response. "You have my good wishes," she said, "and anything else that you may need."

"And you have my blessing," said Tonar.

"And they have mine," said Bilt, coming forward. "It is good for me to have someone expert on ways of Runchot these days. Now that Confederacy is becoming important nation. Don't you you agree, Sae Becha, my friend?"

"I suppose so," said Rilsin dubiously. Bilt was right about one thing, the Confederacy was growing into a power.

"I have good advisor about Saeditin, you know, my friend." Bilt was grinning broadly.

"Do you?" Rilsin was confused. She knew Bilt's penchant for humor, and she sensed a punch line coming.

"Indeed, yes. Solstice Warrior give me good advice. But I must let Warrior return home."

Rilsin frowned. Bilt's Saeditin was fairly good, and she had never had any trouble understanding him, but now there was a language barrier. She had heard of the tradition of the Solstice Warrior, but she could not understand what an odd northern custom had to do with Saeditin. She was about to ask him, in Wilfrisin, to explain, when Bilt did so, smiling, in Saeditin.

"Sola Dira is Solstice Warrior," he said.

Everyone in the tent listened raptly to Bilt's telling of Sola's adventures. Rilsin understood now why Sola had not wished to be present this morning; he was not a man who enjoyed this sort of attention. And it was adding to his reputation as a magician, a detail of which he would definitely not approve, but there seemed little help for it.

"And so it was," Bilt continued, "that Sola Dira, Solstice Warrior, not only bring north back together and save our new nation, but also save Suncat, Reniat SaeKetti, the sign of peace and help," Bilt paused for a moment, searching for the right word, "cooperation, between Saeditin and Confederacy. And," Bilt concluded, "together we bring SaeKetti Suncat home. Confederacy never have better friend than Saeditin. Now our ties are stronger."

Soldiers and nobles, Saeditin and Runchot and Confederates, forgot their differences and applauded, for the moment becoming simply Bilt's audience. Rilsin smiled and caught the corresponding twinkle in Bilt's eye. The big northerner could not only tell a tale, he knew how to use one to cement his diplomatic position.

"Well done, First Man," she said softly, under cover of the applause. She heard him chuckle.

Eventually, the business was concluded, and she was able to get away. The sun was high overhead, and the snow was turning mushy underfoot. Spring was surely coming. She wanted to find Sola and Reniat, and there were other matters that she did not wish to handle in a public audience.

Reniat was easy to find, being just where Rilsin had left her. She was in the care of the trooper designated temporary nursemaid and bodyguard to the SaeKetti, a young woman thrilled with the honor but not overawed, who had left a child of her own back in Petipal. Rilsin picked up her daughter and hugged her. In the time she and Reniat had been separated, Reniat had grown, and she walked and even ran now, and she had more words, in Saeditin and also in Wilfrisin. Rilsin regretted not seeing her child grow into these things, but the regret dwindled beside her gratitude and relief at having her back. She took Reniat with her as she walked around the camp, with Chilsa following them. It was at the edge of the camp, where she stood holding Reniat, looking up into the border mountains, that she became aware of someone else, someone who stood back, until Rilsin motioned her guard to let the woman pass.

"Ria Cilla," Rilsin said. "I looked for you before, but you did not come to the tent this morning."

"Kirra, SaeKet. I have left the name Cilla behind me, with the sad history I have avenged."

"Ria Kirra, then," said Rilsin, "or is it? Will you come home to Saeditin? I can help you establish yourself in Petipal. You need not continue your business in Runchot."

"I am not coming back, SaeKet. I can see you guessed as much."

"I did. I am more than sorry to lose you." It was true. From an uneducated Saeditin commoner, Kirra had established a new identity and worked her way from slavery to a business owner and a controller of events in a breathtakingly short time. The intelligence required for such a transformation staggered Rilsin.

"I had a reason for what I accomplished." Kirra had guessed the direction of Rilsin's thoughts. "Now that reason has gone."

"What will you do? And will Prince Tonar allow you back?"

"Oh, indeed. The prince has put it out that I killed an enemy of Runchot, not just Saeditin. As for my troops— well, that they turned against Runchot was not my fault, so the prince has said." She smiled, but it was a sad and bitter smile. "As for what I will do, I will continue my business." The bitter smile broadened. "It's what I know how to do, SaeKet."

Whatever Rilsin might have answered was forestalled by Reniat's demand to be put down. Both women watched as the little girl ran on her short legs, her hand in Chilsa's fur for balance, to a rock outcrop where some mineral in the stone glittered in the brilliant sunlight.

"Look, Mama, this rock is singing shiny songs!" Reniat sat down suddenly on the rock, and Chilsa began to bathe her face with his big tongue.

"I am more sorry than I can say that you did not find your daughter," Rilsin said.

"Perhaps I will someday, SaeKet," said Kirra. "At least you have yours again." She put her hand to her heart, turned, and left.

SOLA, AS USUAL, proved to be harder to find. Wherever it was she looked for him, he wasn't there, or he had just been there, and she had missed him. Eventually, Reniat became tired, and Rilsin took her back to the tent. She was frustrated and irritated, in part because she had put off business that needed tending to look for Sola, but more because she was certain he did not want to see her. She could have sent for him, and they would have found him and brought him to her, but she would not do that. She had just settled Reniat for a nap, when the tent flap was thrust aside.

"SaeKet," said the guard, "Dira Sola is here. He says he must speak with you. I told him you were busy, but he—"

"Not so loud!" said Sola, coming into the tent. "The SaeKetti is sleeping."

"Thank you," said Rilsin, to the guard. "I will see him now." She reflected that Sola had a habit of doing this to her, breaking in barely announced after she had given up on seeing him.

The guard closed the tent flap. It was dim in the tent but not dark; shafts of early spring sunlight came in through the window flap, which had been left open. The days were lengthening. Rilsin looked around at the mess; they were preparing to break camp, to go back to Petipal. There was no place to sit except the camp bed, set up in the corner. Rilsin glanced down at Reniat, who was sleeping soundly on her own camp bed, her finger in her mouth. She had always sucked her finger, never her thumb like other babies. Chilsa had stretched out beside the bed and looked up now at Rilsin, his green eyes catching fire the way they sometimes did in dim light. But he knew Sola and liked him, so he yawned and settled down again.

"Lets talk over here," said Rilsin in a low whisper. She cleared a pile of papers from a chest. They were drafts of the treaty she and Tonar had just signed, going back to Petipal for perusal by the clerks and the council.

"We don't really have to whisper," said Sola. "Talking softly is enough. She sleeps through almost anything when she's tired, especially if she feels safe." He followed Rilsin to the chest and perched on it, but he rose again after a moment, unable to settle, nervous about what he wanted to say.

"Sola." Rilsin shifted to keep him in focus; he was pacing. "Stop, Sola, I can't follow you like that. I wanted to thank you for saving Reni, for bringing her home—" She stopped.

"Don't thank me." Sola was more abrupt than he meant to be, but he stopped pacing and looked down at her. He remembered Bilt telling him that Rilsin was afraid to love again. It would seem he felt the same way. He found he did not like looming over her, so he tried to back up a little. His foot struck something and he stumbled, just catching himself.

"What—" He was half-tangled in a length of cloth. It was a cloak, emerald green, slashed with gold. He stared at it for a moment, then dropped it suddenly, as if it were red hot.

"Sithli's," said Rilsin. "Tonar had it sent. No, it's not what you think. The prince meant nothing ill by the gesture. Actually, I don't know what he meant, except that he wanted nothing of hers to remain in his possession. There are several crates that he is sending to Petipal." She paused, staring at the side of the tent as if there were something there to see, surprised to be fighting off tears again.

"I am glad she is gone." Sola edged away from the cloak as if it were alive.

"So am I," said Rilsin, "and yet I grieve for her, too. It's strange, Sola, but I don't think I will ever stop grieving her, in a way."

"The friend you grieve died a long time ago. But I understand, at least a little."

"I'm taking her body back to Petipal. She will be buried with at least some rites." Rilsin sighed and looked at Sola, seeing him again.

"What of Kepit?" he asked.

"There is no sign of her. Everyone is looking for her. Our troops, of course, but also the Runchot and Wilfrisin trackers. She has vanished. I don't understand it. But we will find her, unless she has gone into thin air, like the Evil One."

"And they call me a magician."

They looked at each other for a moment. Then they looked away, looked back again.

"I don't know why we always talk of other matters," Rilsin began.

"This is not what I wanted to talk to you about," said Sola simultaneously.

"Go ahead," said Rilsin.

"Please, say what's on your mind," said Sola at the same time. They both stopped and stared at each other.

"I wanted to tell you what happened with Reniat, when I brought her out through the caves," said Sola. "Not what we did, Rilsin, not all of those things that Bilt told you about. I wanted to tell you what happened to how I felt. I love Reni." He paused and looked at Rilsin, but she said nothing, so he continued. "I know she is the SaeKetti, I know she is Sifuat's child as well as yours. I won't say those things don't matter. They do, but they are not what is important. I love Reni for herself. If anything were to happen to her, it would be as if a piece of my heart were ripped out." He glanced toward the corner bed where the child was sleeping. "I wanted you to know."

"Sola," she began, but he held up a hand.

"Wait, please, Rilsin. That isn't all. I don't know why this is hard for me to say. I suppose I am afraid, and that is a difficult thing for me to admit. It's not just Reniat I love. I love you, Rilsin. I have always loved you, but I let my pride and my resentment get in the way of that love. I promise you I won't do that again." He stopped, swallowed, drew a breath. "No matter what you may feel for me. I know I may have given up any chance I had for your love, but that will change nothing in my heart. I had to say that; I had to get it out." He looked at her. "What were you going to say to me?"

Rilsin stood up, walked away from the chest and from Sola, then turned back and walked toward him again. She stopped and looked at him.

"What was I going to say? Not much," she said. "Or not much that you haven't already said. Just that I have had a long time, and it seemed forever, Sola, to realize how much I missed you. When I thought you were dead I—I couldn't bear it, I began to understand—to understand how much you meant to me, how much I realized that I—damn it. Damn it all to a freezing Runchot hell! I can't say what I feel. I can't even say what I mean! Why does my tongue always knot? What I'm trying to say is that I love you, Sola!" She paused, out of breath. Then she took a deep breath. "Will you marry me?"

He looked back at her, saying nothing, not moving.

"You will still have your workshops; you don't have to give them up, I would never ask that, and I know you won't like all the duties of consort, that's not important. We will manage something. It's just that—Sola. Please, say something. Will you? Marry me?"

He didn't say anything. He did take the two steps to close the distance between them, and then he took her in his arms. Chilsa chose that moment to pad over to them and ram the back of Rilsin's knees with his huge head. A moment later, a little voice from the back of the tent said, "Mama? Mama?"

Rilsin pulled back briefly from Sola's kiss. "Look what you are getting into," she said.

"Good," he said, and drew her back again.